D1634028

F

CLEARY

Yesterday's shadow

£16.99

L 5/9

Jon Cleary

Jon Cleary is one of the statesmen of Australian storytelling. Born in Erskineville, Sydney in 1917, he has been a self-supporting professional writer since the 1940s, working in films and television in the United States and Britain. Seven of his books have been made into feature films and three have been adapted for television. A number of his recent Scobie Malone stories have been optioned for a television series. His most famous novel, *The Sundowners*, has sold more than three million copies, and his work has been translated and published in fourteen countries. He has collected a number of literary prizes including the coveted Edgar Award, the Australian Literary Society's Crouch Medal for Best Australian Novel, and the Award for Lifelong Contribution to Crime, Mystery and Detective Genres at the 1995 inaugural Ned Kelly Awards.

JON CLEARY

Yesterday's Shadow

HarperCollins*Publishers*

This novel is entirely a work of fiction. The names,
characters and incidents portrayed in it are the work of the
author's imagination. Any resemblance to actual persons,
living or dead, events or localities is entirely coincidental.

HarperCollins*Publishers*
77–85 Fulham Palace Road,
Hammersmith, London W6 8JB

www.**fire**and**water**.com

Published by HarperCollins*Publishers* 2001
3 5 7 9 8 6 4 2

A catalogue record for this book
is available from the British Library

ISBN 0 00 710867 2

Typeset in Postscript Linotype Times
by Palimpsest Book Production Limited,
Polmont, Stirlingshire

Printed in Great Britain by
Clays Ltd, St Ives plc

For Cate

Chapter One

1

The past is part of the present, if only in memory. But memory, as Malone knew, is always uncertain testimony.

The first body was discovered by a fellow worker of the deceased at 5.08 a.m. The second body was found by a housemaid at 9.38 a.m. Two murders in one night did nothing to raise the hotel's rating from two and a half stars to three, a pursuit of the management over the past three months. An earthquake would have been more welcome, since insurance was preferable to bad publicity.

The Hotel Southern Savoy was one of several on the square across from Central Station, Sydney's terminal for country and interstate trains. The station itself had been built on an old burial ground, an apt location, it was thought in certain quarters, for some of the deadheads in State Rail. The Southern Savoy's clientele was mixed, but one would not have looked amongst it for celebrities or the wealthy. It catered mainly for country visitors and economy tour parties from Scotland, Calabria and the thriftier parts of Vermont. It had little or no interest in its guests, so long as they paid their accounts, and was discreet only because it was too much bother to be otherwise. It had had its visits from the police (two deaths from drug overdoses, several robberies, a prostitute denting the skull of a customer with the heel of her shoe), but it had always managed to keep these distractions out of the news. But murder? *Two* murders?

'The manager is having a fit of the vapours,' Sergeant Phil Truach told Malone, ringing on his mobile and out of earshot of the manager. 'He seems a nice guy, but he's a bit frail, if you know what I mean.'

'Phil, put your prejudices back in your pocket. Have a smoke or two. Before I get there,' he added.

Truach smoked two packs a day and had been told by his doctor that he had never seen such clear arteries, that Philip Morris could drive a truck through them. 'I'll have them empty the ashtrays. The media are already here. I think that's worrying the manager more than the corpses.'

'The bodies still there?'

'The guy, the hotel worker, he's been taken to the morgue. The woman's in her room, the ME's examining her. Crime Scene are still here.'

Normally Malone, head of Homicide, would not have been called in on a single murder till the circumstances of it had been fully determined. But two murders in the one hotel on the same night, one a male worker, the other a female guest, called for his presence. The homicide rate in the city was rising and everyone who was literate, from Opposition MPs to letter-writers to the morning newspapers and callers to radio talk shows, was demanding to know what the government and police were doing about it. Zero tolerance had become a mantra, even with voters who had never come within a hundred kilometres of a violent crime.

He went out to the main room of Homicide where Russ Clements sat at his desk, which, startlingly, was bare of paper. Usually it looked like the dump-bin outside a paper mill.

'What's the matter? You not accepting any more paperwork?'

'This is what they call – is it a hiatus? I dunno if the system's run outa paper, but I'm not, as they say, gunna make any enquiries. It'll start up again, soon's my back is turned. In the meantime . . .'

Malone and Clements had worked together for more years than they cared to count. Over the last year or two, as Homicide and Serial Offenders, part of Crime Agency, had expanded, they had worked together less and less out of the office. Clements, as Supervisor, the equivalent of general manager, had become trapped at his desk. Computers had proved to be just another form of land-mines, hemming him in. The diet of reports, reports, reports had put weight on him, turned muscle to fat. He was a big man, a couple of inches taller than Malone, and though he had never been light-footed, his tread now was heavy. He was a prisoner looking for parole.

'In the meantime, on your feet,' said Malone. He, too, had begun to thicken as middle age wrapped itself round him, but he still looked reasonably athletic. But he knew he was long past chasing crims on foot. 'We're going over to the Southern Savoy. You can help me count the bodies.'

Clements stood up, reached for his jacket as if it were a lifebelt. 'I thought you'd never ask. Gail, keep an eye on this thing for me.' He nodded at his computer, at its screen as blank as a crim's eye. 'Ignore everything but love and kisses from the Commissioner.'

Gail Lee, one of the four women detectives on the staff of twenty, looked at Malone. 'What's the matter with him?'

'He's light-headed, he's going to be a detective again.'

The two men went out of the room, Malone as usual putting on his pork-pie hat. It made him look like a cop from the 1950s, but it was his trademark, though only in the eyes of his staff. They let themselves out through the security door and disappeared, unaware of the swamp they were to step into in Room 342 at the Hotel Southern Savoy.

Gail Lee looked at Sheryl Dallen, another of the distaff side of Homicide. 'I think they're both into the menopause.'

Sheryl leaned back in her chair, swept an arm around her. 'Won't it be lovely when all this is ours? A woman Commissioner, seven women Assistant Commissioners –'

The three men still in the large room looked up, like pointers that had scented danger. Gail and Sheryl exchanged foxy grins.

Malone and Clements drove through a day as sharp as a knife

against the cheek; a westerly wind had whetted it. Building outlines were as clean as etchings; a lone cloud was like an ice-floe, queues stood at bus stops looking as miserable as if they were queuing for the dole. The car's radio told them the temperature was only 14 degrees Celsius.

'A summer's day in Finland,' said Clements.

'Or in England,' said Malone, and they smiled at each other with Down Under smugness.

Phil Truach, cigarette-satisfied, was waiting for them in the lobby of the hotel. It was not a large lobby; expense had been spared by the developer who had built the hotel. It was crowded now with departing guests, some of whom looked to be in a hurry, as if afraid they might be the next murder victims. There were unwelcome guests: two pressmen and three radio reporters. Malone was grateful there were no television cameramen. Television shots of crime scenes never seemed to show anything but police officers going in and out of doorways as if looking for work.

Truach pulled Malone and Clements to one side; they stood behind a limp palm, the one piece of greenery in the lobby. 'The media want a statement.'

'Stuff 'em for the moment,' said Malone. 'Where's the manager?'

'He's up with Crime Scene. He seems to have recovered. Your wife's up there, too, Russ.'

Clements frowned. 'As ME? What's she doing there?'

'I dunno.' Truach held up a hand as they stepped out from behind the palm and the five reporters pushed forward. 'Later, guys.'

'Is there any connection between the two murders? Is it a serial killer?' She was from a radio station, she chewed on *serial killer* as if it were a liqueur-filled chocolate. Malone remembered the days when all police reporters had been male, eager cubs or hard-bitten hacks. These girls were just as tenacious: 'Or is it just coincidence?'

'Coincidence,' said Malone, stepping into the lift and pressing the button for the doors to close. 'It makes the world go round.'

'She won't learn that till she's middle-aged,' said Clements. 'Who's upstairs, Phil, besides my wife?'

'Coupla uniformed guys, two plainclothes from Regent Street, Norma Nickles and a young guy from Crime Scene.' Truach, like most of the older cops, still used the old term instead of Forensic. Police teams, like football teams, were constantly being re-named. 'Your wife and a guy from the morgue. And Deric, the manager. D-E-R-I-C, he spelt it out for me.'

'Phil, I think you're homophobic,' said Malone.

'They rub me up the wrong way,' said Truach and all three of them laughed.

They were on their way to a homicide, a double homicide, another job of work. The mood changed only when the dirty work began: the wonder at why a particular life had been taken, the informing the relatives of the victim's death and how it had occurred.

Romy Clements, Deputy Director of Forensic Medicine at the morgue, looked in surprise at her husband. He returned the look. They hadn't met over a corpse in several years.

'What are you doing here?'

'What are *you* doing here?' he said.

'I have four of my staff off with 'flu virus.'

She was in a white coat, was wearing plastic gloves, but the clinical look didn't detract from her own looks. She, like Russ, had put on a little weight, but middle-aged spread was still a few years ahead of her. She had that comfortable, comforting appearance that some women achieve in their late thirties when life is going well for them. But Malone always found it remarkable that she had reached that assurance. Her mother had died only a short time after coming to Australia from Germany. Her father, never wanting to leave Germany, was serving a life sentence for serial killing. Yet somehow, with the help of Russ, she had come through all that to self-confidence. The Clements' marriage was a harbour for both of them, their five-year-old daughter their beacon in the centre of it.

She nodded down at the body on the bed: 'Strangled. No rape, but there'd been intercourse. Dead eight to ten hours, I'd say.'

The room was crowded and even after all these years Malone wished the crime scenes provided more breathing space. He looked at Des Shirer, the senior man from Regent Street, the local station. He never neglected protocol, it was part of the axle-grease of co-operation.

'What've you got, Des?'

Shirer was in his late thirties, but he had none of the comfortable look that Romy had. He was thin, fidgetty, had awkward movements as if on wires: crime, you knew, would eventually wear him out. 'I've talked to Deric, here –'

Deric was not what Malone had expected from Phil Truach's description. He was in his early thirties, thick blond hair, regular features and what looked like muscular shoulders under the dark jacket. Definitely not a man who would have the vapours.

Till he spoke: it was a high girlish voice and at the moment was quavery: 'She –' He looked down at the still exposed body of the woman, then quickly looked back at Malone. 'She's registered as Mrs Belinda Paterson – that's what her credit card said. Some address in Oregon, in the United States. She booked in yesterday about 6 p.m., said she was staying just the one night. I wasn't on duty, but our reception clerk said she sounded a very nice lady. Not a – well, you know.'

'A hooker looking for business?' said Clements.

Romy looked at Norma Nickles, the other woman in the room besides the dead one. 'That's how they divide us up – nice ladies or hookers. I'll see you at home, *Liebchen*,' she said and gave Clements the sort of smile that has cut a thousand throats, mostly lovers' and husbands'.

'No, we don't think she was anything like that,' said the manager and for a moment the quaver was gone from his voice.

'If she was a hooker, she'd done all right at it.' Norma

6

Nickles was a slim graceful woman who had once been a ballet dancer. She had descended from *entrechat* and *sur les pointes* to down-to-earth, flat-footed examination of crime. And was a star at it. 'Her suit is top quality, Donna Karan, bought at Bergdorf Goodman's in New York. Cashmere sweater, Ferragamo shoes. Her topcoat is vicuna, it doesn't come any more expensive in cloth, right, Doctor?'

'The best.' The two women looked at the coat thrown over a nearby chair. Romy put out a hand to touch it, then realized she was wearing the plastic gloves. 'I don't think even hookers can afford them. Not in this town.'

'This lady had money,' said Norma Nickles.

'What's the rate here?' Malone turned back to the manager.

He had been looking down at the body; he jerked his head up as Malone spoke to him. 'How much? A hundred dollars a night for a double with bath, like this front room. Less than that for group bookings.'

Malone gazed down at the body now being zipped into a bag. The throat had a dark collar of bruising, the face was puffy and distorted, her mouth enlarged by the smeared lipstick. But it was evident that she had once been, only yesterday, a good-looking woman.

'I'd say she was thirty-five, maybe forty, no more,' said Romy, peeling off her plastic gloves. 'She's looked after herself – or been well looked after. She was what you men call well preserved.'

'Was she American, do you think?'

The question was addressed to the manager, who had shut his eyes for the moment as the bag was zipped up. Now he shrugged, spread his hands; the gesture was slightly effeminate. Pull your head in, Malone told himself, and your prejudices. He was not homophobic, but he came of a past generation that carried notions as dated as flares and sideburns. But then he had other prejudices: cricketers who patted each other on the bum (bonding, he was told they called it); the same cricketers who threw the ball high into the air when they took a catch (show-boating, he called it);

footballers who hugged and kissed each other when a try or a goal was scored; mates who thought half a dozen beers was a blood bond (which made him un-Australian). He would get used to fluttery hands eventually.

'Our reception clerk thought so,' said the manager. 'But so many these days try to sound American, don't they? De-BREE for debris, stuff like that.' His own accent was English and sounded genuine. Not gen-u-ine.

'Anything in her handbag?' Clements asked Norma Nickles.

'Just the American Express card, her compact, a packet of condoms –'

'Any used in the intercourse?' asked Malone.

Norma shook her head. 'No.'

'There's semen in the vagina,' said Romy.

'Good. If we pick anyone up we can lecture him on the dangers of unsafe sex. He may not know what DNA can do to him. What else?'

'Her watch, a Bulgari – like I said, this lady had money. A string of pearls – expensive, too.'

'May I interrupt?' said Romy. 'We're ready to take the body away.'

'When will you do the p-m?' asked Malone.

'Not till tomorrow. I have four others lined up ahead of her, including the man they took out earlier. We'll do them in turn.' She looked at her husband: 'No remarks about Teutonic thoroughness.'

'Never entered my head,' said Clements innocently.

'You're coming to dinner tomorrow night?' she asked Malone.

'We'll be there,' said Malone; then looked at the manager who had raised his eyebrows. 'Life goes on, Deric. We're not cold-blooded bastards.'

'No. No, I guess not.' But he didn't look convinced.

As the body was put on a stretcher to be taken away, Malone moved to the window and looked out. On the other side of the square the tall Italianate clock tower of the station reared like an

8

unintended memorial above the dead in the old burying ground. Malone remembered reading somewhere that water from a creek that had run through the burial grounds had been used to make the best-tasting beer in the early days of the colony. Drinkers of it often finished up in the graves beside the creek, adding no advertisement for the beer. In the middle of the square, complementing none of the surrounding buildings, was a steel-and-glass construction that, for want of a better name, was called a bus shelter; those who stood under it said that the only thing it protected them from was the pigeon-shit of the birds that squatted on it. It looked as out of place as a glass condom on an altar, but that was the way the city was going. The dead in the burial grounds would, metaphorically, piss on it from a great height.

Central Square was not Sydney's most glittering scene and he wondered why a seemingly wealthy American woman would have come here to this hundred-dollar-a-night hotel when more expensive and luxurious hotels, with much better views, were available only ten-minute cab rides from here. Then he saw a man get off a bus lugging a heavy suitcase and he turned back to the manager.

He waited while the body was taken away and Romy went out of the room, brushing her hand against Clements' as she went. Then he said, 'Where's the lady's luggage?'

'There wasn't any,' said the manager.

'You let people check in here without luggage?'

Deric looked embarrassed; he moved his hands again. 'Reception uses its discretion. My girl thought Mrs Paterson looked – well, okay. Not a hooker. But . . .'

Malone waited, aware that everyone else in the room had paused.

Deric said, 'People check in here sometimes for meetings – they don't want to meet in more conspicuous places –'

'Inspector,' said Shirer, 'Norma mentioned what was in Mrs Paterson's handbag. Expensive stuff, she said – the watch and the pearls. Yet she signed for a safe deposit box downstairs –'

9

'Did you know that?' Malone asked the manager.

'No. They didn't mention it down at the desk –'

'We haven't looked at it yet,' said Shirer, 'but why didn't she put the watch and pearls in it? Or anyway, the pearls?'

'What time did you come on duty, Deric?'

'I got here at, I dunno, five-thirty, quarter to six. They called me as soon as they found Boris' body –'

'Boris?'

'The cleaner,' said Shirer. 'Boris Jones.'

'Boris *Jones*?' Malone managed to remain expressionless. 'Righto, Deric, let's go down and have a look at what's in the box. The key in her handbag, Norma?'

Norma Nickles ferreted in the crocodile-skin handbag, held out a key. 'That it?'

'That's it,' said the manager and looked almost nervous as he took the key.

Before he left the room Malone asked, 'Any prints?'

'We're still dusting,' said Norma. 'The report will be on your desk this afternoon.'

'Not mine,' said Malone. 'Russ'.'

'Thanks,' said Clements and looked at Shirer. 'The chain of command, Des. Does it ever get you down?'

Shirer looked at his junior man, smiled for the first time. 'Not really, does it, Matt?'

Matt just rolled his eyes and looked at the two uniformed men, who, bottom of the heap, kept their opinion to themselves.

Malone went down in the lift with the manager. Deric was quiet, looked worried. 'What about Boris? Our cleaner? God, two of them the same night! Management has already been on to me – you'd think it was *my* fault! Do you think there's any connection? I mean between the two murders?'

'Do you?'

'Me? Why would I connect them? The woman's a total stranger –'

'Let's hope she's not,' said Malone. 'That always makes our

10

job so much harder. We solved a case last year, took us seven years to identify the victim –'

'Oh God,' said Deric.

In the lobby Malone paused to give a non-committal comment to the media hawks, throwing them a bone that they knew was bare. 'Is that all?' asked the girl from 2UE. 'Who is Belinda Paterson?'

Someone at the reception desk had opened his or her mouth. 'That's all we have at the moment, her name.'

'No address?' This girl knew that bones had a marrow.

Malone looked at the manager, who said, 'No local address. Just an address in the United States.'

'So she's another tourist who's been –'

But Malone had pushed the manager ahead of him into the latter's office and closed the door before he heard the word *murdered*.

'Oh Jesus, Inspector, I can see and hear 'em on tonight's news –'

'Deric, if they hang around after we've gone, you tell them nothing, okay? Nothing. Just refer 'em to us. Now where's the safe deposit box?'

Deric went into an inner room, not much larger than a closet, and came back with the flat metal box. He opened it, then looked at Malone and frowned. 'That's all? A passport?'

Malone picked up the black passport, opened it. He had seen one or two like it before: a diplomatic passport. He saw the photo: the dead woman alive, looking directly into the camera as if challenging it. He read the name and the particulars, then he closed it, took a plastic bag from his pocket and dropped the passport in it.

The hotel manager could read expressions on strangers' faces; it was part of his training. 'Trouble?'

'Could be. Keep it to yourself till I check. It'll be better for the hotel, I think –'

'If you say so. But –'

'No *buts*, Deric. Have you been in this business long? You're English, aren't you?'

Deric had sat down, as if all his strength had suddenly gone. 'No, I'm Australian. From Perth. I used to be an actor. I went to London, worked there off and on for –' He shrugged. 'For too long. I was out of work more than I was working. When I was out, I used to work as a waiter or nights on the reception desk in hotels. Five years ago I gave it up, the acting, and took a hotel management course –' He appeared to be talking to himself. Abruptly he shut up, then after a silence, he said, 'I thought everything was going sweetly for me.'

'It still can, Deric. None of this is your fault. In the meantime –'

He went back upstairs, besieged again by the reporters. He knew they had a job to do, but they pressed their case too hard, as if history itself would stop unless they got the news to the voters immediately.

'Tell us something, Inspector – *anything*! Are the murders connected?'

The lift doors closed and he looked at the two couples riding with him and they looked at him. Both couples were elderly, all four of them seemingly past excitability.

'We've heard about the murders –' He was tall and thin and grey-haired with a face like a wrinkled riding boot: from the bush, thought Malone.

'Don't let it spoil your holiday.'

'We're not down here on holiday,' said the male of the other couple, a stout and weatherbeaten man with faded blue eyes; it was obvious now that the four of them were together. 'We're here for a funeral.'

Malone cursed his loose tongue, was relieved when the lift stopped. 'Sorry. My condolences.'

'You, too,' said the tall thin man, as if police grieved for all murder victims, and the lift doors closed on them.

Malone shook his head at the crossed lines of the world and went into Room 342. Phil Truach and the two Regent Street officers had gone, but Clements was still there with the two Crime Scene officers and the two uniformed men. With the bodies gone from the hotel, everything was looking routine. Out in the hallway there was the sound of a vacuum cleaner at work, taking the marks of the police team out of the carpet.

'Anything?' Malone asked.

'We've got enough prints here to fill a library,' said Norma Nickles with the fastidiousness of an old-fashioned housekeeper. 'The maids seem to be a bit light-handed with the feather-dusters.'

'Tell Deric on your way out. Did you get a print off the flush-button in the toilet?'

'Yeah, there's one clear one.'

'Then maybe that's the one we want. We nailed a feller years ago that way. A bloke usually has a leak before or after sex.'

'Really?' said Norma, who had known the true worth of the advertisements in the tights of male ballet dancers. 'I didn't know that.'

'They also have a leak after murder,' said Clements. 'It's the excitement.'

'You men,' said Norma and all five of them grinned at her.

'Righto, Russ,' said Malone. 'Let's get back.'

'Anything in the deposit box?'

'Nothing. Where's Phil?'

'He's downstairs with the guys from Regent Street, they're interviewing the staff. You wanna question 'em?'

'No, you and I had better get back to the office.' His expression didn't change, but Clements, the old hand, read his eyes. 'Let's have the report soon's you can, Norma. Take care.'

He and Clements went down in the lift, squeezing in with half a dozen guests who recognized them as police and fell silent as if afraid of being questioned. The two detectives strode through the lobby before the reporters could waylay them again. Malone saw the manager standing behind the reception desk, staring at them as if they were guests who had trashed their room and refused to pay their account. Police are rarely welcome guests, certainly never in hotels.

Their unmarked car was parked in the hotel's loading zone. A van had just pulled up and its driver leaned out of his door and yelled, pointing at the sign, 'Can't you buggers read?'

The two detectives ignored him, got into the car and Malone drew it out from the kerb, resisting the urge to give the middle finger to the van driver who was still yelling at them. Only then did Clements speak: 'What have you come up with?'

Malone took the plastic envelope from his pocket, but didn't remove the passport. 'This. We've got trouble, mate. We take this to Greg Random and then to Charlie Hassett before we let anyone else see it.'

'So she's not –' Clements looked at his notebook; he still carried it like an old family heirloom. 'Not Mrs Belinda Paterson?'

'No. She's Mrs Billie Pavane. She's the wife of the American Ambassador.'

2

'Shit!' said Charlie Hassett, Assistant Commissioner, Crime Agency. He looked at the passport as if it were his dismissal pink slip. 'It's our turf, but we're gunna be over-run by our Federal blokes, the CIA, the FBI, Foreign Affairs . . . You're absolutely sure this is the dead woman's, Scobie?'

'Yes, sir. It's hers. I saw her before they zipped up the bag and took her away. It's hers, all right.'

Clements had gone back to Homicide to prepare for the blizzard that would soon be coming out of Canberra. Cold weather had been coming up from the south all week, but there would be no snow sports for the New South Wales Police Service. Malone was wishing that he had taken his vacation, which was due; or even his long service leave, which would give him time to disappear to the other side of the world. Lisa, his wife, had

14

been talking of a trip home to Holland and that now seemed an appealing faraway place. Instead he was now sitting in Assistant Commissioner Hassett's office with Chief Superintendent Greg Random, head of the Homicide and Serial Offenders Unit.

'Charlie, I'm not going to have my men pushed around by outsiders.' Random was the guardian angel of his men and women, though if he had any wings they had been folded and stored in a cupboard. Tall and bony, with a stiff brush of grey hair, he was as dry as the dust on the Western Plains where he had grown up and he would have greeted Lucifer with the same laconic regard as he offered to other, lesser crims. He would not be bending the knee to any Hierarchy from Canberra. For him, anyone down there, whether politician, diplomat or bureaucrat, was a foreigner. 'I want you to let them know that from the start –'

'Greg, relax –' Hassett made a downward motion with two large hands. He had started on the beat thirty-five years ago, when doubt had never entered his still developing mind; his powers of persuasion had consisted of a sledgehammer for closed doors and a bunched fist for closed faces. He occasionally dreamed of the simplicity of those days, but these days there was no sharper mind in the Police Service. He wore his reputation as a hard case as some men, and women, wore their power suits. The sledgehammer had been put away and in its place was a perception as sharp as a professional woodchopper's axe. 'I'll talk to the Commissioner and we'll get the barricades up. We're not gunna be over-run by outsiders. But we've got to get this news down to Canberra – how're you gunna do it?'

'We'll start out with the proper channels, just to show we're not obstructive,' said Random. 'I've talked it over with Scobie. When we leave here we're going down to the US Consul-General. We'll give him the news, tell him we've already got the investigation under way and he can let Canberra know. We'll let them know – in a nice way, of course – that the case is ours.'

Hassett looked at Malone. 'You're not jumping for joy, Scobie.'

'Would you be, sir?'

The Assistant Commissioner grinned. 'You want a loan of my sledgehammer? It's over there in the closet. I've had it gold-plated.' He stood up. He was of what had once been the medium height for police officers, five feet ten inches, and he had thickened; he still suggested the battering-ram he had once been. 'Now I'm gunna give the Commissioner the bad news. Good luck. My regards to the Consul-General. He's a nice bloke and he's gunna hate this as much as you.'

Random and Malone drove down to Martin Place, in the business heart of the city, parked the car in the basement of the MLC building and rode up to the fifty-ninth floor. Money rustled like a breeze in all the floors beneath, but here on the fifty-ninth diplomacy, at citizen level, was the order of business. Passports, trade and general enquiries: nothing that made waves. The two detectives, when they produced their badges, were checked through security as if they were close relatives of the US President and were shown into the Consul-General's office before they could comment on their welcome.

'You've got news of her?'

Consul-General Bradley Avery had been an All-American quarterback before he had given up throwing passes and taken to receiving blasts from Washington. He was as tall as Random and Malone and had shoulders that looked as if he still wore the pads that Malone always found ridiculous on gridiron players. He had dark curly hair and a broad black face just the pleasant side of plain.

'Our embassy called me this morning – got me at home before I was out of bed –'

'We're talking about Mrs Pavane, the Ambassador's wife?' said Random.

'Yes. Yes, of course –' Then Avery waved the two detectives to chairs, came round his desk and sat his haunches on it. 'She's

16

been missing since yesterday morning. She caught a nine o'clock plane out of Canberra for Sydney and she hasn't been since she got off it –'

'You didn't have a consulate car out at the airport to meet her?'

'Yes, there was one. The embassy called after she had left and ordered the car. But she didn't meet it –' Then he stopped, reading the atmosphere for the first time. 'You've got bad news?'

Random nodded, looked at Malone. 'Tell him, Scobie. It's your case.' Planting the territorial imperative early.

Malone recited the bad news. 'That's the bald fact, Mr Avery. What puzzles us is what was the Ambassador's wife doing in a hundred-dollar-a-night hotel under an assumed name?'

Avery had listened in silence, without expression; but now he let out a long hiss of breath, as if he had been holding it in. 'Holy shit! Does the media know?'

'Yes. There was another murder last night at the same hotel, one of their cleaners. If it hadn't been for the double homicide, I don't think the press would have been down there. It would have got a three-line mention in the news brief in tomorrow morning's papers, that's all. But now –'

'Do the media know who she is?'

'Not yet. So far the hotel management doesn't know. I didn't let the manager see this when I took it out of the safe deposit box –' He took the plastic bag containing the passport from his pocket. 'All they know so far is that she was American.'

Avery held out his hand. 'I'll give that back to the Ambassador.'

Malone looked at Random, who said, 'It's our turf, Mr Avery. It's a New South Wales Police Service job, I'm afraid. I wish it weren't, but that's the fact of the matter.'

'Does it have to be?' Avery was not belligerent. He just had the look of a quarterback seeing tackles coming at him from either side.

'I'm afraid so. We'll co-operate with anyone you bring in, but

17

it's our case. We'll be as discreet as possible, but it won't be too long before the media has a field day.'

'Did your security people check yesterday when she didn't turn up?' asked Malone.

'We-ll, no-o.' Avery looked abruptly tentative. 'We didn't send anyone out there after the driver came back and reported he hadn't found her. We phoned Canberra and they said to leave it to them. They're very secure about security down there,' he added and sounded undiplomatic.

'What do they have down there? CIA, FBI, what?' asked Random.

Avery closed up: 'I think you better ask them.'

'How long has the Ambassador been out here?' asked Malone.

'Two months. He's still finding his feet. Don't quote me,' he added and almost managed a smile.

'Is he a career diplomat?'

Foreign ambassadors made little or no impact on the country outside the limited circle of Canberra. They were wraiths that occasionally materialized. Like now.

'No. I should imagine half the State Department had never heard of him till the President submitted his name. I'd never heard of him . . .'

'You're being very frank, Mr Avery,' said Random.

'I'm getting on side,' said Avery, and this time his smile widened. 'Look, you want the facts. I'm the one who's gonna be closest to you in this, so I'll fill you in all I can. Mr Pavane was a big supporter of the President in the last campaign, raising enough money to wrap up Missouri and Kansas for the President. He comes from Kansas City, his family has been there for years. He was president of one of our biggest agrobusinesses and he was picked to come out here because we always seem to be at odds with you on meat and agricultural tariffs and subsidies. Again, don't quote me.' He went round behind his desk, sat down, looked glad to have a chair beneath him. 'I'll call our embassy now. They'll have someone down here this afternoon.

18

I'll tell them it's your turf, as you call it, but you may have to explain it to them yourselves.'

'We'll do that,' said Random. 'You might tell them while you're on the phone that Inspector Malone and I have the backing of our own Assistant Commissioner and our Commissioner himself. Inspector Malone will be doing the leg-work, I'll be running the investigation. But behind me –'

'I get your point, Mr Random,' said Avery. 'Does your Premier and your state government know yet?'

'They will by now. The Commissioner will have told the Premier and the Police Minister.'

Avery looked at Malone. 'You look worried, Inspector. Clouds are gathering?'

'I think so. Where were you before your posting to Sydney?'

'Belgrade.' Another smile, but this time a wry one. 'I see your point. Okay, I'll do all I can to help you. But I hope you understand – consular men are down the totem pole compared to embassy staff.'

'I feel the same way about Police Headquarters.'

'You survive,' said Random, then looked at Avery. 'We'll wait till you've talked to the embassy. Just so's we know, right from the start, where we'll be going.'

'I think I better get my two senior staff in here first.' Avery spoke into the intercom on his desk: 'Jane, will you ask Mr Goodbody and Miz Caporetto to come in? *Now*.' He switched off and sat back. But he was not relaxed. 'You're right. What was Mrs Pavane doing in a cheap hotel under an assumed name? She didn't strike me as like that – I mean the cheap hotel.'

'What do you know about her?' asked Malone.

'Nothing. Except that she was a charming, good-looking woman who always looked a million dollars, as they say. I gather she had made quite an impression down there in Canberra on the cocktail circuit. I met her twice and she looked to me as if she was going to be a great help to the Ambassador.'

'And what's he like?'

But then the door opened and Mr Goodbody and Miz Caporetto came in. Avery waved a finger at the door and Goodbody turned and closed it. Avery stood up and introduced the newcomers; there was obvious rapport between the three of them. Then he said, 'This is Chief Superintendent Random and Inspector Malone from the New South Wales Police Service. They have bad news. Really bad news. They have just found the Ambassador's wife in a hotel up on Central Square. Murdered.'

Gina Caporetto sat down suddenly in a chair which, fortunately, was right behind her. Mitchell Goodbody stood stockstill, one foot in front of the other, as if caught in mid-stride. Then he said, '*Murdered?*'

Malone had heard the echo countless times. Violent death was beyond the immediate comprehension of most people: at least the violent death of those they knew. Consular officials, like police, must have experience of tragedy, but, he guessed, it was the tragedies of strangers. And they would not have expected personal – well, semi-personal – violence here on their doorstep in a freindly city.

'How? Was she – murdered by some stranger?' Goodbody had a soft Southern accent. He was short and thin and looked as if he might be perpetually worried. He had thick fair hair, cut very short as if he had just come out of boot camp, and a long thin face that would reach middle age before the rest of him. The sort of worker who would always see that the office wheels never stopped turning. 'Which hotel was it? Central Square?' He frowned, as if it was remote territory.

'The Southern Savoy,' said Random.

'The what?' Gina Caporetto was a blonde Italian-American, her birth roots north of Milan; it was an unfortunate name, a reminder of an Italian defeat in World War I; but the two Australians in the room had never heard of it. In any case men, and women, would hardly remark her name; instead they took note of her body and, eyes rising, her quite attractive face. She wore a beige knitted dress that looked as if she had put it

20

on wet and it had shrunk. 'I've never heard of it – no, wait a minute. Last year, during the Olympics, there was a big group from, I've forgotten where, New England somewhere, they were booked in there. I went up there once –' She, too, frowned. 'She was – *there*?'

'It's a hundred-dollar-a-night place,' said Avery. 'Superintendent Random tells me the circumstances aren't – well, not the best. She was found naked in her room. She'd been strangled.'

'You are sure it's Mrs Pavane?' Goodbody's accent seemed to have thickened with shock.

'Certain,' said Malone and held up the plastic bag and the passport.

'Do the media know?' Gina Caporetto had recovered her poise, which was considerable.

'Miss Caporetto is our press officer,' said Avery.

'They know there's been a double murder –'

'A *double* murder?' Goodbody seemed to be making a habit of the echo.

'We don't think the other homicide – a hotel cleaner – is connected to that of Mrs Pavane. But we've only just started our investigation –'

Gina Caporetto looked at Avery. 'Shouldn't our people be handling this?'

'I'm afraid not,' said Random, getting in first. 'This is our turf, Miz Caporetto. We'll welcome co-operation, but that's all. I don't know the set-up at your embassy –'

'I'll explain the situation to Canberra,' said Avery. 'I'll call them now. Maybe you could offer Mr Random and Mr Malone some coffee, Gina? Take them into your office while I call Canberra. You stay with me, Mitch. This is just between ourselves till I've talked to the embassy.'

Goodbody still looked shaken: the wheels had come off and he had found himself with no jack. 'They'll be all over us –'

'No, they won't, Mitch,' said Avery warningly. 'Go ahead, Gina, give the gentlemen some coffee.'

21

Gina Caporetto led the two detectives out of the big office into a smaller one on the other side of a lobby. The secretary at the desk outside Avery's room looked up enquiringly, but Ms Caporetto just shook her head.

She closed the door to her office and went to an old-fashioned percolator on a hot-plate. 'I make my own coffee. We Americans think we make the best coffee in the world. But –'

She smiled and Malone said, 'Don't quote you. Did you ever meet Mrs Pavane?'

'Cream or black? Sugar?' She brought them their cups, then took her own behind her desk and sat down. It was a neat, comfortable office; but Malone wondered how comfortable it would be for her in the coming days. Even the ubiquitous Stars and Stripes on a small standard in a corner looked limp.

'Yes, I met her, once down in Canberra just after they had arrived and twice up here. I took her shopping one day and another day I took her to lunch. She was trying to get the feel of – well, Australians, I guess.'

'But?' said Malone.

'But?' She paused, with her cup held in front of her face like a mask.

Greg Random said, 'Miz Caporetto, we cops read what is unsaid. It comes with experience – in other circumstances we might have made good diplomats.' He looked sideways at Malone. 'Except Inspector Malone, who is notoriously undiplomatic.'

'Nice coffee,' said Malone diplomatically, holding up his cup.

Her first smile had been forced, a muscular effort, but now she appeared a little more relaxed; she shook her head and smiled at both of them. She looked like a sex bomb, but she had a cool mind that could always control it.

'Yes – but. I just, I don't know, I felt she wasn't entirely a stranger here.'

'Did you query her on it?'

22

'Yes. Diplomatically.' Just a faint smile.

'And what did she say?'

She took a memory pause; then she said, 'I'm being mean, but it was like she was making up an answer. Then she said she had been out here eight or nine years ago on a quick business trip. She had stayed at the Regent.'

'Five-star,' said Malone. 'So why did she choose the Southern Savoy this time? It'd be struggling to pick up three stars.'

'Did she let her hair down when you took her to lunch?' Random had finished his coffee.

She got up, took his cup and poured more coffee for him. 'Not really. We weren't exactly girls on an equal footing – she was the Ambassador's wife.' She came back, sat down, paused again as if she realized she had spoken in the past tense: *was* the Ambassador's wife. 'She seemed to have tightened up after that first shopping visit. She wasn't rude, but she was – well, *distant*. As if suddenly she had taken a dislike to, I dunno, Sydney or Australia. It happened after this guy spoke to her.'

'Which guy?' Random had almost finished his second cup. Slow in almost everything else, he was a quick coffee drinker, not a sipper.

'We hadn't started lunch when this guy came up, said, "Aren't you –" I didn't catch the name, he sorta mumbled it the way –'

'The way Australians do,' said Malone. 'My wife is always telling me to open my mouth. She's Dutch.'

'Well, yes,' said Ms Caporetto, trying to sound polite. 'Well, anyway, she just froze him. She just said a blunt "No" and he apologized and sorta limped away.'

'Did you get a good look at the man?' asked Malone.

'Not really. I was looking at her. He was short and, I'm not sure, bald. He stopped by for just a few seconds. The place was crowded and he just sort of disappeared.'

'What happened then?'

'Even at the time I thought it a bit strange – she just made no comment. She didn't look at me, picked up her menu and,

I think I've got it right, said, "I'll have the oysters and the barramundi."'

'So she knew about our oysters and our fish?' said Malone.

'Well, yes, it seemed so. But she'd been in Canberra a coupla months – no, at that time a month or maybe five weeks – and maybe they'd told her what was best.'

'What else do they have to talk about down in Canberra?' said Random. 'Where did you have lunch?'

'At Catalina. It was a Friday, all the eastern suburbs ladies were there.'

'What do you know about her back in the States?'

'Nothing. I knew nothing about the Ambassador till we heard he was coming. He's from Kansas City. I come from Philly – Philadelphia. Anything west of the Mississippi is still Indian territory to us.'

Just like us, thought Malone, though on a smaller scale. Sydney's eastern suburbs thought of the western suburbs as Indian territory. 'What's he like?'

'Charming. He's no hayseed or cowboy –' She stopped, shook her head again, looked squarely at the two men. 'Why am I talking to you like this? Because you're cops?'

'Not necessarily,' said Malone. 'Because, like us, you want to know who killed the Ambassador's wife.'

She pondered a moment, then she nodded. 'Okay. As I said, he's no hayseed. He graduated from the University of Missouri, then he went on to Oxford, England – he was there two or three years behind President Clinton. He's very much okay and the word from Canberra is that he's very popular and respected on the diplomatic circuit. Being a US ambassador is not the easiest job in the world, no matter where you are.'

'What is the security set-up? Is there an FBI agent at the embassy?'

'No, he's here at the consulate – that's the posting. But he went down to Canberra last night when Mrs Pavane didn't return there.'

24

Malone glanced at Random. 'Did you know there was an FBI man stationed here?'

'Yes. It's not top secret, but it's not broadcast. So far we've had no dealings with him.'

Malone felt uneasy, but said nothing. Then Consul-General Avery came in. His face was stiff, but he seemed to have recovered from the shock that Random and Malone had brought him. He looked ready for business, unsettling though it might be.

'I spoke to our Chief of Mission first, then the Ambassador came on the line. It's floored him – he sounded as if I'd hit him with a ten-pound hammer. He's coming up right away – they've got a plane standing by. He'll be here in an hour, an hour and a half at the most. Where is Mrs Pavane's body?'

'At the morgue,' said Random. 'If you could meet him at the airport and take him there – it's out at Glebe. We'll let them know to expect him. He'll need to identify the body. Then we'd like to see him.'

'Meet him here, will you? We'd like to keep him away from the media for as long as possible, at least till he's got over the shock. Once it's on the wire services or the reps here of our bigger papers . . .' His brows came down, his mouth twisted and for a moment he looked ugly. Then his face cleared and he looked at his watch. 'Say one-thirty?'

'We'll be here,' said Random, then turned to Gina Caporetto. 'We won't identify Mrs Pavane till we've talked to the Ambassador. We'll keep her out of the news till then. But then –'

'Then,' said Avery with the voice of experience, 'the fan starts whirring.'

'I'm afraid so,' said Random. 'Inspector Malone will be handling it. He's a good man on fans and what sometimes flies out of them.'

'Shit,' said Malone, but under his breath.

Going down in the lift, in the long drop from the 59th floor, Malone felt his spirits descending, too. There were only the two of them in the lift and he said, 'Given my choice I think I'll take the hotel's cleaner and the knife job on him. You can have Mrs Pavane.'

'You have no choice, chum. My Welsh mother used to say –'

'Forget it. You Welsh are a melancholy lot.'

'So are you Irish at times. Like now.'

3

With Celtic pessimism Malone believed in the invasion of the irrational into the orderly. But he did not always accept the toss of the coin by God or the gods, whichever one believed in. He would not accept the second toss of the coin.

He dropped Random off at Police Centre and drove on back to Homicide in Strawberry Hills. There were no hills and there had never been any strawberries, but the voters of Sydney lived and worked in other areas with names just as illusory: Ultimo, Sans Souci, Como. God set a bad example for developers when He named the Garden of Eden.

Malone rode up to the fourth floor, let himself in the security door and found Phil Truach sitting with Clements, waiting for him.

'How'd you go?' asked Clements sympathetically.

Malone told them of the visit to the Consul-General's office. 'I think it's going to be a really bad headache. Let's talk of something simpler. How'd you go, Phil?'

'I haven't come up with much. Nobody saw the cleaner knifed – he was well and truly dead when another guy found him. He wasn't popular, but I didn't get the idea that anyone there would want to top him. He was found in the room where they keep all the cleaning equipment. There didn't appear to have been any struggle – all the buckets and mops and things were neatly stacked. Unless the killer put everything back . . . Crime Scene have dusted the room for prints. They'll let us know.'

'Who was he?'

Truach looked at his notebook. 'Boris Jones, aged forty, his card said. He was a Russian, they said, but he'd changed his name. Mrs Jones is in there –' He nodded towards one of the interview rooms. 'I went out to see her, she lives out at Rozelle. She asked who was in charge and I said you and she said you were the one she wanted to talk to.'

'Why me?'

'I dunno. Ask her.'

'How's she taking it? His murder?'

'She's pretty calm, considering.' Truach looked towards the closed door of the interview room. 'She's been bashed. A black eye and some bruises.'

'The husband did it?'

'She didn't say. Just said she wanted to talk to you. She hardly said a word all the way back here. She's got a friend with her, a Mrs Quantock. She does all the talking.'

Malone stood up. 'Righto, I'll talk to her. But she's your girl. I've got enough on my plate with the Ambassador's missus. Russ, make sure that Regent Street has got the names and addresses of everyone who was booked in last night at the Southern Savoy. They can start doing the donkey-work, checking everyone on the hotel's register.' Then he looked at Clements' still-clean desk. 'Get ready, mate. That desk is going to see more paper than a ticker-tape parade.'

'I can't wait,' said Clements and slumped further back in his chair.

Malone went into the interview room, motioning Gail Lee to follow him. It was standard procedure that two officers had to be present during an interview; he chose Gail because of the two other women in the room. In the climate of women he, with a wife and two daughters, was showerproof; but heavy weather was another matter. Not that he expected heavy weather in this room: that was to come when he met Ambassador Pavane.

The two women were sitting side by side at the single table

27

in the room. One was in her mid-forties: age and measurement: there was a lot of Mrs Quantock and she looked ready to use her weight and experience. The other woman was slight, dark-haired and would have been attractive but for the damage to her face.

'Well!' said Mrs Quantock; she had a voice for shouting over backyard fences, several of them. 'We've had to wait long enough!'

'I'm sorry, Mrs Quantock. There was another murder at the same hotel –'

'Another?' She looked at Mrs Jones. 'Delia –?'

Delia Jones looked across the table as Malone sat down. 'Hullo, Scobie.'

Malone was accustomed to shock; it came with a policeman's lot. But not for the shock of meeting Delia Bates, the long-forgotten love of twenty-five years ago, now the widow of a murdered man. Recognition had not been instant: twenty-year-old Delia was partially hidden in this woman with the battered face sitting opposite him.

'Delia –' Involuntarily he put his hand across the table to press hers. 'Jesus, I didn't know –'

'You know each other?' Mrs Quantock was the sort of friend who would never be left out of any relationship. She would intrude with the best of intentions, swamping the friend with rescue efforts, throwing lifebelts like hoopla rings. She glared at Malone: 'You didn't know what sorta bastard he was? He's been belting her all their married life, in front of the kids –'

Delia, still with her eyes on Malone, put her hand on her friend's arm. 'It's okay, Rosie. We haven't seen each other in twenty-five years.' As if she had counted every one of them. 'He knows nothing about Boris. He's married and has got kids of his own.'

Malone was aware of Gail Lee observing all this with what he called her Oriental lack of expression (though never to her face). She was half-Chinese and she had never succumbed

28

to the temptation to favour her Australian half; serenity is not an Australian expression, at least not amongst the city voters, and she always looked serene. At the moment her face was blank.

Malone was a private man and he did not like his private life exposed; not even that of twenty-five years ago. He had been in love then; or thought so. Till he had gone to London and met Lisa, and then Delia and all the other girls he had known had dropped out of his mind. He had come back to Sydney (he had that year been on another case that had taken him into diplomatic territory; he had gone to London to arrest the Australian High Commissioner, another ambassador, for murder), had spent two days finding the courage to be decent, then met Delia and told her it was all over, that he had fallen in love, deeply, with another girl. Delia had looked at him, saying nothing, then she had got up from the table where they had been at an outdoor café and walked away without a word and out of his life. He had sat there, feeling an utter bastard; then there had been the deep feeling of relief (an honest emotion that bastards can feel) and he got up and went down to the old GPO and booked a call to Lisa, still in London. He would never be able to explain that to Gail Lee. Nor had he ever fully explained it to Lisa. Girls one has slept with should be left undisturbed.

'I dunno,' said Mrs Quantock, 'I dunno how you can sit there so bloody calm, like nothing's happened –'

'I was always calm, wasn't I, Scobie?'

'Not always.' Remembering how she had been in bed.

'No, not always.' For a moment there was the hint of a smile at the corner of her bruised mouth; then it was gone: 'I didn't show it, but I wasn't calm when you told me you were going to marry another girl.'

'Delia, please –' He had taken his hand away from hers.

There was silence in the small room; even Mrs Quantock seemed engulfed by it. Then Gail Lee said quietly, 'Mrs Jones, do you know anyone who would want to kill your husband?'

29

Delia looked at her as if seeing her for the first time; she glanced back at Malone, as if waiting for him to say something, then looked at Gail again. 'Yes.'

'Who?'

'Me.'

'Oh, for Crissake, Delia!' Mrs Quantock moved even closer to her, grabbed her friend's hand. 'Don't be so – so bloody cool! Your life's been hell –'

Delia pressed Rosie Quantock's hand again, stared straight at Malone. 'I killed him, Scobie. I stabbed him, I dunno how many times.'

There was silence again but for a gasp from Mrs Quantock. Malone sat back, gathering himself together, trying to find the cop who had been lost in himself for a minute or two. 'Delia, if you're going to make a confession to killing your husband, I'll have to turn that on.' He pointed to the video recorder. 'Then we'll have to warn you –'

'I know. I watch *The Bill*, *Law and Order*, all those shows –'

'We have to warn you anyway,' he said and did so. 'Righto – What's the matter?'

'You still say that.' Again the small smile. 'Righto.'

'Yes, I guess I do. Now I'll put the question – did you kill your husband Boris Jones?'

'Yes, this morning at the hotel where he worked, the Southern Savoy. In the room where he kept all the cleaning stuff.'

'Was it self-defence? Did he bash you?' He should not have put leading questions like that; he was still coming back out of that dim distant past. The coin had been spun again, the irrational had invaded the orderly again.

'He bashed me before he went to work last night.' She put her hand up to her face almost automatically: as if she had been doing it for years.

'You went to the hotel, followed him to work, to kill him?' said Gail.

'Hold on!' Rosie Quantock was there again, throwing lifebelts.

30

'If you're gunna question her like that, she needs a solicitor. Keep quiet, Delia, don't tell 'em any more.'

'It's all right, Rosie –'

'It's not all right! For Crissake, love, think of yourself and the kids!' She looked at Malone: as Delia's old lover, not a cop: 'Tell her for her own good –'

Malone switched off the recorder. 'We'll have to hold you till you get someone here to brief you, Delia. We'll send you over to Police Centre, to Surry Hills, and they'll hold you there. Do you have a solicitor? Better if you can get one who has some experience in this sort of thing. A conveyancing solicitior isn't going to be much good for you.'

'We'll get one,' said Rosie Quantock. She's a pain in the arse, thought Malone, but she's the sort of friend everyone should have. 'I'll take care of it, Delia. I'll take care of the kids, too. And get on to your mother –'

'How old are the children?' asked Gail.

'Eleven and twelve, a boy and a girl.' Delia looked at Malone, read the question in his face: 'No, I didn't start late. Boris was my second husband, they're his kids. I have a daughter who's twenty.'

'Where's she?' asked Malone.

'In England – London. With her father. He's English, a teacher.'

English, Russian: because she had been jilted by an Australian? 'Do you want us to get in touch with her?'

She shrugged, the calmness still there. There was just a faint shake of the head, not of negation but of wonder, as if she were only just coming to realize the seriousness of her situation. She gazed at Malone for a long moment, then she said, 'We never thought it would come to this, did we, Scobie?'

He was all cop now, the only protection. 'No, Delia, we didn't . . . Detective Lee and another officer will take you over to Surry Hills.' He turned to Rosie Quantock. 'How soon can you get a lawyer for her?'

'Give me an hour.' She could raise an army in an hour, you knew it would not be beyond her.

'Don't rush, get a good one. Detective Lee and the other officer will then question Delia –'

'No,' said Delia.

He looked at her. 'No what?'

'You're the only one I'll talk to.'

'Delia, I have another homicide to look into –'

'No.' It was more than calmness now, it was cold adamancy.

He took a deep breath, trying to remain calm himself. 'Righto, but it may not be till late afternoon before I can get back to you.'

'That will do,' said Rosie Quantock and stood up, putting an arm under Delia's. 'Buck up, love. It's not over till the Fat Lady sings.'

'She used to be in the chorus at the Opera House.' Again there was just the hint of a smile at the corner of the bruised mouth. She looked almost relaxed again, as if the only point that had worried her was that Malone might not question her. And now he had promised that he would.

'Were you a Valkyrie?' Gail asked Rosie Quantock and Malone could see that she was trying to keep the mood light.

'What else? Come on, love. We're still ahead.'

She would not give in, she would be raising spirits, like flags.

Chapter Two

1

After the women had gone, Sheryl Dallen going with Gail Lee, Malone called Clements and Phil Truach into his office. Clements examined him frankly and Malone stared back at him.

'You've got a problem,' said the big man and lowered himself into his usual seat on the couch beneath the window. Out on the ledge a pigeon looked in at them with an impersonal eye.

'You're right, a big one.'

'She did her husband?' said Truach.

'Yes. But this is personal – for me. Delia Jones is an old girlfriend of mine. We went steady for almost a year. She expected me to marry her.'

Clements frowned. 'Delia – Bates? Bateman? You brought her once to a party. *Her?*'

'Her. Delia Bates.'

'No problem,' said Truach. 'I'll handle it, you don't need to come within a mile of her.'

'That won't work, Phil. She won't talk to anyone but me. I tried her with Gail, but no go. I'm just starting to remember how stubborn she could be.'

Clements, the personal friend, said, 'Does Lisa know about her? I mean before you married her?'

'I mentioned her once or twice – just joking, I think. Do you talk about your old girlfriends to Romy? Do you tell your wife about them, Phil?'

'What old girlfriends?' said Truach. 'I was an altar boy till I met her. Of course, there was Father Mulcahy –'

'Righto, lay off. This is no time for joking –'

'Sorry. So she was the one who did the damage? Because he belted her?'

'Evidently he's been doing it for years. He had a go at her last night.'

'So it was self-defence?' Clements, like most cops, was sympathetic to battered women.

'They must of had a fight at the hotel,' said Truach. 'Maybe he tried to belt her again, her following him to work. The room where he was done, everything was in its place when we looked at it. But Norma Nickles rang in with a preliminary report. There were prints, blood on them, on a lot of the stuff, the buckets and mops and things. As if someone had picked it all up and put it back in place.'

'That could be her.' Memory was coming back. She had been wild and uninhibited in bed, but once out of it she had been as neat as a drill sergeant, a place for everything and everything in its place. She had dressed with almost convent-like neatness, then made the bed that they had wrecked. They had joked about her passion for order. Neither of them had known then that her life would be totally disordered. Or so it looked. 'She was like that. She could make a rugby scrum look neat.'

'Then that could save her,' said Clements. 'She gets a good lawyer, they plead the bashing and the self-defence –'

'We can make it look –' said Truach.

'Phil, don't make it look like anything but the facts. I don't want some prosecutor tearing you apart . . . She was my girl-friend, but that was twenty-five years ago. We've both had our own lives since then. I've been the lucky one . . .'

Clements stepped out of his cop's role: 'Are you gunna tell Lisa?'

'Whom –' He had been coached by Lisa who, like most educated foreigners, had more respect for English grammar than the natives. 'Whom do you think she is going to be interested in, an ex-girlfriend who's murdered her husband or the murdered wife of the American Ambassador?'

34

'The Ambassador's wife,' said Truach. 'That will be the one all over the news tonight —'

'You're kidding. You're still influenced by Father Whatshis-name. She will ask me about Delia and so will my daughters. And even Tom will look at me with new interest. They know I've never looked at another woman since I met Lisa and they think my life before her was just a blank. Or at worst I spent all my time with blokes.'

Clements stood up. 'Let's put Delia on the back burner for a while. It's time you went down to the Yanks again, to meet the Ambassador.'

'I think I might ask for a transfer to Fingerprints.' Malone got to his feet, feeling stiff and aged. 'Nothing there turns round and bites you. Call Greg and tell him I'll pick him up.'

The pigeon on the window ledge had been joined by four others. They sat there sheltering against the south wind, looking over their shoulders at the humans inside, their heads bob-bing as if in gossip. Malone leaned across and banged on the window and the pigeons took off, caught at once by the wind.

'Bloody birds, crapping all the time on that ledge —'

'Simmer down,' said Clements. 'Don't take Delia down with you to the Yanks. Leave her here with me and Phil.'

Malone nodded appreciatively. 'Yeah, you're right . . . Phil, get someone to check the restaurant, Catalina, where Miss Caporetto took Mrs Pavane for lunch. Get the names of all male guests that day. Restaurants always ask for a contact number, case you don't turn up. We just have to hope they kept their booking list for — how long was it?'

'Two weeks,' said Clements, who had put it all on the computer.

'Righto, get on with it. We'll try and find that bloke.'

'I don't want to keep harping on her,' said Truach, 'but what about Mrs Jones?'

For a moment the name meant nothing: it was as if he were

trying to shut Delia out of his mind. 'Let's hope she comes to her senses and talks to Gail and Sheryl.'

'Yeah,' said Clements but didn't sound encouraging. 'It would be nice if someone would come in and talk to us about the Ambassador's wife.'

'Fat chance,' said Malone and left to pick up Greg Random. Out of the corner of his eye he saw the pigeons come back to the window ledge. They knew better than to be blown about by the wind.

Random came out of Police Centre, got into the car beside Malone and said without preamble, 'I've set up the Incident Room here at the Centre – that way I can keep an eye on things. I've asked your two girls, Gail and Sheryl, to run it with the senior sergeant from Surry Hills. We'll treat both murders as the one investigation till we've got things sorted out. Gail told me the woman who knifed her husband won't talk to anyone but you.'

Malone told him why, as he drove through a snaking river of drivers who raged at everyone else for their own frustrations. 'I've got to get out of it somehow, Greg.'

'Do the media know about the relationship?'

'Not yet, not unless she wants to tell them. Gail tells me she was photographed, by the press and by the TV cameras, when she was brought in from Rozelle. At that time she hadn't been charged, she was just the widow of the murdered man. You know, the usual hearts-and-flowers thing. They wanted to photograph her two kids, but they'd been taken away by their grandmother. It's a mess, Greg.'

Random said nothing more till they had parked the car in the basement of the MLC building and they were walking towards the lifts. Then: 'Keep her at arm's length. Get any closer and you're off that case.'

'You couldn't make me a better offer.'

There were only four people in the Consul-General's office besides Avery and Ms Caporetto. Malone had expected the

Ambassador to bring an entourage. Newsreel clips of delega-
tions to conferences, football teams running into a stadium,
preparations for war: all had shown that Americans never arrived
under-manned. More was better: it was a second national motto.
Like sweat, resentment was building up against the possibility of
his turf being invaded. Even if, given his druthers, he'd druther
be in Tibooburra, the State foreign legion outpost.

'Ambassador Pavane,' said Avery, and the tall, handsome
blond man stepped forward and shook hands with Random and
Malone.

'I've identified – my – my wife.' The break in his voice was
barely perceptible. 'This is Walter Kortright, our DCM. Roger
Bodine, our RSO. And Joe Himes, FBI.'

Initials, initials, thought Malone, and his puzzlement showed.
As it did with Random.

'Sorry,' said Pavane, reading their faces. 'Walter is our Deputy
Charge of Mission. Roger is the Regional Security Officer. He
works with your Federal Police, when called upon.'

'And Mr Himes?' asked Random.

Pavane didn't answer, just looked at Himes. The Ambassador
looked suddenly tired, as if he wanted to be shed of his role.
He was well-built, looked very fit and had a presence; but at
the moment, Malone felt, it was all facade. The man had been
punched hollow by the death of his wife and the manner of it. He
was above politics, investigation politics, at the moment. Himes
could answer for himself.

'It's your turf, Superintendent.' Himes understood the term;
he also obviously understood the territorial imperative. Malone
abruptly remembered movies where American local officers
resented the intrusion of the FBI. Himes might, just might, be
easy to work with.

He was a thickset, black-haired man with a husky voice and
eyes that once might have been fearless but had learned caution.
'I'll help all I can – when asked.'

'Same here,' said Bodine, the RSO. He looked as if, like Avery, he had been a football player; but not a quarterback, not by at least two halves. He was b-i-i-i-g; and fat. The diplomatic party circuit had got to him, his security was ungirdled. He had a voice that went with his build, like an internal landslide.

'What's the media situation?' Kortright was a soft-featured man with thinning blond hair and an almost incongruously dark moustache, like a military character struggling to get out of an appeaser. His question had little bite to it.

'So far,' said Malone, 'they only know Mrs Pavane under the name she registered at the hotel. Mrs Belinda Paterson.'

'Who?' Pavane was puzzled.

Malone looked at Random, who nodded; then he said to the Ambassador, 'Mr Pavane, could I see you alone?'

Now there was puzzlement on the faces of Kortright and Bodine. Himes was blank-faced and Malone recognized a law officer who had been in a similar situation, telling secrets best left unrevealed.

Pavane looked at the Consul-General, who said, 'Use Miz Caporetto's office.'

Malone and the Ambassador went out and crossed to the press secretary's office. Malone closed the door, turned to find the Ambassador had sat down heavily in one of the chairs in front of the desk. The coffee-pot was on the hot-plate, but this was no time for offering coffee. Something stronger might be better, but there was nothing in sight in the room. Malone sat down in the other chair and waited till the older man at last looked across at him.

'Sorry, Inspector. I'm still coming to terms –'

Malone decided to ease his way into the situation: 'Did your wife tell you where she was going in Sydney? Why she was up here?'

'She was going shopping. And to the Art Gallery. She phoned me, but I was out and my secretary spoke to her –'

'When was this?'

'I think she said two-thirty. My wife said to tell me she'd be

back on a later plane than the five o'clock one. That was all.'
He was looking at Malone, but his gaze was almost blank. 'I
just don't understand –' Then he made a helpless gesture with
a big hand. 'It's just not like her –'

Malone said gently, 'I'm afraid I'm going to tell you something
that will further upset you. That's why I asked could I see you
alone –'

Pavane waited, a hand tightening on the arm of his chair.

Malone always hated this intrusion into another man or woman's personal life: 'There had been intercourse before your wife
was murdered –'

The hand tightened even more: 'She'd been raped?'

'No, sir. The Medical Examiner said there was no evidence
of that – rape always shows. Bruises, marks, things like that.'

The hand fell loose. 'Jesus Christ, you know what you're
saying?'

Husband to husband, not cop to diplomat: 'Yes, sir. And I hate
telling you this. But it may be our only clue to who killed her.
They are taking semen samples, there'll be DNA tests when we
have a suspect –'

Pavane waved a hand, not wanting to hear any more. He looked
older, but age is a ghost that comes and goes till finally it settles.
At last he said, 'You know what you're saying? You are accusing
my wife –'

'Sir, please –' Malone held up his own hand. 'I'm not accusing
your wife of anything. I hate scandal and I'm not interested in it.
All I want is to find out who killed her.' He was about to add:
and why. But now was not the moment.

Pavane sat silent and at last Malone said, 'You were surprised
when I said she was registered as Mrs Belinda Paterson. Was that
her name before you were married?'

'No.'

Again a long silence, then Malone said, 'What was her
name?'

A deep sigh; then Pavane's gaze focused again. He frowned,

drew in a deep breath: 'Page, Wilhelmina Page. But she was always called Billie.'

'You never heard her mention the name Paterson?'

'Never.'

'She had a credit card in that name.'

'I never saw it. She had an American Express card as my wife, Mrs Billie Pavane, but I never checked her account. She was a good businesswoman, she was experienced.'

'Tell me something about her.' Still gently.

Pavane took his time, as if he had been asked to open a very personal diary. 'We've been married two years – very happily married. My first wife died six years ago and I thought I'd never marry again. Then . . .' He turned a direct gaze on Malone. 'Are you married?'

'Yes. Very happily. I have two daughters and a son, all grown.'

'I have a son by my first marriage. He disappeared after his mother died. We never got on –' He stopped. 'Do you want to hear all this?'

'I want to hear about your second wife. Had you known her long?'

'No, not that long. She came to Kansas City – that's my home town – about four years ago. She was a business consultant with our largest bank – handled public relations, things like that. I met her through politics – we were both raising funds for a local senator.'

'You said she came to Kansas City – where did she come from? Her credit card gave an address in Oregon.' He took out his notebook, checked. 'Corvallis. Is it a big town? Was she a business consultant there?'

'It's not large. The State College is there. She was born there, her father worked for the college – not an academic, he was just some worker around the grounds.'

'She went to college? Graduated there?'

'No. Her parents were killed in an auto accident when she was

40

– I'm a bit hazy here – seventeen or eighteen. She was an only child. She left Corvallis and went out to San Francisco. Look, why all the background?'

'Mr Pavane, we're puzzled why she booked into a hundred-dollar-a-night hotel, under an assumed name. I take it that isn't the usual sort of hotel she'd stay at?'

'No-o. I'm just as puzzled as you are. We've never been short of money. I'm comfortable –' Meaning he was wealthy; or, in Australian terms, rich. 'Billie liked the best – she was frank about that and I didn't mind. My first wife was the same. Women are like that.'

He wasn't entirely a diplomat: the three Malone women would have had reservations about him after that remark. But Malone was diplomatic: 'Yes, I guess they are. Had your wife been married before? She was what – in her late thirties?'

'Thirty-eight. No, she hadn't been married. She'd had boy-friends, but she had never settled for a husband. She was too busy making her career, she said. I – well, I accepted that. I didn't talk about my first wife and she didn't talk about her ex-boyfriends. You're a married man, you know how it is.'

Not yet: I haven't been home so far. 'You said you met in politics. Did she have political ambitions?'

'No, not at all. Not as far as running for office. We were working together on last year's presidential campaign – there were hints of an ambassadorship for me and that excited her. We thought of one of the smaller countries in Europe. Denmark, maybe – I'd been to Copenhagen when I was at university in England and I'd liked it. Then the President named Australia – he thought I had certain talents, connections, that would work out here.'

'And your wife liked that? I understand she'd been out here.'

Pavane looked puzzled again. 'Who told you that?'

'Miss Caporetto. She went to lunch with your wife and your

41

wife told her she'd been here on a quick business trip some years ago.'

Pavane shook his head emphatically. 'Miss Caporetto must've got it wrong. My wife didn't want to come here.'

'Why not?'

Pavane almost smiled, took his time. 'Do you want me to be frank or diplomatic, Inspector?'

'Frank, sir. I'm not so nationalistic that I think this is Utopia. One of our Prime Ministers once said not to forget we were at the arse-end of the world. Or words to that effect.'

The Ambassador did smile this time, though it was an effort. 'Those were the words my wife used. Though she pronounced it ass-end.'

'In the end she changed her mind?'

'It took a lot of persuasion on my part.' He was silent a long moment and Malone let him take his time. Then: 'How much do we have to tell the media?'

'Just the facts, sir. How she was murdered, who she is. Nothing more than that. We don't have to tell them what happened beforehand.'

Pavane was grateful: 'You're an understanding man, Inspector.'

Malone nodded in acknowledgement. 'Why did she come to Sydney on this particular trip?'

'She wanted to go to the New South Wales Art Gallery. There's an exhibition on there – the best of Australian art. Back home in Kansas City she's on the board of the Nelson Gallery – that's our main gallery. My father bought and donated paintings to it. She's on leave of absence, but she'd told the board she would look at this collection – we don't see much Australian art in our Mid-West.'

'Righto, sir. We'll see if she ever got to the gallery. As for what I've told you about last night, we'll keep a lid on it as much as possible.'

'Is there likely to be a leak from – well, the morgue staff?'

'The DDFM –' He grinned, trying to lighten the mood. 'The Deputy Director of Forensic Medicine, she did the post-mortem –'

'I met her at the morgue.'

'She's a close personal friend of me and my wife and she's the wife of my second-in-command at Homicide. She would sack anyone who talked out of turn to the media.'

'Good enough. I apologize for questioning them. Will you tell Joe Himes?'

'I'm afraid I'll have to, sir, if he's to work with us. But no one else.' He stood up, put out his hand as the other man rose. 'I'm sorry, sir. I'll do everything I can to keep the dirt out of this. It's not going to be a tabloid carnival.'

'I'm going back to Canberra this afternoon. I want the body of my wife shipped back to Kansas City – I'll go with her. Dr Clements, your friend, said they would release her within the next day or two, soon as the post-mortem is finished. There'll be a press release put out from the embassy when I get back this afternoon. It will say as little as possible.'

'We'll try to do the same at this end, sir. You'll be coming back from Kansas City?'

Pavane hesitated. 'I'll think about it. I really loved my wife, Mr Malone – we were very happy together. I have to get used to the idea that she is gone.' Just before he opened the door to go out he turned. 'Thanks, Mr Malone.'

Malone could only nod.

2

The Consul-General's office was a bustle of departure. Random left at the same time as the Ambassador, DCM Kortright and RSO Bodine. Malone and Himes borrowed Ms Caporetto's office again. Malone stood at the window gazing down on Martin Place at the ants coming back from lunch. There had been the usual lunchtime concert in the small amphitheatre in the middle of the tree-lined plaza and the musicians were packing their gear and moving on to – what? And what were all the human ants scurrying to? From here on the 59th level destiny was a distant prospect. He turned back to Himes: 'Joe, what are your feelings on destiny?'

Himes was seated in the chair behind the desk, the *presiding* chair. *Pull your head in, Malone, he's not taking over.* 'I never worry about destiny. That's for judges and juries.'

Malone grinned: he was going to like this man. 'Righto –'

'Righto? I thought only upper-class Englishmen said that. You know – "Righto, old chap."'

'If I'd been born an upper-class Englishman, my dad would've strangled me at birth. He's never been near Ireland, but he's an Irish patriot – more so than my mother, who was born there. No, righto has just stuck to my tongue since I was a kid.'

'What do you say when things are okay?'

'Okay.'

Himes gazed at Malone and after a long pause said, 'I think you and I are gonna get along, Scobie.'

'I hope so, Joe. We're going to need help – a lot of it.' He sat down, then told Himes of the intimate personal side of the Pavane murder. 'We're not putting out anything about that – our media would make a meal of it.'

'Not just yours. Ours, too.'

'There's something else besides the sex bit. Mrs Pavane has some mystery about her, something that seems to puzzle even the Ambassador. Does the FBI have a bureau in Oregon?'

Himes smiled; he had big white teeth that seemed to alter the whole set of his face. Almost impish, like a boy of long ago suddenly appearing in the man he had become. 'We've got 'em all over. The local cops think we're a pain in the ass.'

Malone returned the smile. 'We think the same about our Feds here. Anyhow, can you have them trace –' He looked at his notebook again. 'Mrs Pavane's maiden name was Wilhelmina

44

Page, but she was known as Billie. She also used an American Express card under the name of Mrs Belinda Paterson. Home address, Corvallis. Her parents, who were killed in a car accident, lived there – roughly, I guess, in the late seventies. Her father had some sort of job at the State College, a groundsman or something.'

'I'll get on to that pronto.' He looked at his watch. 'Unless they're having an early night.'

'The FBI sleeps?'

Again the smile. 'Not as much as the CIA.'

In heaven the seraphim criticize the cherubim, who look down on the thrones: the original bureaucracy.

'Anything else?'

'Mrs Pavane told Miss Caporetto, one day at lunch, that she'd made a quick business trip to Sydney some years ago. The Ambassador says that can't be right. But at the lunch some feller came up, tried to speak to Mrs Pavane, but she just wiped him. Is there any way you can trace if a Miss Page or a Mrs Paterson came to Sydney eight or nine years ago? We'll check with our Immigration.'

Himes made a note. 'I'm told there was another homicide at the same hotel. Any connection?'

'We don't think so. It's a domestic. I'm on my way now to question the wife.'

'I don't envy you. In my job I never got caught up in domestics, not like local cops. This one –' He shook his head as if in disbelief. 'This one's the closest I've ever been to a domestic.'

'Joe, a domestic for us is when the husband kills the wife or vice versa.'

'I know. But from what you've told me, this isn't the usual security thing. Terrorists, someone with a grudge against the US – it looks like nothing more than plain murder. To which Mrs Pavane might've contributed by being where she was in that flea-bag.'

'It's not a flea-bag, Joe. It's just a hotel where the rate is about three or four hundred dollars a night less than she'd be used to paying. What do you know about her?'

'You couldn't meet a nicer woman. She had – what do they call it? – the common touch. I know no more about her than what I saw down in Canberra – the embassy staff love her. She'd have been checked by the FBI back home before she and the Ambassador got the appointment – it's standard procedure –'

'They missed somewhere along the line. They didn't link her with Mrs Belinda Paterson.'

'The FBI is thorough –'

'Joe, I'm not criticizing. I'm stating a fact, that's all. Mrs Pavane apparently has had three names – I'd like to find out which was her real one. Then, maybe, we can start tracing her killer.'

'You think it was someone from her past who killed her?'

'I haven't a clue, Joe. But it would be better if it were, wouldn't it?'

Himes stood up, looking weary. 'I dunno, Scobie. There are no good aspects to murder, are there?'

'I'm not sure of that, either. I've seen some bastards who were better dead than alive.' He, too, stood up. They both looked weary enough to be at the end of a case rather than the beginning of it. 'What if the bloke who killed her didn't know who she really was? She had all her valuables up in the room with her. Only her passport was in the safe deposit box. Didn't she want him to know who she was?'

'I hate the thought she might just have been there as a pick-up. Are you gonna ask the Ambassador what their sex life was like?'

Malone grinned without humour. 'I think I'll leave that to Foreign Affairs.'

3

On his way out Malone looked in on Consul-General Avery. 'We've started, sir. But there's a long way to go.'

46

'I once played in a Rose Bowl game. We were behind thirty-eight to nil at the end of the second quarter.'

'Did you win?'

'No, but we gave UCLA a helluva fright.'

Malone shook his head. 'I've spent all my police career trying to give crims a fright. It never works, not with the pros. This feller who killed Mrs Pavane, he's way ahead at the moment.'

'You sound pessimistic.'

'No, just realistic. It's a cop's philosophy.'

Ms Caporetto rode down in the lift with him. She was wearing a thick brown coat and the sort of tea-cosy hat that he thought was worn only by seven-year-olds with fashion-conscious mothers. She did not look demure, nor as innocent as a seven-year-old, but the body was not visible to be whistled at.

'I'm on my way to see your Premier.'

'Is he getting into the act?'

'I don't think so. It's a courtesy call on our part. We want to ask if everything can be played down, if and when the questions come up in Parliament.'

'Not *if*. *When*. Another twenty-four hours and the Opposition will be asking why we police haven't wrapped it up. It's par for the course. Never be constructive when in Opposition.'

'I love working here. You're such a primitive lot.' But as she stepped out of the lift she gave him a smile that said it was a compliment.

He drove back to Police Centre and Delia Jones. The day had turned grey, but the clouds were still high, scarred by wind. Down at street level another wind chased paper down the gutters, straightened people into mannikins as they turned corners into it. A day for a grey mood.

He first went into the Incident Room, where Gail Lee and Sheryl Dallen had finished the display board. There was not much: a few photos, names, diagrams. There would have been less if the coverage had been of only a single murder.

'Not much, is there?'

'Did you get anything new from the Ambassador?' asked Gail Lee.

'Just that Mrs Pavane has a murky past. No,' he said as both women raised their eyebrows. 'Nothing dirty. It's just that even Mr Pavane can't tell us much about his wife before he married her.'

Then he looked at the photo of the dead Boris Jones. Even in death there was a look of cruelty in the broad Slav face; or was that his own imagination, a desire, too late, to protect Delia? 'What would you say of a bloke like that?'

'A bastard,' said Sheryl. 'But some women would find him attractive.'

'Mrs Jones must have. How is she?'

'A bit edgy,' said Sheryl, 'but nothing much. She's more worried about her kids than about what she's done.'

'Her lawyer turned up yet?'

'Mrs Quantock's brought in a solicitor from out their way, Balmain. She and Mrs Jones have been arguing about who'll pay – evidently Mrs Jones has got nothing. It looks like it might be a Legal Aid job.'

Legal Aid did its best but it could never afford the talent that could turn a no-win case into an acquittal. 'Righto, I'd better see her. You come with me, Gail.'

'Do we keep both murders on the one board?' asked Sheryl.

'I hope not.' He would like the Jones murder dropped off the board altogether. 'We'll see what she has to tell us.'

'Not us,' said Gail. 'You.'

'Don't remind me.' He looked at both of them. 'You know I'd rather walk right away from this?'

'Of course,' said Sheryl and he saw at once that their support was genuine. And it was more acceptable because they were women. This was not blokey mateship.

He took Gail into the interview room with him. He was annoyed but not surprised when he saw Mrs Quantock sitting to one side of Delia and the woman solicitor. Rosie Quantock sensed his annoyance for she said at once, 'I'm here for Delia to lean on.'

'That's okay, Mrs Quantock, but don't interrupt when I'm questioning Delia.' He sat down, looked at the solicitor across the table. 'G'day, Pam. Are you taking Delia's case or are you here just for now? I understand she has asked for Legal Aid.'

'I'm here for the whole term.' Pamela Morrow was an old foe, but a friendly one. She and Malone had met years ago when she had been a law student leading demonstrations against this, that and everything and he had been a new police recruit trying to handle gently a woman trying to kick him in the balls. She was a short dumpling of a woman with red hair cut in a bob with bangs and with bright blue eyes that, he knew, could be as challenging as Rosie Quantock's. 'I'm on the board of the Women's Protection League. We're taking Mrs Jones' case. Right through from now to acquittal.'

He grinned. 'You haven't changed, Pam.' Only then did he look at Delia. 'Pam and I are old mates.'

'Old Home Week,' said Delia and smiled as if she were here on no more than a traffic charge. He caught a glimpse of the girl he had once been in love with. She had been a pretty girl rather than beautiful; chocolate-boxy, his mother had called her. Prettiness, he knew, faded quicker than beauty; but the years had been too cruel to her. 'We're not going to be any trouble, Scobie.'

'Tell us what happened.' Not *me*: *us*. He had to keep Gail in the frame to protect himself.

'Tell him *everything*,' said Rosie Quantock. 'How he's been belting you for years –'

Malone looked at Pam Morrow, who looked at Rosie Quantock. 'Please –'

'Sorry,' said Rosie, but you knew it was just an empty word. 'But she's gotta tell him everything –'

'I will,' said Delia, hands folded together on the table, steady as two interlocked rocks. She nodded at the recorder: 'Is that on?'

'Yes,' said Gail. 'Everything you say –'

49

'I know.' The composure was so complete; Malone had to admire her. 'Well – where do I begin?'

'At the beginning,' said Malone, knowing he was making a concession.

'Well, Boris and I have been married fourteen years. He's from Leningrad – or what do they call it now?'

'St Petersburg,' said Gail.

Delia didn't look at her; her gaze was solely on Malone. 'Yes, there. He was a merchant seaman – he came to Australia twice on a ship. I met him, I liked him, he liked me –' She stopped for just a moment, her gaze still focused on Malone; then she went on, 'The third trip he jumped ship and stayed on.'

'He was an illegal immigrant?' asked Malone.

'I guess so. They never came looking for him – he got papers, I dunno how. We were happy –' She stopped again. She's making points, Malone thought; but ignored them, just looked back at her. She went on again, 'I had the children and then things started to go wrong –'

'I'll say they did,' said Rosie Quantock. 'Ten bloody years –'

'Mrs Quantock,' said Pam Morrow warningly.

'Sorry.'

Delia continued: 'He wouldn't let Melissa near the house – she was my daughter from my first husband.' Again the look; again he made no comment. 'Then the – the belting started. I ran away, twice, with the children. But he came after me each time –'

'Why did you go back to him?' asked Gail.

Delia shrugged. 'Ask any battered wife why –' For a moment she looked at Gail; then she turned her gaze back to Malone. For the first time there was a plea in her voice: 'That's what I've been, Scobie. A battered wife.'

He wanted to reach across and press her hand, but refrained. 'Go on. Tell us about last night. Did you go in to the hotel with the intention of killing him?'

'That's a leading question,' snapped Pam Morrow. 'Try another one, Inspector –'

'No, it's all right,' said Delia. 'Yes. I took the children to my mother's, told her I was going in to tell Boris I was leaving him for good. I wanted him dead, but I don't think I intended killing him.'

'Where did you get the knife?' Malone was wishing he were out of here.

'I dunno. It was there in the room – I just picked it up –'

Malone said nothing further; it was Gail who asked, 'Why? Why did you pick it up?'

'Careful, Delia,' warned Pam Morrow. 'You have to be exact about this. It was after Boris hit you, wasn't it?'

'You're advising your client,' said Gail.

Lay off, Gail! Malone almost shouted.

'That's why I'm here,' said Pam Morrow. 'To make sure she gives you the exact facts, the exact truth.'

Delia took her time, still looking at Malone as if there were just the two of them in the room. Then she said, 'It was after he hit me – here and here –' She pointed to the bruises on her face; still calm, as if they were no more than skin blemishes. 'He gave me the black eye before he left home.'

'Bastard!' said Rosie Quantock.

'There was a struggle?' Malone was leaving the questioning to Gail.

But Delia was still speaking directly to him: 'Oh yes, we fought. We knocked things over – I picked them up and put them back after I'd stabbed him –' She smiled at him, like the old Delia of long ago; he was beginning to wonder if the composure was a pose. 'Neat as usual, remember? But I was just trying to get myself together – I mean, I knew I'd killed him, he wasn't moving –'

'What did you do then?'

'Just a minute –' Malone said. 'What time was this, Delia?'

'Some time after midnight – he'd broken my watch when we fought last night.' She looked at it now on her wrist. 'You gave it to me, remember?'

He didn't remember and he wondered why she mentioned it.
'That was eight-twenty last night. It's stopped.'

Malone nodded to Gail, who went on, 'So you tidied up the store room – what did you do with the knife?'

'I dunno. I forget.'

'How did you leave the hotel?'

'I went out a side door into that alley, that lane, that's there – I didn't want to meet any of Boris' mates. I waited for a taxi outside the hotel.'

Romy had said that Billie Pavane had died eight to ten hours before she was examined: that put *that* murder around 1 a.m.

Malone said, 'While you were waiting for the taxi, did you see anyone come out of the hotel?'

If Delia was remembering anything it wasn't what she saw outside the hotel last night; she had a faraway look, remembering the distant past. Remembering the bruising Malone had given her when he had jilted her? Then her gaze focused and she looked at Gail and said, 'What?'

'Inspector Malone asked you a question,' said Gail.

'Oh.' Then she looked at him again, this time almost impersonally. He repeated his question and she said, 'Yes, a man.'

'Can you describe him?'

She shook her head. 'Only vaguely. A taxi pulled up and he tried to grab it. But I got the door open first –' Now she gave him a very personal look, leaning forward. 'I wasn't thinking too clearly, Scobie – you can understand that, can't you? You must know how in shock I was?'

He didn't ask how he was expected to know: he knew.

He said nothing, and she went on, 'Why do you want to know about the man?'

'The other murder?' said Rosie Quantock, who had been silent too long.

'Would you recognize him again if you saw him?' Malone said.

'Would it help you if I did?'

52

'Hold on a minute,' said Pam Morrow. 'You're not using Delia as a witness to that case while we're still talking about her own case.'

'No, I'd like to help,' said Delia, looking directly at Malone as if they were alone in the room.

She's too eager, he thought. But he said, 'Go on.'

'He was, I dunno, medium-sized. Not as tall as you, not as beefy –'

'Thank you.' He didn't grin, but the four women did.

'Well, you're not beefy, I suppose. You haven't changed much, really. Anyhow, he was slimmer than you. Or I think he was – he was wearing an overcoat, a dark one. And a hat.'

'What sort of hat?'

'I dunno. Just a hat. Not one of those broad-brimmed ones, the Akubras. I wasn't looking at him to remember him –' For the first time she sounded testy; he remembered she could get short-tempered about small things. But never the larger things, like being jilted . . . 'I'll remember him if I see him again.'

'It could've been one of the hotel workers,' said Gail. 'Going off duty. Do you know any of them?'

Delia shook her head. 'No. I've never been near the hotel till last night. Boris never wanted me anywhere near where he worked.'

'Didn't want his mates to see he was a wife-basher,' said Rosie Quantock. 'A real bastard. Bottom of the heap.'

'How long had he been working at the hotel?'

'Two – no, three months. He lost his last job – he worked for a bricklayer. They didn't get on.'

'He bashed him, too.' Mrs Quantock couldn't help being helpful.

'I think this has gone on long enough,' said Pam Morrow and snapped shut her briefcase as if to close all argument. 'Are you going to charge my client?'

'Yes,' said Malone, not looking at Delia. 'She'll be held here overnight and arraigned tomorrow morning, probably down at Liverpool Street.'

'What about bail?'

'That'll be up to the Crown Prosecutor. We won't oppose it.'

'Thanks, Scobie.' Delia reached across and pressed his hand. He felt an inward flinch, but didn't draw his hand away.

'How's she gunna raise bail?' demanded Rosie Quantock. 'She hasn't got a cracker, nothing.'

'Do you own your own house?' asked Gail.

It was Mrs Quantock who answered, with a loud dry cackle. 'She's renting, for Crissake! She'd have trouble raising a hundred dollars –'

'Rosie, please –'

'No, love. This is no time for bloody embarrassment. That arsehole's given you nothing –'

Malone turned to Pam Morrow. 'Can the Women's Protection League help?'

'We'll see. We'll plead self-defence, so maybe the beak will be lenient. If he is, we can cover it.'

Malone stood up, switched off the recorder. 'I'm sorry, Delia.'

She looked up at him. 'For what?'

He left that unanswered.

4

He went home in gathering darkness that suited his mood. He always looked forward to coming home to the house in Randwick; he valued *home*, like a comforting mental condition. It wasn't just the love he found there under the Federation gables but the normality; when he stepped in the front door and closed it behind him he was shutting out Crime, with a capital C. Not that Crime in today's world was *ab*normal. It was just that, most days, he didn't have to bring it home with him.

'Another bad day?' said Lisa as he kissed her cheek.

Women, he was convinced, were born with antennae hidden somewhere in their secret skulls. 'What about you?'

She had worked for the past three years as a public relations officer at Town Hall. Her original assignment had been with the Olympics, but that long headache was now past; the Olympics had been a success, two weeks of excitement and euphoria, and now the city was slowly and reluctantly adjusting to the downturn in the boom. Like the post-coital blues, she had described it to him, though she had never put that in one of her press releases.

She was at the fridge, taking out the beef burgundy she had prepared last night. 'Half an hour to dinner. I just have to heat everything. Open the wine.'

They were alone in the kitchen. This was family night. Claire and her husband Jason, Maureen and Tom would all be here for dinner. Claire had been married a year; Maureen had moved out to live with two girlfriends earlier this year; Tom, who loved a new girl every week but loved his mother's cooking more, was still living at home. Malone knew how fortunate he was to have a family that was not dysfunctional.

'Nobody's here yet?'

'No. You want to shower before they arrive? Tom rang to say he's on his way.' Tom was in his last year of Economics at university. 'He had a date with his tutor.'

'A *date* with his tutor?'

'She's twenty-eight and a dish, he says. I don't think he's doing market research with her. Or maybe he is. Move over.'

He shifted along the kitchen bench to make room as she put vegetables into a pot. He picked up one of the two bottles of red wine, then put it down, folded his arms and leaned back against the bench. At ease – like hell: 'I met an old girlfriend today.'

'Which one?' Sounding as if he had told her he had met an old pet dog. Or bitch.

'Delia Bates.'

Then she looked at him, her hands about to open a bag of rice. 'Ah.'

'That all you have to say?'

'Till I hear what else you're going to say.'

Women: they could weave barbed wire out of words. 'We're holding her for homicide. She stabbed her husband this morning.'

She cut the bag of rice, with a knife. 'Will she get off?'

'I dunno. They're pleading self-defence.'

'How did she feel? I mean, you arresting her?'

'I didn't take her in. Phil Truach did that. I interviewed her. She won't talk to anyone but me.'

'That must have been nice.' She poured the rice into a dry saucepan, white B-B bullets that hit the metal with a clatter. She put down the knife, a long-bladed kitchen knife with blood on it. 'Or was it uncomfortable? I would have been if I'd been there.'

'You weren't there! I'm more uncomfortable right now. Christ, darl, imagine how I felt –'

'I am.' She put the saucepan down on the bench, gave him her full attention. 'She was in love with you, once.'

'Christ, what a memory!' Foolishly, he was getting angry. 'Twenty-five years ago.'

Delia had been the only girl he had ever talked about. Not at length and reluctantly, as if (he thought now) there had been guilt at leaving Delia. It seemed, now, that Lisa remembered what he had forgotten. Women and elephants . . . but now was not the time to voice that comparison. He was already offside in the argument.

'That's what I'm thinking about,' said Lisa. 'You come home and tell me about a domestic, your girlfriend of twenty-five years ago killing her husband, and you don't mention the other homicide that's been on the news all day. The murder of the wife of the American Ambassador. Or aren't you on that one?'

Then the cavalry's bugle blew; or the doorbell rang. 'I'll get it,' he said and almost galloped down the hallway to open the door to Maureen, Claire and Jason.

The girls kissed him; Jason shook hands. His son-in-law was

56

three or four inches taller than he, had bulked out since his marriage; Claire was as good a cook as her mother. *His* mother was in jail, doing life for, with her lesbian lover, having murdered Jason's father. Malone suddenly determined there would be no further talk this evening of domestics. He had warm affection for Jason and suddenly was protective of him.

Maureen, the TV researcher for *Four Corners*, was not interested in domestics or small talk. If and when she married, her husband had better not bring his secrets with him. 'How about that homicide, the Ambassador's wife? Are you on it, Dad?'

'Unfortunately. Excuse me, I'll have a quick wash under the armpits. I've just got in.'

He peeled off into the bathroom, pondered for a moment taking a three-hour soak in the bath. Instead, he stripped off his shirt, had a quick swab under the armpits, washed his face, dried himself, then looked in the mirror. Transfer tomorrow, he told himself. Fingerprints, Traffic. Anywhere to get out of Homicide.

He put on a clean shirt and a jumper. When he went out to join the family. Tom was just coming in. He wore jeans, a black leather jacket and carried his motorcyclist's helmet under his arm like a big black skull. He, too, was taller than Malone. Little Me, thought Malone, and felt self-sympathy itching like a rash.

He helped Maureen get the drinks. She was an attractive girl, dark-haired and good-figured and, Malone guessed, she wore her boyfriends out with her restless energy. He sometimes wondered where she got it from. 'Who dunnit? The Ambassador?'

'Don't joke, Mo. None of your ABC anti-US bias.'

'We're impartial. We're anti-everyone but ourselves.'

'Relax, Mo,' Claire told her sister. She had her mother's blonde looks and composure; their Zuyder Zee look, as Tom called it, never making more than small waves. 'You're not on camera now. Is it going to be tough, Dad?'

He nodded, sipped his beer. The three men were drinking beer; the two girls were on white wine. Out in the kitchen the cook was probably swigging sweet sherry. All at once Malone began to laugh.

'What are you laughing at?'

'Nothing, Just a thought.' He took another sip of his beer, then said, 'It's going to be tough. You media are going to make a meal of it, Mo.'

'I know. News are already running around hooting their heads off.' *Four Corners*, the show she worked on, never ran around hooting; it took its time doing demolition jobs on corruption, maladministration and unsocial justice. He hoped it would never come within coo-ee of the Pavane murder. 'You're in for it, Dad. Sorry.'

'Are the Americans co-operating?' asked Tom. 'You got the CIA, the FBI on your back?'

'No, they know it's our turf.'

'Dad,' said Maureen, 'if we decide to look into Australian–American co-operation or lack thereof –'

'Raise that question again and I'll find something to pin on you, okay?'

'Lay off, Mo,' said Claire. 'You're so bloody morally correct since you joined the ABC –'

'Let's all lay off,' said Malone. 'How are you making out with your tutor, Tom?'

'Who told you about her? Mum, I'll bet –'

'You're dating your tutor?' both his sisters asked. 'You're going for an older woman? What's she teaching you?'

'How to be economical in bed?' suggested Jason.

This is what I like to hear, thought Malone, family chi-acking. No violence, no bashing . . . Then Lisa came to the doorway. 'Dinner is ready if you layabouts are?'

The girls were instantly on their feet, rushing to help her. The three of them went out to the kitchen, Tom went in to have a quick shower (where's he been? thought Malone. In the tutor's bed?) and Jason picked up the glasses and put them on a tray.

'How's work?' Malone asked.

'Quiet, there's not much around.' Jason was an engineer with a large construction company. Since the Olympics there had been a general turn-down, a bubble deflated if not entirely pricked. 'I take it yours is not going to be? Quiet, I mean.'

'Quiet? Oh, we'll keep it that way as long as we can, our end. But the bloody media . . .' He stood up, suddenly feeling weary again, put his empty glass on the tray. 'How's your mum?'

'I dunno. Philosophical, I guess you'd call it. She never mentions Dad, though. Nor Angela Bodalle, for that matter.' Olive Rockne's lesbian lover and fellow murderer was doing her time in another jail. 'Mum hopes to be out in eighteen months. She's been a model prisoner, they say.' He paused in the doorway. 'Do you ever think about her?'

'Often – when I see you. I never got any pleasure from putting her away, Jay.'

'I know that, Scobie. I'm just happy to have you as a father-in-law.' Then he turned quickly and went out to the kitchen, the glasses rattling on the tray.

Malone gathered his feelings, which were suddenly like warm coals. Affection from the young is not a cheap gift.

Dinner was not as awkward as he had expected. The Pavane murder was discussed and everyone was sympathetic towards him for the headaches it promised. Lisa smiled at him from her end of the table, but (why was he so suspicious?) it could have been a public relations smile. The four young ones dominated the conversation, banter flying across the table like party crackers. It was only when relaxation had set in over coffee that Maureen said, 'What about the other murder at the hotel, Dad?'

'What about it?'

'Are you on it?'

He looked along the table at Lisa and she gave him the same smile: it *was* a public relations smile, as empty as a clown's laugh. 'Yes, I'm on it. For the time being.'

'It's just an ordinary domestic,' said Lisa, reaching for an after-dinner mint, biting into it as if it were part of him.

'Then why are you on it?' Claire looked at her father. 'With this other *big* one?'

He looked along the table again at (Mona) Lisa: the smile was smaller this time. He didn't know what made him say it: 'I knew the wife, the one who did the killing. She was an old girlfriend.'

At which they all looked at Lisa, not him. Maureen said *Wowie!*, Tom smiled broadly, Jason looked as if he would rather be out on a construction site and Claire pursed her lips. Lisa finished the mint, repeated the Mona Lisa smile and said, 'Small world, ain't it?'

Claire looked at each of her parents in turn. 'Which of you wants me to represent you? I think we're heading for another domestic.'

He cranked up a smile, gave it to Lisa along the table. 'She's been married twice since I knew her.'

'She do them both in?' said Tom.

Maureen hit him with her fist. 'Pull your head in. This is serious. Why are you on the case, Dad? Just because she's an old girlfriend?'

'Golly,' said Lisa, 'I forgot to ask him that.'

'No, I'm not.' Then he began to wonder if he was. 'She won't talk to anyone else but me. Nobody else in Homicide.'

'You can't blame her for that, Mum,' said Claire.

'Who's blaming her? Or anyone?' She took another mint, bit into it.

'Has she changed?' asked Maureen the researcher. *Get all the facts, we'll sort 'em out later* . . . 'Would you have recognized her?'

'In the street? No.'

'Why did she kill her husband?' asked Jason and it was obvious it was a difficult question.

'He never reads reports of murder cases,' said Claire, pressing his hand.

'For obvious reasons,' said Jason and for a moment the ceiling fell in.

'Sorry,' said Claire, squeezing his hand hard; then she looked around the table. 'What else can we talk about? Who's Randwick playing on Saturday?'

'Eastwood.' Tom played fullback for the local rugby club. 'You coming?'

'We'll be there,' said Jason who, like a good engineer, was sensitive to atmospheric pressure. 'Let's do the washing-up.'

He stood up, gathered some of the coffee cups and went out to the kitchen. The girls followed him, taking plates. Tom sat a moment, then he, too, rose and went out to the kitchen. Malone and Lisa looked at each other along the length of the table.

'She hasn't raised a spark in me,' he said. 'It was all over twenty-five years ago.'

'I know that.' The smile this time was her own; and his. 'But if I told you I'd met an old boyfriend, what would you do?'

'Pinch him. For loitering with intent.' He got up, went along the table and kissed her. 'I love you.'

'Nice,' said Claire from the doorway. 'Now may I finish clearing the table?'

5

Billie Pavane's murderer sat in his $400-a-night hotel room and looked out at the city that he had once hoped to conquer. Conquest of a city had been everyone's (well, everyone *he* knew) ambition back in the eighties and it still lingered, like a pungent dope smell, even now in this first year of the new century. It was not only Sydney that had the infection: it was there in London, New York, Paris; it was there in Toronto where he now worked. He had read that the richest man in the world was now worth more than all but the six biggest economies and everyone (well, everyone *he* knew) thought Bill Gates was God, only richer. The old ambition was still there in Billie's killer, like a dormant cancer: greed had once been good and, he heard it all the time, it was coming back into fashion. But not for him. He had a wife and three children (him: who had never wanted to be even a godfather) and they hamstrung him, if unwittingly, with their principles and decency. At least Billie (he had never called her that back in the old days) had had none of those handicaps, principles and decency, back when things had been going so right. Moralists of the world don't realize the handicaps that pragmatists have to face.

He had left Sydney fourteen years ago with almost $500,000 as his share of the – well, call it scam, if you want to be moralistic. He had not been burdened with conscience; in the run-up to the 1987 crash no one could spell the word. He had said no when Billie (he would have to start thinking of her under that name) had told him she wanted to have his child; the last mantle he would have placed on her was that of motherhood. Parenthood, for Christ's sake? He didn't want to be a father, even if he didn't have to live with her and the kids. He had paid for the abortion and been surprised when the doctor insisted on actual cash rather than Diners Club Card; he had lived to the extreme in those days on his credit card, flashing it like a fairy wand. Billie (would he ever get used to that name?) had been violently bitter when the abortion had gone wrong, as if he were to blame. He had never before seen that side of her. She had always been gay, conscienceless, in the Bollinger-bubble of all the money they had been making. The chill between them turned to freezing point and he wondered how he was going to get away from her. It was just then that he learned that a wise man from the East, from Bellevue Hill actually, had begun selling his holdings. If the richest man in the country was getting out of the market then it was clear, to everyone but the fools, that the boom would not last, as the fools predicted, till Christmas.

Without telling anyone, he had already transferred the bulk of his money to a bank in Liechtenstein. He sold up the rest of his holdings and without saying goodbye to anyone, least of all Billie, he had walked out of the office one Friday afternoon and caught a plane to Bangkok and from there to Paris. He had been good at French at school and he had kept up his study and practice of it because he liked the sound and nuances. Within a month of landing in Paris he had a job with a French bank as an investment adviser. He changed his name and his appearance. He had had the anonymous good looks of male models found in mail-order catalogues, spoiled only by a broken nose. He had worn the nose, broken in a university rugby match, as a badge of honour; it lifted the macho image of wheeling-dealing brokers. The nose was rebuilt, he had his hair cut short in the French style; he was still anonymously good-looking, but any visitor from Sydney would have to look twice at him to recognize him. He spoke French with barely an accent, not easy for an Australian – not the best linguists in the world. He dressed Parisian, even took on French manners. Sydney and everyone there, even his pharmacist father, with whom he never got on, and his sister, snug and smug in a happy North Shore marriage, began to fade from memory. He was as self-contained as he wished to be.

There were affairs, of course. Then one proved difficult and dirty. There was another abortion and the girl, from Brittany, a hard-headed region, threatened to go to the bank and denounce him if he did not marry her. Whether the bank would have listened to her was debatable; but, in a moment of Dom Perignon-induced weakness, beside her in bed, the worst place for secrets, he had told her things about his past that he thought she would never remember. He had forgotten, or didn't know, that many Frenchwomen, inspired by Ninon de Lenclos, wrote diaries. He had resigned from the bank and left for Canada. He felt an utter bastard, but self-recognition does not necessarily mean being conscience-stricken. Guilt is only a comfort blanket for those who want to wear it.

In Toronto he went to work for another bank. It was not the most exciting city, especially after Paris, but he had had enough excitement for the time being. Then disaster, in the form of romance, struck: he fell, really, truly, in love. She was French-Canadian, Catholic, beautiful and she was helplessly in love with him. They were married when she was two months pregnant (the Quebec nuns had not taught her to keep her knees together) and he had settled into the sort of life he had laughed at back home. Upper middle class, country club, even church-going: sometimes he stepped outside himself and wondered what had happened to him. His hair began to turn grey, he had to watch his weight, he had two daughters and a son. The past slipped off the map of his life.

Then on a business trip to Chicago, sitting in a hotel room just like this one, he had switched on the television and seen an interview, relayed from Kansas City, with Billie (the first time he heard that name) and her husband, the ambassador-elect to Australia.

Just as today in this room he had switched on the television and on the midday news had seen the woman who had caught sight of him as he was about to step out of Billie's room in that flea-bag hotel. There was no mistaking her. They had stared at each other long enough to identify each other.

Chapter Three

1

Delia Jones was arraigned next morning and released on bail provided by the Women's Protection League. With the court lists as crowded as they were it could be another two years before she was brought to trial. Justice sees no injustice in taking its time, which is one reason why judges rarely die of heart failure.

'Who was the magistrate?' Malone asked.

Gail Lee had gone down to the court, though she had not been Mrs Jones' escort. 'Mrs Pulbrook.'

'A dragon. She hates men.'

'So do I. Occasionally.' She left his office and went out to the main room, sat down at her desk and stared at her computer as if willing it to come up with a compendium of men's faults. Malone was glad to see it remain blank.

He had no computer in his own office, looking on it as a watchdog that might turn on him. He sometimes recalled, with nostalgia but no regret at its passing, the old 'murder box' that Clements had kept. A battered cardboard shoe-box into which pieces of evidence had been stuffed like family memorabilia: the good old days . . . He went out to Clements, who sat staring at *his* computer as if it was sending him nothing but ransom notes.

'Bad news comes quicker on this thing,' he said. 'Does Bill Gates know?'

'What's the bad news?' said Malone, as if there wasn't enough of it. He sat down, looking relaxed but stiff inside.

'The Pavane job. Our Feds think we should invite them in and some secretary from the embassy says her boss, the DCM –' He looked enquiringly at Malone.

'Deputy Chief of Mission. His name's Kortright.'

'He wants daily reports, whether restricted or otherwise. Hourly, if we can give them. Stuff him and them.' He swivelled in his chair, leaned forward on his desk. 'I'm not gunna sit here like some bloody listening-post –'

'Simmer down. You're going to be working with me. This needs at least two senior men on it. Turn your paperwork over to –'

'Not me,' said Gail Lee from her nearby desk.

'Nor me,' said Sheryl Dallen from behind Clements. 'You need two senior women with you and we're them.'

Then Phil Truach, smug after two cigarettes down in the parking lot, came in, sat down, put down a shopping bag beside him and said, 'Bad news.'

Clements looked at his computer. 'Not on this. Not more shit.'

'You'll have it on it eventually. I went down to the Southern Savoy this morning, do some cleaning up, a few things I thought we might of overlooked –'

'And we had?' said Malone. Why were premonitions hovering around him like starving crows?

'I went back into the store room where Mrs Jones did her husband.' He was addressing Clements, not Malone; almost too obviously. 'There were no knives in there, never have been. Not a chef's kitchen knife. Jones evidently was as neat as his wife – his sidekick said Boris had a place for everything and everything in its place. No knives.'

This is going to get worse, thought Malone and remained silent. He was aware that the two girls were leaning forward but not looking at him, ignoring him as if he were not there.

'There was no knife missing from the hotel kitchen – I had the chef count every one. Then I went out to Rozelle, saw Mrs Jones.'

You had no right to do that, Phil. But of course he did.

'I asked for a look at her kitchen. She asked me did I have a search warrant – just like a professional. Or do they watch too many cop shows these days?'

'Go on,' said Clements, aware of Malone's silence.

'I said no, I didn't have one, but I could get one without any trouble. She let me in and I made for the kitchen. There was a matched set of knives, in one of those wooden holders, on a bench beside the stove. I asked her which one she'd used to knife Boris. She kept her mouth shut, but after a minute she took one out and handed it to me. She hated my guts, but she wasn't gunna do me, too.' He reached down to the shopping bag and took out a plastic bag; in it was a long-bladed kitchen knife. Only then did he look at Malone: 'Sorry, Scobie. It looks as if she went in to the hotel to kill Boris. She had the intention all along.'

There was silence for a while, everyone looking at Malone. Even the four other detectives at their computers were still, as if what had come up on their screens was not what they had expected. It was Clements who at last said, 'Looks like we'll have to tell the DPP, get them to appeal to have the bail revoked.'

Malone still said nothing because he could think of nothing to say; then Sheryl said, 'She's got two kids – what about them?'

'They're the ones I'm thinking of,' said Truach, who had four children of his own. 'What if she tops them and then tops herself? She could be depressed enough,' he said, looking again at Malone as if to say, *I'm trying to find excuses for her, boss.* 'It wouldn't be the first time it's happened.'

There was another silence; the room was carpeted with thin ice. Then Sheryl said, 'I saw the kids last night, at Surry Hills. That Mrs Quantock brought 'em in to see her – the duty sergeant let 'em talk to her. They're not three- and four-year-olds, they're kids who understand what's going on. She loves 'em and they love her – you should of seen them. She would never harm them. Not even by topping herself.'

'She's already harmed them,' said Malone at last, feeling he had to say something, remembering the effect on Jason Rockne and his younger sister when their mother had been indicted for murder.

'Well, yes,' said Sheryl, glad to be able to talk to him direct. 'But she wouldn't *murder* them.'

'How well did you know her?' asked Gail.

There was no rank in this talk and Malone, though selfishly tempted, did not pull any. He wanted help here, not antagonism. 'Pretty well. But that was twenty-five years ago.' And a man never really knew a woman. Adam hadn't known Eve and it had been that way ever since. 'You're right. I don't think she would harm the kids any more than she has.'

'So what do we do?' asked Clements; then answered himself: 'We'll let things stand as they are.'

Truach was the only one not convinced, though he was not going to argue. But, holding up the knife in the plastic bag: 'What do we do with this?'

'We can't withhold evidence,' said Malone, but lamely.

'Why not?' said Sheryl. 'We'll produce it when she goes to trial. Give her counsel time to rebut it, if they can.'

'I think we should at least talk to the DPP,' said Truach.

'Leave it with me,' said Clements and put the plastic bag with the knife in the bottom drawer of his desk, where Malone knew it would stay till Clements decided it was time to produce it.

'Okay,' said Truach; did he look relieved? Malone wondered. 'But we'd better keep an eye on her. Get the locals to look in on her occasionally. Not just wait for her weekly check-in with them.'

'She has to report to them once a week,' said Gail.

'I know,' said Truach. 'But if they call in on her, maybe once or twice a month, have a cuppa with her, no heavy stuff, they can keep an eye on the kids. How did they feel about their father?'

'I talked with Mrs Quantock last night. She holds nothing back – about him, anyway. The kids were dead scared of him, Phil. He was a monster. A real fucking *monster* –' For a moment she lost her customary calm; even Sheryl looked at her in surprise. 'Let's leave her alone!'

Clements looked at Malone, who said nothing; then he stood up. 'Okay, meeting's over. Sheryl, you go out to Balmain, they cover Rozelle, and ask them to keep an eye on her, go to the house maybe once or twice a month. Just a drop-in call.'

'Do we tell 'em what we know about the knife?'

Clements didn't look at Malone this time. 'No, that's our business.'

Truach got to his feet. 'I need a smoke. I'll be downstairs.'

He went out of the room, the odd man out. But as he passed Malone he pressed the latter's shoulder, an intimate gesture that was out of character for him. Nobody said anything and Malone got up and went back into his own office. Clements followed him, said, 'You're off this case. No more Delia Jones, okay?'

'Am I being soft on her?'

'Don't ask me, mate. I have a dozen girls I could be soft on if they came back into my life. With Delia, let Sheryl and Gail do the deciding. They trust her not to do any more damage.'

'I'm still not sure –' Then he threw up his hands. 'Righto, I'm off it till she comes to trial. I'm sorry we made things so awkward for Phil –'

'Forget it. This isn't the first time evidence has been withheld till we wanted to produce it. In the meantime –'

'Yeah, in the meantime. Where have we got on the Ambassador's wife?'

'Romy phoned through a preliminary on her p-m report. The stomach contents show Mrs Pavane had a very good dinner – Japanese cuisine – some hours before she was done in. Where? Who with?'

'The girls can look into that, too.' Then his phone rang and he picked it up. 'Malone.'

'Joe Himes, Scobie.'

Malone waved Clements to a chair. 'What've you got, Joe? If anything?'

'I stayed last night at the Southern Savoy – incognito, I think is the word they use. I wanted a look at the place, thought I might pick up something by osmosis.' Malone made no comment and Himes said, 'You don't appreciate?'

'Joe, Osmosis was the Greek feiler failed the police entrance exam. We just use suspicion and interrogation.' He rolled his eyes at Clements. *Bloody Yanks*. 'What did you pick up?'

'Okay, no osmosis.' Himes still sounded good-humoured. 'It's not the sorta hotel takes any notice of its guests unless they ask. But I guess that's the way it is nowadays, hotels. You pays your money and they don't give a fuck what you do, so long's you don't burn the place down. If Mrs Pavane made any noise while she was being strangled, no one heard it. Or wanted to hear it.'

Malone sighed in agreement. 'That's the way it is, Joe. Nobody wants to be involved. You got anything else?' He tried to sound patient. He liked Himes, but he didn't like interference. 'The consulate got anything to add?'

'I talked to the consulate driver – he went out to meet Mrs Pavane. She was supposed to come out of the terminal to where he was waiting for her – local rules say he can't go into the terminal and leave his car unattended. She didn't show. He waited ten minutes, then got a baggage handler to keep an eye on the car while he went in to look for her. A ground hostess said she'd seen a woman like the one the driver described come off the plane, but she hadn't taken much notice of her –'

'Wait a minute. An ambassador's wife – the *American* Ambassador's wife – flies up from Canberra and nobody takes any notice of her?'

'Scobie, I queried that.' Himes seemed to lose his good humour for the moment. 'She'd have got special attention on the plane, but at this end – Scobie, there were two Cabinet Ministers on that plane. Who gets the attention – Cabinet Ministers or an ambassador's wife? There were six or eight guys waiting for the Ministers –'

'Righto, Joe, I get the point. So Mrs Pavane just slipped out of sight?'

'The ground hostess thought – *thought* – she saw the woman, she didn't know who she was, go off with a man, but she couldn't be sure.'

'Did anyone do any checking *yesterday* morning when she went missing?'

'They contacted your Feds at lunchtime, but then it was called off when Mrs Pavane phoned her husband – or rather, she got his secretary. All she said was that she would be catching a later plane back than she'd booked.'

Malone switched continents: 'What have you heard from your FBI mates?'

'They expect to tell me something tomorrow. They're already down in Corvallis.' Himes was starting to sound not aggressive but certainly more definite, as if to say the FBI, *we Americans*, were not dragging their feet. 'If there's anything more to find out about Mrs Pavane, they'll find it.'

'I'm sure they will, Joe –'

'What have you come up with?' Definitely an edge to his voice now.

'We're tracing the feller who tried to speak to Mrs Pavane at the restaurant a couple of weeks ago. And we know she had a Japanese meal the night before last, some time before she was murdered. We're doing a trace through them, the better ones.'

'Okay, I'll be back to you soon's I hear from our Portland office.' He hung up, the line cold in Malone's ear.

Malone put down the phone. 'I've trodden on his toes . . . Put someone on that Japanese restaurant trace. What are you grinning at?'

'You said she'd had a Jap meal before her murder. We'd have had a mess if she'd had it *after* the murder.'

71

'Don't be such a bloody smartarse. Or are you trying to lighten my mood or something?'

'It needs it.' Clements stood up. 'You're getting shit on the liver again –'

'Hang on. Sorry. Sit down. Now what have we got on who had lunch at Catalina that day the stranger thought he recognized Mrs Pavane?'

Clements sat down again. 'Andy Graham is on it.'

Graham was Homicide's bloodhound; he would follow a trail to the moon. He was big and awkward and always in a hurry, but he produced. Some men, like seamstresses in invisible mending workrooms, can weave loose threads together till a pattern is regained or established. Andy Graham, for all his blundering rush through life, had patience. And the seamstresses, searching for a loose thread, would have agreed that patience was necessary. They would not, however, have tolerated any canine comparison. No woman would want to be referred to as a bloodhound bitch.

Then Malone's phone rang again: 'Scobie? It's Romy. I've just finished the p-m on Boris Jones – you'll have the full report this afternoon. But there is something interesting –'

Malone waited.

'– Mr Jones had sex with someone, I'd say not long before he was murdered. He hadn't washed his penis, there was dried semen on it.'

Malone took his time: 'You're suggesting Mr Jones might've had sex with Mrs Pavane and then strangled her?'

'I'm not suggesting anything. I'll let you know when we get a DNA report on her from Biology at Lidcombe. You're still coming to dinner tonight?'

'We'll be there.' *If only to keep life on an even keel.* He hung up. 'That was your wife.'

'I gathered. Good news or bad news?'

'I dunno. Mr Jones had dipped his wick not long before Mrs Jones did him in.'

Clements thought about that for a long moment; then he said,

'It's against the odds. Why would an ambassador's wife take on some rough trade with a guy she couldn't have known? A cleaner.'

'Again, I dunno. Why would a film star pick up a street hooker, instead of a call girl, to go down on him? That happened. I've been in this game long enough never to make guesses about why people do things. You're the same.'

'Okay, the first thing we do is find out if he had it off with his wife before she stuck the knife in him. I'll send Gail and Sheryl out, that'll be better than you and me leaning on her.'

'Infinitely.'

'It's long odds, but if he did get into bed with Mrs Pavane and then killed her, you'd better get off both cases right now.'

'I couldn't think of a better idea.'

2

Ambassador Stephen Pavane had hardly slept for two nights. Love is debilitating, the cynics said; but they were the ones, almost invariably men, who had been unsuccessful in love. He was no cynic and he had been successful in love several times, but he agreed: love could be debilitating. He had loved Billie with a passion that continually surprised him. He had loved his first wife, but her slow death from cancer had been a preparation for grief and loss. It had brought a void in his life, but it had not been as deep as he had expected; it had been like the filling-in of a grave from the bottom. When the headstone had been placed above her it had somehow been a release. Not a joyous one, but a relief nonetheless. There had been empty years afterwards and then Billie had come along. It had not been love at first sight, not for him, though she had said it had been for her. She had been good at flattery because in most instances she had meant it. Then, abruptly and deeply, he had fallen in love with her. And now . . .

'What?' He was in his office with Kortright, his Deputy Chief of Mission.

'Stephen –' Pavane had insisted that at their level there was no need for formality when they were alone. 'You're not listening to me. Why don't you go back to the private quarters?'

'Walter, if I go back there, what do I do? Sit and stare out the window?' He sat up straight, did look out the window for a moment. It was a cold Canberra day, the trees bare, a white haze that looked like a dusting of snow on the surrounding hills. One of the Marine guards crossed the lawn, bent over against the wind in a most un-Marine-like hunch. Last night's weather report had said there had been heavy falls at Perisher and Thredbo up in the mountains and he and Billie had been planning a weekend of skiing. He looked back at Kortright. 'What were you saying?'

Kortright had a bad habit of making his patience look obvious. He still had some way to go to achieve the bland hypocrisy of a true diplomat; he was aiming for the British or French models, but he had some years of learning ahead. 'Roger Bodine thinks he should go up to Sydney.'

'Joe Himes is there. The Sydney police don't want us interfering.'

'Roger is aware of that. But he thinks this may be more than – than just an ordinary case of murder.' He had been fortunate so far in his postings, at embassies where Americans had not been in danger.

Pavane gave him a hard eye. 'It's not an ordinary case, Walter. It's my wife, the wife of an ambassador. You're a professional diplomat, but sometimes –' He gave up, realizing his grief was turning into random anger. 'Go on.'

Kortright had remained bland at the insult; he was enough of a diplomat to have progressed that far. 'There are religious fanatics threatening to kill Americans wherever they are –'

She slept with whoever killed her: but he couldn't tell Kortright that. Eventually it would come out, but he still hoped it would not be necessary. The hollowness in him deepened.

Still he managed to say: 'There are no religious fanatics in this country, Walter – their religion is sport, but they don't shoot the players the way South Americans do. Walter, she checked into that hotel alone – don't ask me why, I can't explain it. *She* booked the room. There's a much simpler explanation than some religious fanatic luring her there to kill her. But don't ask me what it is.'

'So we keep Roger out of the scene?'

'For the time being, yes.' He had no trouble sounding firm. He was protecting Billie. Or himself?

'Well . . .' Kortright closed the folder he had brought in, though he had taken nothing from it. But it struck Pavane now that his DCM always carried a folder, almost like a talisman. He was still a bureaucrat at heart, though they can be liars like diplomats. 'There are hundreds of messages of sympathy. I'll see that a general acknowledgement is prepared.'

Pavane had come to like Canberra in the two months he had been here, despite its isolation from the mainstream of Australian life. It *was* isolated. But then so were Islamabad and Brasília and they were much more important postings. It was Billie who had described Canberra as a multi-racial country club, with everyone paying their dues and with the two senior members the Americans and the British. But waves, he knew, would already be in the making; as in any country club. There would have been ripples last night at the reception at the French Embassy. There would be a rising swell this evening at the Israeli Embassy. And, a long way away, at those other country clubs, Mission Hills and Kansas City.

'Roger has asked for diplomatic security and got it,' said Kortright, as if reading his thoughts. 'There'll be no announcements from the Sydney police without talking to us first.'

'Good. The Aussies can be co-operative –'

'Sometimes.'

Kortright's mouth did not make a *moue* of contempt, but the dark military moustache seemed to bend in a curve downwards.

He had said nothing to Pavane and he did his job extremely well, but the Ambassador, before leaving Washington, had learned as much as he could about the people he would be working with. Kortright was marking time, waiting for the posting to an *important* capital. London or Paris or Rome, somewhere where sophistication was not suspect and an object like Jackson Pollock's *Blue Poles* would not be treasured as much as the Elgin Marbles or the *Mona Lisa*. He was not a snob, just that he had been to Harvard. Pavane, if he stayed, would not be sorry to lose him. *If he stayed*: it was the first time the thought had entered his head.

'My wife's body will be released tomorrow. I'd like to be on a plane tomorrow night with it.'

'We've made several bookings with United –'

'No, charter a private plane – I'll pay for it. I don't want to be sitting amongst a lot of passengers with my wife's body in the hold.'

'No, of course not.' Kortright was not all State Department; he could be genuinely sympathetic. 'How long will you stay?'

'I don't know, Walter. After the funeral, I'll go on to Washington, talk to the President. A week, ten days at the most. I'll be back –' He ended in mid-air. He could not talk about the future till he found out what had happened in the past. Billie's past . . .

When Kortright had gone, Pavane got up and walked to the window. The embassy was on a small hill, a Southern Georgian construction that had both amused and pleased him when he first saw it. One looked for Spanish moss hanging from the local eucalypts and darky retainers humming spirituals to arriving embassy guests. But he had recognized at once that it was a statement; other embassies declared their origins. Even the Chinese had looked to their past, with dragons and pagoda-like rooflines in the design of their embassy.

He had looked forward to this post, though he had known it would be no bed of roses, at least not all the way. There

76

were matters of defence to be discussed and investment, too; the Australians were running hard to jump aboard the carousel of globalism. But trade was the bogey that kept cropping up all the time, especially in terms of wheat, meat and cotton, which were his business interests. The Australians were like old-time pirates in their trumpeting of free trade. They chose to ignore the local pressures on Congressmen back home, seemingly unaware that the farm lobby didn't care a damn whether a Congressman was a Democrat or a Republican, so long as he did what he was told or he'd be out at the next election.

Still, in his short time here he had come to enjoy working with the Australians. They were civilized, to a certain extent, and no more devious than the politicians back home in Missouri and Kansas. There was a bluntness to them that he admired and that reminded him of stories his own father had told him of Harry Truman and, before him, Jim Pendergast. They understood the true nature of politics and he was reminded again of another man back home, the Irish sage from Kansas City, Jerry Jette, who had said, 'Political science is to politics what botany is to neurosurgery.' The natives here in Canberra understood that and he had felt at home with them.

And now, for the moment anyway, it all meant nothing.

3

'Where's Inspector Malone?' said Delia Jones.

'He couldn't come,' said Gail Lee. 'He's caught up in the murder of the American Ambassador's wife.'

'And she's more important than me?'

'No, she's not, Delia. But there are pressures – he's got everyone and his brother on his back.'

'You dunno what it's like,' said Sheryl Dallen.

Delia stared at them; then appeared to be mollified. 'Okay, but why's he sent you? Are you going to be harassing me all the time

I'm on bail? One of your guys was out here this morning without a warrant –'

'That's why we're here, Delia.'

The two women detectives had come to this semi-detached cottage in a back street of Rozelle. The small suburb, like so many inner sections of colonial Sydney, had been part of a land grant; the welfare state was invented for the upper classes long before it filtered down to the poor. Rozelle was originally called West Balmain after its lucky grantee, William Balmain, the colony's Principal Surgeon. To get a land grant was a better return than anything provided by Medicare to latterday medicos. The land was sub-divided and sub-divided again; terraces of workers' cottages sprang up like hedgerows. In the 1870s the area got its most imposing institution, the Callan Park asylum for the insane; the locals, though out of their own wits on poor wages, were not impressed. The old asylum is now a writers' centre, not much of an improvement in the opinion of the drinkers at the local pubs.

Gentrification was round the corner in some of the other streets, but here the lowly-paid and the pensioner widows and widowers with thirty or forty years' residence still held their ground. This house had been built in the days when sunshine was kept out for fear it would fade the curtains; the windows were narrow, like defence slots in a castle that had shrunk. There was a small neat garden at the front of the house and Sheryl had wondered to Gail who had tended it, Boris the cleaner or Delia the neat one.

They were in the small kitchen; it was neat and clean. The saucepans that hung above the stove, Gail had noted, were not expensive ones; the magazine on the table was *New Idea*, not *House & Garden*. There was no lingering smell of cooking, though this kitchen, she guessed, had been in use for over a hundred years. Everything was worn, but everything was spotless. Delia might be a battered wife, but she was not a slatternly one.

78

'We're not here to harass you,' said Sheryl. 'Just to ask a question or two. Did your husband play around? You know, with other women?'

Delia didn't frown or look surprised or annoyed; she could have been asked if her husband played bowls. 'Yes.'

'You knew?'

'It took me a long while to find out. But yes, I found out about two years ago.'

'Anyone in particular?'

'No.' She was composed again; Gail had to admire her. 'He'd have a woman for a week or two, then dump her.'

'Boris sounds a real shit. Why –?' Then Sheryl waved a hand at herself, as if trying to sweep away her disgust. 'Sorry, Delia. I shouldn't have said that.'

'Why did I marry him? Sometimes I wonder, myself. He was, I dunno, comforting, I guess you'd call it. When I first met him. I needed that, I'd just broken up with Hugh, my first husband –' Then she leaned forward, not eagerly but as if wanting to make sure: 'You're both sympathetic to me, aren't you?'

'Well –' Sheryl leaned back; police sympathy was not something to be handed out like a leaflet. 'Delia, you killed your husband. You had that intention all along –'

'No, I didn't!' For a moment the composure was gone.

'Delia –'

'You don't understand. You should of brought Scobie – he'd of understood –' Then she collected herself, gathering the pebbles that had burst out of her like shot. 'No, I shouldn't of said that. Forget I said it – I don't wanna get him in trouble. I *didn't* intend killing Boris –'

Gail had noticed the calendar on the wall above the small fridge. Dates were circled in red, several days apart. 'What are those dates?'

Delia turned her head, stared at the calendar as if she had not looked at it before, then turned back. 'I was keeping count.'

'Keeping count?'

'When he bashed me. It used to be once a month, six weeks. But lately –'

'You took the knife with you,' said Gail, almost gently.

'Yes. Yeah, I took it – to frighten him. And to frighten *her*.'

'Who?'

'I dunno. Someone at the hotel. Why, what do you know?'

'Delia,' said Gail, still gently, 'Boris had sex with someone not long before you stabbed him. Was it with you?'

'Of course not! Jesus –'

She shook her head fiercely. A lock of hair fell down and she pushed it back: *neatly*, Gail noted. Delia Jones would have been a good-looking girl when Inspector Malone would have known her; the looks were still there, vague, as if behind a frosted glass. The dark brown hair had hints of grey in it; the brown eyes were dulled (or hurt); the figure was thin but once might have been rounded. She was bruised and battered, but somehow she had not totally surrendered.

'If it was someone else, would you know who it was?'

'No, I dunno. It could of been one of the women worked there on night shift –'

'Or one of the guests?' asked Sheryl. 'A woman on her own looking for company?'

'I don't think so. Boris was a *cleaner* – why would some woman, a guest, pick him?' She sounded choosy; but she had picked him. 'No, it was someone who knew him or knew he worked at the hotel. I dunno any of the staff. I suppose there'd be some women there who'd let Boris put the hard word on 'em. He wasn't bad to look at and he had – I suppose you'd call it charm.'

'Bullshit,' said Sheryl, but she said it to herself.

'Where was he when you got to the hotel?' asked Gail. 'Did you ask anyone where he was?'

'No. I went looking for him. He was upstairs, I think it was the third floor. Yes, it was.'

'On the third floor? That –' Gail stopped.

'What?'

'That was where the American Ambassador's wife was murdered,' said Sheryl.

'What?' Delia said again; then was silent. Out beyond the small back yard a voice called, *Delia*! It sounded like Mrs Quantock, but neither Delia nor the two detectives took any notice.

Then Delia looked at them: 'You're not suggesting – Oh God! No. No!' She shook her head again, determinedly. 'She wouldn't have – have looked at him. A *cleaner*? In his overalls, with his hoover and his bucket and mop? No.' She was emphatic. The lock of hair fell down again and this time she didn't push it back. 'No, he was in the corridor, hoovering, when I got up there. I came up by the stairs, I didn't take the lift. I asked him why he hoovered at night, when the guests were asleep, and he said he did it because he was told not to. He was like that. You didn't tell Boris what he could and couldn't do.'

He certainly had charm, thought Sheryl.

'That was why he never lasted long in a job. And then –'

'And then what?'

'Then he'd take it out on me and the kids. You know what it's like. Or do you?'

'No,' said Gail and Sheryl, both unmarried and not living with partners.

'Did he hit you then, when you came up looking for him?' said Gail.

'No, not then. Down in the store room, when we went back down there. He finished hoovering, kept me just standing there, and then we went back downstairs.'

'What a bastard,' said Sheryl. 'So you rule out that he'd been into Room 342?'

'That was where she was? Where is it? I mean, on that floor?'

Gail closed her eyes; the room came back out of memory. She opened her eyes. 'At the end of the corridor, on the right-hand side. Looking out on Central Square.'

Delia was searching her own memory, though she didn't close her eyes. 'A man came out of there, that room – well, he half came out. I remember staring at him and he stared back. Then he stepped back inside, he closed the door again.'

'Was it the same man you saw outside the hotel when you were waiting for a taxi?'

'I dunno. It could of been. If it was, when he came out looking for the taxi, he was wearing an overcoat and a hat. The guy in the room, he had grey hair. I remember that.'

The two detectives looked at each other, but said nothing.

'He was definitely there.' Her voice had changed, was precise. 'In that room, 342. But as for Boris – no. I don't know who he had sex with, but it wasn't with Mrs Whatsername. No way. He hated Americans. He was still Russian like that, still fighting the Cold War.'

Gail and Sheryl stood up. 'We'll be in touch, Delia –'

Delia suddenly looked perturbed. 'Oh God, I'm sorry – I should have offered you coffee or something –'

'Delia, it doesn't matter –' Gail all at once felt sorry for her. She wondered what background Delia came from that, even in these circumstances, she felt hospitality was important. Her speech at times was slovenly, but it was as if from weariness rather than habit; there were hints in the voice, as a moment ago, of education, even elocution. 'Stay out of trouble. Take care of your children.'

'They're not going to revoke my bail, are they?'

'I don't think so,' said Gail, but she couldn't sound optimistic.

'Things will work out, Delia,' said Sheryl, but she sounded no more optimistic than Gail.

Out in the street the two detectives paused by their car. Gail looked up and down the narrow roadway; there were only a few cars parked by the kerb on one side of the road. The houses were all small and one-storied, aged by a century or more of storm, heat and, in some cases, neglect. Under the dull grey day they had a melancholy air to them. As if they knew they were doomed: the developers were just out of sight, bulldozers at the ready.

'Do you think Boris might of killed Mrs Pavane because she was an American?' said Sheryl.

Gail looked at her across the roof of the car. 'He'd have raped her first – he didn't do that. No, I don't think he had anything to do with Mrs Pavane.'

'Then are we gunna look for the woman he had sex with?'

'I suppose we'd better,' said Gail. 'But do you care?'

Then they were aware of Rose Quantock standing at the gate of the house next door. 'You're not gunna leave her alone, are you?'

Gail walked across to her. 'Rosie, we're only doing our job. Detective Dallen and I aren't going to ride her into the ground. We're here just to find out more about Boris.'

'An arsehole. Absolutely. I'd hear him belting her and the kids and I'd hammer on the wall –' She seemed ready to burst with emotion; there were tears in her eyes. 'Jesus, she had to kill him to save herself and the kids! Can't you fucking understand that?'

Gail put a hand on the big plump arm on top of the gate. 'We do understand, Rosie. We see this sort of thing as frequently as you did – more so. We're not going to ride Delia, I promise you.'

'What about the male cops? That Inspector Malone?' She wiped her eyes with the back of her hand.

'He's on her side, too,' said Sheryl from beside the car.

Gail looked at her, frowned warningly; then looked back at Rosie Quantook. 'Go in and sit with Delia a while.' She turned to go back to the car, then stopped. 'Were you really with the Opera House chorus?'

Rosie Quantock gestured at herself, at her surroundings; but somehow managed a smile. 'You'd never believe it, would you? I had a voice, a good one, but never good enough to get outa the chorus. Twelve years, singing me head off. I just never had the education or the ambition. But I enjoyed it, it was better'n working in a factory or behind a counter. I married one of the stagehands – another arsehole, though he never belted me –'

She'd have floored him, thought Sheryl.

The three of them stood there, contemplating the arseholes that men were, then Gail said, 'Look after Delia, Rosie. Sing her a song or two.'

'Something from *Lucia di Lammermoor*? Around here I can do a very good mad scene, any day of the week. Look after yourselves.'

She had recovered her spirits. She went in to help Delia recover hers. The two detectives got into their car and drove away. Looking back in the driving mirror Gail wondered why the street suddenly looked empty.

4

The Clements' home was Victorian, a solid double-fronted, one-storied residence that, ever since it had been built back in 1892, had looked aggressively at anyone who had wanted to change it. The front bedroom projected like a challenge from the rest of the frontage: we're here and here we stay. The house looked out across a small reserve and the calm backwater of Iron Cove; beyond the water the land sloped up to the old asylum. Here was middle-class territory and melancholy, if any, was something one felt when real estate prices fell.

The house *had* been changed: Romy had had reverse-cycle air-conditioning installed. But each room still had its own fireplace and now the Clements and the Malones sat round a fire in the big living room. The dinner table had been cleared, the dishes rinsed and put in the dishwasher for Romy's cleaning woman to wash and put away tomorrow. Romy and Lisa were finishing off their wine, Clements was sipping his after-dinner cooling ale and Malone, who would be driving when he and Lisa left for home, had decided he had had enough for the evening.

Somehow, in the idle way of after-dinner chat, the conversation had got round to demonstrations and police involvement in them:

'I asked this guy,' said Clements, 'pointing out to him I wasn't anti-conservation, just anti-conservationists, I asked him why they were were protecting the hyper-active sloth or the double-pouched kangaroo or something. I asked him if he felt emotionally or materially deprived because there were no more dinosaurs or brontosauruses –'

'And what did he say?' asked Romy.

'He didn't say anything. He kicked me in the crotch.'

'And what did you say then?' asked Lisa.

'I pinched him. I said he was under arrest for despoiling a protected area.'

The two foreign-born wives looked at each other. 'They have lovely simple minds,' said Romy. 'Do you think that's why we married them?'

'I think so,' said Lisa. 'To maintain our European superiority. I think I'm still a Dutch imperialist at heart.'

'I'll second that,' said Malone. 'Have you noticed, Russ, that the Devil is always portrayed as a man? I think the Old Testament was written by women.'

'Of course,' said the women.

Malone loved them both. Then he suddenly realized, though the thought was a simple and obvious one, that he would never have truly known either of them if he had come back to Sydney from London twenty-five years ago and married Delia Bates. And felt a selfish sense of relief.

'Let's change the subject,' said Romy and did: 'Excuse me talking shop, Lisa –'

Lisa waved a dismissive hand, but didn't look enthused.

'What's happening on the Pavane case?'

For a moment Malone had been afraid that she was going to mention the Jones case. 'I think things would have been simpler if you hadn't told us she'd had sex just before the murder.'

'Not much simpler. There's still that mystery, what was she doing in that particular hotel and under an assumed name?'

'It's going to be awful for the husband when that comes out.' Lisa, too, had been afraid that the Jones case would be mentioned. She joined in with relief: 'It will come out eventually, won't it? These things always do, these days.'

'It'll come out,' said Clements. 'It will have to, as evidence, if we nail the killer on a DNA test.'

'What if she'd had sex before she got back to the hotel?' said Romy. 'And the killer was waiting in the room for her?'

'Don't complicate things,' said Malone.

'Mrs Pavane had been around, as they describe it. When we did the p-m we found she'd had an abortion, a bungled job that had made a mess of her uterus.'

'A recent job?' asked Malone.

'No, I'd say not. She couldn't have had children.' Then she looked at him sympathetically: 'It can't be easy talking to the Ambassador. Not if you have to mention that to him.'

'Will you mention it at the inquest?'

'Not necessarily. But you might have to say something to him about it.'

Going home through the cold night, under a broken moon, Lisa said, 'Is it time to retire?'

He looked at her in surprise. 'I'm too young. I'd lose a stack in superannuation –'

'I don't mean retire from the Service. Retire into a softer job. Give up on other people's troubled lives. Sit at a desk and make faces at a computer.'

'I wouldn't be easy to live with, you know that.'

'I'd put up with it. I hate to see you taking these cases as if – as if they were personal.'

'Are we talking about the Ambassador's wife? Or Delia Bates?' They had pulled up at a traffic light. A car full of yelling hoons went through the lights, horn blasting, but he ignored them. Traffic fatalities were not Homicide business, he thought cynically; then gave his attention back to Lisa. 'Is that what you mean by personal?'

'I wasn't thinking of her.' But she had been.

The lights turned green and they moved on; but their conversation had the brakes on. They rode in silence for five minutes, till they were crossing the Anzac Bridge, its cables above them like a giant net ready to catch the sliding moon, before he said, 'Mrs Pavane seems to have told her husband nothing, or practically nothing, about herself. How much did you tell me about yourself?'

'As much as I wanted to,' she said. 'Come to think of it, I don't think you ever asked.'

Come to think of it, he hadn't. Her life before she married him had been richer, fuller than his own. The wealthy Dutch parents, the finishing school in Switzerland, the high social life in London on the diplomatic circle: he hadn't wanted to know, as if afraid to compare it with his own mundane, working-class background.

'You never asked me much about me.'

'No. What would it have been? Cricket, football, girls, beer parties with your mates. I fell in love with *you*, not your background. As you were, at that moment.'

He put his hand on her knee, squeezed it. 'The best way. The way I felt about you.'

They rode on, in a comfortable silence this time, up through the city and out towards Randwick. When they drew up outside their house she said, 'Think about going into another division.'

'No,' he said. 'I'd rather be troubled by people's lives than by a computer.'

Chapter Four

1

The Pavane case was at a standstill, though the media did its best to keep it moving. Diplomatic circles did not get much of a run in State capitals; they are as peripheral as a species that not even conservationists could care about. No editor could tell you the number of embassies in Canberra nor the names of 95 per cent of the ambassadors. But this case was a juicy fruit and they were determined to squeeze every drop from it. Even the talkback hosts were inviting their listeners to voice an opinion and the experts way out there at the end of the airwaves were not backward in coming forward. The only opinion-makers withholding their pens were the cartoonists. The case was not yet a joke nor fit for jokes.

Chief Superintendent Random was not joking as he addressed the morning conference in the Incident Room at Surry Hills:

'We've got to get our finger out. The Prime Minister has been on to the Premier, he's been on to the Police Minister, he's been on to the Commissioner, he's been on to Assistant Commissioner Hassett and he's –' He gave his thin grin. 'I'm at the end of the line and I'm black-and-blue. What's your score, Scobie?'

'Nil-all, sir.'

'You mean bugger-all?'

There was a murmur of laughter, though no one felt in good humour. The display board hung on one wall like an art exhibition that no one appreciated. The two homicides were part of the one exhibition, but everyone knew that Random was not talking about the Jones murder.

'I guess so,' said Malone. 'Agent Himes says he has something –'

Joe Himes, seated beside Malone, said, 'I've heard back from our guys in Portland, sir. Oregon. It doesn't tell us much – just adds to the mystery. I'll talk it over with Inspector Malone and you'll have the report in an hour, after I've made a coupla calls to Canberra.'

'Are they still wanting to get in on the act?'

'I think the Ambassador has got a rein on them, sir. I'll be talking direct to him.'

'Is he going back to the States?'

'Tonight. Mrs Pavane's body is being released this morning and he'll be on a chartered flight tonight with it.'

When the meeting broke up Malone and Himes moved into a side room. Malone had noticed that the FBI man had kept to himself while the strike force in the Incident Room was waiting for Greg Random to arrive. He had the look of a man not quite sure that he was welcome. But he relaxed now with Malone.

'Good news or bad news?' said the latter.

'Bad news, maybe it ain't. Good news, it surely ain't.' Himes took a fax sheet out of his pocket, smoothed it out. Malone had remarked he had a certain deliberation about his movements, as if nothing was presented till he was certain of it. 'Mrs Pavane had been checked. The usual thing is not to go back further than ten years on a spouse, unless there is evidence that she had a record at college or around that time. Involvement in demonstrations, that sorta thing. She was clear up to ten years ago. Worked for a mutual fund in San Francisco a coupla years. Then with a public relations outfit same city, three years. Went to Kansas City then, worked for MidWest National, the biggest bank there, doing PR work. Was working there and also doing volunteer political fund-raising when she met Mr Pavane. The investigation is always done by a single agent and it's left to his judgement. He passed her as clean.'

He paused and Malone said, 'And then?'

'Yeah, and then.' Himes again smoothed out the creases in the sheet, as if some lines might be hidden in them. But Malone was sure he had read and re-read the sheet. 'Our Portland guys went down to Corvallis, Mrs Pavane's supposed birthplace. As Wilhelmina Page, the name she used at those jobs I've just mentioned, the one that's on her marriage certificate in Missouri. Billie Page. Her father was supposed to have worked at State College at Corvallis. No record of him. No record of a Wilhelmina Page being born or registered in Corvallis. No record of her ever having attended the local high school. Before June 1991, when she went to work in the mutual fund in 'Frisco – zilch. She didn't exist.'

'You mentioned the marriage certificate. How much information does she have to give on that?'

'Not much that would help us. If she's over eighteen, all she has to do is produce some form of identification, a driver's licence, passport, something like that. There's no blood test required in Missouri, not that that would help us. She would have had to appear in person to sign the application and plunk down fifty dollars. Then she can marry the Devil himself. Or anyone who wasn't on an FBI Wanted list.' For the first time he grinned. 'As your boss described it, Scobie, we've got bugger-all.'

Malone took his time; he could smell thin ice again. He was going to be giving Ambassador Pavane more information than the man would want to hear.

'Joe, you said you'd be talking to Canberra. Ask the Ambassador if the RSO – Roger? Roger Bodine – if he can go through Mrs Pavane's personal belongings. See if there is a diary, something out of her past that'll give us a clue to who she was back before 1991.'

'Scobie, that's too delicate. Roger Bodine's a real pain in the ass – he takes everything so fucking seriously, as if he's the only one preventing World War Three. Washington's full of guys like him. But he's gotta live with the Ambassador when Mr Pavane comes back. Better that you ask one of your Federal agents to do it – that keeps it out of the personal contact frame –'

'Joe, I'm trying to keep this as localized as I can. You, me and the embassy. I'll go out to the airport tonight and tell him myself. It'll be a helluva time to do it, but better to get it over and done with. If the mood's right, I'll ask him about going through her belongings. Let him know I want to see him, will you?'

'Sure.' Himes looked relieved. 'How's that other case going, the one at the same hotel?'

'The wife's been arraigned – she's confessed to doing the husband.'

'You on it?'

'Up to a point.' He thought he owed it to Himes to be frank: 'The wife was an old girlfriend of mine. I'm trying to stay out of the personal contact frame.'

Himes whistled softly, nodded sympathetically. 'It ain't always easy, is it? I was once on a case till I found out I was chasing my wife's cousin. I got off it just in time. It was a total fuck-up – he was innocent. But boy –' He shook his head, grinned broadly, the boy there again in the man. 'My wife beat hell outa me. Good luck and stay outa the frame.'

Then Gail Lee came to the doorway. 'Andy is on the phone.'

Malone picked up the phone on the desk, asked for the call to be transferred. He motioned for Himes to wait, then Andy Graham came on the line:

'Boss? I'm down in Spring Street.' The heart of the financial district. 'I think we've come up with the guy who was at Catalina that day, spoke to Mrs Pavane. He works for a firm of stockbrokers.'

'You spoken to him yet?'

'Yeah, but he refuses to say anything. I think you'd better come down here and lean on him. I'm in the lobby –' He gave the address. 'He's gotta come down in the lifts or the stairwell if he wants to shoot through. He dunno I'm still hanging around.'

'I'll be there in ten, fifteen minutes at the most. I'll have Agent Himes with me.'

On the way downtown Malone said, 'This feller may be a dead loss.'

Himes nodded, said nothing. He knew the geography of blind alleys and dead ends; it was part of police work. They never taught it to you at the Academy, but like Malone he had learned it from experience. He kept his eye on the road now, appreciative of Malone's careful driving. 'I'm a nervous passenger.'

Malone grinned, liking him more by the minute. 'Join the club. Whenever I'm in a car and not behind the wheel, I've got my feet buried in the floorboards.'

Careful driver though he was, he was a careless parker, being a police officer. He parked the unmarked car in a No Standing zone and led Himes into the lobby of the Homestead Finance building. It was a new building, all marble and brass and a small forest of greenery in the lobby that was changed weekly, like a uniform. The building itself stopped almost any sunshine from reaching down into the roadway outside, but the developers had costed the bottom line of sunshine and it was a minus.

Andy Graham, tall and big, with a large face saved from being plain by lively blue eyes, came towards them. He was awkward, but he could move surprisingly quickly.

'He hasn't come down, boss.' He nodded good-morning to Himes, then addressed Malone again: 'His name's Vokes, Giuseppe Vokes –'

'Who?'

'That's what I said when he told me. He's an associate partner in Buller & Arcadipane and he's a nephew of Arcadipane. His mother's Italian. The firm have two floors, the 11th and the 12th. He's a little guy, he's about Mrs Pavane's age, I'd say, and he's snooty.'

'Towards cops or just towards everyone?'

'Cops, I think.'

'Where'd you get his family background?'

'I've got a mate on the stock exchange –'

Malone, by accident rather than design, was surrounded by staff who had mates, even in jail. 'Righto, let's go up and lean on him. Joe?'

'Righto,' said Himes, making it sound like a foreign word, and they rode up to the offices of Buller & Arcadipane on a width of smiles.

They got off at the wrong floor, the trading floor. A glacier of computers stretched away into the distance; heads were visible above the crevasses like mountaineers who were refusing to surrender. There were shouts, but not shouts for help: the market was going up, who needed rescuing? Giuseppe Vokes, recognizing Andy Graham, got up from behind a computer in the front row and came towards them.

'You have no right barging in here –'

He was short, prematurely bald and with the face of a handsome fox. Just the bloke I'd choose to invest my money, thought Malone, who wouldn't have invested in Fort Knox even in its heyday.

'We're not barging in, Mr Vokes. We have every right as police to come in and ask you some questions. You have the right not to answer them, but don't accuse us of *barging* in. Now can we go somewhere less exposed than this? Everyone thinks we're more interesting than the stock market.'

Heads had risen above the corrugation of computers: the mountaineers sighting rescue? Had the market suddenly started to avalanche?

'This way,' said Vokes and led the way out of the huge room and along a passage to an office. Malone noticed that it was not a corner office. He had learned enough about business to know that a corner office was the horizontal peak of the mountain.

Vokes ushered the three officers in, closed the door, then went round and sat behind a desk. The three visitors sat down, Malone and Himes on chairs, Graham on a couch against one wall. Vokes obviously knew the short man's talent for bringing everyone down to his level. Chairs were not invented only for the weary.

'I have told him –' Vokes nodded at Graham '– that I'm not prepared to answer questions. I know nothing about the American Ambassador's wife.'

'Maybe not,' said Malone. 'But do you know anything about the woman she was before she became Mrs Pavane?'

Vokes had spent a long time in front of computer screens; he could go blank in an instant. 'I've never met the woman. I made a mistake – mistaken identity – that day at the restaurant –'

Malone had been reading bluff from his first day in the Service. 'We're not going to accept that, Mr Vokes, till we're absolutely sure. We'll go back over your career –'

'You can't do that,' said Vokes flatly.

'I think we can. As a member of the stock exchange, your business life is supposed to be an open book – am I right? Do Buller & Arcadipane have any American connections, Detective Graham?'

He knew Graham would have the answer. The younger man looked at his notebook: 'Yeah, they have associate offices in San Francisco and New York with a coupla American firms.'

'You see, Mr Vokes, we've already started. Our friend here, Agent Himes from the FBI, will check if you ever worked with those offices in the States –'

Vokes chewed on his lips, then held up his hand. 'Okay, okay. It's going back a long way – that's why I wasn't sure that day in the restaurant –'

'How far back?'

'Just before the crash, 1987. I didn't know her well –'

'Who?'

'If she is who I think she *was*, her name was Patricia Norval.'

'If you didn't know her well, how did you know her at all? Where?'

'She worked for a firm of stockbrokers – they were in the same building, over on Bond Street, before Buller & Arcadipane moved here.' He named the firm, but Malone had never heard of them. If Clements were here, he would probably be able to name their pedigree: he was Homicide's expert on the stock market and its cowboys. 'They were a small firm – they never made it after the crash in '87. They just folded.'

'What happened to those who would've worked with her?'

Vokes spread his hands; small hands that looked like paws. 'I dunno. They just – evaporated, I guess. I heard one or two of them moved interstate, to Melbourne and Brisbane.'

Himes, with a deferential look at Malone as if asking permission to intrude, said, 'A whole group of brokers just breaks up and disappears? Why?'

Vokes looked uncomfortable. Why do I keep thinking of him as foxy? Malone wondered. 'Mr – Himes? You're asking me to point the finger when all there was was talk, suspicion –'

'We're always at home with suspicion,' said Malone. 'It's our stock in trade.'

'I'll bet,' said Vokes and almost smiled. 'Okay, there was talk that a scam was going on in that office. I don't think the two senior partners knew anything about it. It was this group, three or four of 'em. In the hullabaloo when the crash came, everyone had something bigger to worry about. By the time the exchange had got back on its feet, the firm had disbanded, was gone, and I guess the stock exchange board said forget it.'

'Did they get away with any money from the scam?' asked Himes.

'There was a rumour they took away several million, in '87 dollars. But nobody knew anything for certain.'

'Was Patricia Norval a broker?' asked Andy Graham, who was taking notes.

'No, but you'd often see her on the floor, the main floor and over at the futures exchange. But she never mixed with anyone but the guys from her own firm.'

'What did they do? Rob clients or the firm or what?'

Vokes nodded. 'They were into everything. They were buying and selling clients' stock and pocketing the profit after they'd buy the shares back when the price dropped. You could do it in those days. The rules are much tighter now. There was a boom before the crash, nobody thought it would end. A coupla the guys from the firm – I think one of them was going with Trish Norval –

95

they were dealing in currency, using clients' money. It was a picnic, I tell you.'

'And no one was keeping an eye on possible scams?' asked Himes.

'There may have been, I dunno. If there was, nothing ever came out.'

Himes looked at Malone. 'There was a big hustle on the Chicago exchange back in 1989. We, the FBI, were in on it. We cleaned it up,' he said, scoring a point for the FBI.

'So everyone got out of town?' said Malone, switching the limelight back from the FBI.

'I guess so. The two senior partners, they're dead. There never was any suspicion about them. It was the young hot-shots –' He looked around the three officers, all at once looked less foxy, almost regretful at what went on in his trade. 'There are always hot-shots in this game. They're the ones generate the excitement. They also generate the occasional investigation.'

'Would you know the names of those who worked with her?' asked Graham, notebook still open, pen at the ready.

'They'd be on the stock exchange register for that time.' Vokes was clamming up again.

'I'll look 'em up,' said Graham and one knew that he would.

Just before he rose Malone said, 'Why were you reluctant to talk to us, Mr Vokes?'

Vokes looked at him steadily. 'If you weren't a police officer, wouldn't you want to stay away from a murder?'

'I guess so,' said Malone, thinking of Delia Jones and thinking, I *am* a police officer.

The three police officers left the office. Vokes didn't rise, just nodded as they said goodbye. He was a short man safe in the fort of a chair.

As they went down in the lift Himes said, 'The bureaucrats must be worried. These guys and their computers are gonna run the world this century. Another fifty years and we'll be bowing down to new gods.'

'Not me. Retirement is looking better and better,' said Malone and wished he could push the clock forward. They reached the ground floor and he said, 'Andy, start tracing those who worked with Mrs Pavane – or Miz Norval, whatever we're going to call her. I'll see if someone at Surry Hills has come up with where Mrs Pavane had her Japanese meal just before she was topped.'

'No problem,' said Andy Graham and went off at his lumbering run but still disappearing quickly.

Malone looked after him. 'If I sent him into a china shop he'd break every cup, saucer and plate before he found the door to get out. But if I sent him to the Antarctic to get the name of a particular penguin, he'd talk to a million of them and come back with the right bird.'

'After this posting,' said Himes, 'I go back to take charge of a bureau somewhere – on the East Coast, I hope. Boston or Charleston would be nice. I hope I have your luck with the staff I get.'

They were standing in a square pool of sunshine; the rest of the narrow street was in shade. Malone became aware that the small square of warmth was crowded with about a dozen women, all in black except one, who was in grey, all with mobile phones stuck to their ears: power women who had just emerged from some conference. He had the sudden cock-eyed image that he was in the midst of a misery of Hasidic mourners, on their phones to determine the time of the next funeral. He looked for beards and wide-brimmed black hats, but there were none. Then he was aware that all the women, phones still to ears, were staring at him and Himes, all of them looking threatening, this time calling up reinforcements. Then he shook his head: he was having hallucinations.

'Why do women in business all wear black?' he said, trying to remember what Lisa had worn this morning.

'I dunno,' said Himes. 'I dunno why my wife wears what she does.'

'What does she wear?'

'I dunno,' said Himes and grinned again, proud in a long line of blind husbands.

Malone took the parking ticket from his windscreen, tore it up, dropped it down a grating in the gutter and got into the unmarked car and they drove back to Surry Hills as the group of black-suited women broke up and moved away, some with phones still to their ears as if massaging earache. Malone, watching them in his driving mirror, grinned to himself. He had lost his battle against the progress of technology but it still amused him. Cave-dwellers have a simplicity to them that is appealing. To other cave-dwellers.

Then his car-phone rang: it was Gail Lee: 'We've found out where Mrs Pavane had her Japanese dinner. At Kyoto in Hunter's Hill.'

2

The Queen Victoria Building, the QVB, is one of the city's treasures, a huge Victorian galleried, copper-domed emporium of boutiques, cafés and restaurants. Long neglected, there was talk of demolishing it; it was a nest for unwanted storage, rats and prowling developers. Then Asian developers took it over and restored it to even better than its original glory. Local municipal authorities and developers, blinded by cataracts of the quick buck, had laughed at the folly of the foreigners and went looking for other heritages to pull down. Now, this day, the boutiques, the Olympic boom long over and the tourists gone home, were back to selling to the natives at their half-price winter sales. Windows were plastered with signs – 50% OFF! BEST EVER SALE! – like old-time death notices.

Lisa was in one of the restaurants. It was a ritual that she and Scobie had lunch together once a week, but occasionally she came across here from Town Hall, just across the road, to have lunch on her own. She had worked for two years as the city's PR agent on the Olympics, a two-year headache that no amount of analgesics had ever helped. Now, like everyone else, she was astray. The Lord Mayor, a man afraid of decisions, had talked for the past six months of letting her go. She wasn't sure that she would not welcome the pink slip. City council politics were small wars that gave conflict a bad name and she had grown tired of them.

She was looking at the menu when she became aware of the woman standing by her table. She looked up to tell the waitress she had not yet made up her mind; but it was not the waitress. It was a woman in a long black coat and a black beret.

'Mrs Malone?'

'Yes,' said Lisa reluctantly, wondering if this was another complainant against another of the council's rulings.

'I'm Delia Jones.' She stood awkwardly for a moment, then nodded at the empty chair opposite Lisa. 'May I sit down?'

No, thought Lisa; but said, 'If you wish.'

Delia sat down, almost gracefully. Then a waitress was beside them, waiting on their order. 'What'll it be today, Mrs Malone?'

'I'll have the crab-and-avocado sandwich. And a glass of the usual white.' Then Lisa looked at the woman opposite, heard herself say, 'Would you like lunch?'

'Thank you. I'll have the same.' The waitress went away and Delia went on, 'It must be nice to be known.'

'I come here regularly.' She didn't add: *with Scobie.*

'I can't remember when I last had crab. Scobie used to like it. It was cheaper then. Does he still count his pennies?'

Lisa was gathering her defences. *Defences? What am I afraid of?* She was studying the other woman (the Other Woman?) without being too obvious. The black coat, done up to the neck, was cheap, but Delia wore it with some style; there was a purple-and-green scarf inside the collar, just enough colour to relieve the drab coat. The beret was cheap, the cheapest sort of headgear bar a beanie, but Delia wore it rakishly, pulled forward over one eye. Yes, thought Lisa, she had been attractive, once.

99

'Are you uncomfortable, sitting here with a murderess?'

Lisa was caught off-balance: 'Murderess?'

'I'm old-fashioned.' Delia had misunderstood her reaction. 'I prefer the old terms. Actress, heroine. Though I've never used murderess before. Are you a feminist?'

'No, I don't think so. Well, yes – yes, I guess I am. Up to a point.'

'Are you wondering why I'm here?'

'Yes.' Bluntly.

'Curiosity. He was a nice man. Has he changed?'

'No.' Just as bluntly.

'He was all cop the other day, when I saw him. I couldn't blame him. I was a terrible shock to him. I could see it. Did he tell you about me?'

'Yes.'

Delia said nothing, looked around her. The restaurant was full, every table occupied, everyone concerned with their own troubles, joys, whatever. Chatter filled the room like a smokescreen; one could hide an intimate conversation in it. Then Delia looked out the big window that was the wall dividing the restaurant from the gallery outside. Two young girls came out of a boutique, each with three shopping bags. They looked at the sign that obscured the store's window – 50% OFF! – laughed like footballers who had scored a goal and went swinging their way along the gallery. Delia looked back at Lisa.

'Were you young once?'

'Yes,' said Lisa and was surprised she wasn't surprised by the question.

Then the waitress arrived with their orders, put the plates and glasses of wine down, said, 'Enjoy your lunch,' and went away, leaving her smile behind like a blessing.

'Have you noticed?' said Delia. 'Some waitresses are natural-born? Maybe that's because women are natural-born servers. Are we? But all waiters, they have to be – *made*.'

Lisa wondered if Delia's impression of waitresses and waiters

100

was a memory from the past – from Scobie's day? She didn't look as if she had lately eaten in places where waitresses and waiters held sway.

Delia bit into the sandwich, chewed on it, said, 'This is delicious. I've hardly eaten the last coupla days.'

'How did you know where to find me?'

Delia took her time, enjoying the sandwich. 'I knew where you worked –'

'How?' Lisa hadn't yet started to eat.

'You've been mentioned in the papers – when Scobie was on those two other cases the last coupla years. There was a photo of you – I cut it out –'

Women can read faces as men read maps; they may sometimes mis-read the co-ordinates but they are rarely lost when reading other women. Lisa read Delia's face and suddenly thought, This woman is dangerous.

'I came into town today, just got the idea I'd like to see you. I was going up the steps into Town Hall when I saw you come out. I followed you across here.' She took a sip of her wine. 'I envy you. You know that, I suppose?'

'Mrs Jones –'

'Delia – *please*?'

Lisa ignored the invitation. 'Why did you want to see me?'

Delia, Mrs Jones, looked at her across the rim of her wine glass, took her time. 'I really don't know.' There had been a slight slovenliness to her speech when she had sat down, but now, as if bringing herself up to Lisa's level, or to the level of Delia Bates, she was careful of her delivery. 'Maybe I just wanted to compare notes. On husbands and lovers. He was going to marry me, you know. Scobie.'

'He told me you were never engaged.'

'No-o. But it was understood.'

'By whom?'

'By whom?' She put the glass down. 'By me. We're the ones who make the decisions, aren't we?'

She stared at Lisa, who retreated, said, 'How are your children coping?'

Delia smiled, as if a small victory had been won. 'Okay. My mother is looking after them for a while. They hated their father as much as I did – he belted them, too. There was never any aggression in Scobie.'

Lisa ignored that. Women, with no strength for heavy weapons, fence with more patience than men. 'You have a daughter –'

Delia cut in: 'Scobie's told you a lot about me, hasn't he? Did you enjoy that?'

'Let's cut out the nastiness, Mrs Jones. I didn't invite you to lunch.' Her mobile phone rang, but she reached down into her business satchel and switched it off.

'Always on call, always wanted? That must be nice.' Then she bit into the sandwich again, chewed awhile, then said, 'Okay, no nastiness. Yes, I have a daughter – by my first husband. If I go to jail, she's coming home to help my mother with the other two.'

Calmly told, as if planning a family holiday.

'What does she do?'

'I dunno.' The careful speech slipped away; as if she were tired of the impersonation of a woman gone forever. 'Every time she writes – which isn't often – she has a different job. She's one of the casuals of the world, she tells me. Big deal. You're lucky with your three – they have Scobie as their father. I had no luck – my first husband was a no-hoper and my second –' She grimaced, as if she had bitten on a crab claw. 'The absolute worst.'

'Mrs Jones, are you blaming me for taking Scobie away from you?'

She stared across the table, the almost-finished sandwich still in her hand. 'You did, didn't you?'

Lisa pushed her plate away from her, picked up her satchel and stood up. 'I'll pay for lunch at the desk. Good day and good luck.'

She paid for lunch, went out of the restaurant. Out on the

102

gallery she had to pass by the window where Delia Jones sat. They looked at each other through the glass, imperfect strangers, and Lisa went on back to Town Hall and the small wars there that, she now realized, never touched her.

3

'I tried to get you on your mobile at lunchtime,' said Malone.

'I was busy,' said Lisa.

'I saw a mass meeting of mobiles today – never mind. I just rang to say I'll be late for dinner tonight. I have to go out to the airport, have a few words with Ambassador Pavane.'

'Difficult ones?'

Her antenna is perfect, he thought. 'Yes . . . What did you do for lunch?'

'Just ate. I'll keep your dinner warm. I love you,' she said, her voice lowered, as if there was someone else in her office.

'Same here,' he said, put down his phone and looked across his desk at Gail Lee and Sheryl Dallen. 'My wife.'

'I should hope so,' said Sheryl.

'So what did you find out at this Japanese place at Hunter's Hill?'

'The waiter and the manager recognized her from the photo we showed them,' said Gail. 'They didn't know who she was when she was at the restaurant. It's a quiet place, mostly locals go there. They made no booking, just walked in.'

Hunter's Hill is a small community on a finger of land that juts into Sydney Harbour. It is home to one of the major private schools and a congregation of residents, not all religious, who would not have stared if the Virgin Mary had come to dine amongst them.

'We had to tell 'em who she was,' said Sheryl. 'They were incredibly polite, showed hardly any expression.'

'Very Oriental,' said Gail.

'I'm being polite,' said Sheryl. 'Anyway, we asked them to describe the guy she was with –'

'What did you get?' prompted Malone.

'Have you ever asked one man to describe another?' said Gail. 'Even a Japanese. You're all vaguer than a woman would be –'

Malone showed exaggerated patience. 'What did he look like – vaguely?'

'Tall, middle-aged, they think his hair was grey, but they're not sure. Very well dressed – that's something Japanese men, or anyway these ones, do recognize.'

Malone felt they were looking at him. 'So they'd never recognize me?'

'Probably not,' said Sheryl.

'How did they pay their bill?'

'Cash,' said Gail. 'As if they were covering their tracks.'

'Were they intimate?' asked Malone, then shook his head at their mock look of shock. 'Come on, I don't mean were they having it off on the table. Were they holding hands?'

'We asked that question,' said Gail. 'The waiter said no. But they did look like old friends. When they went out of the restaurant, the guy had his arm round her.'

'Righto, it looks as if they might've been old lovers as well as lovers on the night of the murder. We think we've traced her to a previous identity –' He looked at the notebook open on his desk. 'Patricia Norval. She worked for a small firm of stockbrokers, now out of business. Andy is down at the stock exchange, going through their back register. He'll come up with some names and we'll start sorting them out.'

'Good old Andy,' said Sheryl. 'Sometimes I could love him, only he'd knock me over on the way to the bed.'

'What goes on in the main room when I'm away?'

'Gay abandon,' said Gail and the two of them went out to the main room.

Malone worked at his desk till daylight started to fade, then he went downstairs, got his car out of the car park, drove into the city, picked up Joe Himes and headed out of town for the airport. Rain was pelting down, he drove through silver sheets that obscured everything more than thirty yards ahead, and he wondered if any planes would get off the ground this evening. He was always a cautious driver and this evening he drove as if in a funeral cortège. Other drivers, in cars and heavy trucks, sped by, parting the waters as if they were late arrivals at the Red Sea and Moses was waiting for them up ahead.

'Stupid bastards!'

Then he saw the lights flashing ahead and he slowed down. There had been a multiple-car pile-up; two police officers, slickers glistening in the headlights of approaching cars, were shepherding traffic through. Malone began to wonder how the night could get worse.

He wasn't going to put the car in the airport car park and get wet through making it into the terminal. He parked under cover in the luggage put-down line, showed his badge to a porter, said, 'If anyone moves it, tell 'em I'll pinch 'em. I mean it,' and led Himes into the terminal.

Ambassador Pavane was in a private room off the departure lounge. Malone and Himes were greeted at the door by Gina Caporetto. Malone looked beyond her at the dozen or more people in the room and said, 'Gina, could you see that the Ambassador is left alone with me and Joe? We'll only be ten minutes or so.'

'Serious?' she asked.

'Yes. But private, too. We want to protect him.'

'We all do,' she said and politely, diplomatically, began asking the visitors to step outside for a few minutes. They went out, looking curiously at Malone and Himes but saying nothing.

The two officers were left alone with Pavane and his RSO, Roger Bodine.

'I want Roger to stay,' said Pavane. 'He's going to be my contact while I'm away. I want him to be your contact, too.'

Righto, thought Malone, it's your choice. 'We think we've

come up with something on Mrs Pavane before you met her, sir.'

Pavane looked at Bodine, as if he had changed his mind and was going to ask the security man to step outside. Then he turned back to Malone and Himes. 'Go on.'

Himes then told him of the FBI investigation of the supposed Corvallis background. 'There's no record of her, sir, nothing before 1991 when she went to work in San Francisco.'

Pavane looked around, found a chair and sat down. He was silent for a long moment; the rain beat against the windows, enlarging his silence. Then he looked up at both law officers. 'What other bad news have you? Christ, you deliver nothing *but* bad news!'

They could see his anger, but knew it was not directed at them. His life was falling apart, crumbling off him.

'Get off your feet, gentlemen,' Bodine rumbled solicitously. 'We obviously have some things to discuss.'

Malone and Himes sat down and Bodine lowered himself into a chair like a hippo squatting. Malone wondered how such a grossly overweight man could hold the job he did; Himes told him later of Bodine's record, which was exemplary. Beyond the windows the rain suddenly stopped and a plane took off into the darkness, its lighted windows sliding by like a broken comet's tail.

'We think,' said Malone carefully, 'but we're not sure yet – we think we may have identified Mrs Pavane as Australian. Her name then was Patricia Norval and she worked here in a stockbroker's firm back in the late eighties.' He held off mentioning the office scam; they had no evidence she had been involved in it. Then he said even more carefully, 'She had dinner at a Japanese restaurant in Hunter's Hill the night she was murdered with a man we still have to identify.'

'Jesus!' Pavane leaned back, put a hand over his face, almost as if hiding from the other three men.

Lisa, wider read than Malone, had once remarked to him in other circumstances that Chekhov had said it was important that a human being should never be humiliated. Malone remembered that now and saw the truth of it.

And then he suddenly knew he could not ask the question on the tip of his tongue: *Did you know your wife had had a bungled abortion?* Not in front of Himes and Bodine. Not with his wife's corpse being loaded on to the plane outside there, being taken – home? But where was home for Billie Pavane and Belinda Paterson and Patricia Norval?

Instead he said, 'We're trying to be as discreet as possible, sir. But the mystery of your wife's past life, we can't just leave it –'

'Why not?' Pavane took his hand away from his face.

Malone looked at Himes and Bodine, but they were no help. 'Mr Pavane, that's where your wife's murderer is hidden.'

'You're sure of that?'

Malone could see that the Ambassador was not being obtuse. He was clinging to an image of happiness that had been shattered; and Malone, who had his own happiness intact, could not blame him.

'Pretty sure, sir. It's the only direction we have.'

'This question is academic –' Bodine eased himself forward in his chair. 'Just to take it out of our calculations. You're absolutely sure Mrs Pavane was not murdered by some outfit that was anti-American?'

Malone looked at Himes for that one; who said, 'We've ruled that out, Roger. Whoever killed her, it was personal. Sorry, sir,' he said as Pavane flinched.

Malone put forward a gentle foot: 'Ambassador, did your wife ever mention any trouble in her past life? I mean in San Francisco?'

Pavane thought a while, then shook his head. 'I can't remember anything. Are you suggesting it might have been someone from those days?'

'I don't know, sir. It might be an idea if we got the FBI in San Francisco to look into it.'

There was no immediate answer from Pavane and Bodine said, 'Do we need to do that?'

Uh-uh, thought Malone, I'm in American territory.

Bodine went on, 'If the *National Enquirer* got on to that – and there'd be that sleazy jerk on the internet – I don't think so, sir –'

'I'll think about it,' said Pavane and stood up, heavily, as Gina Caporetto came to the door.

'They're waiting for you to board, sir.'

Pavane thanked her; he had politeness ingrained in him, not the diplomatic sort. Then he shook hands with Malone, Himes and Bodine. 'Keep in touch with me through Roger. Don't do anything about San Francisco till I come back.'

He went out of the room accompanied by Bodine and Gina Caporetto. Malone looked at Himes. 'He doesn't want to know. He'd rather we dropped the whole thing.'

'It's his position, Scobie – he's trying to avoid scandal –'

Malone shook his head. 'It's personal. He's still in love with the woman he married. He doesn't want to know who she was before that.'

4

Some emotions, like steel rails in summer sun and winter wind, run hot and cold. Anger is one of them. Ever since lunchtime Lisa had been running hot and cold. Lovers from the other side of a loved one's life are never welcome; jealousy is another emotion that runs hot and cold. She had come home from the office, decided to wait dinner for Scobie, and had sat for the past hour nursing a gin-and-tonic, looking into it occasionally as if it were a crystal ball that might tell her something. Like all grog, it told her nothing but what she wanted to tell herself.

She looked at the ABC news on television, but there was nothing there to raise her spirits. Calamity provides better images than celebration; Heaven, she mused, would be media-free because there would be nothing worthwhile reporting. She was sinking into a mood where she was glad that Claire, Maureen and Tom were not here to see her.

When Malone came in he looked aged, as if the years had accelerated and wrapped themselves round him. He kissed her and put his arm round her shoulders, holding her tight. She recognized the sign and all the emotion drained out of her. *He was hers.*

'What did you have to tell him?'

'We're killing his wife for the second time. Digging her up and burying her again.'

She kissed him, thinking again but not telling him, *He's mine.* 'I'll get dinner.'

It was steak-and-kidney pie, his favourite, carrots and peas and a glass of red. He poured himself a second glass and said, 'What's for dessert?'

He never neglects his stomach, she thought lovingly.

'I was too tired –'

'You look it,' he said solicitously.

She put down a plate of crackers and three wedges of cheese in front of him. 'Treat your arteries. Brie, cheddar, blue vein.'

The room, or she, felt cold and she turned up the gas heater in the kitchen. Then she sat down opposite him, poured herself a glass of wine and felt the emotion rise within her as the heat did.

'I had lunch today with Delia Jones.'

'Ah.'

'That's all you're going to say?'

'Till I hear what else you're going to say.'

There were echoes in the room but neither of them commented on them.

'I didn't invite her. Well, no – yes, I did. She just came up, introduced herself and, I don't know why, I asked her if she wanted to have lunch with me. At our place in the QVB, our table.'

A dry biscuit crackled in his mouth like static. 'Was it interesting?'

'Yes. Yes, it was. She's still in love with you.'

'No.' He shook his head adamantly. 'No, she's not. She thinks I'm a bastard.'

'Women can still love bastards. I can quote you a long list, from history right up to today. But all right, she's not in love with you. But she hates me because you love me.'

'Darl –' The brie was turning sour in his mouth; he gulped down a mouthful of wine. 'Why didn't you tell her to go to hell?'

'I don't know. I did, eventually. But at first I was curious –'

'At what I saw in her?'

'I suppose so. What did you see in her?' She felt the need for a little masochism. Who was it said, Jealousy is inborn in women's hearts? She would have to look it up. Was it Euripides or St Paul? Some misogynist, for sure.

Scobie reacted like a man: 'Oh, come on! That was twenty-five years ago. I was another – *person*. Simpler, if you like. She was a good-looker, she was good company, she –' He paused a moment; then: 'Are you going to ask me was she good in bed?'

'No. And don't tell me. There were plenty of others –'

He looked at her in surprise. 'Cut it out!'

'Sorry. I didn't mean that –' She reached for his hand. The jealousy drained out of her like a blood-letting. 'Darling, she's dangerous –'

'For you and me? No –'

'No. I don't know what it is, but I saw it in her today. Her life's been a shambles . . . I had to get up and leave her. I paid the bill and walked out. Outside the restaurant, I had to pass her – she looked at me through that window you and I stare out of – it was as if she had already forgotten me. But she hasn't forgotten you –'

'She will.' But he didn't sound convinced or convincing. 'I'll be off the case –'

'Stay away from her. And I'm not saying that because I'm jealous –'

'Are you?'

She considered; then: 'Yes. But I can live with it –'

He turned her hand over in his. 'It's over, darl. It was twenty-five years ago. I don't feel the least spark of interest in her – no, that's not true. I do. I feel sorry for her. But that's all.'

'Watch her. She could make trouble.'

Then the phone rang out in the hallway. He got up, wondering why he felt relieved at the interruption. It was Andy Graham: 'Sorry to call you at home, boss, but Gail said not to call you at the airport –'

'No, Andy. I had enough on my plate out there. What are you going to pile on it now?' He felt utterly depressed. What sort of night was the man in charge out at Tibooburra having? Was he sorting out a fight between two kangaroos? Locking up a drunken emu? I'm getting light-headed, he thought.

'A bit of good news, I hope.' But then Andy Graham was always hopeful of good news; he would look to the UN hurrying to peace-keep Armageddon. 'I've traced another of those guys who worked at that firm of stockbrokers. A guy named Bruce Farro. F-A-R-R-O. He's into software or something now.'

Malone's mood lightened; *someone who can help with our enquiries* was one of the better type of aspirin. 'Why do I think that name is familiar?'

'I dunno. I don't think he'd run around in your – what's the word? – milieu.'

'What milieu does he run around in?'

'The social pages. My girlfriend has pointed him out to me a coupla times. As if I'm interested.'

Malone remembered the name now. 'My daughter Maureen's mentioned him. When she was at uni she did a thesis on social celebrities for her Communications course. She counts the mileage of teeth in the Sunday papers.'

111

He remembered Farro now, though not well enough to have picked him out in a crowd picture. Maureen had said he was double-gaited, fluid, in his sexual choices. One week he would be seen arm-in-arm with a shaven-headed male whose skull looked like a transplant of five o'clock-shadow. Next week he would have his arm round a woman with more hair than a burst chesterfield. Malone hoped there was more to Mr Farro than social celebrity.

But Malone was still bone-weary. 'Andy, does he know you're on to him? Is he likely to shoot through tonight?'

'He knows nothing about our enquiries. He's safe, boss.'

'Righto, I'll see you in the morning, then. Where does he live? We'll drop in and have Weet-Bix and toast with him. Maybe some Vegemite.' He was getting light-headed again.

'In Elizabeth Bay. He has an apartment in –' He gave an address. 'On the water.'

'So he's not short of cash?'

'I'd say not.'

'I'll see you there at nine. Dress casual, Andy – we don't want to frighten him.'

'See you, boss. Have a good night's sleep.'

The phone went dead and Malone could imagine Andy Graham galloping off into the night, bumping into people and things, apologizing, still full and always would be of boundless energy and enthusiasm.

'Good news?' said Lisa.

Malone turned, put his arm round her as she came into the hallway. 'It could be. Or maybe not. I'm not sure how much I want to learn about Mrs Pavane.'

'Let's go to bed.'

'You can take advantage of me. I'll be asleep.'

She jabbed him with her elbow, a lover's punch.

Chapter Five

1

Randwick is on the southern rim of the eastern suburbs; Elizabeth Bay on the northern or harbour rim. Maureen, the social commentator, called the latter area the 'sophisticated but shallow eastern suburbs'. Real estate, fashion and gossip were the interests of the harbour rim; Versace was much better known than Voltaire or Veblen and no one would have known what the latter meant by 'conspicuous waste'. There were stories that during the Olympics, following pressure by the authorities to use public transport rather than their Bentleys and BMWs, some of the sports-minded had been shocked to learn there was no first class on buses. There was a large Jewish population in the area and they did manage to raise the level of discussion and interest in the arts. But the Deep South and the Deep West of Sydney were Ultima Thule (what's that?) to the harbour rim.

Andy Graham was casual: jeans, open-necked shirt, golf jacket. Malone was in slacks, blazer and turtle-necked sweater; he wore a tweed checked cap, which made Graham look at him as if he had turned up in a tiara. Very unofficial – or unofficious-looking, both of them. Malone pressed the button on the intercom and it was almost a minute and two more pressures on the button before an irritated voice asked, 'Yes, who is it?'

'Police.'

'Police?' There was a clearing of throat, sleep being coughed up. 'Did you say *police*?'

'Detective-Inspector Malone and Detective-Constable Graham. May we come up for a few minutes, Mr Farro?'

Another clearing of the throat. 'Show me your badges. There's a security camera right above you. Hold them up to it.'

Grinning at each other, Malone and Graham did so, holding their arms high like a Nazi salute.

'Okay, come up. Top floor.'

A white-haired woman came out of the door as the two detectives lowered their arms, looked curiously at them, walked on, stopped and looked back.

'We've scared her,' said Graham.

'Let's go up and see if we can scare Mr Farro.'

They went into an entrance lobby as cold as marble: the walls and floor were marble. They rode up in a lift that had all the welcoming warmth of a refrigerator. This building had been up only six months; it still smelled of money. They stepped out into a small lobby and Bruce Farro was standing at an open door opposite them.

'Come in, gentlemen.' He sounded more hospitable than he had over the intercom.

He was dressed in cerise-and-blue striped pyjamas and a royal blue dressing gown with a cerise crown on the breast pocket. There was a blue handkerchief in the pocket and Malone wondered whether it was for blow or show. He was slightly shorter than the two detectives, about Malone's age, handsomeness fattening into blandness. He offered no handshake but waved them into his apartment.

It, too, was cold; it had the lived-in look of a *House & Garden* feature. Everything in the big living room was white but for the pictures, all bright abstracts, like graffiti, on the walls. Beyond the big glass doors on to a wide verandah the harbour was steel-blue under the grey skies.

'What's this all about? Coffee? I haven't had breakfast yet. Friday night is always a late night. You know how it is.'

'Indeed,' said Malone, remembering last night.

The living room ran into the dining room which was overlooked by the open kitchen: all white. In summer one would have to wear dark glasses *indoors*. Farro went into the kitchen, talking to them through the gap between an overhead cupboard and the serving bench, then brought coffee to the living room and waved to them again to make themselves comfortable. He was affable, comfortable. Or he was a good actor.

'Is it business? Are you from the Fraud Squad or something?' His teeth were set back in his mouth and his smile seemed to come out of a small cave.

'No, we're from Homicide,' said Malone.

The smile went back into the cave. 'Go on.'

Andy Graham took out his notebook, but didn't look at it. 'Back in the eighties, up till 1987, you worked at –' He named the firm, then waited.

Farro took his time, as if trying to remember the firm or if, indeed, he had worked there; then he nodded. 'Yes.'

'You knew a girl worked there, Patricia Norval. Right?'

Farro again took his time, sipped his coffee; then he said, 'Ah, now I see where we're going.'

'Yes,' said Malone, sipping his own coffee; it was good coffee and must have been brewing for some time. Which meant someone else was in the apartment. 'And you were surprised when we rang your buzzer downstairs a moment ago?'

'We-ll – well, no. I just didn't expect you *here*. How did you get on to me?'

'Detective Graham's parents ran bloodhound kennels, he learned early.'

Farro looked at Graham and smiled. 'Droll.'

'He has the names of everyone who worked at your firm. You're the first we've called on.'

'This is about the murder of the American Ambassador's wife?'

'Yes, it is. How did you know she was here in Australia?'

'I recognized her down in Canberra a month ago. I was down there for my firm. She and her husband were at a reception at the Ministry of Defence, one of our clients.'

115

'Did you speak to her?'

'I tried to, but she stared right through me. You know the way some women can do that.' Malone wondered if he made that sort of remark to his gay friends. 'She didn't want to know me. So I didn't press it.'

'But you were sure you knew her, had worked with her?'

'Yes. How much do you know?' He sounded cautious.

'We'll tell you first what we know about you.' Malone nodded at Graham.

The latter was looking at his notebook now: 'Mr Farro, you left Sydney in 1987, the end of the year. Where did you go to?'

Farro could never be accused of blurting out the truth; or a lie. He said very slowly and deliberately, 'I went to Hong Kong. I was there a year, working with an investment firm, Americans. Then I went to New York, I was there three years. I had a green card, I worked in Wall Street. Then in 1991, I think it was, I went out to Silicon Valley. California. I wanted to learn the computer game.'

'In California did you hear or meet Patricia Norval?' asked Malone.

'I heard of her in San Francisco – well, no, I didn't. Not Trish Norval. She'd changed her name – I can't remember what to.'

'Belinda Paterson?'

'Could've been. I wasn't that interested in her. I didn't try to look her up.'

'Where were you Tuesday night?' Malone hadn't raised or quickened his voice.

Farro once more took his time: 'Tuesday? I was home here, working. Then a friend came, stayed the night.'

'He or she will confirm that?'

Farro looked at him, almost smiled: *so you know my choices.* Then he said, 'I'm sure she will. She's in the bedroom right now.'

'We won't disturb her – not yet. Go on, Andy.'

'When did you come back to Sydney?'

'In 1996. I started up a small software company –'

Graham looked at his notebook: 'Finger Software. You publicly floated it in 1999 and on paper, overnight, you were worth forty million. The Securities Commission looked into it –'

'I was cleared.'

'You gave them the finger?' said Malone. 'Which one?'

Farro held up the middle finger of his right hand and the smile came out of the cave again. 'We're a reputable and established firm. I'm the managing director and we're very well respected by some very reputable clients. If you have them in your notebook, ask them.'

Graham went on: 'When you worked with Miss Norval –'

'I didn't work *with* her. She was just the office manager, she had no dealing with clients.'

'She knew what was going on,' said Malone.

The cave was now just a fissure in a rock-face.

'You see, Mr Farro,' Malone went on, 'we know about the scam you and two or three other brokers were pulling –'

'Would you care to make that charge public? I'll sue you.'

'Oh, we'll make it public if you wish.' One bluffer can recognize another one. 'We'll contact the Securities Commission on Monday –'

'There's a statute of limitations –' The bluff had folded.

'Not on scandal,' said Malone, still bluffing. 'Go on, Andy.'

'There were four of you in – we'll call it the scam, for want of a better word –'

Nicely put, Andy, thought Malone and hid a smile, though not in a cave.

Farro sat quietly, only moving to change the cross-over of his legs. He wore blue velvet slippers, also with the crown emblem on them. He took the handkerchief out of his breast pocket, wiped his upper lip with it and put it back. It was not a blow but a show: it showed he was starting to feel uncomfortable.

'Look, Mr Farro,' said Malone, 'we're not interested in the scam – that's someone's money down the gurgler. We are

Homicide, not Fraud. We're trying to find out who murdered Mrs Pavane – who we now know was Patricia Norval. Did she have a relationship with any of your colleagues? You all left the firm at the same time.'

'Okay.' He was still taking his time. 'This is off the record –' He stared at Andy Graham, who took the hint and closed his notebook. 'There were four of us – the other three were Jack Brown, Wayne Jones and Grant Kael.' He spelled out the last name. 'He's dead, Kael – he was killed in a car accident in Victoria about a year later.'

'Brown and Jones?' said Graham.

'They're common names. Amusing, eh? You're looking for Mr Brown and Mr Jones.'

'I once counted the Joneses in the phone book,' said Graham. 'There were 3822 of them.'

'Droll, eh?' said Malone. 'Come on, Mr Farro, give us their names.'

'I *told* you. Brown and Jones.'

Malone looked at Graham, who shrugged and said, 'They were on the stock exchange register at that time. Where do we find them now, Mr Farro?'

'Your guess is as good as mine. I haven't seen either of them since we split up.'

'Did either of them have a relationship with Miss Norval?'

Again he took his time: 'Probably. She played the field. It was a heady time, back then. I never got involved with her – she wasn't my type –'

Malone refrained from asking what his type was and Farro seemed to notice the reticence; the smile came out of the cave again, but he said nothing. Then there was the sound of a door opening; someone had got tired of waiting to be called. A moment later a woman appeared at a corner of the room in which they sat.

'Bruce?'

'Rita –' Farro rose, went towards her. 'We won't be long – it's just some business that's cropped up –'

118

'While your friend is here with us –' said Malone; he wasn't going to let her escape to be told by Farro to keep her mouth shut. 'Miss –?'

She looked at Farro, her brow furrowed. She had a mass of curly dark hair, a face puffed with sleep and love-making and she was not young and innocent. She was wearing what was obviously one of Farro's robes, a thick terry-towelling gown that fell to the floor and threatened to trip her. She appeared tripped by the two strangers who wanted to know her name.

'Rita Gudersen,' said Farro and seemed to shrug resignedly. 'These gentlemen are from the police, darling. Detective-Inspector Malone and Detective –?'

'Graham,' said Andy Graham, notebook open again. 'Rita Gudersen? How do you spell that?'

'Why?' She had a soft pleasant voice that was strained now by her puzzlement. But she spelled it out. 'What's the matter, Bruce? What's going on?'

'Where were you last Tuesday night?' asked Malone.

Still frowning, she looked at Farro.

'No, don't look at him,' said Malone. 'Look at me, I'm asking the question. Where were you Tuesday night?'

She cleared her throat. 'Here. I came here about – I think it was about ten, maybe a little after. I spent the night with Bruce.'

Farro's smile came almost right out of the cave; he looked as if he had been given a signed blank cheque. 'Well, there you are –'

'May we have your home address and where you work?' Malone ignored him, addressing Rita Gudersen.

'There's no need for that –' said Farro.

'Just routine,' said Malone, still ignoring him, looking at the woman.

She hesitated, then gave a home address in Mosman, on the other side of the harbour. 'Work? I'm with Fairbrother, Milson and Gudersen.'

One of the oldest and biggest law firms in the city. Malone

couldn't remember whether it was her father or her grandfather who had helped found the firm. Or had she married into the Gudersens?

She must have read his mind: 'I am a Gudersen. We handle all Bruce's legal business. Anything else?'

There were several snide remarks that could have been made, but Malone never saw any point in cheap scores. He stood up. 'Thank you, Miss Gudersen. We shan't be bothering you again.'

'Nor me?' said Farro.

'We'll see. Have a good weekend.'

Going down in the lift Andy Graham said, 'I had a few more questions I wanted to ask him.'

'Andy, that will give us a reason for calling him again. When he's not sleeping with his legal adviser. We may need him to identify Mr Brown and Mr Jones. If we find them.'

'Mr Jones wouldn't be our Boris, would he? That would simplify things.'

'No, it wouldn't, Andy. Not for me.'

Malone went home, did some notes for his report, had lunch, then he and Lisa went down to Coogee to watch Tom play rugby for Randwick against Gordon, an old rival. There they were met by Claire and Jason, Maureen and her boyfriend-of-the-week, Clint or Flint or something. His name didn't matter, he would be replaced next week. Malone worried at this production-belt attitude towards her love-life, but Maureen was obviously a good production manager. She appeared to be carrying no neuroses.

'But what if she gets pregnant to one of these blokes?' Malone had asked.

'Relax,' Lisa had said. 'Mo knows how to take care of herself.'

'You didn't. We didn't plan to have Claire, not so soon –'

'I said, relax. When Mo falls pregnant it will be to someone she's in love with.'

'How can *you* be so relaxed? You're condoning free love –'

'Pull your head in, as Mo would tell you. You're assuming your daughter goes to bed with every boy she goes out with. Have more faith in her.'

He had given up, but watched for signs of stress in Maureen; she smiled back at him as if Lisa had told her of his concern. Now today, out of the corner of his eye Malone sized up the latest – Clint? Flint? – and hoped next week's choice would be better. The bugger was actually barracking for Gordon.

But Randwick won, with Tom scoring a try and kicking four goals. As he came off the field he waved to them, then went up the pavilion steps towards the dressing-rooms. Halfway up he stopped and spoke to a woman. Malone, on his way out to the gates, stepped out of the crowd and looked up.

The woman looked like Rita Gudersen; but it wasn't she. She had a lot of dark reddish hair and, from a distance, looked very attractive. She gave Tom a big smile and pressed his arm affectionately.

'That's his tutor,' said Maureen, stopping beside her father. 'She has every professor and lecturer and half the students falling all over her, slobbering like pups. She can pick and choose. We should feel honoured she's chosen our Tom.'

'She's old enough to be his mother!'

'Tell that to Mum. She's twenty-eight, that's all.'

'How do you know all this?'

'I'm a *Four Corners* researcher, aren't I? All we have to do is keep an eye on him, Dad. When he wants to leave Mum's cooking and move out, then'll be the time to squash it. She's not serious about him, she'll move on to someone else. He's her toy boy.'

'That's what I've raised? A toy boy?'

'We can enter him in next year's *Cosmo* Bachelor of the Year. Though his IQ might be too high for it.'

She put her arm in his and he said, 'Where's Clint? Or Flint?'

'He's squiring Mum to the car. He's very polite – they're *very* polite, those Gordon men, when they're off the field. They have mother fixations up on the North Shore.'

'Spoken like a true *Four Corners* researcher. What do you see in him?'

'He has a Porsche. Second-hand, but a Porsche. How's your old girlfriend going?'

'Are you a *Four Corners* researcher or my darling daughter?'

'Your darling daughter. Do you think I'd sneak a professional question in on you?'

'Yes.' They were outside the ground now; the crowd had thinned. Down along the street he could see Lisa and Clint (or Flint?) standing by a silver Porsche. He could imagine Lisa thinking about a spin in it; she had always been a speed demon, always drove much faster than he. 'Your mob are not thinking of doing anything on her?'

'Dad, she's a nobody. I don't mean that nastily. If we were going to do a programme on battered wives – well, yes, we might consider her. But compared to Mrs Pavane's murder? No way. I was just asking was she troubling you?'

'No. But she invited herself to lunch with Mum yesterday.'

'Ah.'

He heard the echo: *Ah.*

'Then she's going to make a nuisance of herself?'

'That's what your mother suggested. Or *told* me – not suggested. You women and your bloody intuition!'

'Never fails. Hullo, Hugh.'

Malone looked after the huge young man who had just passed, football kitbag slung over a shoulder that looked as if it could carry a steel beam. 'Who's that?'

'Last week's choice.'

'What does he drive?'

'He has a second-hand Yamaha with a pillion. Didn't you always warn me to keep my legs together?'

'Never talked to my daughters like that in my life.'

She kissed his cheek as they came to Lisa and Clint (or

122

Flint). 'Take him home, Mum. He's getting parental. Or have you seduced Mum into going for a drive with you? She used to be a dolly bird in London years ago.'

Clint, no student of history, looked blank. 'What's a dolly bird?'

'Clint,' said Lisa, 'if you'd had a Porsche in London in those days you'd have been wearing dolly birds as mascots.'

Going home in the family Fairlane, Lisa at the wheel said, 'She's safe with Clint. He's more interested in cars than he is in girls.'

'Did you see the woman Tom's interested in?'

'Woman?'

'She's old enough to be – Maureen tells me she's twenty-eight. Every bloke at NSW is slobbering over her.'

'Good for Tom.'

'He's her toy boy.'

She looked sideways at him, at the same time swinging out on to the wrong side of the road to pass a laboring Beetle. 'Do you really think Tom's so soft in the head he'd fall for that?'

'It's not his head I'm thinking of. Take your foot off the pedal! You're doing ninety and we're coming up past the police station. Geez – a middle-aged dolly bird and a toy boy!'

'Bless your luck.'

So he blessed his luck by taking her to bed before supper, knowing that if Tom was with the toy-boy fancier he would not be home till late. After supper they watched weak comedians on television; switched over to what was, by Lisa's count, the nineteenth cookery show on TV. Then they watched the late news. A reporter was doing his piece on a small earthquake in New Guinea: 'Incredibly, the de-bree is mostly coconuts as plantation after plantation has been devastated. The scene is absolutely fantastic – there's no other word for it.' Not in his vocabulary, Malone thought. 'So far the death toll is, basically, ten dead –'

And then, as if the call had been waiting all day to spoil their mood, the phone rang. He went out into the hallway and picked it up: it was Gail Lee, not worried but apologetic: 'I'm sorry, boss, but we have a problem. The Southern Savoy called in Regent Street, who called us – I'm on weekend call. Mrs Jones has been making a nuisance of herself here at the hotel.'

'Doing what?'

'Threatening one of the housemaids – says she was the one who had sex with Mr Jones that night. Regent Street want to cart her off in the wagon, but she's putting on an act, getting a bit hysterical, says she won't leave here till she talks to you.'

'Oh Christ!' He saw that Lisa had come to the door of the living room.

'We can manhandle her, if you don't want to come in –'

'No, hold her there. Give me twenty minutes. Make sure there is parking right outside for me.'

'Delia?' said Lisa as he hung up the phone.

'How'd you know?'

'I told you – she's going to cause trouble.'

'Darl –' She had followed him into their bedroom as he got out of his pyjamas. She laid out his turtleneck sweater, went to the closet and took out a sports jacket and slacks. A wife getting her man off to work. 'Darl, she won't after tonight. She's been threatening one of the housemaids, the girl who had it off with Boris the night Delia did him in. They'll revoke her bail, remand her to Mulawa.' The women's prison. 'She's likely to spend all the time in there till she goes to trial.'

Lisa was unimpressed. 'Give her my regards. Tell her you were about to go to bed with me for the second time tonight.'

'That's nasty.'

'I know. And it tastes sweet.'

But at the front door she kissed him, stood there in her robe in the open doorway as he drove away. 'Don't catch cold!' he called to her, but the wind snatched his words away.

He turned on the heater in the car, but it didn't warm him. He couldn't remember when he had last felt so astray; he was like an

124

astigmatic man trying to thread a needle. He had a major murder on his hands, a killing that was cloaked in fog, and now a *simple* murder, a domestic, for Christ's sake, was pulling him into its net because of bait that was twenty-five years old. He had loved Delia back then; or had thought so. He wondered if, had her life since then been happy, she would have remembered him. But he could not ask her that question. He had to tell her to drop out of his life, that he could no longer help her. And yet . . .

Gail Lee, wrapped in a thick camelhair coat and what looked like a matching hat, well dressed enough to be the Commissioner's wife, was waiting for him under the awning outside the Southern Savoy. He pulled the car into an empty space, was tooted by a taxi trying to pull into the same space, got out and crossed to Gail. They went into the hotel, leaving the taxi driver, who had now got out of his cab, shouting after them in a thick spew of words that was spattered by the wind.

In the lobby Gail paused. 'She's in the manager's office with one of the Regent Street guys. They took the wagon away, the hotel thought it was lowering the tone.'

'How is she?'

'Bloody spiky. Won't talk to anyone but you.' She looked at him solicitously. 'I'm sorry.'

He sighed. 'I'm getting tired of this. Righto, let's go inside. Where's the maid Boris is supposed to have screwed?'

'She's in the small office behind the reception desk. Scared out of her mind.'

Guests were coming in the front door, swept in by the wind, tossing chat amongst themselves, everyone looking as if they had had a night that was – 'Fantastic!' said a young man, and his three friends couldn't find a better word: 'Fantastic!'

Malone looked at them sourly. 'Basically, that is.'

Gail looked at the two couples as they got into a lift, then looked back at him. 'I shouldn't have called you.'

He managed a grin. 'I'll talk to the maid later. Let's see what Delia has to say.'

125

There were only Delia Jones and a young uniformed officer in the manager's office, sitting far apart as if there was no connection between them. The officer stood up as Malone and Gail came in, but Delia just raised her eyes without raising her head.

'Evening, sir. Constable Szabo, from Regent Street.' He was short and thickset, barely the required Service height, with wary eyes and a pleasant, nondescript face. At least his eyes were wary of Delia; he had so far only put his toe in the pool of women. 'The lady has had nothing to say.'

Malone pulled up a chair and sat down in front of Delia. 'Have you got nothing to say to me, Delia?'

She had been sitting stiffly in her chair, but now suddenly she relaxed and smiled. She was in her long black coat and her beret and evidently had just repaired her make-up: made-up for *him*. She looked triumphantly at Gail.

'I've said all along that I'll talk to you. Gail, here, doesn't seem to get the message.'

'Detective Lee has a job to do, Delia. Now what do you want to tell me? I understand you came in here to bail up the maid you say Boris had sex with. That right?'

'Yes.'

'And what were you planning to say to her? Or do to her?'

'Nothing. I just wanted to see what sort of trash he liked to poke.'

'Delia —' He wanted to slap her, though he didn't know why. 'What was the point? The maid, whoever she is, wasn't the reason you killed Boris. Or was she?'

She was abruptly cautious; or cunning. One could almost see the change of gears behind the cosmetics. 'I killed him because he belted me.' She put her hand up to her face, touched her mouth, her bruised cheek, both now almost disguised by the make-up. But the gesture was theatrical, as if she had rehearsed it. 'I've said that all along.'

'You had no intention of hurting the woman?'

'None at all.'

Constable Szabo coughed and Malone turned to him. 'Yes?'

'Mrs Jones did attack the maid. A coupla the guests, upstairs, they had to separate them. It was pretty rough, they said. Then reception called us.'

Malone looked back at Delia, shook his head. 'Delia, when are you going to learn? If you want us –' he almost said *me* '– to help you, you're not going about it the right way by lying. Why'd you attack the maid?'

'Are you on my side or not?' It was almost a fierce demand.

'I'm on the law's side.' He stood up. 'Call the wagon, Constable. Lock her up for the night and we'll see she's taken before the Bench in the morning.' He turned back to Delia. 'They'll revoke your bail and you'll be remanded. You'll spend the time till your trial, maybe a year, maybe two, in jail. Think about it, Delia.'

'Okay, okay!' She stood up, stepped towards him; but he moved away. She was wearing a cheap perfume and the heat of her sudden desperation made it smell stronger. 'I was stupid – I lost my block with her – I wouldn't have hurt her, not really –'

He was aware of Gail Lee and Constable Szabo watching him, but it was impossible to read what their gaze was saying. He took the plunge: 'Stay here. Sit down –' She didn't move and he snapped, 'Sit down! Don't call your station yet, Constable. I'll be back.' He jerked his head at Gail and led her out of the office.

He leaned against the closed door and looked at her. She said, 'Like I said, I'm sorry I called you.'

He was grateful for her concern. 'No, it's okay, Gail. But she's going to be a pain . . . Let's talk to the maid.'

She was in the small office behind the reception desk, sitting on a chair in the middle of the room, knees together, hands clutching each other in her lap.

Malone introduced himself. 'You are –?'

'Dolores Cortes.'

She had a thin light voice, made thinner by her fear. She was a Filipina, young, on the verge of prettiness with a sensual mouth and dark eyes that in other circumstances might have been lively, even inviting. Now they were dark and frightened.

'What happened tonight, Dolores?' Malone drew up a chair opposite her and Gail half-sat on a small desk.

'Boris's – Mrs Jones came in – I was upstairs on the second floor, she came up there looking for me, she asked me what I'd done with Boris –'

'And what did you tell her?'

'I didn't tell her nothing – at first. But she was pretty angry – in a quiet way, you know what I mean? Then I told her Boris and me had had – you know.' She looked at Gail, as if she would understand more than this man sitting in front of her. 'I've never done it before – with a married man, I mean.'

'When did it start with Boris?'

'I dunno – a month ago, I think it was. He – you know –' She looked at Gail again and the latter nodded sympathetically.

'Did he attack you, force himself on you?'

'Oh no! Nothing like that –'

'Did it happen only once? And then again on the night he was murdered?'

She looked up at Gail again, then back at Malone. He suddenly had the feeling he was in a Saturday night confessional; she was stumbling over how she was going to tell him she had sinned. 'No, it happened other times.'

'Often? And you consented?'

She nodded. 'Every night.'

Gail rolled her eyes and Malone had to keep his own steady. Life at the Southern Savoy was not humdrum. 'He didn't force himself on you?' She looked puzzled. 'He didn't belt you, like he did his wife?' *Why did I say that?*

'Oh no! I liked him. He was – you know –'

'You told Mrs Jones all this?'

'No. No, I just said it happened the once. If I'd told her

about the other times . . . She's his wife. He was having it with her, too.'

'He told you that? He didn't plead with you that he wasn't getting it at home?'

'No, he liked to – to show off? How many times he could do it.'

Malone leaned back, didn't look at Gail. 'Dolores, have you ever thought about going back to the Philippines?'

'Why? They're just as bad there. Worse.'

'Dolores,' he said patiently, 'let's get away from over-sexed men. Why did you come out here?'

'Because there's work here.' She was practical now, her hands relaxed on her knees.

Gail put the questioning back on track: 'So after you'd told Mrs Jones what you and Boris had been up to, she attacked you?'

'What's gunna happen to her? She'll go to jail?'

'That's not for us to decide,' said Malone. 'Did she attack you?'

She was hunched for a moment now, suddenly less relaxed; then she straightened up, ready for a dive: 'No, she didn't do nothing like that. She just hugged me.'

The two detectives looked at each, recognizing at once the way things were going to go. Malone said, 'Dolores, people had to separate you –'

She was sitting up very straight now, her hands clutching the edges of her chair. 'We were hugging each other, that was all –'

'So you won't lay charges against her?'

'Charges? You mean send her to jail? No, why would I wanna do that?'

Malone pushed his chair back. 'Righto, Dolores, you can go. The office here has your home address?'

'Yeah. They're gunna fire me, they said –'

'Who said that? We'll see what we can do. Jobs are hard to find. Take care and stay away from randy men. Married ones.'

He and Gail Lee went out of the office, stopped inside the reception desk. There was only one clerk on duty, a young dark-haired man who was obviously Asian. Malone, like most of his generation and certainly that of his parents, had the astigmatic eye when it came to separating Asians. This one's name was Jose, said the badge on his tunic.

'Where do you come from, Jose?'

'Manila, sir.'

'Righto, stick with Dolores, don't report this to the hotel management –'

'I already have, sir. Here comes Mr Niven now.'

He had come in the front door. He was wearing a tweed overcoat, buttoned up to the neck against the wind, and a tweed hat. Very English, thought Malone, but a bit actorish. The good-looking face had been polished by the wind, the cheeks shining.

'More trouble? Oh God, is this place developing a jinx?'

'Let's go into your office, Deric. I think we can sort things out –' He looked over his shoulder at the reception clerk. 'Tell Dolores she can go –'

'She hasn't finished her shift yet –'

'Let her finish it,' said Deric Niven. 'I'll talk to her later. In my office, Inspector?'

'Just where I was going to suggest. We have Mrs Jones, Boris' wife, in there.'

'Oh God.'

Malone waited for him to put the back of his hand to his brow. *Come on, Malone.* Why is it that when one is tired, prejudices float up above goodwill? 'We're trying to smooth all this out with no fuss, if we can. Don't lose hope, Deric. We'll keep this one out of the media.' But he avoided Gail's eye as he said it.

They went into Niven's office and Delia, still on her chair, sat up at once. She said nothing, just looked curiously at Niven, then at Malone and Gail.

'You haven't met Mrs Jones, have you? This is Mr Niven, the manager of the hotel.'

'Mrs Jones –' Niven nodded politely, but that was all. She was an unwelcome guest in his hotel.

She just nodded back at him, meeting his frostiness with her own. Then she turned to Malone. 'Can I go now?'

'I'll get Constable Szabo to have a patrol car take you home. Is there anyone there? Your friend, Mrs –?'

'Quantock,' said Gail.

'No, there's no one there. I'm on my own.' She made it sound like utter desolation.

'Where are your kids?'

'With my mother.' She looked at Niven again, then back at Malone.

'Where does she live?'

'Bexley, she still lives there.' She was annoyed. 'Don't you remember, Scobie? You used to take me home in your old Holden –'

He sidestepped that, aware of Niven's lifting his head. 'I think you'd better go there. Detective Lee will call your mother, tell her to expect you –'

'It's late. You take me home to my own place –'

He ignored that. 'I don't think you should go home to an empty house – not after tonight –'

But all at once she was paying no attention to him. She was staring directly at Niven. 'That's him!' Her voice was gritty. 'He was the man tried to take the taxi from me that night, outside the hotel –'

2

As Malone, in his youth, had ventured into the territory known as Woman, he had slowly worked out what sort of woman he would want to live with. In a casual father-to-son conversation he had once told Tom to look for a woman with some mystery to her – 'Don't choose the what-you-see-is-what-you-get sort.'

Tom, at that stage, had been happy to welcome any woman who fell into his lap. But he had said, 'Was Mum like that? Some mystery to her?'

'Yes.'

And now on this cold winter's night he was asking himself had there been any mystery in Delia Bates when he had known her. She certainly was proving now that what you saw was not what you got.

She had been taken out to her mother's home in Bexley (*Don't you remember, Scobie?* she had said, driving the memory needle into him, trying to infect him) and Deric Niven had been brought here to Police Centre in Surry Hills. Malone, before taking him into an interview room, had taken him through the Incident Room. He had paused to speak to one of the detectives on duty, working a ploy that had worked before. Niven had stood beside Gail Lee; he had been manoeuvred to face the flow-chart. There two bodies were displayed in graphic photos such as one never saw in newspapers or on television. He stared at the photos, then abruptly turned away, putting his hand to his mouth.

'You want to be sick?' asked Gail.

He shook his head, was relieved when Malone led him on to one of the interview rooms. He was still in his overcoat, looking as if trying to shrink into it. He slumped down on a chair as Malone and Gail sat down opposite him on the other side of a table.

'You feeling okay, Deric?'

He nodded, sought his voice and found it. 'I had nothing to do with Mrs Pavane's death.'

'I can't remember us saying that you did,' said Malone. 'But you haven't told us all you know about that night.'

There was shouting and swearing outside. The Surry Hills station was part of the Police Centre and the Saturday night cattle round-up was at its peak. Out there were drunks, brawlers, hookers trying to roll clients: all simple law-breakers. None connected with a murder.

'Am I going to be charged with anything?'

'That will depend. Why? Do you want your lawyer?'

He looked at the video recorder, then back at them. 'Not yet. If I talk to you, can we leave that off?'

'That will depend on what you tell us. But for the time being, okay, we won't turn it on. Now, on Tuesday night, early Wednesday morning, were you up in Room 342, Mrs Pavane's room?'

'No.'

'Why did you tell us you were off duty Tuesday night, that you were not at the hotel?'

Niven said nothing. As if he were suddenly feeling stifled, he stood up, pulled off his overcoat and dropped it on the table. Then he sat down again.

'Did you have any connection with Mrs Pavane?'

'Oh, for Crissake!' He twisted his head, like a bad actor; then he looked back at them, leaned forward, another theatrical piece: 'I'm her brother!'

Both Malone and Gail Lee sat back in their chairs: even a little theatrically, though neither of them noticed. Then Malone said, 'Go on. Give us some family history, Deric.'

Niven folded his hands together, sat back and looked at them as if they were some sort of memory bowl. He might have been a good actor once, Malone thought; he knew how to use pauses. Or maybe he was looking for memories that had long since faded.

'I hadn't seen her in almost twenty years. We grew up on a farm outside Albany –' A town on the far south-west coast of the continent, as remote from Sydney as one could get; as remote as the stars from Corvallis, Oregon, and Kansas City, Missouri. 'Our name is, always has been, Niven. But she changed hers –'

'Several times,' said Gail Lee.

He nodded. 'That was her. Always wanting to be someone

133

else. She hated the farm, living on it . . . We raised wheat, at harvest time she'd always disappear –'

'What about you?' said Gail. 'Being gay? You are, aren't you?'

He nodded again. 'My dad, if he was with his mates, he'd walk away when I put in an appearance. I worked as hard as him on the farm, but it didn't make any difference. Then he and my mother were killed – the farm ute ran off the road and hit a tree –'

Malone glanced at Gail, who nodded. Billie Pavane had kept one true fact in her resumé.

'I was seventeen and Trish –'

'That was her given name?' asked Malone.

'Patricia, but she was always called Trish. She was nineteen. Right after the funeral she told me the farm was mine and she left, went to – came here to Sydney. She dropped me a card occasionally, but then they stopped and I never heard from her.'

He stopped, too, and they let him swim in whatever he felt: regret, resentment, whatever. Then Malone said, 'Were you close? Were there other brothers and sisters?'

'No, there were just the two of us. We were never that close, but we never fought. We never confided in each other . . . She liked men. My mother was always at her, people were talking about her when she was only fifteen, sixteen –'

'She had lots of boyfriends?'

'Only the ones with money – or who were going to inherit money. There was money in the bush back then. She was never interested in the road-mender's son.'

Malone said gently, 'You didn't like her, Deric?'

'Oh no! No.' He unclasped his hands, spread them, then folded them together again. 'I got into a couple of fights over her – guys who made snide remarks about her. Gays *can* fight, you know,' he said and looked challengingly at Malone.

'I don't doubt it, Deric. Go on.'

'Well –' He paused, looked puzzled, as if this was the first time someone had asked him to recap his life. 'Well, when I turned twenty-one I sold the farm and went to London. I had enough money to stake myself, to try and be an actor. I never made it. A few jobs in repertory, places like Swindon – God!' He made Swindon sound as if it were down a coal mine. 'Some work in TV – I was in a scene like this once in *The Bill.*' He waved an arm around him. 'A small part. I did some BBC radio work. But I was never going to make a living at it. I stuck at it too long, but eventually I came to my senses.'

'And you heard nothing from Trish all this time?'

'Not a word. I heard, I dunno where, that she'd gone to America, but I didn't know where. I took the hotel management course, spent the last of the money I'd got for the farm, worked on the Continent in small hotels – my French and Italian aren't bad. I had a French partner in London . . .' He stopped, as if that was a chapter in his life he hadn't opened in a long time. He went on: 'Then I came home, worked in Perth, then Adelaide, then I finished up here in Sydney.' He drew in a deep breath and shut his eyes, like a tired reader closing a book that had disturbed him.

Malone and Gail, both patient people, let him stay in that darkness that he had closed in on himself. He would come out of it, they knew, he was *glad* to have someone to tell his secrets to.

He opened his eyes. 'It's a bit late, but I loved Trish. She could be a pain in the arse –' Suddenly he smiled, looked at Malone, who smiled in return. 'Wrong phrase. She could be a pain – but she always stuck up for me. Against Mum or Dad or anyone who picked on me. It's no fun being gay in the bush.'

'So when did you finally make contact with her?' asked Malone.

'I wrote to her when she first came back to Australia, to Canberra. I saw a photo of her when she and her husband arrived – even though it was nearly twenty years, I recognized her.'

'Would someone else have recognized her?'

'You mean someone here in Sydney? Someone who knew her

– what? Ten, fifteen years ago? I don't know. Maybe. But I knew her at once, soon as I saw the photo. I wrote her – I didn't know whether she would reply. But she did – though she asked me not to say anything to anyone till she had seen me.'

'And you didn't tell any of your friends your sister was the wife of the American Ambassador?' said Gail.

'No, I didn't. Is that so strange?'

'Frankly, yes. People gossip, even when they don't mean to.'

'Well, you're wrong.' He was annoyed. 'This was my sister asking a favour of me – the first time in twenty years.'

'I apologize,' said Gail and sounded sincere.

He nodded, like a teacher saying, Let that be a lesson to you. Then he went on, 'She came up to Sydney and I met her and we had drinks. It was a bit – well, *stiff*, at first. Then it was like it was back home. We even talked about the farm, though neither of us was nostalgic for it. Then she told me she'd said goodbye to Trish Niven – she was very frank, like she used to be years ago. She said she'd created a new life and she didn't want it spoiled.'

'She was asking you to keep your mouth shut?' said Malone.

'Yes. Yes, if you want to put it like that. She said we'd keep in touch, but she didn't want it to be known that we were brother and sister.'

'So she was never going to tell her husband about you?'

'I guess not. I was going to ask her about it, but never got round to it.'

'So you agreed to what she suggested?'

'I agreed. Why not? I'm not a vindictive person, Mr Malone. Maybe I didn't admire what she'd done –'

'Did she tell you what she'd done?' asked Gail.

'No-o. But I guessed there was something there that she didn't want to talk about, something that had happened in Sydney before she went to the States. I didn't ask her about it. I said I'd play it any way she wanted.'

'Which meant you weren't going to be introduced into her circle? The diplomatic circle?'

He sat back, more relaxed now. 'Why are you so pissed off about her, Mr Malone?'

Malone didn't answer that, just said, 'Go on. How did she finish up here in the Southern Savoy?'

'We're trying to be better than we are, Mr Malone. Don't put us down.'

'I'm not putting you down, Deric. When I go anywhere, this is the sort of hotel I stay in. I'm not five-star material. Why did she come here, book a room?'

Niven took his time again; he was sizing them up as much as they had been measuring him. 'She rang me Monday, asked could I book her in for one night.'

'Did you ask her why? Why here and not the Regent or the InterContinental?'

'She said she had some business to attend to. She said she would explain later, but she wasn't going to do it over the phone.'

'Was she phoning from the embassy?'

'I don't think so. There was a lot of noise in the background, like a restaurant, I thought.'

'So you booked the room? In what name?'

'She told me it had to be Mrs Belinda Paterson.'

'Deric, you did a lot of lying last Wednesday morning when we were called in. You played dumb to everything we asked you.'

'Well –' There were no theatrical gestures now. 'Well, I was in shock. Really. But . . .' He looked at both of them, leaned forward again. 'With all that media mob out there in the lobby – the *American Ambassador's wife* – Christ, what would you have done? You'd have kept your mouths shut till you'd sorted things out in your mind –'

'That was four days ago,' said Malone. 'You wouldn't have opened your mouth at all if Mrs Jones hadn't pointed the finger at you.'

'You don't know that I wouldn't have –' For a moment

belligerence welled up in him, like bile; then it subsided. 'Mrs Jones, anyway, was mistaken –'

'We'll get around to that. But first – did you see her when she arrived at the hotel? Your sister?'

'No, I was off duty and I thought it better to stay away. Okay,' he said as they both looked sceptical, 'I didn't want to know. I was going to see her Wednesday morning.'

'And ask her then why all the secrecy?'

'Maybe. I don't know. There was twenty years I wanted to ask her about –' He looked suddenly saddened, regretting all the lost years. Whatever sort of woman Trish was, thought Malone, he loved her.

'Did you see who her visitor was? Did anyone?'

Niven hesitated: 'Ye-es. The housemaid, Dolores. I told her to keep her mouth shut, too.'

Malone sucked in air through his teeth. Gail Lee leaned forward as if she might hit Niven; he leaned back. There was silence in the room; outside in the square there was the wail of a siren, the sound of disaster. Then Malone squashed down his temper.

'Jesus, Deric –' He waited a moment till he was fully in control of himself. 'I oughta pinch you now . . . What the bloody hell prompted you to tell her that?'

'I don't know. I – I guess I was trying to protect Trish.'

Malone sighed. 'I hope you keep the hotel's books in better order than you do your thoughts. We might've been four days better ahead if you had – Ah!' He waved a hand in disgust, looked at Gail. 'What are we going to do with him?'

'We'll talk to Dolores,' she said. 'But first – Mr Niven?'

He appeared to be not paying attention; then he looked up: 'What?'

'Why were you here in the hotel at the time of the murder? You were supposed to be off duty.'

He was gathering his thoughts, fumble-fingered as he had claimed to be on the night of the murder. His arm jerked and he knocked his hat to the floor; he bent and picked it up, then carefully placed it on his overcoat. He's acting, thought Malone and wanted to yell at him.

'That – that's what I told you. I *was* off duty. Mrs Jones is mistaken. I wasn't here in the hotel. I'd been to a club down in Bay Street, around the corner from here. You can check, they know me there, it's a gay club. I came up here to the hotel because I knew cabs were always pulling up outside there –'

'Mrs Jones says you were in a hurry, you tried to muscle in on her for the cab –'

'She's mistaken. Come on, look at her! She's just murdered her husband – you talk about my state of mind –' Then he took control of his agitation: 'Yes, I tried to beat her to the cab. But that's the way it is – when did you last step back to let someone else take a cab? It's a free-for-all.'

'I rarely take cabs,' said Malone.

'You take hire cars? On a cop's salary?'

'No,' said Gail. 'Our boss is a notorious tightwad. Taxi drivers would starve if they depended on him.'

'Thank you for the reference,' said Malone.

But the small exchange had softened Niven; he laughed, sat back in his chair. Malone took advantage of the moment: 'Righto, you weren't at the hotel that night. We'll check with the club. When did you talk to Dolores?'

'When she came on duty Wednesday night. I knew she had been working on that floor – I didn't know she had been having it off with Boris. If I'd known that was going on, they'd both been out on their ear . . . I just asked her if she'd seen anything, not expecting her to say anything. But yes, she said, she'd seen the lady in 342 go in there with a man. A guy with grey hair was how she described him, nothing more than that.'

'And you didn't think you should have reported that to us?'

'I would have eventually, I guess. But like I said – I was trying to protect Trish. Stupid, I know. But I've been reading all the reports on the murder and looking at the TV coverage, and you people aren't saying much, are you? Who are you protecting?'

139

Too many, too much, to tell you, mate.

Niven caught the momentary silence, said, 'The American Embassy? The Ambassador?'

Malone ignored the questions. 'Did your sister give you any hint who she was meeting?'

'None at all.' He shook his head, looked relaxed again; he had scored a point with the question on the embassy and the ambassador. 'But I guessed it must have been someone she knew here in Sydney. I don't even know what she did when she worked here.'

'She was with a stockbrokers' office, she was the office manager. We think – we're not sure yet, but we think she might've been involved with one or two fellers in that office who worked a scam and got away with it.'

Malone watched Niven carefully as he said this; but the latter took it without any surprise: 'That'd be Trish. She wanted to be rich – well, have money. That's the way of the world, isn't it?'

'Not with me and Detective Lee.'

'Nor me.' Somehow he smiled and the three pure-at-heart, financially, were bound together.

Malone pushed back his chair. 'Where do you live?'

'Paddington.'

'You got his address, Gail?' She nodded. 'Righto, Deric, you can go. You've been a bloody fool and a bloody hindrance, but if we locked people up for those stupidities the court lists would be chockablock till the *next* millennium.'

Niven stood up, pulled on his overcoat, picked up his hat. 'Can someone give me a lift home?'

'Don't push your luck. Knock someone over for a cab.'

Gail Lee took Niven out and Malone sat on in the interview room for a while. Then he got up, feeling stiff and bony, and went out into the Incident Room. He stood in front of the flow-chart, scanned the photos, the diagrams and the names. Then he added *Dolores Cortes* to the list of names, but he knew in his heart she was no more than a footnote who would offer very little information.

'I look at them boards and I wonder why Christ would ever bother about a Second Coming.'

Malone turned. It was Paddy Finnegan, the duty night sergeant in the Surry Hills station. Balding, overweight, a rock turning to sand, his legs gone, one year short of retirement: but he had the wisdom and disillusion of experience. He would no longer chase a fleeing crim, but he would never shoot anyone in the back. Not even a murderer.

'G'day, Paddy. What do you think I should do? Wipe it all out?'

'Would that solve the problem?'

'No.'

'Don't you wish you were me? Only a year to go and it's all behind me.'

'I'm thinking of applying for a transfer to Tibooburra.'

'I was out there, once – I done a camping trip, on holidays. I was sitting there with one of the blokes from the local and I said, "Is this the end of the world?" And he said, "No, but if you stand up, you can see it."'

It was an old joke, but it was what Malone needed; he laughed. 'Take care, Paddy.'

He drove home to Randwick, put the Fairlane in the garage. Lisa's Laser was parked out in the street, where every wife's car should be when there is only one garage. He had the Australian male's attitude when it came to cars, chauvinistic.

The wind had dropped and the sky had cleared; the moon was unscarred by clouds. He walked through a trench of moonlight between the camellia trees, came up on to the verandah and Tom was just inserting his key in the front door.

'How'd you go tonight with your tutor?'

'You saw her down at the footy?'

'Yes. Not bad, as older women go.'

141

'Three other guys phoned her tonight while I was there.' He grinned. 'I woke up, I was just part of her library.'

'You don't sound too upset.'

'Remember once you told me, always look for some mystery in your women?' He grinned again. 'She has no mystery.'

Malone could have hugged him; but he was not modern enough for that. He pushed Tom ahead of him into the house, closed the door. Was home. Life had its compensations.

3

Billie Pavane's (or Trish Norval's) killer had moved from his hotel. He had learned many things as a stockbroker, one being that a shifting target was hard to invest in. He was the target of the police investigation, if so far unknown, and he had an analytical mind that appreciated police analysis. If they had discovered Billie Pavane's real identity, then it would not be long before they learned the identity of those with whom she had been associated. And she had been closer to him than to any of the others.

So he moved out of the Regent and into a serviced apartment in Wharf West, where short-term guests were welcome and no questions asked other than the status of their credit cards. He was within sight of the harbour and at the opposite end of the central business district from the Southern Savoy, but he knew the linear line of a police investigation could stretch interminably. He did not feel safe.

He had come to Sydney, pulled by the one decent gesture he had made towards his father since he had been a teenager. The irony of it was bitter now.

Julian Baker, the name he had had for the last fourteen years, had kept in touch with his sister, but only tenuously, like a fifth cousin. Once a year they exchanged Christmas cards, as cool as diplomats' visiting cards; she didn't know he had changed his name and they always arrived addressed to his real name at a post office box he had rented in Toronto. Then the letter had come telling him his father was dying of cancer and wanted to see him before he died.

He had waited two days, pondering the letter, then he had phoned Sarah, the first time he had spoken to her in all those years. Her voice hadn't changed, it was still fruity, like that of an old-time actress. 'Ohmigod, how good it is to hear your voice! But you sound so – so different. So – so *American*.'

'Canadian, actually.' Down in the southern hemisphere, no one ever knew the difference. 'How's Dad?'

'Bad. It won't be long. He does want to see you – he keeps asking have I found you –'

'Does he say why?'

'No – just says he has something to tell you. Like a confession, I gather.'

He had no idea what his father, the Presbyterian churchgoer, would want to confess to him. 'What's the cancer?'

'Melanomas. All that golf and gardening –'

He remembered his father, the tall lean man who, as if to escape all the bottled health in his pharmacy, spent as much time as he could in the open air and sun. Which was now killing him.

'Please, *do* come,' said Sarah. 'If you want the fare, Walter and I –'

He smiled at that, unoffended; he could probably buy out Walter and Sarah a couple of times over. 'No, that's no problem. It'll take a day or two – I have some things to attend to –'

'So I can tell him you're coming? It will keep him alive –'

'Yes. Tell him to hang in there –'

'You sound so American –'

'Canadian, actually.' He took his time and she must have thought he had rung off.'

'Are you there?' Pronounced *the-ah*? with the rising inflection.

'Yes.' Another long pause; intuition told him she was suddenly

143

remembering the past: *his* past. 'Sarah, don't broadcast that I'm coming. I'd rather come home quietly –'

There was her own long pause; then she said quietly, 'I understand. Walter will, too.'

Meaning Walter, her husband, would understand for his own reasons. In Toronto the killer had often gone to the public library and looked at the Sydney newspapers, subconsciously looking to see how much of the 1980s was being exhumed. There he had occasionally seen mention of Walter, a successful barrister who, the legal columnists said, had hopes of being a judge. Walter wouldn't want his brother-in-law's past peccadillos, whatever they were, brought out for an airing by the tabloids. Secrecy is an infectious disease, a health hazard Julian Baker appreciated.

He had leave due to him from the bank and he took it; since the country was in the summer doldrums, his absence would hardly be noticed. Then he told his three sub-teen children he was going to Asia on business and they, ready to leave for summer camp in New Hampshire, couldn't have cared if he was going off to Moscow to see if more Russian crooks were looking for a money laundry. It is often forgotten that children can be as incurious as they are curious. It was not so with Lucille, his wife. She was as curious as a tabloid reporter.

He had always believed that truth was a negotiable commodity. So he told her only half of it. Yes, he was Australian as he had told her; but no, both his parents were not dead. He had told her he had run away from home when he was sixteen and he let that lie lie; he did tell her that, no, he was not an only child, he had a sister and it was she who had told him his father, still alive, was dying. He was going back to Sydney to patch up the estrangement from his father.

She was touched. 'I want to go with you –'

'No –' He had to bite back the word so that it didn't sound like an expletive. He loved her, still occasionally looked at her with a stranger's eye and saw what a beautiful woman she was. She had a poise to her and sense of commercial duty that made

144

her a good corporation wife, but she was still her own woman; and his. He put his hand on hers: 'Let me see him alone – first. If everything works out okay, I'll call you and you can come. If it doesn't –' He knew that it wouldn't. If there was a reconciliation with his father, it did not mean he was going to take up life again on the Sydney scene. 'I'll let you know –'

She had then looked suspicious; she was French-Canadian, but more French than Canadian. French wives have been suspicious of their husbands since Clovis' time. 'You're telling me the truth? You don't have an old girlfriend out there?'

'One I knew when I was sixteen? I'm not chasing another woman – forget anything like that.'

There had been one or two short-term affairs, but Lucille had known nothing of them. They had been during the last two months of her last two pregnancies and he had viewed them as nothing more than therapeutic, a flushing of dirty water off his chest. But now he thought of Trish Norval . . .

Lucille kissed him, then gave him a love-bite that raised a welt on his neck. 'If ever I found you with another woman, I'd bite right through your carotid artery.'

He told himself he was lucky to have such a loving, if ferocious, wife and left her and came to Sydney. Sarah and Walter Wexall were at the airport to meet him. Sarah was – what was the word? he wondered. *Matronly*? Walter was – what was the masculine word for *matronly*? Sarah hesitated, then put her arms round him and kissed him on the cheek. Walter shook his hand and patted him on the shoulder as he might a horse.

'My God, how you've changed! Is it *really* you?' Sarah's voice carried; elderly arriving passengers turned back to see if Sybil Thorndike, risen from the grave, had been on the plane.

'It's me –'

Then suddenly Sarah had sobered, her voice lowered: 'But you're too late! Dad –'

She stopped, put her hand to her mouth and tears ran down her cheeks. Walter said, 'He died at the weekend. We told him

145

you were coming, but he couldn't hold out. He seemed pleased, though. He's being cremated tomorrow –'

Walter Wexall might once have been good-looking, but middle age and flesh had taken over. He now had the bland sort of face that is given character by glasses; he wore designer gold-rims. He had a good deep voice, ideal for sentencing when he became a judge, and an assured dignity that was genuine. He was a Senior Counsel and regretted he had been too late to be a Queen's Counsel. QC after one's name sounded so much better than SC.

Driving out of the airport in the Mercedes, Walter said, 'As Sarah says, we wouldn't have recognized you.'

'I had a car accident. They re-modelled my face a little.' Lies slid off his tongue as smoothly as truth; sometimes their sincerity fooled even him. 'And I've gone grey.'

'Worried?' said Walter, as if cross-examining.

'Not at all. I've forgotten my past, if that's what you mean.' He said it with a smile and was met by smiles; insincerity bloomed in the car like paper flowers. 'I just hope everyone else will forget it.'

'Oh, of course,' said Walter and looked relieved.

They dropped him at the Regent, Walter pulling the car into the concourse with the familiarity of a man who came often to this hotel. Julian wondered if he should not have chosen another hotel.

'Get a good night's sleep,' said Sarah, sounding just like their mother. 'We'll pick you up at ten tomorrow morning. The funeral is at eleven. Oh, it's so good to see you again!'

'Likewise,' he said.

'So American!'

'Canadian, actually.' Then he leaned on the roof of the car, lowered his head and his voice: 'I shan't be coming to the funeral.'

'Oh my! Why not?'

He looked past her at Walter. 'I think it would be better if I remained invisible, don't you, Walter?'

Walter was not surprised by the question; he nodded. 'I see your point.'

Julian looked at Sarah. 'I mean no disrespect to Dad.'

She stared at him, then nodded. 'I understand. Come to dinner tomorrow night, just we three. There's so much to catch up on.'

'I'll look forward to it.' He looked past her again at Walter: 'Thanks, old chap.'

Walter understood, as if a password had been exchanged. 'Good to see you back. We'll keep it low-key.'

'The best way,' he said and watched them drive away. The rear of the Mercedes, he thought, looked like Walter: solid and bland.

Next night he caught a cab and went out to Killara, a breeding wetlands for lawyers; children there, it was said, learned the alphabet from the *Law Society Journal*. The houses were as authoritative as courthouses, the gardens as neat as the women residents' hair. There had been one or two drug scandals amongst the local teenagers, but the North Shore is more experienced and adept at putting the lid on the scandal pot than the other, less conservative areas of Sydney. Julian Baker had grown up here under his real name and he knew the environment as well as anyone. He had groped girls from Pymble Ladies College and passed out dead drunk on a green at Killara Golf Club. He was coming back to familiar territory.

Sarah opened the door to him, greeted him with warmth. 'Come in, come in! The boys are here, but they're going out –'

The two boys, in their late teens, looked at him with suspicion: born lawyers, he thought. Or cops. 'Hi,' they said, articulate as two pillar-boxes and left.

'They're going to miss Pa,' said Sarah.

'How did the funeral go?'

Sarah put her hand over her mouth and turned and went out to the kitchen. 'Without fuss,' said Walter. 'The way your father would have wanted. Drink?'

'Sarah very upset?'

'Yes. But she's strong, she's not going to crumble. The living always feel it more than the dead, don't you think?'

'I don't know. I've never asked the dead.'

Walter smiled; he was not going to crumble. 'How do you feel?'

'I wish I'd got here before he died.' It was an honest thought.

Later, when they moved into the dining room, he saw that dinner was prologue. Sarah must have come straight home from the funeral to prepare it, though Julian wondered if there had been coffee-and-cakes for the mourners. His father had had many friends and Julian guessed that Sarah and Walter, always conscientious about doing the right thing, would have held some sort of reception. Nonetheless, Sarah had not allowed herself to be put off from preparing a proper dinner for her long-lost brother. Which, he knew, was how she would be thinking of him. She had always had a touch of the theatrical, though only in her thoughts, never in her behaviour.

There were oysters – 'I remembered how much you liked them' – and beef burgundy and diplomat pudding – 'Remember how Mother used to make it?' The wine was excellent – 'I have a half-interest in a vineyard up in the Hunter,' said Walter – and there was port with the coffee. Only over the coffee did Sarah mention that she had had a caterer prepare and bring in the meal. For some reason he felt disappointed. When they were young she had been so solicitous of him, always his defender. The wine had made him sentimental.

Then they repaired to the living room and the real talk began.

The room was expensively, if conservatively, furnished. It was an upholstered complement to Walter and Sarah. The only odd note in the room was a Jeffrey Smart painting of a desolate Italian autostrada; Julian could only guess that it had been bought as an investment. The other two paintings suited the room: solid spring landscapes, no sign of drought or ring-barked trees. Walter and Sarah had surrounded themselves with security. But then, he reminded himself, so had he back in Toronto. He was feeling mellow, prepared to feel at home with them.

'There is a problem,' said Walter.

'Oh?' Julian was now drinking mineral water, keeping his mind clear.

'Your father left no will. He knew he was dying, but for some reason he kept putting it off. I tried to get him to make one, but he was adamant. He was waiting for you to come home.'

Julian had no illusions: 'To see if I was still the bastard he always thought I was?'

'He never said anything like that. You know what you father was like – he could be very close-mouthed. I'd known him for years before I found out he always voted Labor.' As if he had voted for the Ku Klux Klan or belonged to some satanic cult.

'Perversity, that was all it was. He knew a Labor vote in this electorate would probably be dropped in the dustbin by the scrutineers.' Though he had not known how his father had voted; they had never discussed politics. 'But he can't have left much. The house and maybe the business – can you sell a pharmacy as a going business?'

'The house and the pharmacy are small potatoes,' said Walter.

'His portfolio manager –' said Sarah.

'His *what?*' Julian sat up. 'I know he had a few shares, blue-chip stuff, but not much –'

'The portfolio,' said Walter in a measured voice, as if delivering a court judgement, 'is worth nine and a half million dollars. Give or take a few dollars.'

Julian looked at the glass of mineral water, then said, 'May I have a whisky?'

Walter poured him a whisky from a cut-glass decanter. This was not the sort of room in which bottles were displayed; at dinner the wine had been decanted. 'I had a stiff whisky myself when I was told. We didn't know of the portfolio man's existence. He read of your father's death – evidently portfolio managers read the obituaries –'

'Like lawyers?' But he smiled.

Walter smiled in reply, but it was an effort. 'Yes . . . Did you ever give your dad investment advice?'

'Back in the eighties I mentioned some stocks, flyers that I thought might take off. It was just in conversation – when we talked at all –'

'He must have taken your advice. He was buying and selling for years, evidently, before he took on the portfolio manager. He must have borrowed and borrowed big, but there's no debt now.'

Julian sipped his whisky, trying to conjure up the image of his father as a stock exchange gambler. And yet it could have happened; he had seen plenty of it in the eighties. Cautious men who took a flutter, won, took another flutter and then, caught on the surf, just kept going. Was that how it had happened with his father?

'As I say,' said Walter, 'it's worth nine and a half million dollars. You're interested, of course?'

Nothing stirs a moneyman's interest more than the mention of more money. Does a politician not stir at the rustle of extra votes? Does a priest not tremble with excitement in his cassock when penitents flock to the church after a catastrophe, investing prayers they have dug out of pockets of neglect? The self had always been one of Julian Baker's icons and he was not going to deny it now, even though he was in mild shock.

'Yes,' he said and he was surprised at the evenness of his voice. 'I'm interested.'

'We thought you would be,' said Sarah and managed not to sound tart.

'There should be no trouble in settling everything.' Walter looked settled now. 'You and Sarah are the only natural heirs. We have a good firm of solcitors taking care of everything. I often work with them, they brief me as a barrister. Fairbrother, Milson and Gudersen. You may remember them?'

Julian frowned. 'They're still around? They've been going for *years*.'

'That's what we need, not some of these ambulance-chasers who have sprung up, aping the Americans.'

Julian had begun to suspect there was some anti-Americanism in this household. His father had believed that the last decent Americans had been Abraham Lincoln and James Stewart. He would have to keep reminding them that he was Canadian, if only by adoption.

'They are a firm that knows the meaning of discretion,' said Sarah.

'Of course,' said Julian; but memory was coming back: 'Didn't they handle matters for the stockbrokers I worked for? Won't they recall there was a bit of a stink when we broke up, I mean when my name comes up?'

Walter sniffed, as if mention of a bit of a stink had passed under his nose. 'I said they are *discreet*. What's past is past.'

Walter, Julian felt, would rewrite history in the interests of discretion.

Then Sarah, proving she had learned something from being a lawyer's wife, said, 'You have another identity in Canada, am I right? You never did tell us what you did or have been doing all these years. I always had some idea you were a travelling salesman, always writing to you at a box number.'

'She's exaggerating,' said Walter. 'You don't look like Willy Loman.'

A no-hoper, that Willy Loman. Why had they thought he would be no more than a travelling salesman? But he gave them his sincere smile (a travelling salesman's smile?), at which he was very good. 'What do I have to divulge to these solicitors when we start talking about Dad's estate?'

'All you have to do is prove you are Charles' natural-born and legitimate son. We'll attest to that. It would be better if you could stay till all the paperwork is processed – there will be the usual advertisement when someone dies with no will, but

151

we don't expect any claimants coming forth –' Walter smiled over his whisky. 'Your father has surprised us all by being a gambler, but I don't think he is going to surprise us further with some illegitimate heirs showing up.'

'He always thought I was a bastard.' But Julian smiled again and went on, 'Yes, I have another identity in Canada. My name now is Julian Baker –'

'Julian?' said Sarah. 'I like that.'

'I'm happily married to a French-Canadian girl, Lucille, and we have three kids, two girls and a boy. But do Fairbrother and company need to know that?'

'We shan't ask why you want to keep it quiet –' said Sarah.

'Oh, you can ask and I'll tell you why. It would mean that I should have to do an awful lot of explaining to Lucille and the kids – I've told her part of the story, but not all. And I don't want to have to explain to the bank where I'm a senior vice-president. When I left here, I decided on a fresh start with a fresh name . . . You'll understand, Walter?'

Walter, who had spent most of his life defending clients with something to hide, nodded, understandingly if not sympathetically. 'If you have a good, *solid* life now –'

'I have. Julian Baker is a well-respected pillar in Toronto. I want to stay that way. The old past is long past.'

'Of course,' said Walter and Sarah and looked relieved. As if their future was assured.

That had been a week ago. But temptation, like an itch in the groin, had not allowed the past to remain where it was. He had phoned Trish Norval (or Billie Pavane) in Canberra and as he had expected she said she would see him, just for old times' sake.

Chapter Six

1

There was no progress in the Pavane homicide over the next five days. Malone asked Joe Himes to come out to Homicide and there on the Monday morning he told the FBI how much more they had learned about the past life of Mrs Pavane.

'Who tells the Ambassador when he comes back?' asked Himes.

'He's coming back?'

'So Canberra says.' Himes was still wearing his trenchcoat, as if, having just come in from the rain, he saw another storm rising. 'I think we should call our FBI office in Kansas City and let them give him the bad news.'

Malone for a moment was tempted; then saw that Himes, though far from cheerful, was kidding. 'Do we tell Roger Bodine?'

Himes considered for quite a long moment; he looked out the window at the rain, then back at Malone. At last he said, 'Not yet. Stall him if he asks. I think we should protect the Ambassador as long as we can.'

'Bodine wouldn't talk, would he?'

'Scobie, in any organization secrecy is just molasses in a sieve – sooner or later it seeps through.' He smiled, the first time since arriving. Malone remarked again how boyish the heavy-set man could suddenly look; except for the eyes, which were still cautious. 'I made that up when I first went into the Academy. It was one of the first lessons I learned there, though it wasn't in the curriculum. Roger has a secretary, who has a friend or husband, who has . . . You get the drift.'

'I have to tell my boss, but I'm not putting it on paper or the computer. But eventually . . .' He, too, looked out the window as if there might be some message there. But the rain was smearing the window, the view was dim. 'Righto, we sit on it as far as Canberra is concerned. But if they find out we've kept it from them, the embassy blokes, I mean, you take the kicks, okay?'

'We've been doing that for years. The only one who ever loved us was J. Edgar. But none of us loved him. *I* didn't.' He stood up, buttoned up the trenchcoat; he looked as wide as two commissionaires. 'Our San Francisco office is trying to find out more about Wilhelmina Page's stay in that city. Or was she Belinda Paterson while she was there?' He put his hands in his pockets, looked dejected. 'Why am I afraid they'll find out more than we want to tell the Ambassador?'

'Joe, what if Mrs Pavane was at the hotel because the bloke had picked it? Say he was blackmailing her –?'

'And she paid him off by going to bed with him?'

'It's happened.'

Himes thought about it for a moment. 'Possible. But if he was blackmailing her, was that all she was paying him? Sex?'

'No, he could've been asking for money, too. Can you look into her bank account, see if she'd had any large withdrawls lately?'

'Scobie –' Himes looked disappointed, as if he had credited Malone with more intelligence. 'Do you expect me to go to the Ambassador and tell him I want to look into his wife's bank account, that we think she may have been paying off a blackmailer?'

'Now that you mention it –'

'Scobie, if *you* want to approach him –'

'No, thanks. Sorry I brought it up.'

Himes shook his head at the denseness at the lower levels of police work and left. Malone picked up the phone and rang Pamela Morrow.

'Pam, we've been having trouble with your client, Delia.' He

154

told her about last Saturday night. 'Tell her to pull her head in or she's going to finish up in Mulawa. She won't like it out there amongst some of the girls.'

'Husband-killers, especially those who've been bashed and belted, some of them are looked up to in jail.' But then she sighed, almost like a moan. 'But Delia can be a pain. Sometimes the ones you are trying to help are the worst of the lot. What was she like when you knew her? Or shouldn't I ask that?'

'I'd rather you hadn't. But, okay – she could be demanding. We usually did what she wanted to do, not what I wanted.'

'Most women try for that, didn't you know?' There was what sounded like a soft laugh; then she said, 'Is she still insisting on seeing you?'

'Not any more, Pam. I'm putting my foot down.'

'I've heard that before. First lovers are the biggest suckers.'

'What are you now? A marriage counsellor?'

'You're married, aren't you? Happily married? That's Delia's beef. Look after yourself, Scobie. Find another case to occupy you.'

'I have one –'

'Of course. How's it going?'

'Don't ask.'

Tuesday, Wednesday, Thursday went by. Five more murders: two domestics, two bikies executed, a gay bashed to death by a drunken homophobe. A week's working calendar, while the rest of the voters went to their offices, their factories, their trucks and buses and courier bikes and complained to fellow workers how tough life was. Homicide was called in only on the bikie executions and Clements assigned two detectives to the case. Malone, Andy Graham and Gail Lee and Sheryl Dallen remained on the Pavane strike force. The Jones murder was taken down from the flow-chart and Bruce Farro's name was added to the Pavane name-list. At the top of the list were still: Billie Pavane, Belinda Paterson, Wilhelmina Page and Patricia Norval. A quartet swimming in and out of each other like shadows.

Friday Andy Graham struck pay-dirt: 'Boss, I think I've traced Wayne Jones. He's got a website up on the Central Coast, he runs a sorta stock market consultancy, as far as I can gather. He's at Woy Woy.'

'Woy Woy? That's a financial centre?'

Woy Woy was a tiny community eighty kilometres north of Sydney that had for years slept undisturbed; it fronted a long wide bay known as Brisbane Water and its population, many of them retired pensioners, hardly gave a thought to the city slickers further south. Then the city slickers discovered the region and over the past thirty years the Central Coast had bloomed (like an atomic bomb, thought the old Woy Woy residents) and lush bush disappeared to make way for mini-mansions, vacation and conference hotels and retirement villages for the better-off. The surviving Woy Woy originals put out in their small rowing boats, tossed a line to the fish and watched the money floating through the area like a plague of locusts. Land prices soared and expensive cruisers began appearing on Brisbane Water like an invading armada, their wake hitting the edges where the locals floated like the sound of a slap in the face. The natives, sea-sick, rowed their boats back to shore and their modest weatherboard cottages. One pensioner, offered a small fortune for his 'shack', shot the would-be buyer in the leg. The local police sergeant, born and bred in the area, called to arrest the gunman, was told, and accepted, the plea that the shot had not been fired in anger at the insult of the offer but the insult of his home being called a 'shack'. No charges were laid and the slicker, hobbling, went back to the city and bought water-front at Hunter's Hill, where the natives are not gun-happy. The National Rifle Association in the United States sent a message of congratulation to the gun-toting pensioner, who wondered what they were on about, and the Real Estate Institute of New South Wales countered with a claim for police protection. Malone wondered if Wayne Jones was up there scamming the transplanted city slickers.

'Does he know you're on to him, Andy?'

'Nup.'

'Righto, we'll leave him till tomorrow morning. We'll have another casual Saturday visit. Pick me up at eight at home in one of the office cars. Bring the blue light and the siren, in case we're held up on the freeway.'

'Right!' said Andy Graham and Malone could already hear the siren and see the flashing blue light.

The rain cleared overnight and Saturday was a cold, ice-blue day with a moderate wind to remind the voters that winter was still around. Graham picked up Malone and drove the eighty kilometres to Woy Woy with reasonable recklessness, using the siren and the blue light only once. They slid off the freeway and down the long hill, past stunted trees that had pushed up through the rocky escarpment, to the wind-scabbed Brisbane Water.

Wayne Jones' house was not a shack. It was double-fronted brick, Spanish-styled, on a wide lot that faced east across the bay. He opened the teak door to a chime that played some notes inside the house. He was either expecting someone else or careless of security, and looked at them in expectation.

'Clients? Mr –?'

'No,' said Malone. 'Police.'

Jones frowned, which was a regular expression that Malone had come to recognize when the word *Police* was sprung. He looked at the two strangers in their casual clothes, like golfers who had come looking for a missing ball, then said, 'Police? It's not bad news? My wife –?'

'No, not bad news. We just want to ask a few questions, Mr Jones. I'm Detective-Inspector Malone and this is Detective-Constable Graham. We're from Homicide.'

'Homicide?' This time the frown was even deeper.

'May we come in?' Malone showed his badge: 'Just in case you doubt us –'

'Of course, of course.' He stood aside, closed the front door behind them, then led them through the house and out to a large sun-room that looked out on a wide terrace, a swimming pool and a jetty where a medium-sized cruiser was moored. Mr Jones wasn't short a quid, Malone noted.

'What's it about?'

Jones waved them to a chair. He was young-middle-aged, with prematurely grey hair and a lean, long-jawed face. He was dressed in a brown cashmere sweater and tan cargo pants, with more pockets than a billiard-table and not even a pencil in any of them. He wore bright yellow socks and tan desert boots. He was a fashionplate but at the moment he looked rather cracked.

'Homicide? Your beat's murder, isn't it?'

'Yes,' said Malone and nodded to Graham.

The latter opened his notebook and read Wayne Jones' history back in the 1980s. 'That all correct, Mr Jones?'

'I don't like that word *scam*. I could sue you for that –'

'Mr Bruce Farro threatened us with the same line,' said Malone.

'I haven't spoken to Bruce in – God, what is it? Fourteen years. I see him occasionally in the papers, all those whingdings you have down in Sydney –'

'Not us,' said Malone.

Jones smiled weakly; he would always try to be affable, a salesman. 'No, I guess not . . . Why are you bothering us? Me and him?'

Malone gave him a quick run-down on the Pavane murder.

'Holy shit!' Jones swung his head back and forth like an animal. It was a most peculiar movement and Malone wondered where he had picked it up. Rock-and-roll singers did it, but Jones, Malone guessed, would neither rock nor roll. 'That's how Trish Norval finished up – wife of the American Ambassador?'

'You're surprised?'

Jones stopped the head-rolling. He looked out at the water, at the white scabs that were rising as the wind increased. A small tourist ferry cruised past, half a dozen winter-wrapped sightseers staring out like prisoners on their way to exile. Gulls crawled up the wall of the wind and a jet-skier swept by, spray trailing him like a broken wing, a petrol-driven petrel. Then Jones turned back to the two detectives.

'No, on reflection, I'm not surprised.'

'Were you,' asked Malone, 'close to her?'

Jones had thin eyes that almost closed when he smiled. 'I'm glad you asked that while my wife isn't here. I took Trish out a coupla times – yes, we went to bed once, as I remember. But she had other fish to fry. And she fried them.'

'Jack Brown and Grant Kael?' said Andy Graham, notebook still open.

'You've done your homework.'

'Bruce Farro helped,' said Malone.

'He would. Bruce was always ready to put the knife in.'

'You trusted him while the scam was on. Or did he put the knife in and you walked away with nothing?'

'I can still sue you, you know –'

It was Malone's turn to smile. 'Wayne, this is just between you and us. All we are interested in is who murdered Mrs Pavane – Trish Norval. Where were you last Tuesday week, around midnight?'

The question was put without any raising of the voice, but it was like a thrown knife. Jones reeled back; or sat back. 'Christ Almighty – what does that mean? Where was –? I don't fucking know – yes, I do! I was at a business seminar in Gosford. I was there till, I dunno, eleven or eleven-thirty. Then I came home. I can give you names to check –'

'What exactly do you do, Mr Jones?' asked Graham, pen at the ready.

'I'm a stock market consultant. I have a list of clients, here and around the world – I cover all the major stock exchanges. I don't buy or sell –'

'Like you used to,' said Malone.

'You *have* done your homework.'

'Without benefit of website or internet. Is that how you handle your clients?'

159

'Yes. I do exactly what stockbrokers do – what I used to do. Only I don't buy and sell any more. Except my own investments.'

Malone looked around, then out at the cruiser, then back at Jones. 'It pays.'

'Yes, it pays and it's all above board –' The affability slipped, he was angry. Then he seemed to realize that how he made his living did not concern them. They had, as he had said about Trish Norval, other fish to fry. The effort to settle himself was plainly visible: 'Look, I haven't seen Trish since 1987. That's the truth.'

'Did you ever hear of her?'

'Never. Someone told me she'd gone overseas, but I didn't know where. I went to New Zealand till – well, till things blew over. Yes, there *was* a scam and we got away with it. I'm not proud of it – I was younger and I got carried away like so many back then –' Then he stopped, tilting his head as if listening to what he had just said. Then he smiled wryly: 'Sorry. I'm starting to sound – pious? Conscience-stricken? Maybe I am – but I never gave the money back. We always told ourselves we weren't robbing anyone, just using someone else's money. Banks do it all the time, don't they? I kept it and used it and now I like to think I'm respectable and honest.'

'We'd never think of contradicting you,' said Malone. 'But we're Homicide, not Fraud. We never have to worry about morality – it usually doesn't come up in murder cases.'

'They teach you sarcasm in Homicide?' Then Jones seemed to relax. 'Look, Inspector, don't let's cross swords. I'm sorry to hear Trish Norval is dead – *murdered*. But I had nothing to do with it. I wish I could help, but I can't –' The head rolled again.

'That leaves Jack Brown,' said Andy Graham.

'What about Grant Kael?'

'You didn't know? He was killed in a car accident in Victoria. It must of been while you were in New Zealand.'

'Poor guy.' Jones looked genuinely concerned. 'He was dotty

160

over Trish, but she never gave him a look-in. He was the – well, I guess he was the quietest of us all.'

'So that leaves Jack Brown,' Graham repeated.

Jones shook his head, just a gentle shake this time; he looked completely relaxed now. 'He went overseas, that was all I heard. He got out before the rest of us. Just walked out one Friday, I think it was, no goodbye, no farewell drink, nothing. Jack was the most self-contained bastard I ever met. But there was a thing between him and Trish. She was as shitty as the rest of us when he walked out. Maybe more so.'

'So you've heard nothing of him since then?' asked Malone.

'Not a word. But wherever he is, unless he's dead, Jack will be doing all right. He was the smartest of us all, he was the one who planned the –' He smiled again, eyes thinning. 'The scam.'

'He had no family here?' said Malone.

'I think he did, but he never talked about them and we never met. Like I said, he was self-contained. I could never see what Trish saw in him.'

'You're implying they were pretty close?'

Jones nodded. 'Office gossip.' He was silent a while, trying to recall those years. It was obvious he had not thought of them in a long time, putting them behind him. 'There was a hint there had been an abortion, but I never took much interest – it was girls' gossip.'

'Never reliable,' said Andy Graham and the three chauvinists looked at each other and nodded. 'But go on, Wayne –'

'Like I said – I never took much notice. By then Trish and I were history. Pretty small history. I don't think she would remember me.'

'She won't now,' said Malone.

'No.' Jones looked at the two detectives. 'The wife of the American Ambassador – how did she get that far?'

'We're still working on it,' said Malone and stood up. 'Righto, Mr Jones, thanks for seeing us.'

Andy Graham took his time getting up. 'Mr Jones, what do you know about a firm called Finger Software?'

There was no mistaking Jones' look of caution. 'Why?'

'It's run by your old mate Bruce Farro. You must of known that.'

Malone said nothing, just a bystander with a stake in the game.

'Yeah,' said Jones, still cautious, 'I've had a look at it. For my clients.'

'And what was your advice?'

'I don't think I have to tell you that – it's confidential –'

'We treat everything as confidential,' said Malone. 'Or would you like a trip back to Sydney while we do our own checking and then get you to verify what we find out?'

'Come on, Mr Jones,' said Graham. 'What you tell us isn't gunna affect your clients.'

Jones still said nothing, looked out towards the terrace and the gulls battling the wind. He rolled his head again in his peculiar motion and Malone said, 'Come on, Wayne. It's just between you, us and the gulls.'

Jones turned back. 'I wouldn't touch Finger with a forty-foot pole. It's falling over – it's got a mountain of debt and it's losing contracts. Bruce Farro is up to his arse in trouble and it couldn't happen to a nicer shit!'

Malone looked at Andy Graham. 'That's all we needed to know, Andy . . . Thank you, Wayne. Enjoy the rest of the day.'

'Will that be all?' Jones all at once looked anxious.

'We'll see what comes up. Do you work here at home?'

'No, I have an office over in Gosford. I have a guy working there this morning, covering New York and Chicago. This job, you work six days a week. I'm on my way over there now. How did you find my home address?'

'I never query Detective Graham's methods. I think if ever he left the Police Service, he'd do very well in the stock market.'

Jones smiled again, but weakly; he was suddenly less comfortable, as if the past, like the wind outside, was rising. 'If you want to see me again, could you make it at my office?' He flipped open a box beside a phone on a side table, took out a business card and handed it to Malone. 'I'd rather my wife – well, you understand? I wasn't married when . . .'

'We understand,' said Malone and handed the card to Graham. 'The firm you worked for disbanded after the 1987 crash. Where would we look for their records?'

Jones pondered, then said, 'I guess the best place would be the lawyers we used.'

'Who were they?'

'Fairbrother, Milson and Gudersen. They're still around, I think.'

Malone and Graham drove back to Sydney into a wind that was like a heavy surf. But they were happy. Graham used the siren and blue light only twice, almost like shouts of joy.

2

Two days later Wayne Jones was in his office when he got a phone call. What he took to be an American voice said, 'My name is John Blake. I'm an investment adviser in Chicago. I'm out here looking at possibilities for clients of mine. Your name was given to me – apparently you know the market up, down and sideways.'

'We do our best,' said Jones.

'I understand that we'll have to register with you if we want to use your services. But just to give us an example of the information we'd be buying, would you advise me to buy into – just a moment.' There was a sound that might have been that of paper being turned over. 'Finger Software. Do you know anything about it?'

'I wouldn't touch it – Mr Blake? Is that it?'

'Yes, Blake. You wouldn't care to enlarge on that advice?'

'I will, if you come to see me, Mr Blake. I'm running a business –'

'Of course. Well, I'll be in touch, make an appointment.'

The line went dead. Jones sat back, not taken in. Who was so interested in Bruce Farro and his dog of a company?

Then his wife appeared at the door of his office, hung as usual with shopping bags. 'Sweetheart, my credit cards have run out –'

'All five of them?'

'Yeah. Crazy, isn't it?' She was ten years younger than he, still beautiful and he had made the mistake of marrying her for her looks and her inconsistencies. But he still loved her, mainly because he was too busy to go looking elsewhere. 'What's the matter? You look worried.'

'It's nothing,' he said. 'I just thought of someone I used to know.'

'Not a girl?' But she was smiling, sure of him.

'No, not a girl.' He took out his chequebook. 'How much do you need?'

'Why does a husband always say, How much do you *need*? *Want* is the word, sweetheart.'

3

The funeral director, a veteran of big events, thought the funeral a huge success; but, a man of taste, he did not mention his satisfaction to the Ambassador. The Episcopalian Bishop performed the service, the University of Missouri choir sang the hymns, the State Governor read the eulogy and the ghost of Harry Truman walked over from Independence and stood in a corner. The Secretary of State flew in from Washington with an entourage of such size it was thought he had just stopped off on his way to an international peace conference.

Twenty-three senators, representatives and State assemblymen who had been financed by the Pavane family attended; they sprinkled themselves amongst the mourners, for there is nothing more off-putting to citizens, even in the United States, than a congeal of consuls. Kansas City society was there and all the directors of the Pavane agricultural and commercial empire. Private jets flew in from Omaha, Oklahoma City, Dallas and Denver; St Louis, a rival city to K.C., just sent faxes. A sky-writer offered his services for a message on the heavens, but Stephen Pavane, also a man of taste, had scathingly rejected such an idea. Billie Pavane, entry into this world hidden in a dark cloud, went out of it in a blaze of glory.

She was buried in Union Cemetery, amongst Stephen's fore-bears. The original were French fur traders who came west from the post at St Louis and arrived at the Missouri; the family name then had been Pavan. They had settled on either side of the Big Muddy, as the local Kanza Indians called it, and gradually their holdings had grown. The dead Pavanes, including Stephen's parents, were buried with their feet facing east in the belief they wouldn't see God if their backs were turned. Billie, only a social guest of God, was buried with her feet in the proper direction.

The wake, though it was not called that, the Ambassador being an Episcopalian, was held at the Pavane mansion on Ward Parkway, *the* thoroughfare in Kansas City. Stephen's two brothers and his sister hosted the gathering, while the widower stood in a corner and wondered again at funerals being for the living, not the dead.

He was joined by Chief of Police Terence O'Malley. 'My condolences, Stephen. Nobody here believed it when we got the news.'

O'Malley was all bone-and-gristle, with a ginger crew-cut and eyes too bright and frank for a cop. He ran a police force that was highly regarded, even by criminals; it had not always been so in Kansas City. Stephen Pavane could remember his grandfather telling him stories of the K.C. force in the days when the Pendergast machine ran local politics. At one time there had been seventy-five ex-cons on the force, none of them rehabilitated; squad cars often carried liquor in their trunks for bootleggers. All that had been cleaned up and Chief O'Malley was the image of what the voters wanted in a police chief.

'Who's handling it out in Australia? The murder?'

'There's an FBI man in Sydney –'

O'Malley wrinkled his thin nose. 'They're never much good twenty-five miles out of Washington.'

Pavane smiled. 'Terry, you know they're better than that. Anyhow, it's really in the hands of the local New South Wales cops.'

'What are they like?'

'As good as yours.' Too good, perhaps: they were uncovering more than he wanted to know. 'They're pretty modern out there.'

O'Malley's grin was a widening slit in his thin face. 'I've heard they're ahead of us on some things. Identification imaging, stuff like that. You going back there?'

'I have to talk that over with the Secretary. Excuse me, Terry.'

He left O'Malley and crossed to the Secretary of State, took him by the arm and led him out on to a wide terrace that looked out on a large garden and a tennis court. The terrace was crowded with mourners, all on their third or fourth drink, and the two men went down into the garden and crossed to the chairs beside the tennis court.

'So what do you want to do, Stephen?'

Benjamin Market was a New Yorker, a Wall Street lawyer who recognized that the rest of the world resented the United States, but knew where to come when it wanted money. He was small and neat and amiable, a Jew whom even the Arabs liked and trusted. He had been married three times and had learned diplomacy the hard way; that is, domestically. He

166

and Pavane were old friends, though separated by regional differences.

'Take your time in making up your mind. The Aussies have got other things on *their* minds, with an election coming up. That's when foreign affairs become irrelevant.'

Pavane had always liked this small, unfussed man. 'No, I'll go back at the weekend, Ben.'

He looked down towards the south. There had been storm warnings this morning on the radio; tornadoes were beating their way up from the Gulf of Mexico. They could do no more damage then he already felt.

'Ben – I have to tell you . . .' This wasn't easy, not even to an understanding friend, who still had an official position to safeguard. 'There are some things about Billie that may come out that I didn't know about. I'd like to be there to handle them if they do.'

'What things? I have to ask, Stephen. Not because I'm personally curious, but – well, you understand . . .'

'I'm not sure, yet. But – well, Billie wasn't who I thought she was.'

'Who was she, then?'

'I don't know, Ben. That's what I have to go back and find out. At first, when their cops out there started telling me things, I didn't want to know. But now . . .'

'Is it serious stuff? I mean, political?'

'No, it's nothing like that.' But how could he be sure?

Market looked down to the south; the sky had begun to darken. He was an urban man, but even he knew that the swift tremble of birds in the still air was not a good omen. He looked up at the tall man beside him.

'How do you find the Aussies?'

'Oh, you never have any trouble finding them. It's like Washington – there are no retiring people in Canberra.'

'You know what I mean –' He was not an insensitive man, he knew when to be patient.

167

'Ben, it took me a little time. They're very sensitive to criticism. They'll ask, "What do you think of Australia?" You think they want an honest answer. So you tell 'em, but try to be polite. But that's the last thing they want. They bridle, as if you've raped their grandma.'

Ben Market nodded. He had been around the world enough times to know that foreigners never really wanted to know Americans' opinion of them. The Brits and the French, he guessed, had never been asked their opinions of lesser breeds. Their superiority had been too self-evident.

'Stephen, I'll appreciate it if you do stay on out there. The Aussies can be a pain in the ass at times.'

'They say the same about us.' Then he smiled.

'What's funny?'

'An old joke out here in the boondocks. The hen says to the farmer, "An egg may be breakfast for you, but it's just a pain in the ass for me."'

'You still have your sense of humour.'

'Barely,' said Stephen Pavane.

4

Fairbrother, Milson and Gudersen were one of those law firms that had more partners than a cotillion ball. Its offices were in Phillip Street, where lawyers are more numerous than pigeons and briefs were tool of trade, not underwear. The offices covered enough floors to suggest a small government department, but no jeans and open-necked shirts and trainers were tolerated here. Fairbrother, Milson and Gudersen were *old* school, though they charged new school fees.

Monday morning Malone and Graham presented themselves at the reception desk. No casual clothes this time, but suits and ties and Malone with his trademark pork-pie hat. The receptionist was certainly not jeans-and-trainers; she was sleek as a fashion model but healthier looking. She had the fluting vowels of one of the eastern suburbs' private schools.

'Do you have an appointment with Miz Gudersen?'

'No, we're police. Usually we don't make appointments.'

She gave them a smile that showed what she thought of police wit. 'I'll check if she can see you. You may be lucky.'

'We usually are,' said Malone and gave her a smile that showed what he thought of snooty receptionists.

Ms Gudersen was free if not welcoming. She was power-suited in clerical grey offset by a yellow silk blouse. Her face this morning was not puffed from sleep or love-making; the wild tangle of hair was drawn back in a smooth chignon. Her voice was as crisp as that of a platform announcer: 'You have five minutes –'

'We have as much time as it will take,' said Malone. 'Don't let's get off on the wrong foot, Miss Gudersen.' He waited for her to tell him *Miz* Gudersen; but she didn't. She gazed at him steadily, measuring an opponent; then nodded. 'We're working on a murder case. Unfortunately, those sort of cases can't be hurried. You may know that.'

'I do only civil cases.'

She sized them up again, then waved the two of them to chairs. Malone noted that she had a corner office, which meant that she was a senior partner; probably by inheritance. The office itself was standard old school: lots of timber panelling, glass-fronted bookcases, an antique desk that had probably been used by her father and her grandfather. The only bright note in the room was a Lloyd Rees painting of a harbour bay, but even the artist was dead.

'The Pavane case? Is Bruce Farro in trouble?' She spoke as if, though she slept with him, Farro was just an acquaintance. Or a client.

'No,' said Malone. 'We are looking for someone who worked with him back in the 1980s. We believe Fairbrother etcetera did their legal –'

'Fairbrother, Milson and Gudersen,' she said and smiled; she was relaxed now, almost hospitable. 'I like to get a mention. I'm the last of the Gudersens.'

'I'll remember that,' said Malone and smiled in return. Then, because he didn't believe in letting his junior officer sit there like a shag on a rock, he said, 'Detective Graham has the man's name.'

'Jack Brown,' said Graham. 'We'd like to know where he is.'

'That was when?'

'Last seen 1987,' said Graham.

She shook her head. 'I was very junior here in those days, I'd just graduated. I knew no one there at that firm of stock-brokers.'

Malone had been watching her. At the mention of the name *Jack Brown* the hand on the desk had closed into a fist, but otherwise there was no reaction. However it was enough for Malone to ask: 'But you know of Mr Brown now, right?'

'You're stepping outside your brief, Inspector –'

'You know that I'm not.' The tones of both of them were even. 'Where is he now?'

'I don't know.'

'But you've seen him recently?'

'Inspector, you've heard of lawyer-client confidentiality –'

Malone grinned wearily; it was like listening to a joke repeated time and time again. 'Yes, I've heard of it. All we want to do is ask Mr Brown a few questions –'

'I'll see what can be done. Now, if you'll excuse me –?'

Going down in the lift, surrounded by other travellers, Malone said nothing to Andy Graham. But out in the street, in the cold sunlight, with lawyers striding past, gowns flapping in the wind, clerks trailing behind with trolleys packed with books, as if they had just come from a legal supermarket shopping spree, he snarled, 'Jack Bloody Brown is somewhere here in Sydney! Find him, Andy!'

'Where do I start?' For once Graham looked like a bloodhound that had lost its nose.

'He must've had a family before he left here. Find 'em! Go back back to Farro and Jones, find out if Brown had a mother or father or siblings!'

'Siblings?' Graham suddenly grinned; it was almost impossible for him to remain depressed. 'If I called my sisters siblings they'd kick me for talking dirty.'

'Get cracking!'

Malone stalked off, forgetting that he had come here with Graham in an office car. Uncharacteristically, temper was getting the better of him; he had either aged suddenly or reverted to adolescence. He had walked a hundred metres before he realized where he was heading; he turned, looked back and saw Andy Graham driving off. Reluctantly, he hailed a cab, got in the back and refused to enter into conversation with the talkative cab driver. At Strawberry Hills he got out and paid the exact fare, counting out the last coins.

'Have a nice day,' said the cab driver, a Greek. 'Fall under a truck.'

Back at Fairbrother, Milson and Gudersen the phone had been picked up as soon as the two detectives had left the room. Rita Gudersen said, 'Get me Mr Wexall.'

5

When Malone got up to his office, Clements was waiting for him: 'You look as if you've got shit on the liver again.'

'Righto, stop laughing. What have you got?'

'Nemesis – I have to laugh every time I hear that. Who was Nemesis?'

Malone had looked it up: 'The Greek goddess of vengeance. She'd kick you up the bum if she were here. Get on with it.'

'Simmer down, mate. Well, Nemesis, she's just rung in. She

may be the goddess of vengeance, but she's cocked things up. That fingerprint they found on the flush-button at the Southern Savoy, it was a woman's print. She had a record, so they started looking up her record and the report got temporarily lost. She was the housemaid found the Pavane corpse. She went into the bathroom and vomited in the toilet, then flushed it. They've interviewed her now and it's got us nowhere.' He sat down opposite Malone, took his time: 'You got nowhere, too. Right?'

'No, we've narrowed it down. Jack Brown. Find him and maybe – *maybe* – we'll know who did in Mrs Pavane.'

'And then you tell Ambassador Pavane and he won't want to know. And the shit goes from your liver to the fan.'

'Nemesis might've gone out with you if she'd known you.'

'I think her other name is Delia Jones. She's rung twice, wanting to speak to you. Only you. I told her you were no longer on her case.'

6

Claire Malone (she still used her maiden name at work) saw the Notice of Intended Distribution of the Estate of Charles Brown while looking through the Legal Notices in the daily newspapers. She did not know her father was looking for Charles Brown's son and she passed on to other notices that might concern any of her clients. It was Andy Graham, dogged as usual, who pressed both Bruce Farro and Wayne Jones till Farro remembered that Brown had once mentioned that his father was a chemist somewhere on the North Shore. From there, though it took him another two days, the trail led to Jack Brown's sister, married to Walter Wexall, SC.

'I know Wexall's reputation, boss. He wouldn't have defended Jesus Christ – too radical. If Jack Brown is Mrs Pavane's killer, Mr Wexall will divorce Jack Brown's sister.'

172

'Have you got in touch with Wexall or his wife?' asked Malone.

'I thought you'd like to do that,' said Graham, straightfaced.

'You'll get on, Andy,' said Malone and the younger man grinned.

Malone rang Wexall's chambers, only to be told: 'Mr Wexall is in court today.'

'Where?'

'Darlinghurst. Central Criminal Courts, Number 4.'

Malone and Graham drove over to Darlinghurst through another fine but cold day. When Malone had come out of the house this morning he had been greeted by a fire of camellias and azaleas, Nature showing she was not all cold heart. The sun had no warmth, but it was bright enough to throw shadows. Only the shadows in the courts were darker.

There were half a dozen bikies outside Court 4, sun glinting on their studded black leathers like on molluscs on dark rocks. They looked at the two detectives, recognizing them for what they were, and turned away with contempt. Inside the court two bikies were being charged with murder. One was bearded and long-haired and ear-ringed, the other clean-shaven and close-cropped and unmarked; they looked unrelated, as if in the dock on separate charges. Their defending counsel was Walter Wexall.

Gowned and bewigged, sonorous voice rolling like muted thunder, he was impressive; but ten minutes inside the court and Malone saw that Wexall was fighting a lost cause. Twenty minutes later the court rose for lunch and Malone and Graham followed Wexall out into a corridor. Malone signalled to one of the court sheriffs and they were ushered into a side room.

'You're not on this case, are you, Inspector?'

They had met a couple of times on other murder cases, but they were on formal terms.

'No, Mr Wexall. We're on the Pavane case, the American Ambassador's wife. You've read about it.' *As who hasn't?*

Wexall raised an eyebrow above the gold-rimmed glasses.

Malone had been in enough court audiences to know that barristers were all actors manqué; they used gestures, expressions with measured abandon. 'Why me?'

'We understand your wife's maiden name was Sarah Brown. Did she have a brother, Jack Brown?'

Wexall had taken off his wig and gown, looked reduced without them; or was he reduced by some sudden unease? 'Yes.'

He's going to make this difficult. 'We want to talk to him. Is he in Sydney?'

'I'm not his lawyer –'

'We know that. That's why we know we won't be breaking any lawyer-client confidentiality.'

Wexall saw his mistake. 'Why do you want to question him? Is it something to do with the Pavane case?'

'Yes.'

Wexall frowned at the shortness of the answer, waited as if expecting more; then he chewed his lip. 'Is he in serious trouble?'

'We don't know. But he knew Mrs Pavane –'

The eyebrow went up again. 'When? Where?'

'I'm afraid we can't tell you that, not yet –' *Not till I've told the Ambassador.* 'All I can say, Mr Wexall, is that we think he can help us in our enquiries.'

Wexall smiled at the old cliché. 'In what way?'

'You *are* defending him, aren't you? Maybe not for a fee, but because he's your brother-in-law.'

Wexall looked at him, then at Graham, who had remained silent, then back at Malone. 'I could refuse to answer –'

'You won't, Mr Wexall. You know the law better than I –'

'So he's in trouble?'

'Not yet, no. Do you know where we can find him?'

Wexall chewed his lip again, then nodded, more to himself than to the two detectives. 'He's staying at the Regent. Under the name of Julian Baker.'

'Thanks, Mr Wexall. Nothing may come of this – we're not out to spread it to the media –'

'You have to do what you have to do – who said that? Gary Cooper or John Wayne?' He was looking for humour to prop him up.

'You have to do the same, I'm sure. How's it going out there?' He nodded in the direction of the courtroom.

'Hopeless, I fear. But one keeps trying.'

At five thousand bucks a day, why wouldn't one? 'Good luck. We'll let you know how we get on with –' He looked at Andy Graham.

Who had jotted down the name in his notebook: 'Julian Baker.'

'Do you know why he has changed his name?'

'Ask him,' said Walter Wexall and barely refrained from washing his hands.

When Malone and Graham came out of Court 4 the bikies were still there, munching on hamburgers and sandwiches, looking like horseless knights without their Harleys. The two detectives walked across to their car and Andy Graham said, 'They stick together, don't they?'

'Who?'

'Bikies.' Then as he got in behind the wheel: 'I don't think Mr Wexall is gunna stick by Jack Brown.'

They drove down to the Regent and Malone waited in the car while Graham went in to enquire after Mr Baker. He was back within two minutes. 'He's gone. Checked out the morning of July 17.' He got in behind the wheel again. 'That was the morning after the murder.'

The hotel commissionaire tapped on Malone's window and he wound it down. 'Yes,' he said absently, mind stuck in the mud of frustration.

'Would you mind moving your car, sir? There are three taxis waiting to come in behind you.'

'Would you remember a Mr Julian Baker, a guest here? He checked out just on two weeks ago.'

'No, sir, I can't place him, not the name. Would you mind moving on, please?'

Graham eased the car down the ramp. 'Where to now? Back to Darlinghurst?'

'No, back to the office. Check with Immigration, see if Julian Baker has left the country. Check with all the airlines, see if Julian Baker booked on an interstate flight. Then if you were taking your girlfriend out to dinner this evening, tell her you'll be late. We're going up to see Mr and Mrs Wexall. We'll give Mr Wexall time to get home.'

'Where do they live?'

'I'm depending on you to find out.'

Chapter Seven

1

Julian Baker had not told Sarah and Walter why he had moved; and he had not told them where he had moved to. All he had said in a phone call to Sarah was, 'I've moved. The Regent was a bit too public – I almost bumped into two guys I used to work with.'

'Where are you?' she had said.

'I'll let you know when I've settled.'

'Jack –'

'Julian.'

'No. It's a nice name, but I'll never get used to it. Jack, why all the hide-and-seek? I spent years writing to a box number. Now –'

'If ever you and Walter come to Toronto –' He hoped to God they wouldn't, though he didn't believe in God. 'If ever you come, you'll understand what I'm trying to protect, Rah.'

He hadn't called her that since they were children and she noticed it. 'Rah. That was a long time ago, wasn't it? Where did it all go?'

He had no answer to that and hung up. Then he had stared at the phone, cursing it. If he hadn't picked it up that morning at the Regent and called Canberra . . .

She had hesitated, then said yes, she would meet him; as he had guessed she would. She had been surprised at his call, but not cool. They had been a drug for each other, an addiction that was still there. It had been sex and nothing else. She had tried to tell him, when she fell pregnant, that it was love; but he hadn't believed her because he knew she was as selfish as himself. Love, he had read at university, was a mutual selfishness and he had told her he had no argument with that. She was still bitterly hating him when he had walked away from her and later he would wonder if the pregnancy had been planned.

Hate survives; he knew that, too. But when she called for him in a cab at the Regent and he got in beside her, she pressed his hand and kissed him on the cheek and he knew the evening was going to be fine. He didn't query why she had insisted on calling for him, instead of the other way round.

'We're going to a Japanese restaurant in Hunter's Hill.'

He noticed she now had an American accent. He had once read that Australian actors were considered the best at imitating American accents; and she had always been something of an actor. For himself, he had cultivated a mid-Atlantic accent. Both of them, he thought, were still intent on disguise.

'Nobody will know us there.' She had dropped her voice, as if she suspected the cab driver had his ears pinned back.

He was studying her in the dim light of the cab. 'I'd have still known you.'

'I'm not sure I'd have known you. But you still look good.' She squeezed his hand.

'Likewise.'

The restaurant, it seemed, had been designed for those who wanted to be discreet. Nobody made entrances here; *paparazzi* would have been as welcome as terrorists. Julian didn't know where Trish (he called her that and she did not mind, smiling as if at the memory of a long-lost relative) had learned about Japanese food; she did the ordering with confidence, but allowed him to order the wine. The dinner went smoothly and halfway through it, after the second glass of wine, he knew the evening was going to end in bed.

He was surprised when she told him where she was staying. He did not know the Southern Savoy, but then the hotel scene had changed a lot in the years he had been away. As, indeed, had Sydney itself.

'Where is it?'

'On Railway Square. It's a two-bit hotel, but clean and nobody asks questions.'

'How did you get on to it?'

'My brother manages it.'

'Your brother? I didn't know you had one. Won't he broadcast who you are and where you're staying? Hotel managers are always looking to advertise.'

'He doesn't know who I'm meeting. He's not the sort who wants to let everyone know who his sister is married to. Are you married?'

He nodded. 'Three kids. Have you any children?'

That was a mistake. She put down her wine glass and her eyes were suddenly cold. 'The abortion buggered up my uterus. You knew that.'

'No, I never –'

Her accent was abruptly Australian, the past catching up with them for the moment. 'I can never have children, thanks to you.'

He had to look elsewhere to avoid her stare. He looked towards a waiter without seeing him; unfortunately, the waiter saw him and came towards them. 'Something wrong, sir?'

'Eh? No. No, everything's fine, thank you. Beautiful meal.'

'Thank you, sir. It is our pleasure to please.'

The formality sounded almost like a joke. But Julian was at ease with other races, always had been; right now he was very much not at ease with one of his own. The waiter bowed and went away and he looked back at her. 'I'm sorry. A bit late –'

'Yes. Very.' She stared at him a moment longer, took a sip of her wine. Moved it around in her mouth, as if tasting him as well as it. Then her gaze softened, just a little. 'It's over. My husband –'

'What's he like?' he said hurriedly before she could tell him that her husband had always wanted children.

'You'd like him.'

179

'Ambitious?'

'Not so's you'd notice. He doesn't need to be. He has every-thing he wants. Including me,' she said, but smiled widely.

'He's lucky, then.'

'Thank you,' she said, as if he had handed her a bus ticket.

But as they waited outside the restaurant for the cab that had been called, she said, 'Do you want me to drop you off at the Regent?'

'Or?'

'Or you can see me home to the Southern Savoy.'

'Will your brother be there?'

'No.'

'I'll see you home to the Southern Savoy.'

They sat close together in the cab, saying little, their hands saying everything for them. They walked through the deserted lobby of the hotel, nobody in sight at the reception desk, and waited for the lift. Going up in the lift to Room 342 he said, 'You didn't get your key.'

'I didn't hand it in,' she said and held it up.

'You planned this. You were never a planner.'

'I am now. Have been for a long time.'

They had not forgotten each other's bodies; nor had the bodies changed that much. Sex is an exploration as well as an exploitation; they mapped each other like besotted cartographers. When they finally fell apart they were as exhausted as Burke and Wills. They lay, not under a coolibah tree, but under the light of a cheap bedside lamp, and looked at each other, not with love but a coldness that each managed to hide.

'Still good?' she said at last.

'Still good.'

'Better than your wife?'

Then he knew the hate was still there and he should never have picked up the phone to call her. 'Let's leave spouses out of it. I'm not going to ask you about – what's his name? Stephen?'

'Oh, you can ask me about him.' She rolled over on her back, pulled the sheet up on her; as if to say one didn't talk about one's husband with everything exposed. 'I love him.'

'Good,' he said, not yet hating her. 'And I love my wife.'

Neither of them smoked, so there was none of the stagecraft with cigarettes after intercourse. And there was no smoke to the dialogue: 'Do you give her a good life? I don't mean this –' She gestured at the bed.

'I think so. I've done well –' He hadn't meant to say that: he was not normally boastful.

'So have I.' She sounded boastful; he waited for her to throw out her chest, but she kept it under the sheet. 'I married a rich man, Jack.'

'I always knew you would.' He managed a smile.

'No, you didn't. You didn't give a damn who I married. So long as it wasn't you.'

It was time to get dressed; he began to draw on his shorts. He had his back to her when she said, 'Whoever you are now, whatever you've done, I could ruin you, Jack.'

He said nothing for a moment, stood up and turned round. Then: 'I could do the same to you.'

She shook her head; her dark hair fell down and she pushed it back. 'What could you tell them? That I'm not who I said I was? You have no idea where I've been or what I've done in the last – what is it? Fourteen years? When we were with the firm, I was never under suspicion like you and the others, Bruce and Wayne and Grant – I wonder if they're still around? Who cares? You don't, do you?'

'No.' His voice was flat as he pulled on his trousers.

'They interviewed me and I came out virgin pure –'

'Does your husband know all about you?' He was pulling on his shirt.

'Yes.' She's lying, he thought; but wasn't sure. 'But not about you and me.'

'You're lying –'

'How would you know? I'll tell your wife about you and me –'

181

It was then that he hit her; when suddenly he really hated her. If she had not hit back, coming out of the sheets like an animal out of a burrow, had not fought him with her own hatred, he might have stopped. Rage vomited out of him and, later, he would be confused as to what actually happened. When he drew back from her she was dead.

He sat down on the side of the bed, trembling. He looked at her, then looked away. He sat there for almost ten minutes, not moving. Then the discipline that had run most of his life seeped back into him, like water hardening into ice; he was not shattered, he was not going to go to pieces. He stood up, finished dressing unhurriedly. He thought criminally: had he left any fingerprints anywhere? He wiped the bedhead, avoided looking at her; the dressing-table; the chair over which he had hung his clothes. He went into the bathroom, relieved himself, put a piece of toilet paper over his finger before he pushed the flush-button.

He came out of the bathroom, looked around him, satisfied himself he was leaving nothing of himself in the room but the marks of his fingers on her throat. Then, handkerchief in hand, he opened the door and looked out and straight into the face of a slim woman staring at him over the shoulder of a man in overalls with a carpet-cleaner. He closed the door, leaned against it on the inside.

Five minutes later he opened the door again, looked out. The hallway was deserted. The woman and the man in overalls had gone. He stepped out, closing the door behind him, and went looking for fire stairs as a way out of the hotel.

He knew nothing of the fact that he had left his DNA print in the vagina of Trish Norval.

2

Malone changed his mind at the last minute: 'Andy, you've got the night off. I'll take Gail with me to see the Wexalls. Two

182

boofheaded cops walking in on Mrs Wexall might upset her too much – we'd get nothing out of her.'

'I've never thought of myself as boofheaded.' Graham grinned; he was becoming sophisticated. He did not object to being replaced by a woman; he had a girlfriend who, with due diligence (she worked for a firm of accountants), was educating him in the skills of women. 'I'll tell Louisa what you said – she'll be disappointed. Here's the address.'

'Enjoy your date with Louisa.'

'I always do. I listen to only half what she's telling me, but isn't that the best principle?'

'All the time, Andy,' said Malone and was glad Lisa and his girls could not hear him.

Gail Lee was not happy when she was told she would be on duty for a couple of hours this evening. 'I wish you'd told me sooner – I was taking my mother to the opera –'

Instantly he regretted he had not given her more notice; but Andy Graham was already gone. 'I'm sorry, Gail. But I need a woman on this visit –'

'It's okay.' She sounded ungracious, but in the cool way that only East Asians can achieve, 'My sister can stand in for me.'

'What's the opera?'

She looked at him in surprise; she knew he was not an opera-goer. '*Don Giovanni*. It's supposed to be a comic opera, but I always cheer when the hero is dragged down to hell.'

'You drive. I'll ride in the back with the airbags.'

But he rode up to Killara with her in the front seat. She had done a stint with the Highway Patrol before joining Homicide and she drove fast but with skill. He, as usual, rode with his feet in the floorboards.

'How would you go in a Ferrari?'

'Highway Patrol would never catch me.'

Now that the base had been broadened and she was on the Pavane case as well as the Delia Jones one, she had softened her coolness. Young detectives, if not the older ones, prefer cases that are not open-and-shut. As if they are still sitting for exams.

The Killara street was not a setting where one would come looking for a murderer; or news of one. It was tree-lined, the street-lamps shining through them like stage lighting, throwing shadows that held no menace. There were no cars lining the street. Every house had its garages; some had curved driveways where cars were parked. Large deep gardens fronted the houses like moats.

But here in secure suburbia there was still a need for security, it seemed. Gail pressed a lighted button and a voice over an intercom demanded, 'Yes? Who is it?'

'Police,' said Gail. 'Detective-Inspector Malone and Detective-Constable Lee.'

The voice was a woman's. 'Police? What do you want? Just a moment.'

Gail looked at Malone, who said, 'She's checking with hubby if we're okay. Here he comes –'

Walter Wexall's voice was the sort that never crackled, not even over an intercom. 'What is it about?'

Malone leaned into the intercom: 'Mr Wexall, I'm not going to talk to you through this thing. Will you please come to the door?'

'I'm freezing,' said Gail. 'I left my coat in the car.'

'Here he comes.'

The front door opened and Walter Wexall stood behind the security door, outlined against the lighted hallway behind him. 'I don't appreciate being intruded on in my own home, Inspector –'

'Will you ask us in, Mr Wexall?' Malone managed to keep the sharpness out of his voice. 'Detective Lee is freezing.'

Wexall opened the security door, suddenly relaxing as if realizing his stiff attitude would get him nowhere; or as if, belatedly, realizing his impoliteness. 'Come in. I apologize. I don't welcome even clients here at my home –'

'I understand, Mr Wexall.' Malone decided to be polite, too. 'I never invite crims home.'

184

Wexall was not all stuffed shirt; he had a sense of humour. He laughed and stood aside, gave a theatrical gesture. 'Come in, come in. Sarah –'

She came down the hallway, a galleon of a woman beside the very slim Gail Lee. 'It's about Jack? My brother?'

'Just a few questions –' said Malone.

They were led into a large living room as comfortable and secure as a furnished vault. The evening was still young, just gone seven, and it struck Malone that he and Gail had probably interrupted the Wexalls' dinner. But if that were so, the Wexalls made no mention of it.

They were polite; but they were not offering coffee or drinks. 'Did you see my brother-in-law?' asked Walter.

The two detectives were seated in deep armchairs; Sarah Wexall sat opposite them in a matching lounger. Walter stood in front of the fireplace, where logs burned, warming his backside. He had his hands clasped behind his back and, almost Victorian-like, he dominated the room. But Malone cut the legs from under him:

'He wasn't at the Regent. He checked out the morning after the murder we're investigating. I think you knew that, Mr Wexall.'

There was a silence but for the hiss of flames. Sarah looked as if she was about to say something, then changed her mind. She glanced up at her husband, but he appeared to be gazing at the painting on the wall above Malone's head. Then he looked down and said lamely, 'We were hoping to be kept right out of it. You caught me off-balance this morning –'

Malone didn't buy that, but made no comment. Wexall had been too long a court performer to be caught off-balance; he was an actor manqué, but not a failure in measured delivery. He had been playing defence counsel this morning and he still was.

Gail Lee looked at Sarah: 'Mrs Wexall, do *you* know where your brother is? Is he still in Sydney?'

Sarah hesitated, glanced at her husband again, then said, 'I

185

think so. I've spoken to him a couple of times on the phone, but he wouldn't say where he was.'

'You didn't find that strange?'

'Well –' Then she looked again at counsel for advice, but Walter was silent.

Gail persisted: 'You didn't find it strange?'

'Yes . . . No, not really.' Sarah was having difficulty with her voice. 'We hadn't spoken for so long – fourteen years. We were – are still getting to know each other again –'

'Where has he been the last few years? Those fourteen years?' asked Malone. 'We know he left Sydney in 1987 –'

'Paris,' said Walter, taking over from Sarah; she looked at him with gratitude, almost non-wifely. 'Toronto. He works for some Canadian bank.'

'Walter –' Sarah suddenly changed her mind.

'Darling –' For the moment the two detectives might not have been in the room. Walter moved away from the fireplace, sat on the arm of the lounger and took her hand. 'He has to defend himself. We can't do it for him.'

'I know –' Her face looked doughy, ready to fall out of shape. 'I just can't believe he would have anything to do with – with –' She flapped a hand helplessly, looked at Malone and Gail Lee. 'With what you're investigating.'

Malone fed them a crumb. 'We don't know he has anything to do with it. But we're working our way through a list and he's on it.' He looked up at Walter. 'You know that's the way we work, by elimination.'

Walter hesitated, then nodded. 'Yes. Of course.'

'Have you seen him at all in the past week or ten days?'

Again there was hesitation. Walter looked at a loss in his own home; at a Bar table there would have been papers to shuffle, junior counsel to consult. Then he said, 'We had a session at our solicitor's –'

'Fairbrother etcetera?'

'Yes. We're dealing with the estate – their father, my wife's

186

and Julian's – Jack's – he died two weeks ago. Intestate. With no will, there are things to be cleared up.'

'He keeps in touch, then?'

'Yes,' said Sarah. 'We've had a meeting at the solicitors. He calls every two or three days.'

'Never saying where he's staying?'

'No.' Then tentatively, almost fearfully: 'Can you trace those calls?'

'Unfortunately, no. Once you put down the receiver, that wipes the call.' Then Malone looked at Wexall: 'We'd like to put a tap on your line.'

That was an idea that did not appeal to Wexall: 'No. No, I can't allow that –'

'Mr Wexall –' Malone was all patience. 'We can go to a magistrate or judge –'

'They'd never agree.' He knew his standing with the Bench.

'Maybe not, but they'd ask questions why we wanted it and we'd tell them in detail. Gossip flies –'

'There are judges who'd give you hard labour for such a slander –' But once again he eased out of the stiffness that seemed to come and go like an arthritic attack. He said almost plaintively, 'You're threatening us.'

'No,' said Malone. 'It's the situation that's threatening, not us. You know that.'

Wexall said nothing, looked at Sarah, grimaced, then looked back at Malone: 'All right, you can put a tap on the line.'

'Walter!'

'Darling, please –' He was standing again in front of the fireplace, no longer looking Victorian and dominant. 'We can't obstruct them . . . What you hear on the line, Inspector, it will be kept under strict control? Wire taps are always being leaked.'

'I promise I'll have the head of any bloke who leaks anything. I have reasons why we don't want this case spread around.'

Wexall never missed a point: 'It might harm the American Ambassador?'

It was Malone's turn to hesitate; then he nodded. Abruptly he went off on another tack before any more questions about the Pavanes could be asked: 'Do you have a recent photo of your brother, Mrs Wexall?'

She shook her head. 'Nothing. I think there might be one or two of him as a teenager, but he's changed. A lot.'

'What does he look like now? Describe him.'

'Well . . .' She had to take her time, as if describing a stranger. 'He's tall – I don't know, six feet, six-one.' No centimetres for her. 'He's well-built, he seems to have looked after himself. He's – yes, I think he's good-looking?' She looked at her husband, who nodded. 'He has grey hair. He dresses – American, I suppose you'd call it.' She would always be conscious of dress; had she been around at the time, she would have described what Anne Boleyn and Marie Antoinette had worn on their last outings. 'You know, those button-down shirts that always look as if they haven't been ironed –'

Malone was glad he was wearing his soft collar with the stays. Beautifully ironed.

'Yes, American –'

'Canadian,' said her husband.

'Well, they're much the same, aren't they?'

'Not quite.' He turned back to Malone. 'He's distinctive, Inspector. He has a very – a very self-contained look.'

'He was always like that,' said Sarah. 'Even as a boy. Self-contained, that's Jack.'

Malone and Gail Lee asked a few more questions, but they had the feeling the Wexalls had been drained dry, both of them. At least for this evening. The two detectives stood up and Sarah rose with them, rushing, but politely, to sweep them out of the house.

At the door Malone said, 'We'll have the tap on your phone first thing in the morning. If Jack – or Julian – calls tonight, advise him to come in and see us.' He handed Wexall his card. 'It'll save a lot of bother all round, tell him.'

'Did he know –' said Sarah. 'Did he know the Ambassador's wife?'

'Yes. Tell him we know that.'

He and Gail went down the garden path, the wind threshing the trees above them, and out to the car. Once in it, with the windows wound up and the heat turned on, Malone said, 'Righto, up to Gordon, that's the local shop. We'll get them to put surveillance on the house while I rustle up some blokes from the strike force.'

'Do we stake out the Fairbrother office, too?'

'Yes. One way or another we're going to have Mr Baker, or Mr Brown, talk to us. Even if we have to follow him to Toronto. Get Andy to check which Canadian bank Julian Baker works for.'

'I'll do that,' said Gail. 'I'd like a trip to Canada. As compensation.'

'For missing the opera?' He grinned. 'Sorry about that.'

'This is starting to sound like one. Only there's no music.'

3

Five minutes after the two detectives left the Wexall house the phone rang. Walter picked it up: 'Yes? Jack? Sorry. Julian . . . No, I'm okay. The police have just been here.'

There was silence for a moment; then: 'What did they want?'

'To talk to you – about the American Ambassador's wife.' Sarah, standing beside him, went to say something, but he waved her to wait. 'Julian, I think we'd better talk –'

'What about?'

'You.' He took his own pause, then said, 'And what you're involved in.'

Another long pause; then: 'What makes you think I'm involved in anything?'

'Julian –' He would come to hate that name. 'My whole career has been based on sizing up people – from how they act, what they say, what they *don't* say. Don't let's beat about the bush over the phone. If we can help –' He glanced at Sarah and she nodded. 'If we can help, you'd better see us. Soon.'

'I'm not coming up there –'

He's guilty of something. But Walter didn't pursue the thought, shying away from it. 'No, not here . . . Get in a cab and come to your father's house. We still have the key. We'll meet you there in half an hour –'

'Walter –'

'Jack –' *Never mind Julian.* 'If you want us to help – or understand – meet us at the house in half an hour.'

He hung up and turned to Sarah. 'He's hiding something.'

She clutched his arm as if wanting him to hold her up. 'I can't – I just can't believe –'

'Don't believe the worst – don't believe anything till he's talked to us. Give him the benefit of the doubt.' But he now had no doubt himself. No proof, not a shred of evidence, but no doubt.

'Oh, I'm so glad the boys are away for the night –'

On a school camping trip, learning about hazards and how to cope.

'Don't worry about them. We have ourselves to think of.'

He put on a turtleneck sweater and blazer, she a cashmere cardigan and camelhair coat; they would have dressed for a garage sale. He got the Mercedes out of the garage and they drove down the North Shore to Lindfield. As they pulled into the driveway of the house where Sarah and Jack had grown up, a woman came out of the neighbouring house. There are faces at windows even in the best of districts.

'Can I help? Oh, it's you, Sarah!'

'Just checking a few things,' said Walter while Sarah was trying to find something to say.

'Are you going to put the house on the market?' Despite the cold, Mrs Next-Door wasn't going to waste the opportunity to pick up crumbs of news. Real estate was important, it had to

190

be kept in mind, no matter what the circumstances. You never knew who might move in next you.

'Too soon to think of that,' said Walter and took Sarah's arm and steered her to the front door.

Inside the house, with a couple of lights switched on, they stood and looked at each other. They were suddenly assailed by memory, though they had not come here looking for memories. But all this around them was part of what they were trying to protect. This was the house where he had courted her (she still used the old-fashioned term), when he had been a law student and she had been a doctor's receptionist. They had built their life in a pyramid of blocks and the pinnacle, so Walter had been advised, was only a year or two away. And now . . .

It was a widower's house, a bachelor's by marriage. Sarah's mother had died twenty years ago and her father had refused a live-in housekeeper (telling them he couldn't afford one, while the money piled up in his portfolio) and had settled for a cleaning woman who came in twice a week and re-arranged the dust. There were no flowers in the vases, no life-style magazines on the coffee table, no scarves (Sarah's mother had loved scarves) lying around. There were books everywhere: spy novels, histories, biographies. But, oddly, there were no books on investment nor copies of business magazines. As if, when they came to visit, he had been hiding his secret interest. As for women he might have entertained here, no trace of them had been left. It struck Sarah only then that her father, in his own way, had been as self-contained as Jack.

Jack (she would never get used to Julian, though she liked the name) arrived twenty minutes later by cab. When they opened the door to him he stood a moment, as if reluctant to enter the house where he and his father had argued so often.

'Who's the woman next door? She wanted to know if she could help me.'

'Mrs –' Walter named the woman. 'Full of good works. Come in before she hops the fence.'

'What's happened to the North Shore? It used to mind its own business.'

'It never did. It was just subtler in the old days.'

Jack (Julian) stepped in the door. He was wrapped in a dark overcoat and his hair was a grey mess. Walter closed the door against the wind and the police, wherever they might now be.

'What's this about?' Julian (he had shucked off the old name, despite what his brother-in-law might say) smoothed down his hair. He opened his overcoat, but didn't take it off as he followed them into the cold living room. 'It must be serious –'

Don't act innocent, thought Walter. 'Jack –'

'Julian.'

'No. Jack. Because this concerns us as much as you, because the mess that's building up around us – *us*, Jack – must have started a long while ago, when you were Jack Brown. Did you know the American Ambassador's wife?'

'Mrs Pavane,' said Sarah, who now remembered the name.

'Christ, it's cold in here!' He wrapped the coat round him, but didn't do it up, and sat down in the worn green leather chair that had been his father's favourite. 'Did Dad still persist in not having air-conditioning?'

'You know what he was like,' said Sarah.

'Jack –' said Walter, persisting.

He looked up from the deep chair, sighed, then said, 'Why did the police come to you?'

'They traced Sarah as your sister – don't ask me how. I know this Inspector Malone, he's no fool. I think they know a lot more than they told us. Did you know Mrs Pavane?'

'Not as Mrs Pavane, no.' He took his time: 'We used to go out together years ago. It was nothing serious – you remember what it was like in those days, everyone having a good time –'

'We were married –' It was difficult to tell whether Sarah was being prim or regretful. 'I had the boys –'

Walter said, 'Did you see her the night she was murdered?' It was a prosecuting counsel's question, direct and blunt.

192

Sarah had sat down, but Walter was still standing. Julian looked at her, then up at him. 'Whose side are you on, Walter? Are you working for the police?'

'No, I'm not. I'm on *our* side, if you want to put it that way. Sarah and me. Have you seen her since you landed back in Sydney?'

Who would have recognized him that night, would identify him as being with her? The Regent's commissionaire, the staff at the Japanese restaurant, the cab drivers? No. Only the woman who had stared at him as he had opened the door of Room 342.

'No. I phoned her down in Canberra, just to congratulate her. We had a chat, a friendly one, and that was it.'

'So you weren't with her on the night she was murdered?'

'Darling –'

Walter didn't look at her, continued to stare at Julian. As he did at defendants in the dock. 'I have to ask it, Sarah. Jack knows that.'

'Of course you do,' said Julian, all at once seemingly relaxed, self-contained. 'No, I wasn't with her. Wasn't I here, having dinner with you?'

'No,' said Sarah, reluctantly.

He's amazing, thought Walter. In a courtroom I would be battling him for hours.

Julian gestured helplessly. 'Then I don't remember. I haven't been out much, other than coming to see you, going to the lawyers . . .'

'Why did you call Mrs Pavane?' asked Walter. 'After all these years?'

'Wouldn't you call an old friend if he got to be a judge or a Cabinet Minister? I knew Mrs Pavane when she was Trish Norval, we worked in the same office. We were friends, we went out together a few times. But I haven't seen her since I left here all that time ago. I spoke to her, but that was all.'

He's lying, thought Walter; but they had to accept it. So far he had not let himself think that his brother-in-law might be a

193

murderer. But Jack was lying about something . . . 'Well, that's all we wanted to know.'

'Why couldn't you have asked me over the phone? Instead of dragging me all the way out here?' But he didn't ask the question belligerently, more as if he were puzzled.

God, thought Walter again, he *is* so self-contained. 'I wanted to ask you face to face. It's the way I work, Jack, you know that. Or you should.'

'You've made your reputation while I've been away, Walter. I've never seen you in court. But now – are you satisfied? Now we've been face to face?'

Sarah said, 'Jack, don't let's fight –'

'Rah, I'm not fighting,' he said evenly. 'I'm just upset that you thought I might have had something to do with this – this –' for the first time he missed a beat '– murder.'

'It's not us,' she said defensively. 'It's the police.'

'You seem impressed by them,' said Julian, looking at Walter. 'They weren't a very impressive lot back in the eighties. Corrupt cops in cahoots with criminals –'

'They're different now, they've cleaned up the Service – there are still a few bad apples, but not many. This Inspector Malone knows much more than he's told us. If you have nothing to hide, I'd advise you to go and see him.' Then Walter tried to lighten the moment, backing off, seeing how upset Sarah was: 'That's free advice. Normally I charge a whopping fee.'

Julian smiled at both of them, stood up unhurriedly. 'I'll think about it. In the meantime, there's another meeting tomorrow morning, that right? Will that be the last?'

'I think so,' said Walter. 'There are a few papers to sign, then the administrator can go ahead settling the estate. You should get your share, two to three months at the outside. We'll put this house on the market –' He waved a hand around the room.

'Do we have to?' said Sarah. 'I'd like to keep it for one of the boys, either one. I was born here.' She looked around her, as if looking for her lost girlhood. 'We both were.'

194

'No,' said Julian. 'We were both born in hospital. Sell it, Walter. What'll it bring?'

'Eight or nine hundred thousand, the agents say.' He's still greedy, thought Walter. 'We'll sell, if that's what you want.'

'That will be the last link, then,' said Julian and looked at Sarah. 'Except for you.'

She wasn't sure what was in his voice: warmth, indifference, what? So she said nothing. There was an emptiness in her that she had never felt before, not even when her father died. She had looked forward so much to the reunion with Jack, hoping he had changed. He had, but for the worse, it seemed.

'We'll see you tomorrow morning,' said Walter. 'Nine o'clock. I'm due in court at ten.'

'A winning case?' asked Julian.

'No, a losing one. Two bikie murderers, guilty as hell. But I tried –'

'I'm sure you would have. Can you give me a lift back to the nearest station? I'll catch a train back to town.'

'We can drive you back to town –' said Sarah.

'No, the train will do.'

'So you're still staying somewhere in the city?'

'Yes,' he said with a smile, but offered no more.

They drove him to Lindfield station, he kissed Sarah on the cheek and shook Walter's hand and they left him and went home to Killara. They went to bed and Walter tossed and turned all night. He was egotistical, pompous and wrapped in leaves of social values as many and thin as those of a lettuce. But he had a conscience, a value with no price.

In the morning, at seven-thirty he rang the number Malone had given him at Homicide.

A man's voice answered and Walter asked for Inspector Malone. 'I know he won't be in his office at this hour, but it's urgent I speak to him. This is Walter Wexall, Senior Counsel.'

'The barrister? I can't give you the boss' home number, that's

195

definitely not on. Give me your number and I'll have him call
you right away.'

Walter gave his home number, put down the phone and looked
at Sarah, who had come to the door of their bedroom. 'I have to
do it, darling. It's a matter of conscience.'

'You've thought everything through? What it might do to
us?'

'Everything. It won't affect me at the Bar. Or going to the
Supreme Court –' He put out a hand and she took it. 'There'll
be some awkwardness with our friends –'

She was almost afraid to ask the question: 'Do you think *he*
murdered that woman?'

'I don't know –' But he did. Then the phone rang: 'Wexall.'

'You wanted to speak to me, Mr Wexall?'

'Yes, Inspector. Nine o'clock this morning, at the offices of
Fairbrother and company. He'll be there. And, Inspector . . .'

Malone, at the other end of the line, waited on the long pause.
Then: 'Yes?'

'Inspector, could you not let him know I called you?'

'Mr Wexall, I'll take all the credit. And thank you – I know
this hasn't been easy for you.'

Walter put down the phone and wrapped his arms round the
weeping Sarah.

4

Malone tossed up in his mind whom to take with him: Andy
Graham or Gail Lee. Then he decided that it was Graham's
dogged work which had brought them this far.

So he and Graham were waiting in Rita Gudersen's office
when Julian Baker came in. Walter and Sarah Wexall had not
yet arrived and Mrs Gudersen had been surprised when Malone
and Graham told her why they were here.

'I think it'll be better if we meet him here in your office, rather than outside. We don't want to upset your other clients.'

'Why did you have to choose *here*?'

'Because we knew he'd be here.'

'Who told you?'

'No one. We just worked on deduction.'

She gave them a sour smile. 'Who are you trying to kid? Okay, but no fuss, understand?'

'No fuss,' said Malone. 'Unless Mr Baker starts it. What name has he been using with you?'

'John Brown – though he's called Jack all the time.' She walked to the big window, sat down on its ledge and looked back at the two detectives. And Malone looked at her. She was a good-looking woman, successful, possibly had everything she wanted. Then he wondered why she would want to spend her time with a shonk like Bruce Farro; but he had long ago given up trying to fathom women. To be honest, he might somehow have made things easier with Delia Bates all those long years ago . . . Then Rita Gudersen said, 'Is he – is he connected to the murder of the American Ambassador's wife?'

'We don't know. That's what we want to ask him.'

She smiled again, less sour this time. 'I'd hate to cross-examine you in the witness box.'

'I'm a novice compared to Detective Graham.'

Andy Graham smiled and took the compliment. Then Mr Brown was announced by Rita Gudersen's secretary. He came in, overcoated, hat in hand, and pulled up sharply when he saw the two strangers.

'I'm sorry, Miz Gudersen. Am I too early?'

'Not at all,' said Malone and introduced himself and Graham. 'We'd like to talk to you, ask a few questions.'

'What about?'

'Not here, Mr Brown –'

Julian looked at Rita Gudersen, who had moved back to her desk but was still standing. 'Did you arrange this?'

197

'No, I did not, Mr Brown. We are not in the habit of ambushing our clients –' Her voice was like a double-edged sword.

He dipped his head. 'I apologize.'

'Miss Gudersen had nothing to do with this,' said Malone. 'We'd like you to come up to Police Centre with us. We shan't keep you any longer than is necessary.'

'I can't come now. Can't it wait? I have a meeting –' He looked at Rita Gudersen. 'Are my sister and her husband here?'

'No.' She was playing her part better than Malone had expected from her early attitude towards him and Graham. 'Mr Wexall phoned – they've been held up. They'll be twenty or thirty minutes late.'

'You'll be back here by then, Mr Brown,' said Malone. 'Do you mind coming with us?'

'And if I do mind?' For a moment there was a show of belligerence; then he thought better of it. 'Okay . . . Tell the Wexalls I'll be back here before ten, Rita.' Then his face stiffened with shrewdness: 'Walter told me he had to be in court at ten. So he won't be coming?'

He's guessed who gave us the word, thought Malone.

'I wouldn't know about that,' said Rita Gudersen.

He studied her, then said, 'Okay, we'll get everything signed and sealed. I'm booked out this afternoon for San Francisco.' Then he looked at Malone. 'Ready, Inspector?'

The bastard's cool. 'All the time, any time. It's the Police Service motto. Right, Detective Graham?'

'All the time, sir,' said Andy Graham.

198

Chapter Eight

1

'Delia,' said Rosie Quantock, 'you gotta find yourself something to do. A job or something.'

She was wearing the burden of Delia and her crime and the care of Delia's two kids, but it hardly showed. She had been a battler all her life, coming from a large family with no money; she had had her dreams, but they had always been beyond her reach. She had had a voice that, in other circumstances, might have at least got her out of the chorus; but she had never had enough money to hire a top coach, she had never been quite good enough to win a scholarship, she had been a union organizer and management had always shied away from her, fearful that if they promoted her she would have organized Sutherland, Pavarotti and only God knew who else. She had married a stagehand and retired, but still went to the Opera House, stood in the wings and sang silently every note with those on stage. She had surrendered but no one but her husband knew.

Delia Jones looked at her two children. 'What d'you reckon? You want me to work?'

The boy and girl looked like each other and both looked like their mother. If there was anything of their father in them, it was only that their cheeks were wider than their mother's. They both had her dark hair and the girl had her mother's lively, pretty mouth. The boy had a quiet countenance to him, as if always waiting for tomorrow.

'It'd help, wouldn't it, Mum?' said the girl. 'I mean, it'd give you something to do, instead of sitting around, moping all day.'

'You think that's what I do?' She loved them and was tolerant of their criticism.

'Yeah,' said the boy. He was eleven years old, but already he had put a foot inside the door of adulthood, opened for him by his warring parents. 'Get a job, Mum. It'd give us more money to spend.'

'You need it, the extra money,' said Rosie Quantock. 'You dunno how long this – this thing is gunna drag on. Are you behind in the rent?'

Delia didn't answer and the girl said, 'Yeah. The man was here yesterday and Mum sent me to the door –'

'Dakota, you talk too much,' said her mother, but wearily.

They were seated round the kitchen table, the breakfast things still in front of them. Morning light streamed in the curtainless window, but it did nothing to relieve the drabness of the small room. In the past two weeks Rosie Quantock had noticed that Delia had grown careless about housekeeping. The woman who, even when battered and bruised, had kept the small house as neat as a cell no longer appeared to care. But the calendar, with those battle days circled in red, had disappeared from the wall above the fridge. A certain amount of housekeeping had been done.

Delia looked at her friend. 'Rosie, what would I do? They don't want me back where I used to work – like when I take calls on the board, people are gunna recognize who I am.'

'Change your name,' said the boy.

'Calvin, I can't do that.'

'I'm gunna change mine,' he said.

'What? Calvin or Jones?' said Rosie Quantock, who had no children of her own, and smiled at him and rubbed the back of his neck. Then she looked at Delia with real concern. 'Go down to the job office this morning, love. Take anything they offer you. But get off your arse, get out and do something!'

'Rosie's right, Mum,' said the girl. 'While we're on holidays, I'm gunna do some baby-sitting.'

Delia looked at the boy with a tired smile. 'And what are you gunna do?'

'I dunno. I could mow lawns, only grass don't grow in winter. Maybe I can wash someone's car.'

'Well, wash all these things up first,' said Delia and rose. She led Rosie Quantock to the front door, opened it and stepped out into the cold sunlight. 'I really appreciate you trying to help me, Rosie. But it isn't easy, going into places where people recognize me. I see 'em nudging each other – *There she is.*'

'Stuff 'em, love. The only ones who wouldn't be on your side would be the men. The women understand. You had the guts to do something some of them might want to do.' She opened the front gate, stepped out. 'Go and register for a sole parent's pension.'

Delia laughed. 'Rosie, I'm a sole parent because I killed my husband!'

'Don't matter. You'll be dealing with bureaucrats – they're only interested in facts, not reasons.'

Delia smiled; her smiles now all looked tired. 'You're on your own, Rosie. I dunno what I'd do without you to buck me up.'

'You need bucking up.' Rosie closed the gate. 'Go out and get yourself some money. Only don't hold up a bank or some guy flashing his money around.'

'You think I might do that?'

'I wouldn't blame you, love –' She was smiling, not tiredly.

'You never blamed me for – for what I did to Boris.'

'He had it coming to him. I'll never blame you for that. Neither will the kids. If it hadn't been him, it would of been you that some day would of finished up dead.' She was inside her own gate now, talking over the small dividing fence. 'Now go and get a job, pay the rent, buy the kids a meal at McDonald's or Pizza Hut. Get yourself a life again. It's gunna be a long wait till you go to trial.'

She went into her house, closing the front door as if to say there was no further argument. Delia leaned on her own front gate and looked up and down the narrow street. A few cars were parked along one kerb: nothing new, nothing that would excite the revheads who went to motor shows: four wheels, an engine, a means of escape for a day or two to something better than this. She had dreamed of better than this, she was convinced; twenty-five years ago came back to mind like an old movie. Scobie had been in the dream, she had told herself over the past weeks. They had been more than lovers, they had been deeply in love. He had proposed to her, she could hear the words even now . . . Her mind whirled, just as it had when she had driven the knife into Boris.

She clutched at the gate to steady herself. Her gaze had blurred; she blinked and tried to clear it. Slowly she recovered, still holding to the gate. Then her mind cleared, her legs strengthened and she was all right. She must not let the kids see her like this . . .

'Mum?'

She turned her head. Dakota was in the doorway. 'Yes?'

'Calvin's out the back, he's burning Dad's photo. The one you threw out.'

'Let him go. If that's what he wants to do –' She felt a sort of mad glee.

Dakota looked at her, then the lively, pretty mouth curved in a smile. They were mother and daughter.

Delia smiled back. She loved both of her children so much. She would get another job, find money somehow to give them a good life . . .

2

Before he left home that morning Malone had called Gail Lee at her flat in Leichhardt. He had never been to her home nor she to his; they lived three lives, only sharing the one at Homicide. Once or twice he had thought of inviting Gail and Sheryl Dallen home to meet his girls and Tom, but decided against it. Police life had enough skeins to it without getting them tangled.

'Gail, you and Sheryl go out and pick up Delia Jones, bring her in to Police Centre.'

'Something on?' Gail sounded as if she might be brushing her teeth, her usual clear speech was indistinct.

'We're picking up Julian Baker. I want her to have a look at him in a line-up, but don't tell her that.'

'What if she won't come?' Her voice was clearer, the question clearer still.

'Tell her I want to talk to her. That'll bring her in.' He hung up and turned round to find Lisa leaning against the wall only feet from him. 'Ah.'

'Yes – ah. Another little tryst?'

'I'm just going to ask her what she's doing this weekend. I thought we might have her over for dinner.'

She peeled herself off the wall, came to him and put her arms round his neck. 'Will she be a help in the Pavane case?'

'I'm hoping so. If she can pick him out of a line-up –' He kissed her. Then cocked an eye over her shoulder at Tom standing in his bedroom doorway.

'I wish you wouldn't do that in front of the kid,' said Tom. 'You're worse than a Spanish movie.'

'It's his hot Irish blood,' said Lisa. 'You should be so lucky to have some.'

She went down towards the kitchen and Tom grinned after her. 'You're lucky, aren't you? We both are.'

'How's your tutor?' asked Malone.

'Like as if we'd never met. We just nod to each other in class.'

'She doesn't resent you jilting her?'

'I didn't *jilt* her. I just didn't renew my subscription. I heard you then on the phone – your ex-girlfriend coming to see you?'

For the first time he could remember he looked with suspicion at his son. 'What does that mean?'

'Nothing.' Tom looked surprised. 'What – oh, come on, Dad! What do you think I'm doing? Spying for Mum? It was just a question, that was all. I heard you say the other night she wouldn't talk to anyone but you –'

'Righto –' Malone waved an apologetic hand. 'She's a bloody nuisance, if you want the truth. But she's a witness and I have to talk to her.'

'A witness? I thought she was a killer?'

Malone had said enough; Delia kept tripping him up. 'I'll tell you about it when it's all over.'

'No, you won't,' said Tom; then smiled. 'Mum'll have your balls if you mention that woman again.'

'Mum would never have thoughts like that –'

'You kidding?' said Tom and, grinning, went into the bathroom.

Where did the innocent four-year-old go, the one who used to greet me with 'Friend or fuzz'? He just wished he could not renew his subscription with Delia. Had his own life been so simple when he was young? But he knew the question had been answered in Delia's mind. She didn't think so. She had never thought of him as part of her library. It only came back to him now that he had broken her hymen. Where had he read that first love is never forgotten? He would have to handle Delia with kid gloves, which were not a uniform issue with police.

Now, gloveless, he was escorting Julian Baker into Police Centre. 'A few questions, Mr Baker, and you can be back at your meeting and then on your way home to – Toronto, is it?'

'How do you know so much?' Baker had regained his good temper, though he was not affable.

'It's a computer world, Mr Baker. There are no secrets any more – you must know that. They're hacking into the Pentagon. Next thing they'll be hacking into the Vatican and nothing will be secret any more . . . In here?' He led Baker into an interview room, gestured for him to be seated. 'Detective Graham and I have a few questions about Mrs Pavane. You remember her? She used to be Patricia Norval.'

He and Andy Graham sat down on the other side of the table from Baker. The latter looked at the video recorder, but made no comment. Then he stood up and took off his overcoat, folded it and laid it over the back of the empty chair beside him. Then he sat down again, shot his cuffs and laid his hands flat on the table. It was an act and Malone had to admire it.

'Yes, I knew Trish. Who told you?'

'We've been visiting some of your old workmates,' said Malone. 'We know something of what went on in those offices – the scam, gossip, stuff like that –'

'What scam was that?'

This bastard is so cool. 'It's none of our business, Jack –'

'Julian.'

'Sorry. Julian. It's none of our business, we're Homicide, so we won't go into it. Patricia Norval – or Mrs Billie Pavane, which was who she was when she was murdered – she's our business. Did you see her after you came back to Sydney this time?'

'No. I phoned her in Canberra, talked for about five minutes and that was it –'

'Yes, we know that. We checked the phone records from your room at the Regent.'

'You're thorough,' said Baker, unworried.

'Yes, you'll find that we are. Go on.'

'I just congratulated her on how well she'd done. From office manager to ambassador's wife.'

'She must have enjoyed hearing you say that. You're a snob?'

Baker smiled. 'Who isn't, to a greater or lesser degree? You must consider yourself better than some people?'

'Only crims. So you thought you were better than Patricia Norval?'

'Not really. We just had different standards.'

'We know about the scam you were involved in,' said Andy

Graham. 'You were the prime mover. That was part of your standards.'

Baker had been ignoring Graham up till now. He stared at him, then looked back at Malone. But the latter had seen the tightening of the jaw. *He's self-contained,* the Wexalls had said of him. But every armour-plating has a weakness somewhere: Malone had seen it so often.

'Mrs Pavane had an abortion years ago. Was the child yours?'

Nothing showed in his face; which was a mistake, Malone thought. He should have been surprised or indignant: *anything.* 'I knew nothing about any abortion.'

'Did you kill Patricia Norval?' Malone said quietly while the armour was still being adjusted.

'No.' The answer was as soft as Malone's question.

He's too self-contained. 'Where were you the night of July 16?'

The brow furrowed: *he's a good actor, too.* 'I think I had dinner at my hotel, the Regent –'

'No, you didn't –' Graham came in almost too quickly. 'You had dinner at a Japanese restaurant in Hunter's Hill with Mrs Pavane.'

Baker shook his grey head. 'You're wrong. I haven't been in Hunter's Hill in years.'

'Then you won't mind if we put you in a line-up?' said Malone.

That dented the armour. 'I can refuse?'

'No, you can't. You can have a lawyer come here and advise you, but you will still have to stand in a line-up. We'd also want to do a DNA test on you.'

'A *what*? Why, for Crissake?' The self-containment was falling apart.

'We think you had sex with Mrs Pavane the night she was murdered and you left your semen in her. It's a dead giveaway, Jack. Julian.'

'This is – it's bloody demeaning!' Sex has become a common

206

social habit, like shaking hands; but it is still a practice that brings about varying degrees of reaction. Like hypocrisy, as in Baker's case: 'Jesus, talk about intrusion – Can I refuse a DNA test?'

'We can get a court order. It'll look suspicious, won't it, if you refuse?'

'I don't care what it looks like! If you think I'm going to jerk off for you guys –'

'There'll be no need for that. We can get a DNA identification from a single hair from that nice thatch you've got on your head. We don't go in for crudity here, Jack.'

'Julian –'

'Whatever.' He was chipping away at the armour.

'I want to see a lawyer –'

'Who?'

Baker was silent, re-soldering the armour. Then he said, 'My brother-in-law, Walter Wexall.'

'He wouldn't be available. He's defending a case up at Darlinghurst – he'll be in court this morning.'

'Then we'll wait till the lunch recess.'

'You'll miss your plane this afternoon,' said Andy Graham.

'There'll be others. I'll be back in Toronto before the week's out.'

This bugger's too confident. But Malone knew the old proverb: Confidence goes farther in company than good sense. Experienced crims had proven it time and time again; jails are stuffed with men, and women, who thought confidence was some sort of protection.

'You may well be back there, Jack. In the meantime –' He looked at Graham. 'Check with Mr Wexall, tell him we'd like him down here as soon as the court rises for lunch. Have a car for him.'

Graham rose, went out with his usual rush. Baker looked after him. 'He's an eager beaver, isn't he?'

'You know much about beavers? Living in Canada?'

'Never seen one. I'm not an outdoors man, except for golf. No hunting, stuff like that. Can I go now?'

Malone shook his head in mock disbelief. 'You're a card, Jack. What do you think I am? A bleeding heart that trusts every man? No, Jack, you'll have to stay here, we'll make you comfortable. I'll get you a paper, you can fill in the time reading how unsophisticated we are out here.'

'Get me the *Financial Review*.'

'I don't think they'd run to that, Jack, not here at Police Centre. That'd be more in Fraud Squad's line. Would you like tea or coffee?'

'Tea, black, no sugar. And a biscuit. Do you have any Iced Vo-Vos?'

'You're still Australian through and through?' The Iced Vo-Vo was a national icon, on a par with certain racehorses; generals and statesmen were ignored.

'Only part-way.'

Malone called in a detective from the strike force to sit with Baker, then he went out to the corridor outside the Incident Room. Gail Lee and Sheryl Dallen were there with Delia Jones and a pretty girl about twelve or thirteen.

'Hullo, Scobie,' said Delia, smiling as if she had been invited to dinner. 'You wanted to talk to me? Oh, this is my daughter Dakota.'

North or South? But he couldn't lay his sarcasm on the girl. 'Hello, Dakota.'

'He could of been your father,' said Delia, still smiling.

The girl looked up at him: appraisingly? She was tallish for her age, with traces of her mother in her pretty face; she was an adolescent, but it wouldn't be long before she was older than her mother. The years ahead were already there in her face. 'Hi.'

'Hi,' he said. 'Delia, can I see you alone? Detectives Lee and Dallen will look after Dakota.'

He turned instinctively towards the Incident Room, then changed his mind and led Delia down towards the end of the corridor. There was traffic here and he looked around again, then led her into a small store room. She spun right round, almost a pirouette, then said, 'I killed Boris in a room like this.'

She's nuts, he thought; and looked at her with sharpened eyes. She's bloody *enjoying* this. 'Let's forget Boris, Delia. Why did you bring your daughter?'

'Company. We're very close.' Some refinement was creeping back into her voice, the voice she had had when she had known him; it seemed to come and go like a hoarseness of the throat. 'I wanted you to see her. What might have been, you know what I mean?'

He took a deep breath. 'Delia, that's history now –'

'Not for me.'

He almost took her hand, as he might have for someone grieving; but that would have been a mistake. 'Did Detectives Lee and Dallen tell you why we wanted you in here?'

'They said you wanted to talk to me.'

'No, Delia. What we want you to do is walk up and down a line of men and see if you recognize anyone.'

She looked disappointed, narrowing her lips; then she seemed to shrug off whatever she felt and said, 'A line-up? I've seen it in movies, on TV. I stand behind a glass screen –'

'No, not here. We're behind the times. You walk up and down in front of the line-up, each of the men will have a number, then you come out and write on a piece of paper the number of the man you've pointed the finger at. Only,' he added hastily, 'don't point the finger while you're in there.'

'That's pretty primitive, isn't it? Compared to what you see in the movies, TV?'

'Delia,' he said patiently, 'stop comparing us with the movies and TV. This is real life –'

'TV is about all I get to see –' For a moment there was a whine in her voice. She was wearing her long black coat, but had taken off her beret and shaken out her hair; as if trying to look younger, like the girl of long ago. She swallowed and said, 'What man am I supposed to be identifying?'

'The man you saw coming out of Room 342 at the Southern Savoy the night –' He almost said, *the night you killed Boris.* 'The night the American Ambassador's wife was murdered.'

'So I'm important?' It was hard to tell whether she was being childish or sarcastic.

'You're very important, Delia. But –'

She looked at him; like a wife: 'But?'

'There's been a delay. We can't have the line-up for another two or three hours. Do you want us to take you back home till then?'

'You could take me and Dakota to morning tea. I know a nice place – in the QVB –'

'Delia, I'm not allowed to visit with a witness.'

'That's all I am – a witness?' She was smiling again, almost coquettishly.

'Yes,' he said bluntly. 'Let's go back –'

'No!' She stood her ground. They were close together in the narrowness of the store room; he could smell the cheap perfume she wore, feel the sudden heat of her body. Shelves of paper pressed in on them: charge-sheets, witness reports, pamphlets: they were surrounded by officialdom. But she was determined to keep everything personal. 'You can't brush me off like this!'

'Delia –' He was finding it hard to keep his patience. Too, a happily married man for twenty-five years, he was out of practice with a thwarted lover. He had met women almost every week of his police career who made demands on him: murderers, drug dealers, drug addicts, widows looking for comfort. He had been bruised by the contacts, but none of them had been personal. Still, something was nagging at him: conscience? But he knew, *knew*, he had never thought of marriage with her. 'I'm not brushing you off. It's just the way the system works –'

It was a lie: he had sat and talked with dozens of witnesses.

'Let's stay here, then. We can have a quiet chat – you and me and Dakota. I'd like you to get to know her –'

I don't want to know her! I have kids of my own! But all he said was, 'Let's go, Delia –'

She grabbed his hand. 'Kiss me!'

He snatched his hand away, stepped out into the corridor as three of the strike force men came by. They nodded to him, looked past him and saw Delia in the store room, face flushed, a lock of hair hanging down over her face. Then they went on down the corridor towards the Incident Room. They had just looked in on what Malone knew they would, later in conversation amongst themselves, refer to as another Incident Room.

He went down towards Gail Lee and Sheryl Dallen, who appeared to be entertaining Dakota with stories of how exciting life was in the Police Service. Whatever they were telling her, Dakota was gasping and laughing, hands to her mouth. Then all three turned and saw Malone coming towards them, anger plain as a birthmark on his face. He was hurrying, but Delia, pulling on her beret, was coming behind him at her own measured pace.

'Gail – Sheryl –' He took out his wallet. 'Take Mrs Jones and her daughter out for morning coffee. Or an early lunch –' He took two fifty-dollar notes out of his wallet.

'No,' said Gail and gave him a hard stare. 'It'll be on the office expense account.'

He was suddenly grateful to her: she had saved him from himself. He put the notes back in his wallet, amongst the dust there. 'See you back here at twelve-thirty,' he said and almost plunged into the Incident Room and shut the door.

He waited there, while the strike force men at their desks sneaked curious glances at him, then he opened the door and stepped out into the corridor again. And looked into the equally curious face of Chief Superintendent Greg Random.

'Just missed being run over by a bus?'

'What?'

Random put up a hand and leaned against the wall. 'What's

on your mind, Scobie? They tell me you've brought in this bloke Brown you've been looking for. He proving difficult?'

'No. No.' Malone leaned back against the wall, tried to look relaxed. Be relaxed. 'He's not going to be easy, but we still have a few things to put to him. No, it's Mrs Jones.'

Random said nothing, at which he was very good.

Malone hesitated, then went on, 'I'm off her case, Greg –'

'Wise move,' was all Random said.

'But I want her to identify Brown as the feller she saw that night at the Southern Savoy, coming out of the murder room.'

'And she's refusing?'

'No. No, she's just being bloody difficult.'

'Who with?'

'With me. She thinks she has a proprietary interest in me. You know she was an old girlfriend –'

'Old girlfriends are like scenes of the crime – they should never be re-visited. Old Welsh police proverb . . . I can take you off the Pavane case.'

The two men, bound together by twenty-five years of association, looked at each other. 'You could, Greg. And maybe I'd feel better for it – it's a bloody headache. But who takes over handling the Ambassador, all the diplomatic shit? You want it?'

Random leaned away from the wall, put up a denying hand. 'No, thanks. There's another old Welsh proverb –'

'Stuff the bloody proverbs. And none of your Welsh poets and their wisdom. Do you want to take over?'

'No, I don't. That's one thing about us Welsh – we're more cautious than you Irish. Stay on the job and stay away from Mrs Jones.'

He went on down the corridor and out to the lifts that would take him up to his office, where complications came in triplicate and could be put in the *Out* basket for others to deal with. There were compensations for being a Chief Superintendent.

Malone went into the interview room where Baker, cup and saucer at his elbow, sat reading a morning newspaper. He had obviously just commented on an item to the strike force man sitting with him, for the latter was laughing and had just said, 'I know him – he's a real lair –'

'Who's a real lair?' asked Malone.

Baker, smiling, unworried still, looked up at him, the newspaper still held spread out. 'Bruce Farro. Detective Chatswood says he was on the Fraud Squad before he came here –'

'You investigated Farro?' asked Malone.

Chatswood was a burly young man with shoulders that started under his ears and a red urchin's face that would still be smiling and winking at the world when he was drawing his pension and his shoulders had fallen away to his elbows. 'No, sir. But we had an interest in him for a while – he's always been on the shonky side. We never got anything positive on him –'

'What's your interest in him, Jack?'

'Julian . . . None, really. You know how it is – you see an old mate's name in the paper and you wonder how he's going . . . Is Walter Wexall on his way?'

'He'll be here at lunchtime. Read your paper. Get Detective Chatswood to tell you more about Fraud and how they work. You might find it educational.'

Baker smiled at him above the newspaper. 'I doubt it, Inspector.'

Malone then went out to the small rest room off the Incident Room. Phil Truach was there with two of the women detectives from the strike force, drinking coffee and watching a daytime soap opera on the small TV set beside a microwave oven.

'I should of been an actor,' said Truach.

Today's episode was a weepie, everyone crying, including the men. Tears flowed like a burst water main; everything, including the furniture, looked sodden. Except the masses of hair on the actors. It floated above the flood like a drift of dark clouds, blow-dried and wavy.

'I'd love hair like that,' said Truach, who was almost bald. 'Tossing in the wind, women racing after me to stroke it –'

'While you blew cigarette-smoke in their faces.' Malone winked at the two women, who smiled: you don't have to tell us about men, bald or blow-dried. 'On your feet, Phil. I want five or six fellers for a line-up, all about six feet and not too bulky, all with grey hair blowing in the wind –'

'He once sent me out to look for six virgins,' Truach told the women.

'You still looking?' they said and gathered up the coffee cups, switched off the TV.

Malone made himself a cup of coffee and went back into the Incident Room and sat down facing the flow-chart. The Jones murder had been removed; it was now just papers on its way to the Director of Public Prosecutions. The Pavane murder was still on the chart, like a gallery exhibition gathering dust. Very soon, he hoped, they could start taking down the layout. He looked up as Phil Truach passed behind him.

'Near the end?'

'I hope so, Phil. I put Jack Brown in the line-up, Delia Jones points the finger and that'll be it.'

'You hope.'

'Yes, I hope.'

3

Walter Wexall said, 'I shouldn't be here, Jack. It would have been much better to have had Rita Gudersen send one of their solicitors –'

'No,' said Baker. 'I wanted you. For the family's sake. *Your* sake.'

Wexall looked at Malone, shrugged hopelessly. 'What do you want me to do, Inspector?'

Malone was surprised that he had asked. '*We* don't want you to do anything, Mr Wexall. That's between you and your client.'

'He's not –' Then Wexall sat down heavily beside Baker.

214

'Well, yes, I guess he is. Has he been charged with any-thing yet?'

'Walter –' Baker looked at him with mocking disapproval.

'Shut up, Jack. We're beyond the joking stage.'

'We've charged him with nothing – so far.' Malone was not going to lose control of the situation while these two bickered. 'We want Mr Brown to appear in a line-up and to take a DNA test. He's refused the latter. We can get a court order.'

Baker was sitting very still now; Malone had remarked the coolness turning to coldness. Or was it fear? 'Okay, I'll stand in the line-up, I've got nothing to hide. But the DNA –' He shook his head. 'No.'

'Have you made any statement yet?'

'No. And I'm not going to.'

'If you're not going to say anything, why did you bother to call me down here?'

Baker looked at Wexall; there was no doubt in Malone's mind that he was mocking him. 'I was trying to impress Inspector Malone with the connections I have.'

The two men stared at each other; Malone and Andy Graham could have been out of the room. The tension was palpable and Malone waited for Wexall to erupt. But Walter Wexall had learned from long experience in court that temper never won an argument. Fiery rhetoric could sometimes win a jury, but fiery temper never. He turned back to Malone:

'Where do you have the line-up?'

'Next door, in the Surry Hills station.'

'Are there any media wolves here?'

'I think there are one or two out front.'

'Get rid of them –'

'Mr Wexall, we're not running this case to suit you and your client. We'll get you in next door through the back way, but don't tell me what to do with the media.'

Wexall remained stiff and impassive for a long moment; then

215

he seemed to shrug inwardly. 'I'm sorry, Inspector . . . When he
has passed the line-up test, can he go?'

'If he passes, yes.' He looked at Baker.

'Oh, I'll pass, no fear of that.' If there was any fear, he was
hiding it well.

'We'll still wonder why, if you're denying you were nowhere
near the Southern Savoy hotel on the night of Mrs Pavane's
murder, you won't take the DNA test.'

'It's just personal,' said Baker, pushing back his chair, picking
up his overcoat and hat. 'As my lawyer says, it's an invasion. I
even hated taking blood tests for a doctor . . . Shall we go?'

*He's so bloody confident. But he's going to come a gutser
when Delia recognizes him.*

'I'll wait here,' said Wexall and stood his ground.

'As you wish,' said Baker, but his smile was again mocking.

Malone nodded at Wexall. 'Whatever you wish, Mr Wexall.
Unless you'd like to volunteer for the line-up?'

'No, thanks.' Wexall's mouth twitched, but not with humour.

Baker stopped at the doorway. 'You never did take risks,
Walter.'

'Unlike you, Jack.'

When the two detectives stepped out of the room with Baker,
Joe Himes was waiting for Malone. 'You got a minute, Inspector?'

Andy Graham took Baker down the corridor and Himes looked
after them. 'Who's he?'

'He's the feller murdered Mrs Pavane. Another ten minutes
and we'll be charging him.'

'How do you feel about it?'

Malone caught the caution in the other man's question. 'How
do *you* feel?'

'I dunno, Scobie. As a law enforcement officer – pleased for
you, I guess. I've spent the last few days listening to Roger
Bodine on the line – he's convinced there's more to the murder
than we've dug up. He's sure the Taliban or Colombian drug

216

lords or Russian mafia are behind it somewhere. I'll be happy to prove him wrong . . . But then there's the Ambassador. I wonder how he'll feel when we tell him?'

'That his wife's murderer was his wife's old boyfriend? Not happy, I'd say. You want to tell him?'

'Balls to that. We tell him together – tonight. He's due back late this afternoon and he'll be waiting for us at the Consulate. I got word this morning from Bradley Avery.'

'This is when I'd like to turn the whole thing over to senior officers. The Commissioner – he should be carrying the can now.'

'Scobie, when did you ever hear of a senior officer carrying the can? That's why they breed us, low men on the totem pole. I'll see you at the Consulate at five, okay? Good luck with your suspect.'

'Joe, would you prefer we let this whole thing drop out of sight?'

Himes took his time; then: 'Frankly, yes. It's gonna do more harm than good.'

He turned quickly, as if to avoid more questions, and went out towards the front of the building. Malone stared after him, then Sheryl Dallen came out of the Incident Room.

'Where's Mrs Jones? Not in *there*?' he snapped.

'No.' Sheryl was surprised at his abruptness. 'Gail has taken her and her daughter in next door to the station. Gail is gunna sit with Dakota out the front while Delia does the line-up.'

'You take them for lunch or morning coffee?'

'Early lunch. Dakota ate as if she was starving, like she'd never been in a restaurant with a menu. Delia chose the place – a restaurant in the QVB.' She paused, still unsure of his mood, then said, 'She said she'd had lunch there with your wife.'

He was abruptly all caution: 'She talk about my wife?'

'No. She just made that remark, then she was all sweetness and what-have-you. She can be pretty nice when she likes. She and her daughter get on well.'

'Good. I'm glad there are one or two things in life that don't

217

upset her.' She stared at him and he said, 'Righto, don't say it. But she's been making life bloody difficult –'

'She's okay now. Will I start the paperwork for looking up Mr Baker?'

'Tell Russ to clear his desk.'

When he came in through the back entrance to Surry Hills police station Delia Jones was standing with two of the strike force officers and Senior-Sergeant Garry Peeples, of the Surry Hills staff.

'G'day, Scobie.' They had worked together on another case. They also had another bond: Peeples was a fast bowler, as Malone had been. They were bound by blood, that of batsmen they had hit. 'We're all ready to go. Phil Truach has got five grey-haired guys, middle-aged, in the room there. Where'd he get 'em at such short notice?'

'Phil could find you five grey-haired gay dwarfs at short notice.' At last he looked at Delia: 'Are you ready?'

'Of course,' she said with an executioner's smile.

'I've explained the procedure to Mrs Jones –' Peeples, two or three inches taller than Malone, big in chest and shoulders, towered over those in the small outer room. 'She's not to point at any guy, just take her time, then come out and let us know which one she saw at the crime scene.'

'Take your time, Delia,' said Malone and tried to sound comforting. He knew the task was never easy, except for the malicious. 'Write the number of the man you think you saw on that piece of paper Sergeant Peeples has given you and then give it to me. Above all, take your time.'

'Oh, I will, Scobie. Trust me.' She gave him a wide smile, then actually squared her shoulders and marched into the line-up room.

She slowed once inside the room. Six men, grey-haired, well-built, stood side by side, each holding a square of cardboard with a number on it, 1 to 6. Each had his individual look, but they were distant relatives to each other; Phil Truach, somehow, had picked

218

a gallery in which Julian Baker, or Jack Brown, did not stand out. No accused could claim that the line-up had been loaded.

Delia moved slowly along the line, taking her time as she passed each man. Baker was No. 4; she paused in front of him, then moved on. She got to No. 6, paused again, frowned as if trying to catch a memory; the man's face stiffened and the square of cardboard trembled slightly in his hand. Then Delia turned and made her slow way back down the line. She passed by Baker without looking at him and walked out of the room to where Malone and the others stood waiting for her.

'No,' she said, speaking directly to Malone. 'The man I saw at the hotel isn't in that line-up.'

Malone felt the anger boil up in him, but somehow he sat on it. *She's shafted me! She recognized Brown and she's given him the blind eye!* He looked directly into her eyes and she gazed back at him, a glint of amusement in the gaze. He said quietly but with strain, 'You're sure, Delia?'

'Certain, Scobie. Have I ruined your case?'

'No. We have another witness,' he lied. *Christ, this is like a lovers' fight!* 'Thanks for coming in.'

'That's all you have to say?'

He was aware of the others standing around them; in the margin of his gaze they seemed to have multiplied. Their faces were like stone masks looking at him, not her.

'That's all,' he said and pushed past Garry Peeples and went back to the interview room where Walter Wexall had said he would wait. He went in, leaving the door open, and Wexall got up from where he had been sitting at the table.

'Well?'

'He's in the clear. For the time being.'

'Your witness –?' Wexall knew the value, and non-value, of witnesses. They were no more reliable than cheap barometers.

'She let us down.' *She let me down*: but he wasn't going to say that. 'He's the one, Mr Wexall, he killed Mrs Pavane –'

Wexall held up a hand. 'Hold it . . . Whatever happens to

Jack, I'm not going to be representing him. So I don't want to know –'

'That's what he holds against you, isn't it? You don't want to know –' Then he heard the sourness in his own voice and instantly relented: 'Sorry. I've got shit on the liver – we had him nailed in there –'

Wexall said nothing for a moment; then: 'I think you're right about him – what you're accusing him of. But I can't help, Mr Malone – I don't *want* to help –' He buttoned up his jacket, pulled on the raincoat he had been wearing when he arrived. 'I'm not proud of not wanting to be involved . . . But Jack has never thought of anyone but himself. Let him look after himself.'

He went out without saying goodbye, just a sharp nod, went through the doorway and paused a moment, as if he might shut the door. But he had already shut a door. Jack Brown was outside it, left to see if Julian Baker could rescue him.

Malone remained in the room, standing at the table like a man who had come in expecting it to be laid for dinner and found it bare. Then Sheryl Dallen was standing in the doorway.

'Boss –'

He turned, blinked, drew himself together. 'She sank us, Sheryl. Sank *me*.'

Sheryl didn't correct him. 'It was on the cards. She has it in for you . . . Am I talking outa turn?'

'No, Sheryl, you're right. *Jesus*!' He wanted to bang a fist against the wall, let anger vomit out of him.

'These things happen,' said Sheryl. 'Personal things –'

'I should've stepped right away from her – right from the start –'

'How were you to know it was gunna come to this? Come on, no one's blaming you –' She put a hand on his arm: a *personal* gesture. 'She's gone now, her and her daughter. She's outa the Pavane case now. Gail and I'll look after her –'

It was a physical strain to bring himself together; like lifting the weight of himself. 'Thanks, Sheryl.'

She stepped back from him; the personal moment was over. 'Baker's gone, too – we had to let him go. Do we let him go outa the country?'

'No. Start the paperwork for a court order for the DNA test. We'll get the bastard yet –'

'We can have another line-up, bring in the housemaid or the waiter from the restaurant in Hunter's Hill. He'd recognize him –'

'All he did there was have dinner with her. He didn't kill her at the restaurant. If he gets away from us, he goes back to Canada – he has a wife and kids there. Is he going to run away from *them*?'

'Looks like he's been running for the past fourteen years,' said Sheryl. 'He could go on running . . .'

'Get the court order. Put a tail on him, case he tries to board a plane out of the country – I'm not sure a court order from us would hold any water in Canada. I'll talk to Greg Random whether we let the Toronto police know what we know.'

'It would of been much easier if Delia had fingered him –' Then she stopped. 'Sorry.'

As Tom had warned him this morning, he would not mention Delia again to Lisa.

4

Delia and her daughter left Surry Hills station and walked out into bright sunlight. A wind still blew from the south-west, but they were protected from it by the big building behind them. Delia stood in the sunshine, feeling it as if it were a blessing. She had done the right thing, for herself, if not for Scobie.

'Did you find it interesting in there?' she asked Dakota.

They began to walk down towards Railway Square, where they would catch a bus for home. She would look across to the Southern Savoy hotel, but not tell Dakota that was where she had killed her and Calvin's father.

'Yeah. I think I might do an essay on it for school – social studies.' Dakota was a bright pupil at school; already she had ambition. To get out of the narrow street in Rozelle, out of being poor; but she never told her mother that. They passed a giggle of girls in the uniforms of a private school and she glanced at them, not resentfully but enviously. 'I think I might be a cop. That lady, Miss Lee, she made it sound all pretty interesting. Did you do what they wanted you to do? You know, recognize the man?'

'No, I didn't. Did you see him?'

'Yeah, he came out while I was sitting at the front with Miss Lee. He got the sergeant on the desk to call him a cab.'

Delia stopped. 'He say where he wanted to go?'

'I wasn't really paying attention, except I saw Miss Lee write it down. I took a squint at her pad – Wharf West. Where's that?'

'I dunno. You didn't hear what the man's name was, did you?'

'Yeah. Mr Baker – I heard the policeman on the desk say it when he phoned the cab company. Why didn't they get a cab for us?'

'We're in the doghouse.'

'Why?'

'I'll tell you when I get home.' They were standing on the kerb waiting for the traffic lights to change. They turned green, a sign for her to go ahead with the thought that had just sprung to mind: 'Dakota, you go on home – I'll put you on the bus. I've just thought of something I've gotta do –'

'Mum, let me come with you –'

'No, darling, go home. I think things are maybe gunna look up for us. We'll go out tonight to eat – Pizza Hut or somewhere –'

Dakota wrinkled her nose: she had wide, even lofty ambitions: 'Ah gee, can't we go somewhere better'n that? A restaurant, not

222

a posh one – I liked that place we went to this morning, in the QVB. Let's go there – you seemed to like it –'

'Someone else was paying –' She smiled, to herself, not her daughter. 'Okay, we'll go there.'

Chapter Nine

1

Julian Baker was worried. When they had brought in that woman to identify him in the line-up, he knew he was doomed. He knew, as clearly as if she had spoken directly to him, that the memory of that night at the Southern Savoy, when they had stared at each other from no more than six feet, was as clear in her mind as in his.

All his strength and confidence had drained out of him and he could not remember how he had managed to remain standing. She had come slowly towards him, paused for a moment no more than three or four feet in front of him, looked him in the eye, then passed on. There had been no recognition in her gaze, but there had been in his: he had not been able to hide it. But no cop had been walking behind her; she was alone, the sergeant in charge standing out by the door. She had paused in front of the end man, whom Baker couldn't see; he wanted to turn his head, look to see if the end man, No. 6, resembled him. But, though his eyes hurt with the effort, he kept staring straight ahead. The woman had come slowly back down the line, gone past him without pausing, with only a cursory glance, and on out of the room with the sergeant.

Nonetheless, Baker was worried. Why had she paused in front of him and not in front of Nos. 1, 2, 3 and 5? Why in front of No. 6? When the line broke up, Baker glanced at No. 6. The man looked vaguely like himself, but only to someone wearing dark glasses in a fog. No, she had recognized him, No. 4, but why had she denied any recognition?

He had not seen Inspector Malone when he came out of the

line-up room. The sergeant in charge, Sergeant Peeples, had obviously been upset; his curt dismissal was an insult. One of the women detectives had looked at him, shaken her head in disgust and gone into another room. They had a case against him, otherwise they would not have been so sure that the woman would recognize him.

The police knew more than they had let him know. Who had told them? Walter? Sarah? But they had known nothing of the night of the murder. No, the only hook on which they could hang him was that bloody woman.

He stood at the window of the small service apartment in Wharf West, staring down towards the central business district. He had heard people refer to it as the CBD, everything was initials now; but it had not been called that in his day here. He could not see the street and the building where he had worked, where he had met Trish Norval and this whole mess had begun. Cliffs of buildings blocked the view like monuments pushed up out of the tectonics of progress. No matter: he had finished looking back. He had to protect the future . . .

He had called Lucille as soon as he had got back from Surry Hills police station. It had been 10.30 p.m. in Toronto, yesterday, still part of the past . . . 'I've been delayed, darling. If I can get a business or first-class cancellation, I'll be on a plane tonight –'

'I've missed you so much, *cherie*.' She was fluently bilingual; making love to her was like being in bed with two women. 'With the children away, I'm so lonely –'

'Me, too. I'll see you in a couple of days at the outside. I love you –'

He had hung up, determined to protect *that* life, to put everything else behind him. He was thinking of the future when the phone rang:

'Mr Baker? It's reception. There is a lady here would like to see you.'

He frowned. Another fucking detective? 'Ask her what she wants.'

There was a long silence, then the receptionist came back on the line: 'She says she has a message from the Southern Savoy hotel.'

Who was it? Was it that woman detective who had given him that look of disgust when he had come out of the line-up room? But he knew it wasn't; he knew who it was: 'Send her up.'

He had the door open waiting for the woman when she stepped out of the lift into the small lobby. It was she, all right: same long black coat, same beret, same cool look; but this time of recognition. 'Hello, Mr Baker. Nice of you to see me.'

'Come in.' There was no invitation in his voice, all he wanted was to get her into the apartment out of sight.

She went in past him, waited in the middle of the small living room for him to close the door and come in after her.

'Who sent you? The cops?'

She smiled. 'Hardly.'

'Are you wired?' The movies and television had taught him how the police worked.

She opened the black coat. 'Want to feel me?'

It was sexual, but all he felt was disgust: to his own surprise. 'No, I'll trust you. Sit down.'

He sat down opposite her. They were on upright chairs, no lounging back in armchairs.

'What do you want?'

'You think I want something?' As if to fit in with the apartment around her, Delia was careful with her voice; as if visiting past surroundings. No slovenliness, just clear enunciation, the voice she had had when she had known Scobie.

'You wouldn't be here if you didn't.' His own voice had lost something of his accent, the past creeping in, the vowels flattened.

'I did you a favour today.'

'In what way?'

'I didn't point the finger at you and tell them you were the man I'd seen that night at the Southern Savoy.'

226

He couldn't help but notice how composed she was, unafraid. As if there was nothing more in life to be afraid of. She knew he was a murderer, but she could have been here soliciting a charity donation. He had dealt before with demanding women: Trish; Bernadette, the girl from Brittany; even Lucille could be demanding. He had not had to bargain on a question of murder. Even Trish had never thought of the abortion she had had as murder.

'I wasn't that man –'

She shook her head. 'You were the man, Mr Baker. I could go back and tell Inspector Malone – he'll always listen to me –'

'What do you want?'

'To keep my mouth shut?' She had a pretty mouth, even when demanding. 'Money, Mr Baker.'

'I could ring Inspector Malone and tell him you're here demanding money.'

'Go ahead.' She looked around, then nodded at the phone on the bench that divided the living room from the small kitchen. 'I can give you his number –'

'You seem pretty close to him?' He was buying time, trying to think of alternatives to buying her.

'We were old friends, we were going to be married once –' For just a moment there was an edge to her voice, the pretty mouth turned ugly.

'And you're getting your own back on him?' He could read women as he could read a computer. Unfortunately, like computers, women were not fail-free. But he had read this woman correctly, he saw the answer in her face.

'That's my business,' she said sharply. 'How much will you pay me?'

'How much do you want?'

There was a knock on the door, then a key in the lock and the door opened. A cleaning woman, trolley at the ready like an armoury of weapons, stood there. 'Oh, sorry, sir! I thought you'd checked out –'

227

'Tonight,' he said, barely glancing at her. 'Close the door.'

The woman glared at him, another opponent; then she slammed the door and was gone. Delia smiled at him. 'You're a real charmer, aren't you?'

'Don't flatter me. What's your name?'

'Do you need to know that?'

'Don't bugger me about!' He was getting edgy.

'Delia Jones.'

He frowned, squinted at her. Pieces of jigsaw fell into his mind. There had been another murder at the Southern Savoy the night he had been there with Trish Norval. He had read the story in the newspapers, seen it on television; but all the time it had been separate in his mind to his own case. Something distant, like a tidal wave in the Bay of Bengal or an earthquake in Mongolia. He had seen a TV clip of the woman, face obscured, charged with the murder of her husband – 'Jesus!' he said. 'You murdered your husband!'

'Yes,' she said, sitting primly on the chair, knees together, handbag held by both hands. 'We're partners, in a way.'

'Christ, you have a hide! You kill your husband and you come here –'

'Mr Baker, I've already been charged. I've admitted killing him – he deserved it, every time I put the knife into him.' Her face had tightened, the mouth turned ugly again; the bitterness in her voice soured every word. 'He used to bash me and my girl and boy. You haven't been charged – not yet.' Then the mouth flowered again, the bitterness went from her voice. She smoothed the drape of the coat over her knees. 'It's bizarre, isn't it? You and me, both murderers, sitting here having a little chat. You should've offered me coffee and biscuits.'

She's nuts, he thought. But if she was, she was the sanest madwoman he could imagine. She was sitting calmly on her chair, occasionally looking around like a woman sizing up another woman's home, then looking back at him and smiling.

'Mr Baker,' she said pleasantly, 'I'd like a hundred thousand dollars.'

'Like fucking hell –'

'Don't swear at me, Mr Baker,' she said, prim again. 'That's not going to help. It'll be much better if we have a nice friendly bargain.'

'A hundred thousand? A bargain?' He was surprised at himself: he was becoming hysterical.

'Just for starters.' Then she smiled again. 'Just kidding –'

Jesus, he thought, I've let her take control. He who, even when things had gone wrong, had known when to leave before he lost control. 'What does a hundred thousand buy me?'

'My shut mouth.'

A part of his mind, the moviegoer's mind, heard her and marvelled. Quentin Tarantino wrote dialogue for everyone to use. 'I don't have a hundred thousand, just like that. I'm not that rich –'

'What do you do, Mr Baker?'

He gave her his honest stare, at which bankers are expert. 'I'm in the second-hand car business –'

'Where?'

'In the States. A small town in – in Wisconsin.' The lies were weak, but he had known occasions when truth had been weak. Or sounded so.

She looked around the apartment, then back at him. 'You're lying, Mr Baker.' She opened her handbag, took out a small folder. 'These were on the desk downstairs – I took one.' She read from it: 'One-bedroom serviced apartments, three hundred and twenty dollars a night, plus GST.' Then she looked up at him. 'A second-hand car salesman in a small town in – where? Wisconsin? You can afford something like this? You've been here – how long? You're lying, Mr Baker.'

'You're lying, too.' He was no longer self-contained; he was having difficulty keeping his temper under control. 'You wouldn't keep your mouth shut –'

'I'm honest, Mr Baker. Or I have been up till now. Not that it's got me very far –' She had another moment of bitterness; but he was outside it. 'All I want is the hundred thousand and you can go back to wherever it is, your used-car yard, and you'll be safe. And I'll be comfortable, me and my children.'

He had been leaning forward, but now he sat back in the upright chair. He looked at her steadily, for the first time taking her in whole. He was not reassured by what he saw. She would never keep her mouth shut; she was too poor, too bitter, to do that. He was enough of a chauvinist to be convinced that only one woman in a thousand could keep her mouth shut. This one wouldn't: she would talk to a friend, maybe even a cop – Inspector Malone? Even if she kept her mouth shut, the ante would be upped: another hundred thousand, two hundred thousand, it would go on and on. Give a woman money to spend and she could never stop. Trish had been like that; and Bernadette and even Lucille. He had never had any confidence in women and sometimes cursed his weakness for them.

'I can find out what you really do, Mr Baker. They would of taken down your particulars up there at Police Centre. All I have to do is call Inspector Malone – he'll always talk to me –' There was a peculiar note to her voice that he couldn't fathom. 'I can do it –'

'He's your old boyfriend, you said – what guarantee would I have you wouldn't tell him I was the guy you should have fingered?'

'You'd have to trust me.'

'A blackmailer?' He was regaining a little control, but he wasn't sure what he could do with it.

'Don't start calling me names.' Primly again. 'I did you a favour, Mr Baker. You owe me.'

'How would I pay you? I don't have a hundred thousand dollars here with me. You'd have to trust me to send it to you, to your bank . . . Do you know what happens when large amounts of money, like a hundred thousand, arrive in someone's bank

230

account? The bank has to report it to some government office
– I'm not sure what it's called here. So it can be traced whether
it's money that's been laundered, drug money, stuff like that.'

'How do you know so much?'

'Because I'm a businessman. If you were in business, you'd
know it, too.'

'We could find a way –' He had put her off-balance. She
shifted on her chair. 'You could start paying me now, while
you're here.'

He laughed, even if it had to be forced. 'You think I carry
that sort of money with me? I'm an honest businessman, Mrs
Jones, not some under-the-counter jerk. I have some travellers'
cheques, but I rely mostly on my credit card.'

'I want to be paid,' she said doggedly; her elocution slipped
a cog or two: 'I done you a favour.'

'I'm leaving here tonight, I'm going back to – to Wisconsin.
I'll be out of sight, out of mind –' He didn't believe that, but
he tried to sound convincing.

He could see that she was wavering; but he hadn't frightened
her: 'That's what you think. They know you killed the Ambassador's wife. She was important – they're not gunna let up on you.
They'll tell the FBI or the Wisconsin police about you –'

'So what are we going to do?' He had leaned forward to press
his points, but now he sat back, gathering reins.

'We'll work something out. I'll get your address from the
police, I'll write you –'

'You think they'll give it to you – someone who's up on a
murder charge?'

'I'll get it, don't worry,' she said, but she had lost her
confidence. 'In the meantime, what've you got?'

'What?'

'How much money have you got on you?'

He laughed again, this time without forcing it. 'Christ, that's
a comedown, isn't it? A hundred thousand and now you'll take
pocket money?'

'More than that,' she said. 'All your cash and your travellers' cheques. How much?'

'You're a bushranger, you know that? Mrs Bloody Ned Kelly.'

But all at once he wanted to be rid of her, wanted time to think how to deal with her. He got up, looked in his wallet and took out two hundred-dollar notes. Then he went into the bedroom, got two five-hundred-dollar cheques, came back and signed them. He handed them and the money to her.

'A bank might query where you got them from –'

'I'll cash 'em, don't worry.' She took the money and the cheques and put them in her handbag. Then she stood up, the rough edge of her voice gone again now: 'I'm not being malicious, Mr Baker. I'm just trying to even things out –'

'Who with?'

She smiled, shook her head. 'Just the world in general. I'm not a communist or a socialist – I'd love to be rich. But the gap between rich and poor is getting bigger every day –' She patted her handbag and what she had just put in it. 'This'll close the gap a little.'

'No, you're getting even –'

She held up a hand, almost as if she might put her fingers to his lips. Then she opened her handbag, took out a slip of paper and handed it to him. 'I've written my address there. And my bank – I have an account, but I don't think there's anything in it but bank fees. I'll give you time to get home to Wisconsin and your – you're not a car salesman, are you?'

'No,' he said with his honest stare. 'Actually, I'm in insurance.'

'Well, whatever. I'll give you two weeks and if I haven't got the hundred thousand by then, I'll be going back to Inspector Malone to tell him you're the man I saw coming out of Mrs Pavane's room the night she was murdered.' She looked around the apartment. 'Nice place. You should see where *I* live.'

Then she opened the front door, smiled at him again with the pretty mouth and was gone. He shut the door, refraining from

232

slamming it; then from the doorway of the apartment opposite the cleaning woman stared at him with all the antagonism of – what had she called it? – the gap between the rich and the poor. The bloody no-hopers wanted to take over the world without working for it.

He went back into the living room and stood at the window again, staring out at the windowed cliffs and, buried somewhere in their depths, the site where he had first met Trish Norval and the whole fucking disaster had begun.

He stood there for almost ten minutes, mind working, stumbling over itself, trying to find a pattern. He had to be out of the country before they could get the court order for him to have the DNA test. Once back in Canada there might, just *might*, be some way of avoiding a court order issued in a foreign country; he would embarrass Walter by asking him. He could not raise a smile at the thought.

The immediate danger was Delia Jones. With her pointing the finger, an extradition order could be issued; Canada would not say no to that. Then he reached for the phone book, found a number, punched the buttons:

'May I speak to Mr Farro?'

2

The day after the funeral Billy Pavane came back home to the big house on Ward Parkway. The day was overcast and a wind, coming ahead of the tornadoes in the south like a messenger, was bending the magnolia trees that Billy's mother had so carefully protected and nurtured. Occasionally a window-pane rattled, as if ghosts were trying to get in.

'I'm sorry, Dad. I was hoping to make it yesterday, but we were cleaning up after a fire –'

Stephen Pavane, ill at ease with his son but delighted to see him, said, 'Fire? What sort of fire?'

'A forest fire. I'm a ranger, Dad. With the National Park Service. Up in Washington State, I've been with them a year –'

There was an awkwardness between them; three years' separation there like a long dinner table at which each was afraid to change his position. 'Billy –' It was like an echo, a sad voice calling someone else. 'I'm glad you're back.'

His son had grown, filled out, was a big boy – no, *man*. He had some of the Pavane handsomeness, but his mother was there in him, too: the soft dark eyes, the cleft in the chin, the look of caution. Stephen had tried to give him the best, as he had been given by *his* father. Norma had sent him east to Phillips Exeter, Yale, vacations in France and Italy. She had come from Virginia and it had been as if she were intent on rubbing off the rough Mid-West edges before they appeared. Stephen had objected to none of it; but the boy himself had seemed to resent all the wealth that had paid for it. Or not the wealth: just the means by which it had been obtained. Billy had become a conservationist at Exeter, which, as Stephen tried to explain to Norma, was like sending a boy to the Vatican to learn to be a communist. Jasper County Land had made its money with no concern for conservation and that had been the beginning of the deep rift between father and son. Billy had come and gone from the house after his mother's death, sometimes for a week, sometimes for months. Then three years ago he had walked out after a blistering row and there had been only intermittent phone calls, always short, since then. He had never asked for money, never said more than that he was doing okay. Stephen had lived with a hurt that he had never confessed to anyone, not even Billie, his new wife.

'You haven't had much luck, have you? Losing Mom – and now –'

'I'm still coming to terms with it.'

'Will you go back to Australia?'

'I've decided to.'

'What was she like? I saw a photo of her – someone sent me

234

a copy of the *Star*, when you got the appointment. She was a looker.'

'Yes, she was that. She had personality, too. You'd have liked her, I think –' But he sounded dubious.

'You think I might've compared her to Mom?' He shook his head. 'I wouldn't have done that. Mom wouldn't have minded you marrying again. What was she like – besides the looks?'

He looked even more dubious; he tried to hide it, but failed. He stared out the tall windows at the sky darkening in the south. 'I'm not sure –'

The young man frowned in puzzlement. 'Something went wrong? I read about – about the murder –'

Was Billy, his closest relative, the one to confide in? Or was that gap too wide? 'Billy –'

'I'm called Will now. My girlfriend doesn't like Billy.'

'Oh.' As if his son had been totally alone out there in the wide world. 'Is it serious?'

'Yeah. She works in the Service, she has a degree in botany. We've been together for some time. She's three months pregnant. You're gonna be a grandpa.'

It was the moment that, like a musical chord in a sentimental movie, brought them together. Stephen put out his hand and Will took it, shook it firmly. There was no embrace, not yet. Three years was too big a gap to cover in one leap.

'Congratulations – Will.'

'You, too. You'll like Robyn – she's English, went to Oxford, like you. Her old man teaches at Berkeley –' He grinned. 'No, she's not a radical. She's a conservative, like you.'

'A conservative conservationist?' He grinned in return.

'I'm sorry I never met – Billie. The little bit on her in the *Star* said she came from Oregon.' His grin widened. 'People from the north-west are different. They'll tell you that all the time.'

Was now the time to confide? He took the risk. 'She wasn't from there. She was an Australian. I didn't know –'

Will Pavane waited. He had learned patience; or control. Once he had been headstrong, flaring up like a lightning strike; but that, it seemed, had all been buried. Robyn, if it was she, appeared to have had a settling influence on him.

'I've kept it quiet – partly for my own sake, partly because of the position I now hold. The FBI have been working on it – the police back in Sydney keep coming up with stuff –'

'I don't want to know, Dad, if you don't want to tell me –'

'It's not that.' He suddenly realised he *did* want to tell him; that there was no one closer to him than this stranger come home. 'I'll tell you everything when I know what there is to tell –'

'Is that why you're going back to Australia? To see what more you can find out?'

'I'm not sure. I'm not sure I want to know any more – or anyone else to know –' Then he changed the subject, looked around him. 'While I'm away, do you want to bring Robyn back here?'

Will, too, looked around him. The big living room had all the evidence of the Pavane wealth. The Monet, the Bonnard, the Eakins on the walls; the Sèvres porcelain in the cabinet in the corner; the Louis XVI furniture on the Aubusson carpet: it was a drawing room rather than a living room. His mother had tried to revive what she believed the original Pavane clan had left behind in France; though, truth be known, they had been lower-class artisans and not Sèvres or Louis XVI fanciers. They had brought nothing with them from France and taken nothing down the Missouri other than a French lower middle class talent for making money and keeping it. Will, and his father, had never been comfortable in the room. But he knew that his father was talking about more than this room, this house. *Do you want to bring her back to what you'll inherit?*

'I'll think about it, Dad. What I'd rather do, after the baby arrives, is come out and visit you in – is it Canberra?' He had not much knowledge of Australia, though he had heard there were some pretty gung-ho conservationists out there. None of whom, of course, his father would have met.

Stephen was pleased with the idea; but: 'When I've got everything settled out there,' he said. 'Leave it till then.'

'Sure,' said Will and looked as if he understood. 'What are the cops like out there?'

'Understanding,' he said, but knew that events never paid heed to understanding men.

3

He was wan and tired after the long plane trip. Or was it fear of what he might be coming back to? 'Have you had a tough time, Inspector?'

Malone read the second meaning in the question: *Is it going to be tough for me?* 'Pretty tough, sir. If Agent Himes and I could see you alone?'

'Why is that necessary?' Roger Bodine's tone was sharp. He seemed to have lost weight since Malone saw him last, but maybe that was because today, except for a white shirt and a sober blue tie, he was dressed all in black. Offering not a cheerful note for his boss.

'Because what I want to discuss with the Ambassador is confidential police business. I have to keep it that way till we charge someone with Mrs Pavane's murder.' He didn't know how much Bodine knew about police and legal matters, but he wasn't going to enlighten him. 'I'm not meaning to be rude, Mr Bodine –'

'Perhaps I can stay,' said Deputy Chief of Mission Kortright. For some reason he had shaved off his moustache and now looked totally anonymous. 'I'm a lawyer – I *was* a lawyer – I can give the Ambassador advice if it's wanted –'

'No,' said Pavane; he looked weary, but not exhausted enough to be pushed around. 'Excuse us, gentlemen.'

They were in the Consul-General's room, Pavane sitting behind the big desk and the others, the two law officers, the two embassy men and Bradley Avery sitting in chairs in front of him. Avery stood up, suddenly looking huge and authoritative. He went to the door and opened it.

'We'll be in Miz Caporetto's office, sir. Gentlemen?'

Kortright and Bodine said nothing, rose without grace and went out. Avery nodded to the Ambassador, then went out, closing the door behind him.

'A good man,' said Pavane.

Malone didn't ask which one, but knew. The Ambassador was not at ease with his two senior embassy men, they were too close to home. 'I'm afraid what we have to tell you is not good news, sir. But first – we've discovered who your wife was originally. Where she came from –'

'How did you do that?'

'Her brother is here in Sydney. He's the manager of the hotel where – where *it* happened. The family name was Niven. They grew up together, there were only two siblings, on a farm in Western Australia. Their parents were killed in a car accident, as she told you, only not in Oregon.'

'What's the brother like? Is he likely to want to make something of all this?'

'You mean, is he anti-American? I don't think so. He had a lot of time for his sister, but they went their separate ways. He was an actor in England for some years –' He hesitated, careful of barbed wire that still existed with some: 'He's gay.'

Pavane showed no reaction. 'You can trust him not to want to make something out of this? Sell a story to the media?'

'I think so, sir. I think he has too much respect for Trish, as he calls her.'

'Trish?' As if she were someone he had never met; then, almost as if talking to himself: 'We'll always be thinking about two different women. What else have you come up with?'

'I'll let Mr Himes start off on that –'

'Thanks,' said Himes drily and looked as if he was not going to enjoy his role. 'We've checked and doublechecked the Stateside

238

record of Mrs Pavane. We've come up with nothing new on what we told you before you left to go home. She was never what she told you she was, except for the job she had in San Francisco.'

Pavane looked at them both. 'If I hadn't got this ambassadorship, I'd have never known who she was and probably lived happy ever after.'

Malone nodded, but guessed that Pavane was only talking against the wind. 'Unfortunately, sir, the rest of what we've managed to dig up here is dirt.'

Pavane winced, held up a hand as if warding off a blow. But it was just to ask for time and the two law officers sat there and waited while he picked up his shield. Then he said, 'Do I need to hear it all?'

It was Malone's turn to take time; then he said, 'Unfortunately, I think so. We have a suspect –'

'In custody?'

'No, not at the moment. He's under surveillance. We know – well, we're *sure* he committed the murder, but a prime witness let us down. He's our man, though. He was –' But you didn't tell a man: *he was once your wife's lover.* 'He had a relationship with your wife when she was Patricia Norval, when they worked together here in Sydney. He was the man who had dinner with her the night of the murder and went back to the hotel with her.'

'I'm glad you sent the others out of the room,' said Pavane, sitting very still behind the desk. 'Go on. You mentioned dirt.'

Malone went on, reluctantly: 'There was some sort of scam in the stockbrokers' offices where they worked – our man and three others. We don't know if Mrs Pavane was involved in the scam, but she must've known of it. There was a scandal that was hushed up – it was at the time of the stock market crash out here in 1987. They were lucky to get away with it, but they did. The firm made up some of the missing money and then the office was wound up. The scam men and Mrs Pavane went their own ways. Mrs Pavane to San Francisco, evidently.'

'Jesus!' If he were not so tired, Pavane might have handled

239

the situation better. He was a diplomat, but not a career one; not one of those who could fly halfway across the world, get off the plane, spend three days deciding the fate of a nation, then fly back to his home desk. But then those inexhaustible career people did not carry, as he did, deep personal problems in their baggage. He stared at the two men, then spread both hands helplessly: 'Do we have to pursue all this?'

Malone left it to Himes to answer that, retreating behind national boundaries like a true patriot, running up another flag.

'Sir,' said Himes, 'we won't know that till we get this guy into court on the murder charge. Nobody ever knows what defence lawyers are gonna haul out –'

'Who is this guy?'

Does he really want to know? Malone wondered. 'He's Australian, but he's been overseas for the past fourteen years. He's a banker now in Canada, in Toronto. He's married, has kids, is what I think they call a pillar of the community. He's well related here – his brother-in-law is one of our senior barristers. When we get him into the dock, a lot of innocent people are going to collapse around him –'

Pavane looked at him hard: 'A point I was going to make.'

Malone couldn't resist his exasperation; the tongue got away from him again: 'What do you expect us to do, sir?'

Himes glanced sharply at him, but said nothing.

For a moment it looked as if Pavane was about to pull rank on Malone. But one really decent man recognizes another; it is the code that has held back the corruption of utter bastards. It is becoming a rare gesture in business and politics, and diplomacy wouldn't give it a passing glance. Pavane stared at Malone, then he surrendered and nodded.

'How much have you got on him?'

Why did you have to ask that? 'We're putting it together.'

'You mean you're still collecting evidence?'

'Yes.'

'What else do you mean, Inspector?' If he continued his career as a diplomat Pavane would be a success; he was learning to read evasion. 'What have you got or not got?'

Malone looked at Himes, but the FBI man seemed to have retreated to the other side of the room without moving. *It's your deal, Scobie*, Himes told him silently and shut up shop.

He looked back at the Ambassador. 'I'm sorry I have to tell you this, sir . . . We're getting a court order to have this bloke take a DNA test.'

'Why?'

Malone made himself look directly into the eyes of Pavane, kept his voice as gentle as possible: 'He left semen in Mrs Pavane.'

Pavane shut his eyes and his face seemed to flatten as if he had been physically hit. He sat like that for a long moment, then he opened his eyes, the pain stark in them. 'Jesus, you're really pouring it on, aren't you?'

'Not with any pleasure, sir. I just wish there was another way –'

'There isn't?'

'No, sir. If this witness we had hadn't let us down, there might not have been any need for the DNA test –'

'Who's the witness?'

'A woman. We had the suspect in a line-up and we were certain the woman would finger him. She didn't.' Pavane looked as if he was about to ask a question and Malone hurried on: 'There was nothing we could do about it. We had to let him go. But we've got him under surveillance and we'll grab him as soon as we get the DNA order.'

Pavane sat a while, staring at what lay ahead; then he looked up and nodded. 'Get your man, Inspector. Bring him to justice for murdering my wife.'

'We'll do that. You've come back to stay?'

'Yes. The President and the Secretary of State left it to me. I decided I should finish the job –' Then he smiled, but it was an effort. 'I'd barely started.'

Malone stood up and Himes followed him. They were both experienced men, but they felt awkward. 'Good luck, sir. And Mr Himes and I promise – we'll do our best to keep the dirt out of this case.'

'Thank you, both of you.' Pavane got up, came round the desk and shook their hands. 'But I'm not hopeful. The world is hungry for dirt. We had it in our country just a few years ago. There's something in the Bible – Tell it not in Gath, publish it not in the streets of Askelon. No, but put it on the internet.'

The two lawmen were at the door when Pavane said, 'You said a prime witness let you down. Why?'

Malone had wanted to get out of the room before the question was asked; but he felt he owed Pavane some truth: 'She held a grudge, sir.'

'Against who? The suspect?'

'No, sir. Against me.'

Pavane waited, but Malone wasn't going to tell him any more. 'It's something personal?'

'Yes, sir.'

'Then you understand how I feel?' There was a bitterness in his voice, but Malone couldn't be sure that it was directed at him.

Outside the room, in the outer office, Himes stopped and looked at Malone. He kept his voice low, aware of the secretary sitting at her desk some feet away. 'I'll have to talk to Kortright and Bodine. How much do I tell 'em about Mrs Jones?'

'Do me a favour,' said Malone. 'Tell 'em no more than I told the Ambassador.'

Himes chewed a lip, then shrugged. 'It's your case, Scobie.'

'I wish it weren't.'

4

'Nice place,' said Julian Baker.

'Thank you,' said Bruce Farro, cautious as a householder

greeting a repossession man. 'Things have improved since we last met.'

'Have they?'

Farro ignored that. 'Why here and not my office? You said you had something to discuss. Business?'

'In a way.'

Baker didn't like the apartment at all. His tastes were more traditional, he liked furniture that was comfortable and colours that soothed. He had been influenced by Lucille, who thought taste had gone out the window when French Regency fashion died. But he had wanted to start on a pleasant note, though it was evident at once that Farro was not going to be hospitable. His suspicion was as eye-catching as the scarlet sweater he was wearing, one that didn't fit his complexion.

'I talked with Wayne Jones the other day, though I don't think he recognized me. May I sit down? This may take a little time.' He took off his overcoat, put the small parcel he carried on top of the folded coat as he laid it on a couch. He dropped into a chair and after a pause Farro sat down opposite him. 'You're in need of money, Bruce.'

Out beyond the closed glass doors the harbour was marked only by shore lights and the moving electric gulls of ferry lights. The night was cold, but there was no wind. The room was even colder, despite the fact that the heating was turned on. Farro sat stiffly in his chair, an iceman.

He said nothing and Baker went on, 'Let's be honest, Bruce, you're in deep shit, right?'

Farro said nothing.

'How much do you need to get you out of the shit, Bruce?'

At last, as if only now trusting his voice and his temper, Farro said, 'It's none of your fucking business!'

'True.' Baker nodded in agreement, trying to be fair. 'But I don't want to see an old mate go down the toilet.'

'We were never mates.' Farro now had his voice under control. 'Cut out the bullshit, Jack. You haven't come here to talk about my business. Which I can tell you, is perfectly okay.'

'Now *that's* bullshit, Bruce. I asked Wayne about investing in Finger Software and he told me to lock up my money. Then I rang another guy, Giuseppe Vokes – remember him? I didn't tell him who I was, just said I was in from the States looking into investment opportunities for clients. Said I had ten million as an initial investment and to test their advice, what did they think of Finger? You'd be surprised, Bruce – or maybe you wouldn't. You come in here with an American accent – actually, I don't have an American accent, but they can't tell the difference. You talk American and say you have money to invest and they'll always talk to you – up to a point. Giuseppe said Finger – well, he was pretty rude, Bruce, about where Finger might have been. He said he'd tell me more if I came in to see him. I said I'd do that.'

'Will you?' Farro was abruptly all caution.

'I don't think so, Bruce. I don't need to. I checked your stock exchange price – it's gone down 60 per cent in the past two months. You're getting no new clients and the ones you have aren't as big as you claim. The defence contract, for instance – just one small section, that's all. How much are you in for, Bruce?'

Farro's cave of a mouth opened, but the teeth weren't coming out in a smile. He pondered a long moment, then he stood up. 'You want a drink?'

'A whisky. No water, just ice.' Baker looked around the room again. 'You own this or leasing it?'

'Leasing.'

'How much?'

Farro turned round from the sideboard where he was pouring two Scotches. 'Jesus, what business is it of yours?'

'Bruce,' said Baker, unflustered by Farro's show of anger, 'I'm trying to help you. How much?'

'Ten thousand a month. Here!' He shoved a glass at Baker, the whisky slopping and wetting Baker's hand as he took it.

'Sit down, Bruce, don't get so excited.' He wiped his hand with a handkerchief, then sipped his drink. 'You are in a deep hole. Your company can't be saved, nor its shareholders. But I can save you.'

'How?' Farro had sat down again. He took a deep gulp of his whisky, then settled himself as if ready to talk business. He just wasn't ready for the business to be discussed:

'How much will you charge to murder someone?'

Farro stared at him, then stood up, gesturing towards the door. 'Okay – out! You're fucking crazy!'

'Sit *down*, Bruce.' Baker hadn't moved; he gave the order as he might have to a dog. 'I'm not crazy, I'm perfectly sane and serious. I have a problem and I think you can solve it for me.'

Farro hesitated, then sat down again. He took another gulp of his drink and put down the glass; he had emptied it in two gulps. He was flushed, but not from the drink. Anger, puzzlement were blowing him up. 'Why me?'

'Bruce –' He was patient, but not patronizing. 'You are, as I remember the cricket commentators used to say, in dire straits. You love money, as I do, and you're going to be bloody unhappy when you have none. When all this is gone –' He waved a hand around him. 'I knew you'd listen to me.'

'What's the matter with you, for Crissake?'

'I'm in a situation, Bruce. You know what it's like – everything is going along smoothly, you've got no problems and then – wham! Suddenly you've got a major problem. I guess it was like that for you when your company started to fall apart. You got caught up in all that software boom, that right? Suckers rushing in from all directions to invest in bubbles? You got off the ground with a public float, right? And then the big guys came in, kicked your arse and now you're up to your armpits in debt, right? It's a problem, Bruce, and you ain't the first who's had it happen to him. Nor are you gonna be the last. Now my problem is different – it's not a money problem –'

Farro's temperature had been lowered; his mind was in gear

now: 'This has something to do with Trish Norval, hasn't it?'

'Yes, it does –'

'Jesus, Jack, did you kill her? She was the American Ambassador's wife – I dunno how she ever got that far –'

'No, I didn't kill her, actually.' Good liars half-believe their lies; that is why they can sound so convincing. All they have to have is a good memory, which, when there is nothing concrete to remember is not so easy. 'I was with her the night she was murdered – we'd been to dinner and went back to her hotel. But she was alive when I left her – sleeping –'

'Then what's your problem?' But Farro didn't look as pragmatic as he sounded.

'The police don't believe my story. The main problem, though, is there is this woman . . . May I have another whisky?' He held out his glass. Farro stood up, took it and went back to the sideboard. 'Somebody told the cops a lot of lies about me and Trish. I think that might have been you, Bruce.'

Farro came back with the drink. 'I told them nothing –'

'Bruce, cut out the bullshit.' He took a sip of his drink. 'It's all water under the bridge, anyway. I could tell them a lot about you –'

'They know what we did, you and me and the others – the scam. They're not interested.'

'Not the scam, Bruce. The money – what was it? Three hundred thousand? You took it out of the Jebble trust account. That closed down the firm, Bruce. It didn't bankrupt it, but the two old guys, the senior partners, old Sam and Leslie, they were so disgusted at us young guns, they just folded the firm and retired. They paid the money back into the trust out of their own pockets, folded their tents and departed. They had scruples, Bruce, something you and I knew never had any value. Not in those days. I knew all about what you got away with, Bruce.'

'You have no proof –' Farro could feel the past welling up like a great black cloud.

'Who needs proof? A word here, a word there, it gets around the business community . . . The business community here is still just a small parish . . . The police think I killed Trish, but they've got no proof. But the word gets around – you think that back where I come from, the people there, I work with, go to the country club with, go to church with –'

'You go to church? Jesus, I bet they don't let you take around the plate –'

'Bruce, I've turned over a new leaf. But like I said – the word gets around, you think they're not gonna start looking at me outa the corners of their eyes? When shit hits the fan, Bruce, it doesn't care what it sprays. Now are you prepared to listen to my proposition?' He took another sip of his drink, looked at Farro over the rim of his glass.

Farro got up, went back to the sideboard and refilled his own glass. He came back, sat down. Baker could see the businessman getting his notes together. 'You mentioned a woman. What has she got on you?'

'She saw me coming out of the room where I'd been with Trish – where Trish was murdered. The police put me in a line-up and she was expected to identify me. But she didn't. Which pissed off the police completely. Then she came to me, where I'm staying, and she's blackmailing me.'

'So? Report her to the cops.'

'Bruce –' He was beginning to sound impatient; he didn't want to have to draw cartoons. 'If you were in my place, the chief suspect, would you go back to the police and complain about their chief witness?'

Farro considered this; then he said, 'Murder someone? I'm not a violent man –'

'Of course you're not. Neither am I. But we're both venal men, let's admit it.' He took another sip of his drink. 'I'll give you a million dollars to do it. I could hire a hitman, give him fifteen or twenty thousand, whatever the going rate is. But would I ever be rid of him? Next thing he'd be blackmailing

247

me, just as she is. You and I, Bruce, for a million dollars, can trust each other.'

Shock was the first expression on Farro's face; it was almost instantly replaced by greed. Venality is a quick fertilizer. 'You haven't got that sort of money to throw around!'

'I'm not throwing it around. And I've got it, trust me.' *Four and a half million bucks that I knew nothing about till a week or two ago.* 'I can pay it to you wherever you like. A big deal like that, it would be better if you didn't have it paid into your bank here. You wouldn't want to be suspected of laundering cash, not on top of all your other sins.'

Farro put down his glass on a nearby table. He leaned forward. 'I think you've come here to play some fucking joke –'

'No, Bruce.' Baker stared at him steadily. 'It's no joke. A million bucks to murder a woman – a woman who murdered her husband –'

Farro was completely alert now: 'Jesus – not the woman –? The one at the hotel that night, killed her husband or someone –'

'Her husband. Yes, her. Bizarre, eh? But the police believe her and not me when it comes to Trish's murder. Except that she let them down in the line-up – she said she didn't recognize me. I'll pay you the million dollars in Switzerland or the Bahamas or where you like –'

Farro sat back. He was ruthless, but only in business and romance, where it was part of the game; he could never kill anyone, he had standards, if only out of squeamishness. But he could hire a hitman. His cocaine dealer would know someone who would know someone . . . 'You'll pay upfront?'

Baker smiled. 'Only a percentage, Bruce. Five thousand down –'

'Against a million? Come on!'

Baker had had to raise the cash through Sarah. He had gone to her this afternoon, told her his credit cards, held through his bank, had run out their time; he had, he said, forgotten to check them. He had accounts to settle where he was staying and he wanted

248

to buy presents for Lucille and the children. Without demurral, as if unconsciously making up for Walter's antagonism, she had written him a cash cheque for five thousand – 'Tell my bank to call me if there's any query.' She had kissed him then, a little self-consciously, and he had kissed her back with a feeling of guilt, something he could never remember feeling before.

'Bruce, trust me. I want you to start right away. No wasting time, let's get on with it before this woman changes her mind.'

Farro took his time, seeing beyond the five thousand dollars to the million. 'I'll have to get a gun –'

Baker reached across to the couch, picked up the small parcel on top of his overcoat, opened it. 'This is a Walther .380 –'

'Where'd you get *that*?'

'Bruce, in this town, as in any big town, you can get what you want if you're willing to pay.' He had had to go to American Express to cash a travellers' cheque, but they hadn't asked what he was going to do with the money. 'It took me a coupla hours, but eventually I got this. Unfortunately, you can't fit a silencer to it, so you'll have to muffle the shot as best you can –'

'Jesus, you're so cold-blooded!'

'I always was, up till some years ago –' He thought of Lucille and the kids; but only for a moment. 'I'm reverting to type. Here –' He held out the gun and a small box of ammunition. 'Take it.'

For a moment Farro couldn't move his hands; then he reached out and took the gun and the box. 'I've never fired a gun in my life –'

'You won't need to practise. Just get up close and all you have to do is squeeze the trigger.'

'You talk as if you've done this before. How many people have you killed? You don't belong to one of those crazy American outfits that play war games?'

'No, Bruce, I don't. And I've never killed anyone. I told you – I'm non-violent. Except in this particular case –' He smiled. 'When you kill this woman, you'll be sparing her a long jail sentence – which she'll get for killing her husband. Look at it that way, Bruce. Take the job and the money.'

'Can I trust you?'

'Yes, you can. Give me the name of a bank and the deposit will be there, in cash, tomorrow morning.'

'How do I know the rest of the money will turn up? A million – that's a lot of money to have to spare, Jack.'

But Baker could see that Farro was weakening. 'I have it, Bruce – trust me. It's legit money, no strings to it. You will have the full million within a month of you doing the deed.' Walter had assured him that, with a little push and shove in the right quarters, administration on his father's estate was being put through in a hurry. 'You can close down your software company – I like the name. Finger – a nice touch. You can take what you can snare from it and go and live in Monaco or the Bahamas or wherever you like. Wherever you want to go to escape the shit that's gonna start flying when the shareholders start yelling for your blood.'

Farro seemed unware that he was still holding the gun; then he looked down at it and hastily put it on the table beside him. 'I don't make deals on trust –'

'Neither do I, Bruce. But we both have a lot to lose if we don't trust each other. I'm your salvation and you can be mine. Where's your bank?'

Farro took half a minute to consider. Salvation has tempted sinners, but they are usually attempting to avoid Hell; this particular redemption offered an escape from bankruptcy and scandal. A million wasn't much these days, but beggars can't be choosers. He had no one other than himself to consider: no male or female partner, no parents, no siblings, just himself. He gave the address of a bank in Hong Kong.

'I still have an account from when I worked there back in '88. By the time the million is due I'll have an account in the Bahamas or the Caymans. You won't have any trouble transferring it?'

'None at all. I've been working for banks for the past fourteen years. If you know how, transferring money is just as easy as passing on a virus. As soon as you've done the job on the woman, you can leave for the Bahamas or wherever and count the money as it comes in. Here is the woman's name and address. She was obliging – she gave it to me. Women can be dumb, they're too trusting.'

'Am I too trusting?'

'No, Bruce, we're both bastards. We recognize each other.'

Suddenly Farro laughed, tension slipping out of him like sweat. 'We had good times, once, didn't we?'

'Often,' said Baker, who couldn't remember ever enjoying Farro's company. He stood up, pulled on his overcoat. 'I'm leaving the country tomorrow. Kill her any time after six o'clock tomorrow evening.'

'You haven't told me where you live –'

'Wisconsin, Bruce.'

'You're in a bank *there*? Jesus – Wisconsin?' He tried to remember where it was in the United States, but couldn't. 'That's not exactly the hub of the universe, is it?'

'Trust me, Bruce. I'll be in touch.'

When he had gone Farro went back to the living room and picked up the gun. He handled it gingerly, as if it were alive; he felt himself beginning to tremble and he put the gun down. He slumped into a chair, began to wonder if he would go ahead with the bargain he had made. But a million was a million . . .

5

Malone and Lisa had taken their respective parents to a Hungarian restaurant only two minutes' drive from the Malone house in Randwick. There the goulash and dumplings and the cheesecake had made all six forget the winter's night. Malone had brought two bottles of shiraz and Jan Pretorius brought a liqueur for the dessert and coffee. Brigid Malone had a glass of the shiraz and a glass of the liqueur and began to hum 'Danny Boy'; Malone, shocked at his mother's levity, looked at her and wondered when she was going to break into Riverdance. Elisabeth Pretorius offered to sing a Dutch folk song, but was dissuaded by Lisa. Hans, a conservative, and Con Malone, an ex-communist, agreed that, barring a few exceptions, the politicians of today were enough to warrant non-compulsory voting. Malone sat quiet, enjoying the dinner because of the others' good humour, but not joining in.

The Pretoriuses took Con and Brigid home in their Jaguar. Con, still talking about bloody politicians, sat up front with Jan. Elisabeth and Brigid sat in the back, two dowagers from opposite ends of the social spectrum, bound together by wine and love of their offspring and grandchildren. When the car drew up in the narrow street in Erskineville, Con, suddenly and for the first time in his life drunk with snobbery, hoped the Wogs and the Yuppies and all the other foreigners who had invaded his street would be there to see Mum and him get out of the Jaguar.

Lisa drove herself and Scobie home, six blocks during which they didn't speak. She drove the car into the garage, switched off the ignition and waited.

'Well?' He knew when questions were going to be asked.

'What happened at the office today?'

'Do we have to sit out here to discuss it?'

'Don't get shirty with me – keep that for the office.' He couldn't remember how many times she had told him that. 'Tom's home tonight. You won't tell me what went wrong, not in front of him. And I'm not in the mood for office discussions in bed.'

'Who's shirty now?'

She sat patiently; she had a gift for patience, which, generally speaking, isn't a universal gift. At last he said, 'Delia Jones let me down today.'

A wifely silence is a desert of air; marriages, and life, have been known to perish in it. Somewhere a cat howled, like a lone barracker in an empty stadium.

252

He waited, but she out-waited him. Then he explained what had happened in the line-up: 'We had him nailed – and she just walked right by him. She recognized him, we saw it in his face, but she gave us the finger, not him.'

'She gave *you* the finger.'

He said nothing, and after a moment she went on:

'You should have stayed away from her.'

'Oh, for Crissake!' He was suddenly angry, not so much with her as at the whole bloody situation. 'I'm not on her case – I'm on the Pavane case! How the hell do you expect me to walk away from her? She could've wrapped up the Pavane case for us –'

'Simmer down.' That was what Clements was always telling him: *simmer down.* 'All right, I said the wrong thing. But I told you – that woman is dangerous. She hasn't forgotten what might have been.'

'That's what she said.' He opened the car door, got out. 'Don't let's fight, darl. Not over her.'

She got out, came round to the back of the car and took his hand. 'I'm not fighting you. I'm fighting her. I could *kill* her –'

He kissed her cheek. 'That's all I want – three murders. I love you.'

'You'd better,' she said and kissed him fiercely on the lips, biting him.

Just as Delia would have done if he had let her.

6

As Malone came out of the bathroom, ready to go to bed, the phone rang: 'Inspector Malone? Sorry to call you so late, but I tried you earlier on your mobile –'

He had left it at home, deliberately. 'It's on the blink, Garry. What's the problem?'

Garry Peeples sounded tired. 'A coupla the guys on surveillance on our man Baker, they called in an hour ago. Baker went to see that other guy in your report, Bruce Farro, at his apartment.'

'Where's Baker now?'

'Back at Wharf West. Our guys lost him this afternoon for a coupla hours –'

'How'd they manage that?' He was irritable.

So was Peeples. 'Scobie, when did you last tail someone in a cab and you in your car? He gets outa the cab, crosses the street against the traffic –'

'Did he know he was being tailed?'

'We dunno. Anyhow, they lost him and picked him up again when he went back to Wharf West. They're there now. We've checked the airlines – he's booked out tomorrow afternoon for LA on Qantas.'

'Hold him, Garry. Tell your fellers.'

'What on?'

'Anything you can dream up. Seducing a minor, treason, anything at all. Just so long as it delays him. I don't want him leaving the country till we've got that DNA order. He's our man, Garry.'

'Why would he have gone to see Farro?'

'I hope to find that out first thing in the morning. You going off now?'

'I'm halfway out the door. Scobie – what are our chances with this guy?'

'I never bet, Garry. The only time I ever did, Russ Clements told me about a horse he said couldn't lose. I put a tenner on it at 20 to 1. Halfway down the straight it was five lengths in front. Then the jockey threw himself over the rails. Said a bee had stung him. I wanted to pinch him for false pretences, sodomizing a horse, anything. They had to drag me away in a patrol car.'

'Goodnight, Scobie.'

Chapter Ten

1

Bruce Farro was in trouble. He had gone last night to a café in Kings Cross, having called his cocaine dealer. The café had a reputation for being 'clean', that no drug deals or bank jobs or killer hits were ever planned on its premises. Which made it an ideal place for Farro and his dealer to meet.

'I can't meet your request, Mr Farro –'

His name (he said) was Fidel Salazar and he claimed he came from Colombia (where else?). He was a fidgety little man, always winding his watch, as if telling time to hurry up. He was as sleek as a water rat, with the same sheen to him, and Farro, fastidious about company, wished they could have met in a dark lane.

He claimed to have had a Fulbright scholarship to Harvard and sometimes tried for a Harvard accent. He could lie in five languages and was reasonably evasive in two others. He had a legitimate business as a rug dealer, bringing in imports from such well-known rug capitals as Bogota, Caracas and La Paz. So far the authorities had failed to nail him, but, as in all bureaucracies, failure was not looked upon as a defeat but as a reason for increased budget.

'Not at the moment.' He had a soft voice, a result of selling secretly. 'What you are asking needs due diligence –'

'For Crissakes, Fidel, this isn't a board meeting. All I'm asking –' *All*? He wondered at his own choice of words. 'I'm willing to pay. Why can't you arrange someone immediately? I want it done tomorrow night –'

'Mr Farro, trust me –'

'Fidel, forget fucking trust!' He had raised his voice. The

waitress, passing, shook her head in mock admonishment. He lowered his voice. 'I've had enough of that. Let's get down to business. What's the problem?'

'Well, first we have to discuss my placement fee – I'm acting like an employment office, right?' He didn't smile; Farro realized the little man was serious. 'You'll pay that?'

'How much?'

'Five thousand.' The fee came so glibly that one had to wonder how many hitmen he put in employment each month.

'Jesus, Fidel, no wonder you drive a Maserati! Okay, how much will the man cost?'

'The price varies – this man's a tradesman. Different situations, different prices. Like a plumber. Fifteen to twenty-five thousand, depending –'

Farro thought a while, working out the percentage against a million. 'Okay, when can he do it?'

'I'll talk to him. Excuse me.'

He got up, hurried out of the café. Small men hurrying always look self-important. Big men, so think big men, just look purposeful. Out on the pavement Salazar put a mobile to his ear. There was a few minutes' discussion, then he came hurrying back into the café and sat down. 'He'll do the job. Wednesday of next week.'

'Wednesday of next –! Fidel, I want it done *tomorrow night!*' He had involuntarily raised his hand as if to thump it on the table between him and Salazar.

The waitress, a blonde a stage short of prettiness, appeared above them. 'You want something else, honey?' She was filling in time, waiting to be discovered as a profitable hooker.

Ferro, distracted, looked up at her. 'What? No, nothing. Later.'

'Whatever you say,' she said and winked at Salazar, whom she knew. He winked back, but he might have been closing a lid over a marble.

Farro waited till she had gone away, then he leaned forward

across the table. 'Fidel, I can't wait! I need the guy tomorrow night. I'll pay more – 10 per cent above what he asks –' Even when desperate he was greedy. Or uncharitable.

Salazar shook his head. 'He's adamant, Mr Farro. He doesn't do rush jobs, he says. He likes to plan. He was in the army – you know, Plan A, Plan B –'

'Armies never have a Plan B – they haven't had since fucking Vietnam. Get me someone else, Fidel – *anyone!*'

Salazar shook his head again. 'Too risky, Mr Farro. There are dickheads around town would do it for a coupla thousand, but you're a businessman, Mr Farro – you don't invest in dickheads. No, I advise you to wait for this man. He's an expert, works to a schedule. Does four jobs a year and lives very nicely. He sells insurance the rest of the time.'

I'm being jerked here, thought Farro. He stared at the little man, then stood up. 'Forget I asked you, Fidel.'

'We've never met,' said Salazar. 'See you Friday night for the usual? Good luck with your quest.'

'My quest? Who do you think I am – Don Quix-fucking-ote?'

For the first time Salazar smiled, a pleasant baring of teeth. 'A windmill would be easier than what you're trying to tilt at. I always had a soft spot for Don Quixote – we South Americans do. Good luck.'

And now this morning, with Don Quixote's luck, here were Inspector Malone and a burly man he introduced as Senior-Sergeant Clements knocking at his door. Before he'd had breakfast: 'Inspector! So early? Why?'

'I'm glad we haven't upset you, Mr Farro –'

Not much. 'Not at all. Come in. I often have business breakfasts –'

'Good. This is business. Go ahead with your breakfast. Thanks, we'll have coffee. And Sergeant Clements will have a croissant. Now –'

Farro paused, about to pour the extra coffees. 'Yes?'

257

'You had a visit from Jack Brown last night. Or Julian Baker, as he now calls himself.'

Farro had no trouble looking indignant; which isn't far from looking afraid. 'You're keeping tabs on me?'

'Not on you, Mr Farro. Why did you think we would?'

Farro managed to keep his hand from shaking as he handed across the cups. 'It never crossed my mind –'

'Neither it should,' said Malone comfortably. 'No, we were just keeping an eye on Jack Brown. Why did he come to see you?'

Farro poured himself some coffee, took his time. He had had a mouthful of yoghurt and he could feel it turning sour in his stomach. He managed not to make a sour face. 'He wanted to talk business.'

'He wanted to invest in Finger?' said Clements and, unasked, reached for a warm croissant. He was a pastry man, but only when away from Romy's iron rule. 'What did you advise him?'

'You're interested in the stock market?' Farro was fencing for time.

'He is an expert,' said Malone. 'That's why I brought him along. What sort of business did Mr Brown want to discuss?'

Farro could see his briefcase, with the Walther and the ammunition in it, lying on the couch behind Clements. 'No, he wasn't interested in my company. He wanted to discuss the long-term prospects of some of the blue chip companies.'

'He was looking to the long term?'

'So he said.'

'Did he mention where he had spent yesterday morning?'

'No-o.' Farro didn't pick up his coffee cup, for fear that his hand would shake. 'Should he have?'

'I think he should have – in view of the long term. We had him in a line-up at Surry Hills police station. He didn't tell you *that*?'

Farro looked suitably shocked; he was gradually settling his nerves. 'In a line-up? God, what for?' Then he showed some acting ability: 'He's not –?'

'Not what?' said Clements round a mouthful of croissant.

'The American Ambassador's wife – you don't suspect him of being involved in that? Christ!'

'I'm afraid we do, Mr Farro,' said Malone. 'And frankly, we're surprised he came to see you last night and discussed business and didn't even mention, in passing, that he'd been to see us. Wouldn't you, if you were in our place, wouldn't you think that a bit strange?'

Farro bit into a croissant. There were only two and Clements had been eyeing the second one. Farro had no appetite, but he wanted time, something to chew on while he got his mind in a straight line.

'It wasn't a pleasant meeting, Inspector. We argued – I think it boiled down to the fact that we didn't trust each other. Never did, I guess. We were involved together in that little business fourteen years ago, but we were never close. I'm afraid last night's business chat came to nothing. I was glad to see him go.' Which was the truth and he felt more confident as he said it.

'He didn't mention a Mrs Jones?'

'Who's she?' He was comfortable now; all he had to do was sit them out. 'An old girlfriend?'

'Not of his,' said Malone, not looking at Clements. 'I'm a little puzzled, Mr Farro, I have to say – he was here half an hour and you did nothing but argue?'

'Well, no, not all the time. We – well, we reminisced for a while, I think we were both sizing each other up. And then things got – well, abrasive, I guess you'd call it.'

'You argued over blue-chip shares?' said Clements, mouth clear now. 'I thought no one ever argued over those. Except BHP when it got on the skids.'

'No,' said Farro and drank some coffee, his hand steady now as he lifted the cup. 'We argued over what went wrong fourteen years ago. We agreed to dislike each other and he left.'

Malone looked out to the wide verandah, where a frieze

of five gulls stared in at the three men. 'Do you feed the gulls?'

'My cleaning woman does. The buggers can starve as far as I'm concerned. They crap all over the verandah.'

'You should be in our game, Mr Farro. There's crap all over, everywhere.' He stood up. 'Finished, Russ?'

Clements wiped his fingers on the paper napkin Farro handed him. 'I think we misjudged you, Mr Farro.'

'People are always doing that,' said Farro.

'If Mr Brown comes back for another argument,' said Malone, 'let us know.'

'He won't be back,' said Farro, rising, wishing them to be gone as soon as possible.

'He said that?'

'Well, not in so many words –'

'Did he say anything about leaving the country, going back to Canada?'

'Canada?' Farro hid his surprise. 'No, he said nothing about going anywhere.'

'You're not going abroad?' said Clements. 'On business?'

'No. There's too much going on here.'

'Indeed there is,' said Malone. 'We may be in touch again. Take care.'

When the two detectives had gone, Farro finished his breakfast, drinking another cup of coffee, going over what had been said at this table. He had not stumbled, given anything away; but they had left him with the deep impression that he was still in their notebooks or computers or whatever they used. He got up, went to the living-room door, opened it and shouted at the gulls. They spread their wings and whirled away, but he knew they would be back.

He went back into the room, took the gun and the ammunition out of his briefcase, went into his bedroom and locked them away in the bottom drawer of the desk by the window. Then he showered and dressed, left the breakfast dishes for the cleaning woman and was on the way to the front door when the phone rang:

'Bruce?'

'Jack! I've just had two detectives here asking after you – an Inspector Malone, I've met him before, and a Sergeant Clements –'

'Oh?' A moment's silence. The gulls were back on the verandah railing. 'Why'd they come to you?'

'They've got a tail on you, Jack. They knew you were here last night.'

'What'd you tell them?'

'Oh, come on, Jack! Nothing, for Crissakes! But they told me something – they said you were going back to Canada. Canada? You told me you were living in Wisconsin –'

'Bruce, that's where I do live. You think I want the cops to know? Trust me, Bruce. How are you going on our plan?'

'It's not proving easy, Jack. I think I may have to call it off –'

'No!' The voice was sharp. 'You've got to do it, Bruce. You can't pass up the million, I know how much you need it. The money is yours, Bruce . . . Do it, Bruce. Do it!'

'What'll it matter if they pick you up? They sounded pretty sure they could stick it into you.' *How did I get into this? I'm sounding like an accomplice.* But he knew how. The million dollars floated before him like – what did they call it? Virtual reality. To become really real, when . . .

'They're not gonna pick me up, Bruce. Do it. The money will be yours in a month. Trust me.'

The phone went dead. Farro looked at it as if expecting a delayed message, then he set it back in its cradle. He would find Mrs Jones this evening and kill her.

He reminded himself he had always been prepared to take risks. Which was how he had got into his present financial mess with Finger Software. Another risk would get him out of it. He would begin thinking about Plan A . . .

261

'What d'you reckon?' asked Malone as they walked down to their car.

'I wouldn't trust him with a dollar,' said Clements. 'But I don't think he's gunna be any help on our case. He's no mate of our guy Brown.'

'I'm wondering why Brown would have looked him up.' He took off his hat and slapped it at a gull that was using the roof of the car as a toilet.

'Birds of a feather. Maybe Brown just wanted to see how well Farro had done out of that scam years ago. Money binds.'

'Where'd you learn that? Your stockbroker tell you that?'

'No, a crooked jockey when I used to punt on the horses. Back to the office?'

'Unless you'd like to try Tibooburra?'

They were inside the car now, the windows up against the cold. Clements looked at him. 'You still thinking about Delia?'

'No.'

'Like I said, forget her. She's mine now, but I don't think she's gunna be any more trouble. She crapped in her nest when she gave us the finger in the line-up. I'll get the girls to call on her occasionally, but so long as she reports each week to Balmain, we won't hear from her again till she goes to trial. In the meantime –'

'In the meantime, I've got my own troubles. Next time I have to talk to the Ambassador . . .'

Back at the office Malone spent the next hour wrist-deep in paperwork. Despite the proliferation of computers, somehow paper had not decreased. He looked up with relief when Sheryl Dallen came into his office and put an envelope on his desk.

'The court order for the DNA,' she said. 'We've got him!'

He felt his own lift of excitement. 'Any trouble getting it?'

'The judge raised his eyebrows when I told him why we wanted it.'

'Righto, go down to Wharf West with Andy Graham and pick him up. Take him to Police Centre, then charge him. He'll argue against that, but it'll hold him till we've done the DNA test. I'll get a doctor in from Forensic Biology, we'll get the lab started on it right away.'

When Sheryl had gone, Malone rang Forensic Biology at Lidcome; a doctor would be on his way at once. Then he rang Joe Himes at the US Consul-General's office.

'Joe? We've got the DNA order and they're on their way now to pick him up. You'd better ring the Ambassador and warn him. The shit's not flying yet, but the fan is starting to spin.'

It took Himes some time to say, 'I'm not looking forward to this.'

'Tell him we'll tone down the personal bits as much as possible. It may be a year or eighteen months before Brown comes to trial and maybe by then the Ambassador will be back home. Your ambassadors change with the presidents, don't they?'

'Only some. I think if this hadn't happened, he could have been ambassador, here or anywhere, for as long as he liked. Let me know when you've got Brown in custody. I'd like to sit in while you question him. Just for our records.'

'No problem, Joe.'

'You kidding?' said Himes and sounded morose.

Malone put down the phone as Clements came into the office. 'Sheryl told me the good news.'

'I hope so.' He sat back in his chair. 'When we've wrapped this up, I think I may take long service leave. Lisa is getting fed up at Town Hall. We'll go off on a trip. I've always wanted to see the Andes.'

'Why not the Himalayas?'

'Too crowded. I hear they've got a McDonald's at the Everest base camp.'

263

'No, you just want to get as far away as possible from all the crap we've had the past coupla weeks.'

'You're worse than Lisa for seeing through me.'

'We've been together longer.'

Malone looked after him as he went out of the office. Affection for the big man welled in him. Friendship (he disliked the word mateship, which had become devalued) bound them like a chain.

Half an hour later the phone rang: 'Boss? Andy here. Bad news. Our man's disappeared.'

Malone blued the air for almost half a minute; everyone out in the main room looked up. Then he simmered down: 'What happened?'

'The two guys tailing him were outside in their car, watching both the front entrance and the exit from the garage. They're pretty sure he didn't know they were tailing him –'

'You wanna bet? He knew they were there, Andy. I dunno how, but he must have. He probably –' Then he stopped.

'He probably what?'

'Andy, Russ and I saw Bruce Farro this morning, we told him we knew Brown had been to see him last night –' He stopped again. He had said too much, he did not have to confide in his junior officer.

There was a judgemental silence at the other end of the line. *The two bosses had cocked up things.* It would be all over Homicide within the hour. At last Graham said, 'Well, maybe. Anyhow, he's gone. He checked out just after nine and we can only guess he exited through the service bay – that's around the corner.'

Malone was pulling hard on the reins of himself. 'Righto, you and Sheryl get over to Police Centre – tell the blokes at Wharf West to report there, too. I'll meet you there with Greg Random.'

He put down the phone, looked up to see Clements standing in the doorway.

'We stuffed it, mate,' he said. 'Our bloke's shot through.'

Julian Baker (though he knew in his heart he was still Jack Brown) was not panic-stricken; but he was worried. He was not a criminal (well, not a professional one), so why would he have suspected he might be followed? But, of course, he should have thought of that. He had been too confident, he had thought about Delia Jones and not the police.

He decided that he could not leave Sydney by plane; the police would have all the airports watched. After leaving Wharf West by the service delivery bay, he had walked a couple of blocks, carrying his bag and his briefcase, then hailed a cab. For a moment he had thought of going to Walter and Sarah's at Killara; but that would be stupid, the instinct of a rabbit looking for a home burrow. Then he said, 'Central Railway Station.'

There, he bought a first-class ticket on the express for Melbourne tonight, put the briefcase and bag in a locker, and went out to lose himself for the rest of the day. Where to go?

He went to the movies in a complex in George Street, the main city artery, to a morning and then again to an afternoon session. On both occasions he chose the wrong movies, for he was not a regular moviegoer. The movies featured young actors he didn't know in situations that didn't interest him: coming-of-age kids didn't know what the real world held for them. Older actors, whom he dimly recognized, appeared spasmodically in both movies, either as villains or dickheads, troglodytes from another age. In the afternoon movie the young non-hero (no one could think of him as a hero, surely?) shot one of the dickheads and all the dickheads in the packed audience cheered and stamped their feet. Baker left the cinema feeling terribly old.

As he walked out he looked up and saw the video cameras on mountings above the pavements; he was not to know, but the cameras were meant as surveillance on gangs that had been creating a nuisance in this part of town. He instinctively turned his face away.

He walked back to Central, crossed the square and stood at the top of the sloping roadway that led up to the station. He looked across at the Southern Savoy. What a dickhead *he* had been! He cursed himself and found something unusual blurring his vision: tears. He turned quickly and went into the station.

He retrieved his bag and his briefcase. In the latter, stuffing it till it bulged, were the five thousand dollars he had been going to lodge in Bruce Farro's bank. Well, Bruce wouldn't be needing it now; jellyback that he was, he would call off killing Mrs Jones now the police had been to visit him. He needed the money himself; he dared not cash any travellers' cheques, not till he was out of Sydney. He had his first-class plane ticket for the States, but he would not present it at Melbourne. Too close to Sydney. He might have to go all the way across the continent by train, catch a plane out of Perth for London, go home the long way. Home: sentiment was creeping up on him like a debilitating illness.

The big central ticket hall of the station was not as cavernous as some he had seen overseas; nor as gothic, renaissant or art deco as some. It had a certain dignity and style, but, like all big railway stations, it had an air of loneliness, the hollow breath of departure and goodbye. Tears might be shed in airports, but they were always too crowded, too noisy, for loneliness to stand out.

He passed two railway police officers, who gave him just a cursory glance, more intent on looking for loiterers or the homeless seeking a warm place for the night. He showed his ticket at the gate, then walked down the long platform to his carriage. And now he was seated comfortably, feeling safe for the time being, in a first-class compartment. He had tried for a sleeper, but they were all booked. No matter: he had always been able to sleep anywhere.

An elderly couple came into the compartment, nodded to him,

266

put their luggage in the racks, sat down and each took out a mobile phone. They smiled at each other, tapped in numbers, then looked out the window and said goodbye to their grandchildren. Out on the platform three teenagers, mobiles to ears, waved in farewell. The elderly couple put their phones away, smiled at Baker and said, 'Presents from the grandkids. They think the world can't go round without a mobile.'

'My kids are the same,' said Baker; then looked up at the two big men crowding the narrow doorway.

'Evening, Mr Brown,' said Phil Truach. 'Would you mind stepping out here? Detective Graham will bring your bags.'

Baker stood up, rising like a man crippled by arthritis. He did not look at the elderly couple, but pushed past them and went out into the corridor. Andy Graham went back into the compartment, punched numbers on his mobile and put it to his ear.

'We've got him. Thanks, guys.'

Out on the platform one of the two railway police, mobile to his ear, listened and then gave the thumbs up to Graham through the compartment window.

Graham took the briefcase and the bag down from the rack, was careful not to discommode the elderly couple as he edged his way past them.

'Have a nice trip,' he said.

'Who is he?' said the man, gaunt as a ring-barked tree, country written all over him. 'What's he done?'

'We're gunna ask him about that,' said Andy Graham and went down the corridor after Truach and Baker.

In the compartment the elderly couple took out their mobiles and out on the platform the three grandkids responded.

4

Malone and Clements were waiting at Police Centre when Baker was brought in. The entire strike force of Nemesis was in the

Incident Room and Greg Random had come down from his office. Assistant Commissioner Hassett had been informed of the arrest and he had passed on the news to Commissioner Zanuch, who passed it on to the Police Minister, who in turn passed it on to the Premier. Everyone was happy.

Everyone but Malone. He had brought Clements over from Homicide because he needed support; though he was not quite sure why. There was a feeling of relief that the Pavane case, as far as the police were concerned, was over; once the charges were made the case would become the responsibility of the Director of Public Prosecutions. Yet with the relief Malone felt, there was the feeling of wreckage still to be accounted for. He had, in effect, brought Clements with him to hold his hand.

He and Clements took Baker into an interview room, closed the door.

'It's all over, Jack.'

'Julian –' Then he shrugged. He was still in his overcoat, as if he feared the atmosphere in the room was going to be chilling. He sat down, didn't slump; there was still some backbone there. The eyes were wary rather than hopeful. 'Okay, Jack. But whichever one, I'm gonna fight it all the way.'

Malone threw an envelope on the table. 'That's a court order, Jack. You have to do the DNA test, no argument. You want to call a lawyer?'

Baker/Brown pursed his lips, then shook his head. 'Not now. I'll get my brother-in-law to recommend the best. He may change his mind and come in himself.'

'I doubt it. You don't have to say anything etcetera, etcetera . . .'

The accused looked at Clements. 'Shouldn't he quote that in full?'

'I'll swear that he did,' said Clements. 'You want us to go right through the whole rigmarole?'

Brown gave them a tired smile. He was sick inside and afraid; but he would never show cowardice. 'You're good, aren't you?'

'We try,' said Clements, switching on the video recorder. 'But more often than not, we win.'

'Jack,' said Malone, 'there was five thousand dollars in your briefcase. What were you going to do with that?'

'It's my sister's. I borrowed it because I thought I'd need it to get out of the country. Give it back to her, will you, with my thanks.'

'She'll have to claim it.'

Brown shook his head. 'I doubt she'll do that. Her good name is worth more to her than five thousand bucks. She wouldn't want it on the news that she was here claiming the money –'

'It won't be on the news – we can keep that particular bit quiet. Do you want to make a statement?'

'A statement?' Brown looked genuinely puzzled, but he was acting.

'A full confession to the murder of Mrs Pavane.'

'No, thanks.'

Malone stood up and Clements rose, too. 'There's a doctor outside from the Police Biology Section. He'll take a saliva test . . . You sure you don't want a lawyer present?'

'No.' Brown looked at the recorder, which Malone had switched off. Then he looked up at the two detectives. 'It's all over, isn't it?'

'Yes,' said Malone. 'It's all over.'

Half an hour later, still at Police Centre, he called Joe Himes. 'Joe, we've got him. He hasn't made a statement yet, but I think he's given up. Have you spoken to the Ambassador?'

'Yes, he didn't say much . . . Congratulations, Scobie.'

'Forget them, Joe. Do you mind if I call the Ambassador? I feel I owe it to him.'

'It's always been your case, Scobie. I'll talk to you tomorrow. The embassy number is –'

Malone sat for another five minutes before he lifted the phone again and made the call. There was a delay at the Canberra end before Stephen Pavane came on the line: 'Inspector

Malone? Sorry about that. Security sometimes has its draw-backs.'

'I understand, sir. I have –' He couldn't help the slight hesitation. 'Good news. We've caught and charged our man.'

There was a long silence at the other end of the line. Then: 'Has he confessed? Told you what happened and why?'

'Not so far, sir. But he knows the evidence we have against him. I think he's already given up.' Then he added, 'All we can hope is that we don't have to let everything out.'

'No-o.' The word was drawn out, like a long sigh. 'It has not been easy, but now –'

'No, sir, it has not been easy. But it's over now –'

'No, Scobie –' Man to man, not ambassador to police officer. 'Do you have a philosophy?'

Malone considered a moment. 'My philosophy is that commonsense solves more problems than philosophy.'

'Maybe. But commonsense won't solve this problem.'

Murder is a stream that trickles on endlessly. It is all over only for the murdered one.

Chapter Eleven

1

Bruce Farro was both determined and apprehensive; a disturbing mix. He had come out here to Rozelle after dark and parked in the main street. Subconsciously he was thinking criminally; there is always a sediment of evil that can be stirred up. If he parked in one of the side streets, some resident might wonder who owned the stranger's car; they would do nothing about it, other than maybe break into it, until the police came questioning them. A Mercedes 500 was not an anonymous car. So he parked it in the main street, where there were several restaurants, and went looking for Delia Jones' street and house.

He carried a brown-paper shopping bag and looked like a man who might be taking a couple of bottles of wine to a BYO restaurant. He was dressed in dark slacks, dark golf jacket and blue-and-white trainers: in case he had to run, though he had no optimism that he could run far. He found the street he was looking for, turned down it, realized he was on the wrong side for No. 28 and crossed over. He passed the house without pausing (it was so narrow – Christ, who could live there?), went on down, turned the corner and walked right round the block. He could feel the nervousness in his legs and even his arms felt weak. But as he walked he dug deep and began to dredge up courage. What he was about to do was a terrible thing, but it was her life or his. He would stop breathing without money.

He came down towards the house a second time, paused. Then the door of the house opened, two women were silhouetted against a hall light. One of the women, stout and bouncy as a huge beach ball, opened the gate, shouted back over her shoulder:

'Night, love! Tomorrow's a date, okay?'

'Tomorrow,' said the slim woman in the lighted doorway. 'Night, Rosie. And thanks for everything!'

Farro walked on, past the stout woman as she went in the gate of the house next door. He almost gave up then; determination drained out of him like blood. But by the time he walked round the block again he knew the job had to be done, tonight.

He came down towards the house for a third time. There was no street light here; the closest was at least thirty or forty metres up the street. No doors of any of the houses were open; the night was too cold. A strong wind blew from the south-west, seeming to gather strength as it came down the narrow street. He had to lean back against it as he came down towards the house. He wished he had a silencer for the gun, but hoped that the wind would blow away the sound of the shot.

He pushed open the gate, pushing it right back against the fence that separated the house from that next door, leaving him an open exit. He took the gun out of the shopping bag, then the Homer Simpson foam mask. He slipped the mask on, stepped up to the front door and rapped the iron knocker.

No response; he knocked again. Then a woman's voice inside the house said, 'Who is it?'

Farro had a sense of humour, but it was not sardonic; later he would wonder what prompted him to say, 'Inspector Malone.'

Delia opened the door to him, delight on her face: 'Scobie –'

Farro shot her once, right through the heart, with accidental accuracy. He saw the expression on her face change as she repeated, 'Scobie?'; then she fell back into the hallway. He turned, raced out the open gate and down the street, the wind speeding him along. He ran blindly behind the face of Homer Simpson, horrified now at what he had done.

Malone felt sick when Clements rang him and told him of the third murder. 'Jesus, why weren't we protecting her?'

'Scobie –' Clements was sympathetically patient. 'The only guy who might have threatened her, we have in custody. She reported to the Balmain cops today – they said she seemed in pretty good humour. Nobody had been near her. How would Brown have known where she lived?'

'He could have hired a hitman –'

'He could of. We'll talk to him about it. We'll talk to everyone Brown knows – the guy Farro, the one up at Gosford, everyone . . .' Then there was silence.

'You still there? Russ?'

'I'm still here . . . Mate, you're off this case, understand? I'm taking over, you stay right out of it. You understand what I'm telling you?'

It was Malone's turn to be silent; then at last he said, 'I understand. It's all yours.'

'Try and explain that to Lisa. Goodnight.'

Malone hung up the phone, stood a while in the hallway. He was filled with a mix of feelings; something like relief floated to the top. He wondered why; and was ashamed. He went into the living room, where Lisa was curled up on a couch, an open book in her lap. There was nothing worth watching on TV, she had said, it was all cookery programmes.

'Who was that?'

'Russ.' He sat down on the couch, pushing her slippered feet away from him. She was in a nightgown and dressing-gown, her face fresh of make-up after her shower. Her hair was loose and she looked relaxed and comfortable. He said, 'Delia Jones is dead. Someone shot her.'

Her feet were against his thigh, he felt her stiffen. 'Who? Who shot her?'

He shook his head. 'We – they have no idea.'

He could still feel the stiffness in her. 'Do you have to go out?'

'No. It's not my case. Russ is handling it.' He stroked her instep above the slipper. 'It's got nothing to do with me, darl.'

She gazed at him, then she closed the book and dropped it on the floor. She opened her arms and he leaned forward and kissed her. Neither of them said what each of them was thinking. Someone, whoever he was, had solved their problem of Delia Jones.

3

Clements put every spare detective in Homicide on the Delia Jones murder. The media made a party of it, but Clements contributed only scraps. With Greg Random's approval he made himself the only spokesman and he was as close-mouthed as an Asian general after a coup. A TV reporter asked if there was any connection between this latest murder and those at the Southern Savoy hotel.

'None that we know of,' said Clements and closed the press conference.

Then he and Phil Truach interviewed Jack Brown, who was still being held in the cells at Surry Hills awaiting arraignment that morning.

'Did she get in touch with you after the line-up?' asked Clements.

Jack Brown (or Julian Baker) had never thought quicker: 'Yes.' The police would go to Wharf West, ask questions of the reception desk. 'She came to see me the day before yesterday. About an hour after I got back from the line-up.'

'Why'd she do that?' asked Truach.

'She said she didn't think I was the guy she saw that night at

274

the Southern Savoy, but she wasn't sure. She thought she might have to come back to see you guys.'

'She was screwing you for money?' said Clements.

'That was what she was after. I gave her some travellers' cheques – a thousand bucks.'

Truach nodded. 'We found 'em in her handbag, out at her house.'

'Why were you so generous, Jack?' said Clements.

Brown had been kept in a cell separate from other overnight detainees, but he had not slept well. He had not shaved and his clothes were rumpled. His descent had begun, but his mind was still sharp: 'Look – I didn't feel sorry for her, nothing like that. I dunno, maybe she's got nothing, she's on her uppers, but I wasn't playing St Vincent de Paul. I wanted her out of my hair. She asked for the money, I had it to spare and I gave it to her to get rid of her. If you hadn't picked me up last night, I'd have been gone. Out of the country before she went back to you and tried to screw you guys with her lies. She was a weirdo, I thought. I had nothing to do with her murder.' He held up his hands. 'Nothing at all.'

The two detectives stared at him; he gazed back, not brazenly, just the steady stare of a man telling the truth. Then Clements pushed back his chair. 'Okay, Jack. But what was the five thousand for, the cash you had when we picked you up? You weren't gunna send her that, were you?'

Brown managed an air of patience; he even sighed. 'Look, I was on the train for Melbourne. What do you think I was going to do with it? Post it to her? Meet her down there, pay her some more? I told you last night, I borrowed the money from my sister, it was going to pay my way back home. I repeat, I had nothing to do with killing that woman. I saw her for twenty minutes, no more, but that was enough. She was a trouble-maker. Look for someone else. I'm clean.'

When they left him Clements said to Truach, 'He's either the best liar I've come across or he paid someone to hit her.'

'I'm going outside for a smoke,' said Truach. 'I've got a bad taste in my mouth.'

'Forget your smoke.' Clements had not done this much foot-work in ages; adrenaline had stirred, like fresh water coming up from the bottom of a stagnant pool. 'We've going to see Farro.'

4

Bruce Farro had not come in to his office this morning, said his secretary. 'Mr Farro phoned in – he's not well. He's at home.'

When the two detectives had gone she called Farro. 'There were two cops here, Bruce – a Sergeant Clements and I forget the other guy's name. You okay to see them?'

'They're on their way here?'

'I think so. You want me to come over?'

'No, Darlene. I'm okay – I'm feeling a little better. I'll be in after lunch –'

'You *really* okay? You sounded –'

'I shouldn't have mentioned lunch.'

He had been throwing up all night; Delia Jones' shocked face hung in his memory like a shattered TV image. Decency, respect for others, standards he had forgotten, had come crowding back as if he had fallen back into childhood. The reaction had started as soon as he stumbled out of the Jones' gate and began running down the street. Somehow he had found his way back to his car, had sat in it for ten minutes before he could trust himself to start it up and drive it away. Twice on his way back, after he had come off the Anzac Bridge, he had got lost on the turn-offs. Panic had slowly subsided and he had taken his foot off the accelerator, careful not to be picked up for speeding, and at last found his way back to Elizabeth Bay.

None of the other seven residents' cars had been in the underground garage when he had gone out; the garage was still empty as he drove back in. He didn't remark the luck of

276

that draw; last night he had not been thinking of evading police suspicion. He had, however, got rid of the gun and the Homer Simpson mask; but more because they were a reminder of the horrible deed he had done. Before going up to his apartment he had gone out into the street and walked half a dozen blocks down to a nearby harbourside park. There, making sure he was not observed by any of the druggies who frequented the park, he had thrown the gun far out into the black waters. Then he had ripped the mask into pieces, the big laughing teeth of Homer the last to be torn apart, and thrown them out, like bread to invisible ducks, into the harbour. Then he had come back to his apartment and spent the worst night of his life.

And now he was opening the door to Clements and Truach, two cops who looked as if they had never believed a sworn statement from the time they had graduated from kindergarten.

'Hullo? Inspector Malone not with you?'

'Were you expecting him?' said Clements.

'No, not exactly. I just –'

'He's on another case. Your secretary said you've not been well –'

Somehow, since Darlene's phone call, he had managed to pull himself together; but it had been like trying to make an effigy out of a string bag. The newspapers, which had been spread all over the room as he searched for stories on Delia Jones' murder, had been gathered up and put away in a kitchen cupboard. He was still in pyjamas and dressing-gown, the same outfit he had been wearing when the first police officers had come to interview him.

Coffee was perking on the kitchen bench and he offered cups to the visitors. 'What's the problem this time?'

'You look pretty off-colour, Mr Farro,' said Clements, taking the cup of coffee. 'Something upset you?'

'Something I ate last night –'

'You were out last night?'

'No. No, I was home all night.' He led them to chairs in the living room. He sank down, glad of the support beneath him. 'What's this about?'

'You haven't read the news? Listened to the radio?' said Truach.

Farro was used to the two-man question team; he had faced board teams when selling his company. 'I was feeling too lousy to read the papers or listen to gabby voices –' He sipped his coffee, drew up his defences. 'Can we get to the point? Is this something to do with Jack Brown?'

'Slightly,' said Clements. 'We arrested him last night and charged him with the murder of the American Ambassador's wife. A coupla hours later someone shot a woman who was at the same hotel on the night of the Pavane murder. A Mrs Delia Jones.'

Farro made a good pretence of remembering: 'Delia –? Was she the woman killed her husband at that hotel?'

'You remember her?' said Truach. 'People usually don't remember the names of strangers in a murder case. That's our experience.'

Farro sipped his coffee; he would have to be wary of being too clever. 'Normally I take no interest in murders. But you –' He looked at Clements. 'You mentioned Mrs Jones when you were here with Inspector Malone. The business at that hotel – two murders on the one night, one of them the wife of the American Ambassador . . . How many cases do you have like that?'

'Point taken,' said Clements. 'So you were here all night last night? Didn't go out at all? No one here with you?'

'No, I intended to work, I'd brought it home from the office with me. But I made myself a crab sandwich, out of a tin, and half an hour later I was throwing up . . .' He sipped his coffee again, as if to freshen his mouth. 'It went on till two o'clock this morning. Then I fell asleep.'

'You didn't call a doctor?'

'Have you tried to get a GP at night? I didn't even try. If I'd

thought I was going to die, I'd have called an ambulance. . . .
You've arrested Jack Brown?'

Clements nodded. 'He's in custody. He's being arraigned this
morning and we'll oppose bail. I'm afraid your friend is a goner,
Mr Farro.'

'He was never a friend,' said Farro and felt even sicker; the
million dollars had proved to be a mirage after all. He had
murdered someone for absolutely fuck-all. 'Just a colleague,
someone I worked with a long time ago.'

'So you're not upset? You looked a bit sicker when I told
you that.'

'I'm upset at all you're telling me.' He was becoming more
confident. Unless they had something secret to spring on him . . .
He became more careful again. 'Are you accusing me of something?'

'Not at all,' said Clements. 'But in the police business we
throw a wide net and work our way inwards.'

'Where am I? On the edge of the net?' He knew now that he
was, he could see it in their faces.

'Yes,' said Clements. 'But you're not thinking of leaving town,
are you? Or going overseas?'

'No,' said Farro and almost smiled, though sourly, at the irony
of the question. 'No, I'm staying.'

At the door he asked, 'Has Jack Brown had anything to say?
I mean, has he confessed?'

'Virtually,' said Clements. 'He's looking pretty sick . . . Get
well, Mr Farro.'

'I'll do my best,' said Bruce Farro, but didn't know where
to begin.

Chapter Twelve

News, as it does, has become history; or, as it does, dropped from recall. At the end of the day, still the only deadline for supposedly educated spokespersons everywhere, though they never say whether it is the going down of the sun or the chimes of midnight, murder continues as part of life and Homicide is one department that is never downsized.

Mobile phones, like rabbits and TV cookery experts, have bred and bred till at any moment in any hour a mobile is ringing somewhere in the world. Texarkana Smith, nineteen and an aspiring model, mobile to her ear, crossed a road against the lights, was hit by a truck and killed. Her last words were, 'I'll be in t-OUCH!'

Billie Pavane's life so far has not been publicly traced back beyond her existence in Sydney as Patricia Norval. Jack Brown, however, though indicted, is still on remand in jail and not yet brought to trial. Nobody knows what will come out then, but press reporters are polishing their biros and TV cameramen are sharpening their lenses.

Deric Niven, still unknown as Mrs Pavane's brother, has left the Southern Savoy and is now the assistant manager at one of Melbourne's five-star hotels. He has a live-in partner, to whom he has confided nothing.

Lucille Baker and her three children flew out from Toronto as soon as the news of the arraignment of her husband and their father reached them. They stayed a week, dodging reporters, then flew back home. Lucille, on Julian's advice, is suing for divorce. When they had departed, he wept for a whole day, no longer self-contained.

Walter Wexall is now a judge of the New South Wales Supreme Court and Sarah, having claimed her five thousand dollars without fuss or publicity, is chairwoman of two charities and still well established socially. Scandal is not unknown in Killara, but it is whispered, not shouted, as it is in the eastern suburbs.

Delia Jones' daughter by her first marriage, Melissa, has come back from London and is caring for her half-siblings, Dakota and Calvin, with whom she gets on very well. Rosie Quantook hovers over all three of them like a benevolent Valkyrie.

Finger Software went into liquidation, owing millions of dollars, and Bruce Farro was declared bankrupt. Some irate shareholders suggested looking for a hitman to polish him off, but the idea came to nothing. He is now living in a one-bedroom flat in Erskineville, where Malone was born, rides public transport because he can no longer afford a car and has become a born-again Christian, who occasionally prays for greed to be de-listed as a sin. He still has nightmares at what he did to Delia Jones.

Stephen Pavane has been a success in Canberra, but he has privately asked Washington to replace him before his wife's killer goes to trial. If he is out of the country, back home in Kansas City, he hopes that the media will not indulge in overkill on the background to the trial. He is looking forward to returning to K.C., where Will and his now-bride have come back to await the birth of another Pavane. Stephen himself is still bruised and he knows he will not recover quickly.

Joe Himes is to be posted back to take charge of the FBI bureau in Cleveland. On his last night he went to dinner with the Malone family at Catalina, a waterfront restaurant where Malone's American Express card got a mangling he will still be recovering from next year.

Lisa had bought him a new double-breasted blazer for his birthday, six gold buttons on the front, three gold buttons on each sleeve.

'You look like an admiral in the Liechtenstein navy,' said Tom. 'How many ships did you sink today?'

'I'll sink *you*,' said his father.

'You look like James Bond,' said Maureen and kissed him. 'How many women did you sink today?'

Claire had brought Jason, but Maureen and Tom were without dates: Lisa had insisted it would be *family*. Something Joe Himes appreciated: 'I'm divorced,' he told Malone for the first time. 'I've got two kids, two boys, back home in college. They're at Case, which is in Cleveland. They're both computer freaks. They'll join the Bureau eventually, they tell me, but only if they never have to go out into the field. They'll catch everyone on the internet. It's gonna be a sad, dull world, Scobie.'

'I guess so,' Malone had said. 'But on the internet you don't have to face a man and tell him a lot of things he doesn't want to know.'

The dinner went well. Claire announced that she was pregnant and Maureen at once ordered champagne, French of course, none of your domestic stuff. Jason looked across the table and Malone said, 'Now your troubles begin.'

From the first course Malone's mind had been working like a cash register. Lisa saw the occasional expression of pain and she leaned close to him and whispered, 'I'll go you halves.'

'No, no,' he whispered back without conviction. 'But we won't be coming here again till 2005.'

'It's a date,' she said. 'Just you and me.'

'Definitely,' he said. 'There'll be bloody grandkids by then.'

But he looked around the table and thought how, though financially crippled, lucky he was.

That night Delia Jones began to fade from his mind. But the past is never entirely lost, as he knew.